I0641432

Alistair McNaught was born in Lennoxtown, Scotland and grew up in Bearsden, a burgh on the outskirts of Glasgow. After graduating in history and philosophy at Glasgow University, he moved to Oxford, where he worked as a bookseller for sixteen years before becoming a sales representative for a London-based book distribution company. His first novel, *The Tragicall History of Campbell McCluskie*, was published in 2018. He now lives in Wantage. He is married and has two daughters and a melancholic white rescue cat named Alba.

The City by the Sea

ALISTAIR McNAUGHT

AWEN

First published in 2025 by Awen Publications
12 Belle Vue Close, Stroud GL5 1ND, England
www.awenpublications.co.uk

Copyright © 2025 Alistair McNaught

Alistair McNaught has asserted his right in accordance with the
Copyright, Designs and Patents Act 1988 to be identified as the
author of this book. All rights reserved. No part of this publication may be reproduced, transmitted or stored in any form or by
any means without the prior permission of the publisher.

Cover design: Kirsty Hartsiotis and Iona McNaught
Editing: Anthony Nanson

ISBN 978-1-906900-59-5

To Anthony and Kirsty at Awen
for their unflagging support and critical acuity.

To Chantelle, Ian, Kevan, Laura and Ola
for invaluable feedback upon the work in progress.

And to Sarah, Iona and Heather
for their incredible patience over the years.

He was a man and an artist
of such fearful awareness that
he heard signals of impending
peril where others, deaf to the
truth, felt safe and secure.

Milena Jesenska

Prologue

It was winter when he first came to V. The city lay deep in snow. Nothing could be seen of Castle Hill. It was wrapped in mist and darkness; not a glimmer of light hinted at the presence of the building housing the council offices where Josef K was due to have his interview.

From his hotel room, Josef could see a couple of cars abandoned by the roadside at the foot of the hill. The tramlines glistened below the level of the mist, and the halos of two street lamps were dimly visible further up the slope through the white swathes. No trams appeared while Josef stood at the window. They were cancelled, no doubt, owing to the sudden snowstorm that had blown in from the north earlier that morning.

His phone made a pleasant sound like wind chimes caught in a zephyr. He read a brief text from his mother, wishing him good luck in the interview and expressing her anxiety about the weather and his return journey.

He put the phone down on the long wooden counter that served as a dressing table and desk, on which stood a flat-screen television, two mugs, a kettle and a porcelain container of coffee, tea, milk and sugar sachets. A wide mirror reflected his skinny chest with its penstrokes of hair around the brown nipples. He did not like his face. He considered that his nose was too large and his eyes too close together. His hair was jet black, unruly and thick. Occasionally, as now, he would catch himself at an unusual angle that made him appear handsome, but when he moved, the illusion was invariably shattered. The arrogant self-belief nurtured by the success of his viva collapsed suddenly like a house of cards.

In preparation for his interview, Josef had borrowed a short history of V from the university library in the Capital. From it, he had learned that the name, V, meant 'the city by the sea' in the ancient language of the province. It was the romance of that name – which conjured memories of family holidays on the wild Bohemian Coast – far more than the advertised post in the personnel department of the city council, that had prompted Josef to apply for the job.

Of the interview itself, Josef would later recall little of what was said. There was a panel of four people, chaired by the CEO, Chris – a tall, handsome American with a cleft chin and thick silver hair that belied his youthful face. He was employed by the company that had successfully tendered for the contract of running the city administration. With him was an older bald man, whose clipped accent recalled the television news presenters of Josef's childhood, and two women, one of whom had large brown eyes, thickly lined with kohl, which seldom settled on Josef. She had been appointed to the role of personnel manager only in the previous month. During the interview, she said little, but she took copious notes. The second woman said nothing at all. A thin, nervous character with grey hair coiled into a bun, she did not seem to know why she was there. When she had been introduced to Josef, her full title had been given – an archaic-sounding one composed of obsolete language constructions dating from the glory days of empire.

After the interview, Chris paused to speak to Josef by the famous model of the city, which had been made in the nineteenth century by a toymaker of genius. 'I know Professor A well. He taught me law at Harvard.' Professor A had supervised Josef during his recent studies, helping the young man attain a PhD in international business law. 'He recommended you highly for the job, Josef.' Then Chris looked at the miniature city with an expression of distaste. 'We'll be replacing this model when we renovate these offices.'

'Oh, but I thought it was a tourist attraction,' said Josef.

'A dusty antique, Josef, best displayed in the museum.'

'I'm rather fond of such models.'

'There will be a new model, representing the dynamic modern city, sponsored by several large franchises. It will provide a perfect example of what can be achieved when private and public institutions work together. You of all people will appreciate that. I read your PhD thesis. An astonishing piece of work. Astonishing.'

After Chris left, Josef remained studying the model of the city. The diminutive street descending from City Hall was largely the same as it had appeared that morning when Josef was struggling up the icy pavement on his way to his interview. Each small building was rendered in fine detail. All the gothic decorations were present on the miniature City Hall which to this day gave it the appearance of a medieval castle and suggested the ancient fortress that had given the hill its name. Also present were the classical pillars and pediment of the museum next door. The bookshop, bearing the family name of its founders and owners, still occupied the building opposite City Hall at the top of the hill.

Josef leaned closer to look at the tiny figures on the street, in their old-fashioned clothes, and his gaze moved down the slope of Castle Hill, past his hotel to the cathedral. Just beyond the cathedral, a warehouse stretched along a quay, at the end of which there was a large, tree-lined square. Another hill rose from the far end of the square, on the side of which Josef recognised the building where he had gone to look at an apartment on the previous day.

His gaze returned to the quay with its sailing ships and its miniature stevedores, before following the course of the river through a famous gorge on its way to the nearby sea. He noticed a large villa that stood in its own grounds at the top of the cliff on the north side of the gorge, with a village close by which Josef was sure had now been absorbed by the modern city.

The model stood on a specially constructed table in the atrium near the main entrance. The walls of the atrium were panelled with dark wood, and doors led through to the various rooms on the ground floor where the public came to pay their council house rents, to arrange for special rubbish collections or to apply for local health or education grants. Two rows of lights hung from the high ceiling, and a gallery with a balustrade of the same dark wood as the wall panels stretched around three of the walls, with doors leading off into the first-floor offices.

Josef saw a dark-haired woman emerge through one of those doors, walk around the gallery and disappear. Moments later, she reappeared, descending the main staircase at the back of the atrium. Her nervous gait and slightly stooped posture gave her an unremarkable appearance, but as she glanced at him in passing he was struck by her limpid blue, downward-slanting eyes. Like Chris, she had a small cleft on her chin. Her lips were chapped and shiny with salve.

Josef noticed the unusual filigree of a silver brooch that was pinned to one of the woman's coat lapels. It put him in mind of the circular seashell he had seen on a beach during a family holiday in his teens. He had had no idea what kind of creature it had housed, but much of its outer shell had disappeared, leaving only the intricate supports of its internal structure. On leaning over to take a closer look at the shell, Josef had been stunned by the complex of miniature chambers that he saw there and by the thought that similar structures might lie behind the thousands of discarded and broken shells scattered across the sand. He looked at the patterns cut into the rocks around him by the movement of the tides, and the birds wading along the shore, and imagined the numberless generations of sea creatures growing those variegated shells around their vulnerable bodies. That sudden insight into the mind-boggling intricacy of nature aroused in Josef a vertiginous panic that had never fully left him. He wondered if that was why he was so drawn to models of miniature cities such as this.

The woman made her way through the revolving doors, and he watched her disappear among the late afternoon shoppers.

★

A year later, when he finally moved into his office in the renovated City Hall, Josef wondered if he might see that woman again. In truth, he had not thought of her often during the intervening months. The various departments of the city administration had been scattered in temporary offices across the city while the renovation work was carried out. But as he stood by the new model of the city he hoped that the woman might emerge from one of the glass doors on the first floor.

Now, only the executive offices were above the atrium ceiling in the converted roof space, with panoramic windows of tinted glass giving views across the city. Aside from that roof of slate-coloured metal and tinted glass, the façade of the building was unchanged. However, the interior had been utterly transformed. Galleries now went around the upper six floors of the atrium, giving access to glass-walled, open plan offices, and four glass elevators connected those floors. The executives had their own discreetly placed elevator with brushed-steel doors. The main staircase had been replaced by two modest service stairways hidden behind the scenes. The atrium was now a vast, brightly lit space of glass, white paint and brushed steel.

The new model of the city was made of white plastic. There were no people in the streets, and the cliffs and the river were also white. The only colours on the model were the brand colours of the international cafe chain, fast-food outlet, hotel consortium, restaurant chain and corporate construction giant that had sponsored the model and provided some of the funding for the office renovation. Hence the blue high-rise hotel on the square by the quay; the mauve-fronted cafe in the complex of visitor attractions and restaurants that had been built – together with an innovative footbridge – to celebrate the start of the new millennium; the name of a famous chef written on the lilac façade of the restaurant beside the bookshop on Castle Hill; the yellow letter indicating the fast-food outlet on one of the roads leading off the square. Finally, there was the red and black trademark of a stylised tower above the initials 'ANH', within the V of an open pair of compasses, denoting the corporation responsible for the new apartment blocks running along the waterfront, as well as the new building housing the university politics department situated near the museum.

Josef's gaze followed the road he was about to take down the western slope of Castle Hill, beside which stood the 1960s concrete block where he was currently renting an apartment. He looked back up at the first-floor gallery, still hoping he might see the young woman, then he pulled the lapels of his jacket together and made his way through the now automatically revolving doors and out into the snow.

As the white flakes swirled around him and he made his way through the crowds of students and workers heading home, he recalled the old story of the river gorge, which was said to have been created when G, the patron saint of the city, had hurled the Devil off the summit of Castle Hill. Thinking of his own role in recent months, Josef wondered if the Devil had only been biding his time in that gorge, awaiting the opportunity to assume the form of a handsome silver-haired chief executive with a contract full of honeyed promises.

Chapter 1

APRIL

It all started when Adam F placed a ten-thaler bet on the city football team winning a local derby at odds of thirteen to one. Adam had gone out that Saturday morning to catch up on some work at the office for two hours and then to pick up some groceries on the way home. However, his colleague Karl had also been in the office and had persuaded him that they should go for a drink afterwards and maybe catch the football derby on the big screen in the Crow's Nest Inn.

When Adam phoned Katryn, he knew from the hesitation in his wife's voice that she was not happy.

'Don't get drunk and don't spend too much money.' He could hear a child screaming in the background – Helena, he thought; Kris had no doubt done something to upset her. 'I have to go,' said Katryn. 'Don't forget the groceries.'

'Man, when are you going to replace that phone?' said Karl, sliding through numerous bright images on the screen of his own slim phone with its matt black body of precision-machined steel.

Later, Adam would wonder where the time had gone. Everything had been proceeding coherently and logically. He knew that he had done wrong in staying out, but he had 120 thalers extra in his pocket because Karl had persuaded him to place that bet. Karl had spoken to Katryn on Adam's phone at 6.30 p.m., taking full responsibility for the fact that Adam and he were still in the bar. Adam had heard his wife's tinny laughter on the other end when Karl had flirted with her, but he knew that she would be angry, nevertheless; that he might have to endure a week of the silent treatment. He hoped that his surprise windfall would make a difference.

Now, it was just after half-past nine and he and Karl were sitting in the cocktail bar of the Radion Hotel in Vandrhaf Square. Adam could not recall anything that had happened in the past two hours and he was finding it hard to concentrate on what Karl was saying. He was no longer sure what they were talking about.

'Christ, if she is going to be like that! I mean, it's not as if we go out every week, is it?'

Adam had the feeling that he had bad-mouthed Katryn or that he had been indiscreet. Whatever he had said, it had clearly annoyed Karl. Adam looked around at the deep blue décor of the bar; at the counter with its glittering row of beer taps; at the blue glass lampshades hanging by chains from the high ceiling. He looked at the smartly dressed people. A woman in a purple blouse and black skirt was standing at the bar, talking to the barman, blond hair falling in waves to the small of her back. A grey-haired man was leaning his left elbow on the counter beside her, in a well-cut navy suit, a belly-filled linen shirt and a silk tie, smiling indulgently. A bald man in a maroon shirt was sitting at a corner table, drinking beer from a bottle and tapping the keys of a laptop. A family was gathered round another table for a birthday celebration. A heart-shaped helium balloon with the number 50 on it was swaying above the table, its string having just been tweaked by a teenage girl with a bob, who was wearing a black and white polka dot dress. Some young women were standing in a group near the far end of the counter, laughing and joking, while two of their number exchanged banter with a couple of businessmen sitting nearby.

Adam could not take it all in. Everything kept going in and out of focus; conversations became softer and louder for no apparent reason. He caught a glimpse of his face in the mirror beyond Karl. The incipient bags under his eyes, the flesh that now softened his features, and the way his hair was receding from his temples made him feel washed up and old. He tried to focus on the girl with the bob, and he wondered what his daughter, Helena, would be like when she was older. He felt a catch in his throat when he thought about her, always so neat, always so serious. Confused thoughts followed about his troubled son, Kris.

'I really love my kids, Karl. I r ... really love them, but Kris, you know ... my son, Kris. Kris ... s ... s ... sudge a bully.'

'Drink making you maudlin?' said Karl. 'I'll get us another, compadre. That will sort you out.'

★

Twelve midnight on Vandrhaf Square. An old tramp was sitting in a cafe doorway, wrapped in a filthy sleeping bag, clutching with both hands a half-bottle of vodka in a crumpled brown paper bag, sole witness of the modified BMW pulling up outside the Radion Hotel. A tall, slim woman in a black tailored coat and high heels climbed out of the back seat of the car as the driver wound down the window. He had the rugged features of a matinee idol, with unusually full lips, and spoke in a foreign accent with none of the social niceties.

'Room 616, remember. The usual place at 7.30. Not a moment later.'
The woman barely acknowledged what he had said.

'Before you go, Anna. I wanted to tell you: Georgiy writes that your sister, Sofia, is becoming a real beauty; the jewel of Archaeon. Let us do all in our power to keep her that way – you, me, Georgiy, eh, my pretty? A "veritable jewel", he writes.' So saying, the man drove off with a screech of tyres and a turbocharged roar.

Nothing in her carefully made-up face betrayed her anxiety. She knew the Radion Hotel. She knew the receptionists. They all owed Sergei favours, for one reason or another, and so they would nod her through the lobby to the lift as if she was an ordinary guest. The hotel was an unreal world, totally unlike the usual drab room where she worked, carried on her business, or any of the other euphemisms Sergei employed to give their relationship a veneer of normality. A slave was what she was. Only her lustrous black hair, perfect olive skin, widely spaced almond-shaped eyes, and high cheekbones gave her access on certain rare occasions to the gimcrack splendours of the Radion Hotel.

Men turned to look at her as she made her way to the lift, but she knew enough of such looks now not to trust them. Even the most love-struck of her clients seldom failed to take advantage of her position in the basest manner imaginable.

As for the women, she never encountered any in the hotel who showed the least sign of appreciating their freedom and financial security. Anna was convinced that they were sneering at the cheap cut of her coat and her counterfeit shoes, envying her looks, ignorant of the true horror of her situation. Anna hated the Radion Hotel with every fibre of her being.

The only reward she gained from these occasions was her trip to the cafe on the following morning. As a bonus, Sergei would allow her to order a coffee and a croissant out of her takings. She always arrived at the cafe early. For that brief interval until Sergei arrived, she imagined she was leading a life like the lives of those around her; the life that Sergei had promised her all those years ago in her native village.

The door to room 616 was midway along a corridor illuminated at regular intervals by light panels set into the ceiling. One of the tubes in the nearest panel must have been faulty, for it was flickering slightly and emitting a rhythmic buzzing noise that resonated unpleasantly with the hum of the air conditioning. The carpet was decorated with alternating blue and white zigzags.

These brief moments outside the rooms of this hotel were among the most nerve wracking in Anna's life, because she had no way of knowing what to expect. For the past four years, she had been subject to the desires of all kinds of men, from nervous first-timers and guilty husbands to sadists and serial rapists. There had been one client who would surely have murdered her had Sergei not intervened and beaten him near to death; not because of the pain the man had inflicted on her, but because he had had the temerity to damage company goods.

Anna raised her fist and consciously tried to slow her breathing, before knocking on the door three times in quick succession. A plump man with wispy fair hair opened the door. His small eyes avoided her gaze and he took his time looking her up and down before inviting her in. With an inward shudder of revulsion, she noticed his hairy belly showing between two buttons of his undersized shirt.

'You are way prettier than your photo on the website,' he said, before turning his head and adding, 'Wait until you see her, Adam.'

She froze in the act of unbuttoning her coat when she saw the other man stretched out on the sofa. He struggled to raise his head and open his eyes, but he seemed unable to support the weight on his neck and slumped back on the cushion. He had the slightly worn appearance that she had often encountered, of a handsome man gone to seed, the alcohol reek of failure, but she dearly wished that his companion was out cold on the couch instead of him.

'It is 100 thalers for one client,' she said. 'Not two.' She made no effort to hide her anger.

'Look at him. He's incapable of doing anything.'

'I don't care. The price is 100 thalers for one client.'

'How about 150 thalers?'

She pressed her forefinger against her lips and looked at Adam's inert form. '160 thalers,' she said. 'No less.'

'It's a deal,' said the man, spreading his arms wide and bowing from the waist. 'But for the extra you must at least try to resurrect Lazarus. Now, if you'll excuse me.' He headed to the en suite bathroom.

When he emerged ten minutes later, Anna was sitting on the sofa in her bra, pants, and stockings, flipping Adam's flaccid penis from side to side between her hands. Then, still heedless of Karl, she grabbed it in her fist. Only when she caught the camera flash out of the corner of her eye, did she react to him: 'What the hell do you think you are doing?'

'What's it to you? Or do you want me to post a bad review?' Karl could tell that his comment had hit the mark. 'Yes, my dear, customer satisfaction is your only raison d'être here, if you'll pardon my French. Now leave him be and let's get down and dirty.

★

Adam woke in the small hours, still on the sofa. One of the spare sheets had been thrown over him, but he had no recollection of pulling down his trousers and pants. He had no idea where he was, only that his bladder was full to bursting. Everything was in pitch darkness, so he opened the curtains that he found just above the back of the sofa. Light from the half-moon hanging in the sky above Castle Hill allowed him gradually to discern the shapes of the beds, the wardrobe, the chair, the desk, the wall-mounted TV and the outlines of two doors. One must lead to the bathroom, he concluded.

The extractor fan purred into life as soon as he switched on the lamp above the mirror in the en-suite, and a triangle of light stretched across the room to illuminate the serene face of a woman sleeping in the nearer bed. Adam thought she resembled the actress Anna Karina, and he gazed at her, completely mesmerised, until a frown dimpled her features and she turned over.

He closed the bathroom door and tried to keep the stream of his urine from striking the water in the bowl. He looked awful in the cabinet mirror: greenish skin, bloodshot eyes, receding hair. It was true that he was better built now than in his skinny youth, but he was developing a pot belly, owing to his sedentary life and poor diet. He was only thirty-six, but already he felt that he had lost the good looks that had won Katryn's love. Indeed, her recent indifference made him wonder if those looks had ever been more than a delusion. He took one last disparaging look at himself. Then he switched off the lamp before opening the door, made his way carefully to the sofa, pulled the sheet over his shoulder and was completely unaware of falling back to sleep.

The woman was gone when he woke the next morning. Karl was standing by one of the beds, in his boxer shorts, buttoning up his shirt and whistling.

'Where the fuck are we?' said Adam.

'Oh, you're finally awake. I'm sorry, mate, but you owe me another 75 thalers.'

'What the fuck?'

'Well, your share of the room came out of your winnings.' Karl walked over to Adam and presented the screen of his phone. 'But you owe me for this.'

'I thought I had dreamed her.' Adam took in the photograph of the woman who resembled Anna Karina. Unlike the Scandinavian actor, the woman had olive skin. She was sitting cross-legged in her underwear on the sofa, looking at Adam's face with a bored expression while grasping his penis in her fist.

Both men had still been sound asleep when Anna woke up. As always, it took her a moment to realise that she was in the hotel. Her dream of her home village only added to her confusion.

She looked at the unpleasant fat face of the man sleeping in the bed next to hers. His mouth was open. She could smell a mix of garlic, alcohol and tooth decay on his breath. She remembered his unpleasant demands of the previous evening. In truth, he was no more unpleasant than any of her other clients, but he clearly imagined himself to be an expert lover, utterly blind to the notion that someone else might not share his pleasure or enjoy his caresses.

Grabbing her clothes and bag, she went to the bathroom and decided to risk waking the men by having a shower. It was the only pleasure she could take from the hotel. She rotated beneath the high-pressure spray, enjoying the sensation on her skin, imagining that she was cleansing herself of all the filth and sin. Then, after drying herself and putting on the clean knickers that were wrapped separately in her bag in a small plastic carrier, she took out one of the tampons that she kept in the bag's zippered pocket. Very carefully she pulled open the gummed seal and drew out the tampon and its applicator. With great care, she aligned two twenty-thaler notes from the extra payment she had extorted from the fat man, rolling them tightly around the tampon, before sliding everything back into the wrapper. Finally, she re-sealed the wrapper, using her nail varnish, and returned it to the zippered pocket. She would tell Sergei the client had given her a twenty-thaler tip and hope that he would accept this lie without question.

The low sun swept across the square, stretching out the trembling shadows of the linden trees. Three cylindrical metal pillars marked the end of the quay. Anna made her way through a covered walkway supported by iron pillars on the quayside, where a bar and cinema on her right occupied the former warehouse. A cool breeze pressed against her face, loaded with the scents of spring and the seaside tang of the tidal river that filled the narrow basin beside the quay. Another covered walkway, fronting a newer building that mimicked the general shape of the warehouse, led her to the Millennium Bridge. Turning right, away from the bridge, she passed several restaurants on her left and another old building on her right which now housed a pizzeria. Then she crossed the plaza between a science museum and the entrance to an underground car park, before following another, narrower passage to the mauve façade of a chain cafe, its circular sign containing the white cup and stylised swirl of steam that she recalled seeing for the first time when Sergei had taken her to the bustling capital city of her own country. She had thought herself in love then, with the dashing, sophisticated friend of Georgiy who had swept her off her feet with his mysterious background, intense and haunted expression, kissable lips and film star looks. When they moved to the city, Sergei had become increasingly distant and secretive, until he showed up at their apartment one evening with a black eye and an overweight stranger in a cheap suit. Sergei had scarcely looked at her. He had merely turned to his companion and said, 'There she is. Do not mark her in any way, or Dimitrios will gut you like a pig.' Then he had cast one last glance at her and left without saying another word.

As she approached the cafe, Anna noticed the young woman carrying chairs to one of the outside tables. Her hair was black, like Anna's, but straighter and worn for convenience in a ponytail. She glanced over at Anna and smiled in a friendly manner. Anna was sure this woman hadn't been working here when she had last been to the cafe some two months earlier, on a cold, wet Saturday morning, after servicing the captain of the city football team.

The young woman followed Anna into the cafe and walked around the counter to serve her. Anna took in her emerald green eyes, mauve short-sleeved top, the small silver medallion resting between her clavicles, and the name, 'Daniela', printed on her badge.

'A latte and a croissant to have in,' Anna said in response to the trainee barista's standard question. The croissant was the closest Anna could get to those mouth-watering pastries her mother used to make in her childhood. She noted that Daniela too had an accent – Polish she thought, although the ignorant locals would probably think they both came from the same country. Close to, Anna noticed Daniela's uneven teeth when she smiled. One of them was discoloured. Sergei would never have permitted that. With her looks, he would have paid for a dentist. A cost that would be quickly recouped, as he would have told her in case she thought him soft.

Only two other women were in the cafe at that early hour – both cleaners, to judge by their overalls. One was dark-skinned with a pretty, round face and had covered her hair with a black scarf. Anna envied them their light-hearted conversation which made her think of her own happy childhood before her father had fallen into debt and lost his land. She tried to keep her thoughts within the orbit of those happy memories and the pleasures of the moment, but doubts and anxieties were already beginning to cloud her mind, intruding upon this brief interval of freedom.

She would give anything, she thought, to be able to work in this cafe, but even if she could escape from Sergei she would not be able to get a job here. She had been smuggled into the country illegally with other young women whose only value lay in their bodies. Sergei had made it quite clear to her that she, like the others, would be sent back home by the authorities if she was ever foolish enough to run away, and, in her case, Georgiy would do what was required, of that there could be no question.

Anna looked through the window: first, at the tables and chairs that had been set up outside, within the confines of a tubular steel barrier with weighted plastic bases and mauve-coloured panels; then at the art gallery on the opposite corner, with its window display of abstract paintings, each composed of different-coloured shapes arranged on a deep blue background. Occasional black lines and dots suggested the eyes and limbs of bizarre life forms. Anna took in everything, in a desperate attempt to keep her bad memories at bay and to cancel from her mind the drab room in the brothel to which she would be returning shortly, to be used and abused until late into the night. The two cleaners finished their coffees and left.

Daniela was leaning both elbows on the counter, with her left pinkie curled into the corner of her mouth. She stood up abruptly and smiled when the door opened and a man entered. Despite his unusually dark eyes, full lips and strong jaw, Daniela thought there was something repugnant about him that she could not pin down. He ordered a double espresso and slouched over to the beautiful woman sitting by the window in the short black dress and designer high heels.

Even at that distance, Daniela could detect the fear in her eyes, but she had no idea that the woman lived around the corner from her flat, in a three-storey house above a massage parlour. Neither did she realise that another woman with a severe facial scar, whom she saw on occasions in the supermarket, was employed in that house as a maid, or periodically to service clients with very specialised tastes. None of the women imprisoned in the house with Anna knew what, if anything, the maid had done to provoke the attack, but she was an effective warning to one and all, of what to expect if they ever crossed Sergei.

Once they were settled in the car, Anna handed Sergei the 120 thalers, less the price of a croissant and coffee.

'You're not holding out on me, are you?' There was a threat in his voice, but Anna thought the phrase ludicrous. She wondered where he had picked it up, but then, when she reflected on it, his former terms of endearment had been equally cliché, although she had believed them at the time.

'Where would I hide any money from you?' she said, reverting to their own language, spreading her arms as if to offer him her body. She handed him her bag. He rifled through her toiletries, looked in the plastic carrier containing last night's knickers and unzipped the pocket. Anna fought hard to control her nerves, but then he zipped it up again without comment.

Finally, they both clicked their seat belts and he pulled away from the kerb with unnecessary speed. Instead of joining the main road to the city centre, he took a sharp left and headed between the apartment blocks on the waterfront development. Near the end of the road, he turned left into the entrance to an underground car park and pressed a number into the keypad by the gate. There was a brief crackle from the speaker and a tinny voice said, 'Yes?'

'It's Sergei, Mr F.'

'Ah, you have brought your car.' The gates to the car park began slowly to open. 'Turn right after the ramp and go to the end – bay number 7A.'

It took Anna's eyes a moment to adapt to the yellow glow of the strip lights.

'Where are we going, Sergei?'

'No questions.'

'Should I stay in the car?'

Sergei flashed her a look of barely controlled rage. 'No, come with me.' He freshened his breath with a mint spray and carefully straightened his jacket. 'You showered?'

'What?'

'For God's sake, do not anger me, you fucking slut! Did you shower in the hotel?'

'Yes, of course I did.'

He pushed her roughly in the direction of the lift, where he pressed another keypad.

'Come up,' said the voice in its unsettling metallic tone.

A mirror on the back wall seemed to double the space of the lift and reflected their hastily turned backs. Neither Sergei nor Anna could bear to look at their reflections. Soft music was playing through hidden speakers, twice interrupted by a woman's voice announcing that the doors were closing, and then that they were opening when they reached the seventh floor.

They came out at one end of a glass-roofed corridor separating the two penthouse apartments. The walls on either side were faced with light-coloured wooden planks. Each wall had a door set not quite opposite the other, stained with a reddish varnish. Potted ferns stood sentinel at the far end of the short corridor, where a glass wall, divided horizontally into four panes, gave a view across the apartment block opposite towards Castle Hill with its cluster of roofs and chimneys and the crenellated façade of City Hall on its summit.

A youngish woman in a long black robe and black headscarf opened the door in answer to Sergei's knock. She seemed unable to hold his gaze, keeping her face inclined and saying nothing as she gestured to them to enter. Anna could tell that Sergei was nervous because of the way he puffed out his chest and exaggerated his swagger.

She followed him into a bright, airy space scented with sandalwood incense. It was an open plan apartment. One wall was composed of huge glass panes with a sliding door giving on to a rooftop garden of oak decking and potted plants. A bearded man in a white embroidered skullcap was having breakfast at a round table set near a rectangular pond, planted with reeds, whose sheet of glistening water flowed down an angled piece of slate at the far end. He rose when he caught sight of Sergei. Anna noticed that he was wearing a long white robe. His thin, slightly hooked nose reminded her of the Orthodox priest in her village. There was something, too, of the priest's monomania in his eyes.

'Ah, Mr D. Finally, I can put a face to your voice. Please join me.'

'And you are the famed Ben F,' said Sergei with a fake bonhomie Anna had never heard him use before.

'None other.' Then Ben F addressed the woman in a guttural language, whereupon she approached the table with a white mug, a pot of fresh coffee and a plate of croissants on a tray. Anna was unsure if the invitation was extended to her as well, but the woman clarified things by silently leading her to a chair at the breakfast bar in the kitchen area, where coffee, croissant and figs were set out for her.

Anna tried to make out what Sergei and Ben F were saying. They were speaking too softly for their words to reach her, and it was only Sergei's poker face and occasional intimidating smiles that made her conclude that it was a business meeting. Even from where she was sitting, she could tell that the smiles were little more than a simian display to hide Sergei's unease. There was clearly something about this Ben F that frightened him. The idea distressed Anna. It was as if she were trapped beneath infinite layers of threat and intimidation, each layer more dangerous than its predecessor, and she would waste her life working her way through them without ever reaching the end.

To distract herself from her growing anxiety, she looked at the woman, who was wiping crumbs from the granite work surface by the hob. Then she took in the abstract painting – a swirl of pastel colours – above the log effect fire; the tasteful sofas; the eggshell blue paint on the plastered walls. She had never seen the like outside the magazines that did the rounds of the brothel, but it occurred to her that there was little here belonging to Ben F, save perhaps the bookcase full of books on one side of the fireplace and the laptop on the coffee table.

The men rose, all smiles, shook hands, came into the apartment together, and Sergei said, 'You go with him,' confirming what Anna had suspected all along. The woman paused in her obsessive wiping and cast a brief sideways glance at Anna, but her impassive features gave no hint as to its meaning, and Anna dutifully followed Ben F to one of the natural wooden doors leading off from the sitting room.

She found herself in the master bedroom, which was furnished with the kind of simple luxury of which the Radion Hotel could offer only a crude simulacrum. The air was fresh and redolent of sweet-smelling herbs. The wardrobe and the chest of drawers were expertly crafted in pale wood. Everything was spic and span, save for the top of the dressing table. There, between two brass candlesticks, some objects were carefully arranged in front of a framed family photograph. Anna could not tell what the objects were; only that some had been blackened to a greater or lesser degree and that others appeared to be partially melted. Before she could identify them, Ben took hold of her jaw and gently but firmly turned her face so that it was in profile to his haunted gaze.

'I cannot bear to have you look at me. Will it please you to lie on the bed and cover your face with your dress?'

In fear and trepidation, Anna crossed her arms and drew the hem of her dress up over her head and then kicked off her shoes and lay back on the bed. Part of her thought that it was all over, that she was the price to be paid for whatever deal Sergei had struck. Odd memories of her homeland passed through her mind in a series of highly detailed vignettes: the dirt track winding down from her parents' house to her father's mustard fields with a row of cypresses rising beyond them though the summer haze; the fair-haired tourist eyeing her up in a cafe-bar in the capital city when Sergei had temporarily abandoned her to play pool with his gang; the framed poster on the whitewashed wall of that cafe-bar, advertising a French film of the 1960s – *Vivre sa vie* – which portrayed a beautiful dark-haired actress, whom Anna had longed to emulate; the main shopping street in that city where she used to gaze with frustrated desire at the expensive clothes and designer accessories, utterly unappreciative of the freedom she then enjoyed.

She tried to lose herself completely in those memories in a vain bid to escape the soft hands parting her thighs and pulling aside her pants, the brief in and out and the shuddering climax that were being enacted beyond the veil of her dress.

She lay still for a short while afterwards before uncovering her face. The man was standing at the dressing table with his face turned away from both her and the mirror. All she could see was the outline of his right cheekbone.

'Is your father alive?' he said suddenly, and she thought from the sound of his voice that he had been crying.

'No, he died of a heart attack after losing his farm.'

There was a long pause, before he said, 'I'm sorry.' After another long pause, he added, 'You can go now if you like.'

It seemed to take ages for the lift to arrive after Sergei pushed the call button. Anna could sense his mounting anger and impatience. He was always at his most dangerous when he was afraid, but she could see nothing in Ben F's behaviour to justify his fear, so she wondered if it was the organisation behind Ben F that Sergei feared.

The lift door eventually opened to reveal a young man and woman inside. They clearly had not intended to come to this floor, and they moved to one side to allow Sergei and Anna to enter the lift. The woman, a strawberry blonde with dimpled cheeks and a small up-turned nose, was wearing a dark blue skirt suit that had a name badge on the lapel. A laptop bag was hanging from one shoulder and she was composing a text or email on her phone. The young man was tall, slim and dark-haired. His eyes were small and close together and he was dressed in a casual leather jacket and black jeans.

Anna enjoyed the spectacle of Sergei trying to adapt his violent honour code to the couple's social norms. She was otherwise indifferent to their presence. There was nothing they could do to rescue her from the dismal room awaiting her at the end of the car ride: the sagging bed; the overused bidet behind its rattan screen; the dressing table and the wardrobe with their chipped pine veneer; the faded red carpet; the sinister gap beyond the bedside cabinet between skirting board and floor; the nameless men agog with hateful lust.

She took in the awkward smile directed at her by the man in the leather jacket; sensed the desire in his hastily averted gaze, which belied the courtesies exchanged during their brief descent. On reaching floor five, the speaker in the lift warned that the door would be opening, and the pair left Sergei and Anna with the stiff formalities of newly met business acquaintances.

★

Josef still bore within him the image of the stranger's lustrous black hair and unblemished olive skin. He could not recall ever seeing such a beautiful woman before. He wondered about her relationship to the handsome thug accompanying her, with his lascivious lips, cheap cologne and powerful body odour. Josef concluded that only someone with enough income to afford one of the penthouse apartments could hope to know such a woman and that the thug was no doubt employed as a bodyguard. He imagined her the moll of some wealthy crime lord out of the movies. For a moment the corridor with its anonymous doors and its varnished parquet flooring appeared more dangerous and alluring than was implied in the billboard advertising the development – a black and white photograph of a round ironwork tabletop with an artfully arranged still life of a white coffee cup on a saucer, a pair of designer spectacles and a Mont Blanc fountain pen lying aslant the open pages of an expensive notebook.

The estate agent was still trying to hide from him the inconvenience he had caused her by being late for their appointment. She had had to text several other clients to rearrange their meetings and, judging by the succession of electronic pings and whistles, she was having to make alterations to the order of the meetings to satisfy everyone. She had uttered the word 'lifestyle' several times already, in her attractive provincial accent, but her breezy smile failed to hide her perspiration and anxiety. By the time they reached the entrance door to the apartment, Josef was feeling very contrite and, it must be said, rather put off by her cloying words and nervous excitement.

He was reminded of some of the interviews he had been asked to observe in his legal capacity when members of the council staff had had to reapply for their positions to prove their worth to the new administration. Those interviews had begun to weigh heavily on his conscience, making him cringe at some of the arrogant assertions he had made in his PhD thesis about the disparity between terms of contract in the public and private sectors. He was horrified at the distaste and repugnance aroused in him by the desperation of some of those individuals when they realised they might lose their jobs.

The estate agent opened the door and ushered Josef into the apartment. He found himself in a hallway with four doors in the right-hand wall and a dazzle of light in the opening at the far end.

'The apartment is currently vacant,' she said, and switched on some carefully arranged LED spotlights. She led him to the open plan living area which she considered to be 'the best feature of this very desirable property'.

She indicated the kitchen area that was partially divided from the rest of the space by a breakfast bar. He glanced briefly at the oakwood cupboards and slate-coloured worktops and then turned his attention to the view through the panoramic windows stretching along both exterior walls. He could see the river curving into the gorge on the right and a terrace of multicoloured houses on the clifftop beyond the apartment block opposite.

'That's the benefit of a corner apartment,' the estate agent said, moving closer to Josef, who wondered if this unsought intimacy formed part of her sales technique. She indicated the ample space available for both the dining and lounge areas, before suggesting he might like to go out on the balcony.

Josef looked across at the pale green stucco of the apartment block opposite and then down at the rectangular water feature set in a stretch of glass between the riverside and the end of the road that separated the two buildings. He thought of the model of the city in the atrium of the council offices, with its white styrofoam trees and schematic buildings. It lacked all the precision and complexity of the old model that was now displayed in its own room in the museum with a series of oil paintings mounted on the walls around it which celebrated a visit to the city by the monarch in the nineteenth century.

The noise of a turbocharged engine intruded on his reverie, and he saw a black car emerging from the underground car park below and turning right with a squeal of tyres.

'There's another door leading into the master bedroom,' the estate agent said, touching his arm and indicating the way. The bedroom was similarly bright, airy and bare, with the same light wooden flooring as the living area.

Deploring his lack of experience with women, Josef gazed hopelessly at her rounded calves, her full, shapely figure and the rippling layers of her strawberry blond hair as she walked to the door of the en-suite and switched on its constellation of LED spotlights. An extractor fan hummed into life, and he felt an almost visceral excitement at the possible futures awaiting him in that apartment. He thought of the beautiful woman in the lift and of that woman he had seen after his interview a year and a half earlier. The latter had recently sold him a fantasy novel by his favourite author in the bookshop across the road from his office, and he had momentarily entertained the notion that they had been fated to meet again. She had barely acknowledged him, being preoccupied with some problem with the computer stock system, although he couldn't shake the feeling that she despised his choice of reading matter.

He thought of his current rather dowdy flat in the council block at the foot of Castle Hill, which he rented from the Chinese consortium that had bought the block from the cash-strapped council three years earlier. He could not imagine ever inviting anyone back there. It struck him that this clean, bright apartment offered him the opportunity to reinvent himself completely; to shed once and for all the dried husk of his drab and lonely adolescence.

The estate agent seemed to have an uncanny sense of his interest in the apartment. She was smiling unaffectedly, with no trace of her former anxiety. And there was nothing to prevent him from making an offer. His parents had given him a long-term loan for his deposit and there was the money left him by his childless Aunt Sofia. Consequently, his mortgage had been agreed in principle by the building society holding his parents' savings.

The estate agent suggested that he might like to see the second bedroom. He smiled, nodded, and turned to take one last look through the doorway leading to the balcony. For the first time, he noticed a villa among the trees and foliage near the top of a cliff, beyond the row of multicoloured houses.

★

Stefan J was sitting at the oak table in the kitchen of the villa, reading the Sunday newspaper and drinking coffee. His large blue eyes, aquiline nose, shapely lips and strong cheekbones combined with the sweep of his fair hair to impart a boyish, handsome appearance that fooled people into thinking he was younger and less experienced than he was. His muscular torso filled out his blue checked shirt. He was leaning his left elbow on the wooden arm of the chair and cradling his chin with his left hand. A braided leather bracelet drew attention to his well-toned forearm.

He had just finished eating a bowl of high-fibre cereal and half a grapefruit, the hemispherical skin of which was now lying at an angle on a saucer, weighted down by a spoon. He took his coffee black, not because he liked it better without milk, but because one of his former employees considered drinking coffee with milk to be unmanly.

The sun would not reach the kitchen windows until late afternoon, but he could now admire the play of its light on the trees and bushes that screened the western boundary of the grounds from an exclusive housing development built in the 1930s on land sold by one of the villa's former owners. The sky was a beautiful shade of blue that he wanted to call 'azure', but he was unsure if that word correctly described its colour. It was because of such doubts that he had given up writing in his twenties when he had worked as a bookseller. He reflected that if he had not given up writing he might never have taken the evening computer course that had led him to his current wealth.

Nina, the au pair, appeared, leading Stefan's daughter, Natalia, by the hand. Natalia – in a yellow floral-print dress, with one sock crumpled around her ankle – held back. She had been wary of Stefan since she had come upon him arguing with her mother on the previous afternoon when she had eagerly rushed to show them a snail she had discovered in the garden. He put his paper down, took off his glasses, lifted her on to his lap and moved her dishevelled blond hair away

20

from her eyes. She screwed up her face and leaned away when he tried to kiss her.

'Nina, Daddy smells,' she said.

'That's Daddy's new aftershave,' he said, casting a glance over at Nina, who had opened one of the cupboards and was now tearing off some cling film to put over the other half of the grapefruit which was on a saucer on the worktop.

'Elena said that she has not got time for breakfast. She is meeting a friend for lunch.'

'She didn't say anything to me,' said Stefan, noting the outlines of Nina's buttocks in her tight jeans, shifting Natalia on to his thigh and tickling her sides through her cotton frock. Little white rabbits decorated it, which he had mistaken for flowers. Natalia squeezed her lips together, determined not to laugh.

'I think she had just arranged it on her phone,' said Nina.

'No need to tidy up, Nina,' he said as she put grapefruit and saucer into the fridge. 'I'll do it.'

'Are you sure? There is no problem.'

Stefan released Natalia, who ran to Nina. Despite the presence of his daughter, he found his gaze shifting from Nina's triangular face and thick dark hair to take in the glimpse of cleavage in the opening of her blouse. He immediately looked back at her candid grey-blue eyes. Although her expression gave no hint of encouragement, the sight of her flesh made him feel a rush of excitement and hope. Hope of what, he would not have liked to say; just a vague sense of possibilities opening before him, of mysteries to be plumbed. Sometimes her face appeared feline; at other times it appeared pixie-like and mischievous. It belied the strong determination of her character and fooled him into an unwarranted feeling of protectiveness.

He put on his glasses again and resumed reading the book review. The novel *The Journey to Varnak* sounded fascinating. He thought he might wander into town to buy a copy. The walk would do him good.

'Would you like a fresh coffee?' said Nina. Natalia was now hugging her leg and pressing her cheek to Nina's thigh.

'Well, if you are making one?'

Nina lifted Natalia up, holding her with one arm and settling her bottom on her hip. She carried her across the room and through an archway to the playroom. From where Stefan was sitting, a bright red and green beanbag was visible next to a shelf unit laid out with toys and children's books. Picking up one of the books, Nina settled Natalia on the beanbag.

She flicked through the pages for a moment, before saying, 'Natalia, here is my favourite fairy tale. I want you to look at the pictures while I make your daddy some coffee, and I want you to tell me a story about the pictures. Then I will read you the actual story while I drink my coffee.'

Natalia settled on the beanbag with her knees slightly turned in towards each other and the book open in her lap. When she became aware of her father looking at her, she stuck out her tongue and held the book up in front of her face, until it began to droop from the weight and she returned it to her lap. She quietly began to describe one of the pictures to herself, in a matter-of-fact manner she had picked up from her mother.

Nina collected the saucer with the grapefruit skin and the cereal bowl and took them over to the sink. Stefan interrupted his reading to look at her once more, noting the way her blouse outlined her bra strap when she leaned over to put the grapefruit skin into an antique ceramic jar that Elena had bought for storing peelings and other waste food for composting.

Some twelve years earlier, Stefan had set up an online business selling second-hand books on behalf of booksellers across the world. His love of books had prompted his decision about what product to sell, but it was his knowledge of the latest developments in computer software that led to the company's success. Stefan had recognised that the internet offered an unprecedented medium through which bibliophiles could track down the rare and out-of-print books they coveted, but it was his ability to offer a secure payment method that brought the booksellers flocking to his website. His final innovation was to use customer feedback to regulate the process. It provided a readily available barometer of customer satisfaction that compelled the sellers to offer high standards of service or lose sales to their many competitors.

Six years after launching the business, Stefan sold the company for thirty million thalers to a major internet retailer whose coffers were swollen to bursting with venture capital. Astute investments in other internet companies had allowed him to more than treble that sum, simultaneously providing him and his family with complete financial security and depriving his life of all purpose, or so he liked to tell himself to explain the strange melancholia that had overtaken him in recent years and had alienated his wife. She could not understand why anyone who had experienced such good fortune should have any cause to feel depressed.

They no longer shared a bedroom and he seldom saw her now, since she had started a job in a PR company that frequently took her to the Capital. He owned an apartment there, where Elena stayed most weeknights, but which he himself had not seen for three years.

Stefan stepped through the front doorway of the villa and breathed deeply of the fresh spring air. When he reached the driveway, Elena drove past in her silver Audi. She turned to wave at him and he took in her dyed platinum bob, her amber eyes enlarged by her glasses, and her gleaming red lips. Her smile was so affectionate that he was immediately transported back to the happy early days of their relationship. Stefan let himself out of the side gate just as the main gates closed automatically. He could see his wife's car making a left turn into a side street up ahead, and he wondered whom she was meeting for lunch.

The road led him along the boundary wall of his grounds past the side street Elena had taken, before curving downhill between a series of villas, smaller than his own with more modest gardens, that were positioned at various levels on the sloping ground. They were not as exclusive as the houses built to the west of his property, which commanded spectacular views of the gorge and its famous bridge, but each of the houses he passed was different from its neighbours; variations on a notion of vernacular architecture that had been promulgated in the late nineteenth century and that bore little relation to historical reality.

Some of the houses offered Stefan glimpses of the lives within: a woman in a bathrobe, brushing her hair at an upstairs window; a man hanging a leash over a hook in the porch of another house while a Jack Russell wagged its tail and pressed its nose into his free hand; two young girls with identical haircuts and similar eyes, standing side by side, shoulders almost touching, peering out at him through a ground-floor window of a third house – this one with a steeply pitched slate roof and fairy tale turret.

He tried to imagine what life would be like with that woman – would there be a passion lacking in his own marriage – or those girls: he wondered at the peculiar intensity of their eyes and their passive expressions. He had recently started to take up writing again. The notion had come to him at a private view in the City Museum, organised to unveil the beautiful old model of the city in its new setting.

The renovation of the model had not run smoothly, as was attested by the small printed notice informing anyone who cared to read it that the street and house lights, which had once given the model city a magical night-time appearance, would be restored to operation as soon as the necessary parts arrived. It went on to say that the lights were not part of the original model but had been installed at the end of the nineteenth century by an electrical company eager to supply the city with this novel source of energy.

Stefan had loved the little figures populating the streets, or so he had said to his sceptical wife. The figurines of two men fighting outside City Hall, near a horse-drawn wagon loaded with barrels, had given him the idea of writing a novel set in the nineteenth century during a time of economic uncertainty and anarchist outrages. He had got as far as sketching out some ideas for characters and plotlines before falling into despondency about the project.

Now, thinking about the woman at the window and about Nina in the kitchen earlier, he wondered if he should not write a contemporary love story instead, if he could only think of an original angle. He began to run through some scenarios that had been circling in his head since Nina had come to live with them six months earlier.

The road descended for another hundred metres past the garden of the last villa, before climbing between rows of semi-detached houses to join the main road that led to the city from Selonaskala, the former clifftop village.

It was one of those beautiful sunny mornings in spring, following a clear, almost frosty night, when the light was crystalline and the heat was not too oppressive. It would have been perfect if Stefan could have stopped worrying about what his wife was doing; but none of his compensatory fantasies about Nina could quell his fear that Elena was having an affair.

He made his way past an eighteenth-century mansion that was now being used as an English language college and headed down a narrow road to the western slope of Castle Hill.

A dark brown leather messenger bag was hanging by a strap from his shoulder. In it was an expensive fountain pen, held in place by a leather loop; a ring-bound notebook with a green felt cover, in which he jotted down notes on anything that caught his interest; a leather-bound notebook containing plotlines and character sketches from his abandoned novel; a pocket guide to architecture he had bought to teach himself about the buildings in the city, but which he seldom referred to now; his mobile phone; his wallet. All the items were distributed about the various compartments and pockets in the bag in a specific order that had grown in importance to Stefan since he had started to suspect his wife's infidelity. He had now reached the point where he could not countenance changing it. There were in addition two compartments reserved for temporary items, such as the review of the novel which he had torn out of the Sunday paper. The bag had become for Stefan a small, orderly cosmos in which he found reassurance for his loss of control over other aspects of his life.

He understood that the problems in the marriage were entirely his fault, however much he tried to blame his broker, Anton W. It had been nearly three years earlier. Anton had brokered the deal when Stefan sold his shares in a mobile phone company for ten times what he had paid for them. Anton had invited him for a meal in the Capital to celebrate their mutual good fortune. Stefan and Elena had been between nannies at the time, so Elena had stayed at home with Natalia, who was then only six months old.

Memories of that evening began to run through Stefan's mind as he made his way past the car rental office and multi-storey car park on Castle Hill. It had been the last time he had stayed in his apartment in the Capital. Anton had booked a table in a new restaurant that had been decorated by a fashionable artist, Vasily K, with artworks that were heavily influenced by Joseph Cornell. The broker had assured Stefan that it was the place to be seen, and indeed a famous fashion model was there that evening with her boyfriend – a singer notorious for his anti-social behaviour and heroin addiction. Stefan recalled the sense of freedom he had felt that night as he ate a beautifully cooked rack of lamb and glanced at the fashion model from time to time. She appeared entirely unaffected by the attention she received.

The artwork by Stefan's table had remained as clear in his memory as the fashion model's famous cheekbones and pale blue eyes. It took the form of a glass-fronted rectangular recess in the wall, lit from below by small LED lights set in the base. A photograph of Brigitte Bardot – sitting in a bikini with her legs stretched out and her smiling face raised to look over her shoulder – had been pasted against a dark blue background, with galaxies, stars and planets, painted by the artist's assistants. A painted parrot from an illustrated book was positioned on a cardboard swing in the film star's line of vision and a black and white image of a naked woman with outstretched arms and multicoloured wings, taken from a Botticelli angel, was suspended from the top left-hand corner with a blood-filled prophylactic hanging beneath it. Dozens of small seashells were scattered on the base between the lights.

After about half an hour, conversation with Anton began to dry up. This was only the fourth time they had met up socially, and Stefan realised that they did not really have anything in common. Anton was not married, he did not read and he had no interest in art or architecture. He went windsurfing at a resort near the city of V most weekends in the summer. Otherwise, he played squash, went to the gym, or cycled. Analysing market trends took up most of his time, and his main interest in Stefan arose from the latter's remarkable financial success. Anton found it hard to believe that financial gain had not been Stefan's primary motive in setting up his online business, because he could only comprehend rare books and signed first editions in terms of their financial value or investment potential.

Stefan conceded that he had experienced a degree of excitement during the previous few years when he had successfully gambled on some companies that were at the forefront of computer technology, but he saw little point in accumulating any more money. The thrill had gone out of it. Indeed, the question of what to do with his life now was beginning to fill him with a profound disquiet that he did not want to share with Anton. The sensation of freedom Stefan had felt at the outset of the evening was giving way to a feeling of regret that he was not back at home with Elena and Natalia. He was beginning to wonder what exactly he had expected of the evening.

A waiter came over with the dessert menu. Stefan thanked him and looked over at the fashion model, who was carefully wiping the corners of her lips and checking her appearance in her compact mirror. His gaze took in her boyfriend's wide vacant eyes before returning to Anton's handsome gleaming face.

'What was the point of accumulating all that money if you don't use it?' said Anton. 'I mean, the kind of wealth you have can buy you anything you want; things we ordinary mortals can only dream of.'

As Stefan made his way past some bars and restaurants near the summit of Castle Hill, he could recall only scattered fragments of the subsequent evening. Anton had started to speak about a woman he had encountered in a brothel – apparently the most beautiful woman he had ever seen. The way Stefan remembered it, he had used all kinds of spurious arguments to cajole Stefan into accompanying him to that brothel.

'If money is power, Stefan, then your power is almost limitless. This woman will do anything you ask of her.' His avid expression as he spoke these words would form Stefan's last clear memory of that evening before they arrived at the brothel. They had gone on somewhere else after the restaurant, but, aside from vague images of a taxi ride and of a crowded dance floor bathed in ultraviolet light, Stefan had little idea of where they had gone.

He must have sobered up when they got to the brothel, because he clearly recalled the bedroom where he was taken by a quite attractive dark-haired woman with an exotic accent, a missing canine and a mole by her belly button. The woman Anton had referred to had moved on, apparently, but this dark-haired woman came from the same country as her.

The bedroom had been clean, with damaged plaster mouldings and the kind of furniture you might find in a bedsit, but it appeared to Stefan now to have been an otherworldly place where the restraints governing his life had ceased to have any meaning. His memories of his time there filled him with a queasy mix of shame, self-disgust and scarcely suppressed longing. Initially, the sense of longing had predominated and he had considered the whole episode to be of little consequence, as if it had taken place in an alternative reality that in no way impinged on his everyday life. However, in recent months his feelings of shame and self-disgust had increased to the point where he felt that he had irrevocably damaged his marriage and undermined his sense of self-worth. Despite those feelings of remorse, the memory of that dark-haired prostitute, standing slightly hunched by the bed in her underwear, came back to him now, stimulated by the female university students he passed on the street. And there it was again – the fluttering sensation he had experienced in the brothel when it had dawned on him that all his hidden desires were suddenly permissible.

He breathed in the fresh spring air and looked at the ornamental façade of City Hall with its neo-gothic battlements and turrets, then at the intense blue of the sky – 'azure' was surely the right word, he thought, for that shade of blue. Three young women were standing talking at the entrance to the bookshop. One was wearing a short black dress which had fallen off her left shoulder to reveal her gleaming collarbone and a thin, purple bra strap. Her hair was in a bun with loose ringlets around her face which recalled the hairstyles of the early nineteenth century.

Stefan thought of the review he had read in the paper that morning, of *The Journey to Varnak* by the Hungarian writer Gyula K. It had caught the attention of the media because the author had clearly based his fictional city, Varnak, on V, compounding the association by including a novel within the novel, entitled *The City by the Sea*. All the major newspapers had covered it, so Stefan had not been surprised to find the newly published translation reviewed in the liberal Sunday broadsheet that was delivered to his door – an anachronism, like so many of his current habits, that owed a great deal to his disenchantment with the computer-based medium that had brought him his wealth.

The description of the novel's opening had intrigued Stefan. According to the reviewer,

> it takes the form of a nineteenth-century travelogue with the Hungarian protagonist journeying to the city of Varnak. Once there, he presents his impressions of the city: its customs; its food; its sights; its history; the series of events that leads to his taking up residence in the house of a noble family. It is at this point in proceedings that the author introduces the novel within the novel – *The City by the Sea* – which is given to the traveller by a daughter of the house, and which ushers in a gothic tale of ancient evil and sexual obsession.

It was the reviewer's subsequent allusions to the extraordinary eroticism of the novel that had decided Stefan to buy it, perhaps because of Nina's tantalising presence while he was reading the review. Now that eroticism seemed to infuse the sunlit scene around him – the gothic flourishes of City Hall, the female students, and the young woman with the off-the-shoulder dress and unusual hairstyle, who smiled as she moved aside to let him enter the bookshop.

There were not many customers around and most of them were in the cafe, which was situated up some stairs through an archway at the far end of the room. Stefan had not been in this bookshop for a while and was surprised that he could find only a few books near the entrance. Most of the space was taken up with gifts, cards and stationery. He had to ask a young assistant where he might find *The Journey to Varnak*. The assistant looked puzzled, entered something on a computer keyboard, asked Stefan to spell 'Varnak'.

The assistant's uniform T-shirt had the initial letter of the shop name embroidered on its pocket. A plastic card hanging around his neck bore the name 'Sasha N'. His ill-concealed exasperation annoyed Stefan, who wondered why he had not just ordered the book online. He got out the book review and handed it to the assistant, making little effort to hide his own impatience. Then he was enveloped in a beautiful musky scent.

'Is there a problem, Sasha?' The speaker was a female shop assistant now standing next to Stefan and trying to peer round the edge of the computer screen. Sasha handed her the book review and she walked round the desk to operate the computer. She too was wearing a uniform T-shirt. Stefan noticed the name, 'Hannah D', on the name card.

'A truly marvellous novel, sir. The best I've read in ages. It looks as if we had fresh stock come in on Friday.' So saying, she came round the desk to hand him back the review. Then she smiled, swept out her right hand, fingers spread, tilted her head towards the archway and started walking in that direction. Her long, dark brown hair was gathered at the back of her neck with a purple scrunchie. After a moment's hesitation, Stefan started after her, gazing as he did so at the cluster of freckles on her naked right calf. There was another staircase in the archway, descending to a lower floor where the fiction department was now situated, as she explained to Stefan, half turning to look at him while she walked. He found the slight cleft on her chin oddly attractive.

She was wearing a black pencil skirt, with a slit running some fifteen centimetres up the back seam, but it was nevertheless tight enough to compel her to walk sideways down the stairs. Once they reached the fiction department, Hannah checked various tables offering discounts on books, and others on which novels were arranged by theme. Unsure of what to do, Stefan stood nearby, observing her with growing interest.

The impression made by the way she held herself was of someone who was self-conscious and awkward, embarrassed by her height. However, as he took in the play of light in her blue, downward-slanted eyes, he began to feel embarrassed in turn that he had put her to so much effort to find the book. He was about to tell her that it was not important, when she came over, smiling apologetically, and said, 'I'll just check the stockroom, sir. We are quite short-staffed now and perhaps no one had a chance to put it out on Friday.'

As Stefan smiled and nodded, he found himself wondering what age she was. He reckoned she must be twenty-four, or twenty-five at most. He could not imagine her wanting anything to do with someone his age, and he started thinking of Elena driving away in her car that morning, to her mysterious lunch date.

There was someone at Elena's work, Tomas, whom Stefan only knew by name; she had mentioned him once or twice, in relation to some conflict in the office, to which Stefan had paid little attention. Now, that name began to fill out in his imagination with various physical attributes that he knew Elena found attractive.

It occurred to Stefan that in only two years he would be forty. By any standards, he had been enormously successful. He had incredible wealth. He had that cliché of social success – a beautiful wife and daughter – and yet here he was, waiting for Hannah to return with the nervous anticipation of a lovesick teenager.

'Here it is,' she said, presenting him with the book.

His first thought was that the woman portrayed on the dust wrapper bore a resemblance to Hannah, but that was mainly down to hair colour and bone structure. The downward slant to Hannah's eyes, elongated by her eyeliner, gave her a more Asiatic appearance.

On the book cover the open French windows behind the woman had allowed the artist to render a balcony with art nouveau ironwork and a night-time view of the city skyline, which put Stefan in mind of the old model city in the museum. The woman, wearing a long dress of emerald silk, was presenting to the viewer a book bearing the title *The City by the Sea*. On the small cover painting of that book, it was possible to discern another woman whose face had a similar shape, but whose hair and skin were darker, who was running in a torn medieval-style dress through an apocalyptic scene of collapsing and burning buildings. The whole thing had been done with exaggerated colours and a slightly stylised realism that reminded Stefan of a book, retelling the adventures of King Corvus, that he had owned as a child.

'The cover is quite old-fashioned, isn't it?' said Hannah. 'It reminds me of my mum's old children's books. But it is growing on me.'

Stefan noted the Sunday opening times as he left the shop. Once outside, he called home on his mobile. He loved the sound of Nina's low voice on the phone and the way she pronounced the words slowly with her foreign intonation. He told her that he would be having lunch in town, but to let Elena know he would be home in time for dinner.

He ate lunch in a new restaurant down on the waterfront. Afterwards, he went to the museum to look at the old model city again, and, as he still had time to kill, he started reading *The Journey to Varnak* in the museum cafe.

The museum was just about to close when he made his way out, with no clear idea of how he would approach Hannah, or of what he expected might happen, but he was surprised by the distress he felt when he saw her emerging from the bookshop – now wearing a purple blouse that matched her scrunchie – and greeting a red-haired young man who was standing near the entrance in jeans and T-shirt and putting something into his grey canvas shoulder bag. Hannah kissed his cheek lightly and then took his arm in hers as they headed down the street together, talking and laughing.

Stefan felt sick to his stomach. He wondered what the hell he had been thinking, hanging around outside a shop waiting for a stranger who must be nearly fifteen years his junior. The woman with the nineteenth-century hairstyle had been younger still. He thought of the prostitute, reduced in his memory to a pale phantom, shivering in her underwear, with a missing tooth and a mole on her belly. He had no idea about the circumstances of her life or how she had come to be in that brothel with its bedsit furnishings and broken mouldings. He thought of the pattern of tiny rabbits on his daughter's dress. He thought of his wife living her separate, mysterious life in the Capital. He was overwhelmed by a feeling of self-revulsion and impotence at his irrevocable betrayal and feared that he might embarrass himself by bursting into tears – when he turned and saw a dark-skinned woman in a headscarf walking past. She looked back at him with eyes of such a deep brown that he thought his whole miserable existence could be swallowed up in them.

Yasmin S took in the stranger's desolate expression. She was reminded of the last time she had seen her father, and it unsettled her to recall her father's profound sadness. He must have guessed what was going to happen. The stranger turned and walked away, and Yasmin hurried towards the museum, made her way round the corner to the staff entrance and keyed in the code to open the door.

Mr T, the janitor, was sitting at his desk with his brown work coat hanging over the back of his chair. He was reading a military memoir about the recent war, written by a member of the Special Forces whose platoon, shortly before the invasion, had been dropped behind enemy lines among the arid hills encircling the enemy's capital. The book had rows of creases running down the spine and a photograph of the author posing on the cover in his desert combat gear.

Mr T looked at his watch and looked at Yasmin as she put her bag in her locker. He was a narrow-minded man with a small number of firmly held opinions that it was wise not to question. He viewed all immigrants from Yasmin's part of the world with deep suspicion and deplored the enlightened staffing policy adopted by the council. Yasmin's efficient and professional approach to her job served only to exacerbate his prejudice by unmasking its absurdity. He called her a 'raghead' to her face and made little attempt to hide his contempt when he spoke to her.

Yasmin blamed him for the recent reduction in her hours, but Mr T too was suffering from the changes. His overtime had been cut, with significant loss to his earnings. Moreover, his wife's cancer had recently spread to her liver, and the department administering her health insurance had refused to cover the expensive new treatment offered by the hospital. Mr T knew for a fact that immigrants were being favoured in the allocation of health and housing resources; an article in his newspaper had said as much.

He told Yasmin which rooms she had to do, and to make damn sure she did them properly. He would be checking. She went through to the cupboard where the cleaning equipment was stored, and measured some liquid cleaner into her bucket. It was a new brand of cleaner, which had brought Yasmin's hands out in a rash the first time she had used it. She had been more careful subsequently. On reading the small print on the bottle, she discovered that it had been manufactured by Alcatec Industries, a subsidiary of the ANH Corporation, but the ingredients offered no clue as to the cause of her rash.

That Sunday evening, she had to clean the room in which the model city was displayed. She loved the miniature city and worked quickly through the other rooms so that she could lavish her attention on cleaning it. She had even bought some make-up brushes to clean the dust from its narrow streets. She particularly revelled in the old-fashioned costumes worn by the miniature figures, possibly because she knew so little about the history of the city.

She had borrowed a history of the province from the library, but her brother, Salazar, had flown into a rage 'that she should waste her time on the lies of the unbelievers'. Fearing that he would destroy the book and cost them a fine, she had promised not to read it if he gave it back. And so, when she cleaned the model on this mild spring evening, her ignorance allowed her to imagine the city, populated by these people in their unusual clothes, as being a utopia where the women could pursue their interests and desires unfettered by the constraints of religion and culture, where skin colour made no difference. She pictured herself walking up the cobbled street to the public library. On the model, its walls bore the pristine sand colour of the building's original stonework, which in reality was discoloured by decades of soot and fumes. There, she would be able to pursue her studies untroubled by the deadening prejudice and perpetual anger of her brother, who controlled so much of her life.

Vladik, the collections development manager, came and found her there. A reclusive and shy man in his mid-forties, he found it difficult to speak to anyone, let alone this young Arabic woman. He should have reprimanded her the first time he caught her touching the exhibit, but he loved to watch her cleaning the model, to which he had devoted so much of his time, and he relished the care and delicacy with which she carried out her meticulous task. Observing her gentle movements filled him with a profound sense of calm and a kind of timeless pleasure. He could forget his anxieties about his position and about the increasing budget restrictions. In February, he had sent the finance department a purchase request for a perspex case to replace the inadequate rope barrier protecting the miniature city, but he had not chased it up, fearful of losing these precious moments with Yasmin. Nevertheless, he had been shocked earlier that week to receive a firm refusal of the request, countersigned by the CEO of the city administration.

Vladik's presence made Yasmin feel uncomfortably self-conscious and interfered with her thoughts. However, she was gratified when he told Mr T to go home, insisting that he, Vladik, was quite capable of activating the alarm and locking up. After Mr T's reluctant departure, Vladik said, 'Here, Yasmin, let me show you something.' He dimmed the lights and pressed a switch under the model. Whereupon a quiet hum started up and all the street lamps lit up, together with the windows in many of the houses.

'It is quite beautiful,' she said, suddenly smiling at Vladik, who smiled in return, awkwardly, as if he were trying out a novel expression.

'We are in the process of setting up a timer mechanism to dim the lights at regular intervals, to give the impression of night falling on the city. It looks almost real, doesn't it. See where the lights seem to ripple across the surface of the river.'

★

Yasmin lived with her mother and brother in an apartment in a former villa overlooking the town not far from Castle Hill. There were three rooms plus a kitchen and a bathroom. Her brother Salazar slept on a bed-settee in the living room. Yasmin's bedroom had been created by dividing up a larger room and had no window.

As she approached the building and saw the lighted window on the second floor, she knew that Salazar would be angry at her late arrival. She realised that she could never explain her feelings about the model city or tell him about Vladik's odd behaviour.

On entering the living room, she wondered where her brother had found the money for the flat-screen LED television, on which a football match was showing. Salazar, sitting in his armchair and nursing a small glass of black coffee, was wearing a long white robe that left uncovered a nasty scar on his right ankle, legacy of a serious accident on a construction site two years earlier.

Watching his face reflecting the flickering glow of the television, Yasmin was struck, as usual, by his resemblance to their mother when she was young and happy, before their father's imprisonment. His skin was unblemished, his eyes were almond shaped, and he had their mother's exquisite bone structure and thick, long eyelashes.

Yasmin had inherited her own round face from their father and, despite the beautiful straight nose she had taken from their mother, she could never regard herself as attractive. She was unaware of the many men, like Vladik, who had been entranced by the brown depths of her gaze.

When he finally became aware of her presence, Salazar turned to look at her with an expression of barely constrained rage, and she knew exactly what he was going to say.

Chapter 2

MAY

Franz P was sitting up in bed, reading the introduction to his PhD which he had recently drafted. It had seemed pithy and erudite when he had typed it up on his laptop three evenings earlier. Now it appeared to be clumsy and confusing, full of poorly worded sentences and awkward constructions.

He looked at his clothes scattered across the floor and noticed Hannah's brooch lying near his jeans. It must have fallen off her jacket when she left for work that morning. He would give it back to her when they next met, but, as usual, he had no idea when that might be.

Hannah set great store by her independence. Perhaps it would be a week's time, perhaps sooner, or a month might pass before she called him to arrange another meeting. It was not that she forbade him to contact her, but if he did she invariably offered some more or less plausible reason why they could not meet. He could drop in to see her in the bookshop, of course, but she did not like him coming there unannounced. The last time he did, she accused him of trying to control her. She might even think he had taken the brooch to provide an excuse for another meeting.

Sometimes he would rebel against this situation, and there would be an argument, but it was an argument that Franz could never win. He would always end up apologising to her because he dreaded the possibility she might betray him in a fit of pique. He lived in a state of constant anxiety about what she got up to when they were apart; an anxiety that was only compounded by her refusal to satisfy his curiosity. She was not his property, as she told him when he questioned her about her activities. She was free to do what she wanted without answering to him.

His anxieties about the relationship were further compounded by his deep-seated dissatisfaction with his appearance. He disliked his red hair and pale eyelashes, even if his freckles had faded in recent years. He thought his chin was weak and he hated seeing himself in profile. He was apt to put on weight quickly if he was not careful about what he ate, and he always pictured himself as pale and bloated when lying next to Hannah's slim, well-proportioned body. She was also a couple of centimetres taller than him and he would get very self-conscious when they were out together. He particularly hated the looks directed at him by waiters when they dined out.

As he sat in bed now he suddenly lost all interest in his PhD, his ambition to become a diplomat, the class on Hobbes's theory of government that he had to prepare for the following Monday. All seemed meaningless when compared with his desperate need for Hannah. He thought of her smudged eyeliner and the shadows on the skin beneath her eyes when she had woken beside him that morning. He loved the intimacy of seeing her slightly crumpled morning appearance, which made him feel less inferior, and he now felt the familiar ache of her absence.

When he thought back to the start of their relationship, he could discern no logical progression to his current, humiliating dependence on her. At one moment they had been meeting up regularly, having sex with a mutual pleasure that occasioned little reflection, with an almost blasé disregard for the future, and at the next moment he had been filled with an intense, anxious longing for her, coupled with a visceral dread of losing her to some unknown rival.

He tried to concentrate on his dissertation, but his mind kept conjuring images of Hannah from the previous evening. The fathomless pleasure in her suddenly open eyes. The shadow curving under her cheek when she laid her head on his chest. His doubts had been quashed temporarily by her unexpected passion, but now they returned with renewed vigour, drowning the words he was reading with Hannah's imagined betrayals.

He shut down his laptop, closed the lid and climbed out of bed. His flat consisted of one large room with a kitchen area at one end, and a tiny bathroom barely containing a shower, a miniscule sink and a toilet. The apartment block belonged to the university and had been constructed by the same consortium that had built the new politics department building in which his office was situated. Franz was not sure how much longer he could rent the flat, however, because the university was going to stop paying the rental subsidy that it had been providing for postgraduate students. The lectureship that formed his main source of income was generously paid on an hourly basis, but with only eight hours a week during term time he would not be able to afford the full rent on his apartment without the subsidy. As it was, he had to take a summer job to avoid having to return to his parents at the end of the academic year.

These gloomy reflections preoccupied him as he parted the slats of the blind and peered out at the drizzly day. Even the copper pyramids on the politics department roof looked dull under the grey sky. A woman in a red anorak and turquoise flowery wellingtons was manoeuvring a pushchair around some roadworks on the pavement below. A yellow car was preparing to turn right at the junction further down the hill. There was a hazy mist at street level, and it was colder than was normal for the time of year. He let the slats fall back into place.

The remains of Hannah's breakfast were still scattered on the round dining table. A mug of cold tea stood on the bedside cabinet. Hannah had made it for him before she left, but he had fallen asleep again after taking no more than three or four scalding sips.

On retrieving his laptop from the bed, he noticed the stain on the sheet, marking the place where he had disengaged from Hannah in the early hours of the morning, and he experienced a brief stab of anguished desire. This was soon extinguished by his hunger. He hurriedly replaced his laptop in its case and repaired to the kitchen area. He soon discovered that Hannah had used the last of the bread and milk. A quick inventory of the fridge's contents revealed a punnet of discoloured mushrooms, a small mound of butter under its dome, some raspberry jam, a half-full bottle of salad cream and a scraping of lime pickle in a sticky jar.

He made himself a mug of black instant coffee to assuage his hunger and then had a shower. As he soaped himself under its powerful spray, he remembered Hannah mentioning that her flatmate, Daniela, had taken a job in a cafe down on the waterfront. He would have his breakfast there, he decided, and give Daniela the brooch to take to Hannah. He could not think of a better way to convey his nonchalance about their next meeting.

It was raining heavily when he set out, so he reluctantly put on the light blue pakamac that his mother had given him when he started university. He had found a three-quarter-length suede jacket in a charity shop three months ago. Its leather collar was of a darker brown than the jacket and he thought it made him appear like a Parisian intellectual of the 1960s. But he feared that the rain would ruin it.

★

Daniela looked so different from the last time he had seen her that for a moment he wondered if she was the same person. Her hair was now cut short, with a straight fringe above her carefully shaped eyebrows, and it was only her name badge that allowed him to identify her. Judging by her impassive features, she still had not recognised him and was merely confused that he had not immediately placed his order. Franz, it should be noted, had not changed his hairstyle.

'Daniela, it's me, Franz,' he said after a moment. 'Your hair suits you,' he added as a smile of recognition finally lit up her face.

'Franz,' she said. 'I haven't seen you in a long time. How are things with you?' It was a question that Franz had only recently learned not to answer truthfully.

'Fine,' he said. 'How are you?' He was certain that things proceeded more smoothly for other people when it came to such social interactions, but he found them excruciating. He was intimidated by Daniela's emerald eyes and confounded by the critic hidden within him who judged all his actions according to such fluid standards that Franz could not conceive of the self-recriminations that might follow.

'I am well. And you are still working on your ... who is it?'

'Edward H, the political philosopher.'

'It made me laugh that I thought that you worked with him, that he was your colleague. I think I understand better what you are saying now.'

'Yes, sure. You have a very good command of the language.'

'You put things in such an odd way, Franz. Not like other people.'

Franz heard the door to the cafe open behind him, and he spoke in a rush, without thinking, pulling Hannah's brooch from his pocket. 'Listen, you couldn't give this to Hannah, could you? It must have fallen off her jacket this morning.'

'But she is in the bookshop today.'

He smiled weakly. 'Oh, she doesn't like me to interrupt her at work.'

Daniela looked and smiled at the person approaching the counter behind Franz, before accepting the brooch.

'And can I order a cappuccino with a pecan and banana breakfast loaf?' said Franz.

A severe and stout woman, with grey hair cut in the fashion of an earlier decade, cast an impatient look at Franz before gazing intently at Daniela, willing her to stop serving him.

As he carried his tray to a vacant table by a window, Franz reflected on the fact that some four months had passed since he had last slept at Hannah's flat and seen Daniela. Hannah had then been living in the flat for three months, having moved in shortly after she started working in the bookshop. She had told him that she used to work for the council. Her department produced posters and leaflets offering advice and information about a range of health and social issues. When the department suffered some financial cuts, Hannah had jumped at the chance of voluntary redundancy because she could not abide the working practices imposed by the new regime.

Franz had met her in the bookshop where she had finally found a job, earning less than half her former salary. She had only reluctantly moved out of her flat into shared accommodation so that she could save the last of her redundancy package. Daniela had moved in after the former flatmate moved out in early December. Franz had the impression that Hannah had stopped inviting him there because she was jealous of Daniela's artistic talent, but he thought it odd now that Daniela had taken so long to realise who he was. It struck him that Hannah never mentioned him to her flatmate, and this made him wonder if he really played any significant role in Hannah's life.

A group of French girls were gathered at a neighbouring table. Judging by the luggage they had with them, he concluded they were waiting for their coach to arrive at the nearby pick-up point. He imagined the bus on its way north passing through the fantastical scenery of the Tarent Mountains – an arched bridge glimpsed through the mist of a plunging waterfall, a castle on a crag, the dark forests spreading over the foothills.

Only gradually did he become aware of the bearded tramp sitting across from the girls, who was gazing at them fixedly over his coffee and tugging on his penis under the table through the filthy tweed of his trousers. Franz observed him with a sensation of profound disgust, made all the worse by the disturbing correlation he sensed between the tramp's heedless lust and his own obsessive, unequal desire for Hannah. Franz looked down at the unravelling cuff of his pullover and experienced a sudden sense of hopelessness. He had little to show for all his academic successes, and there were no immediate prospects of improving his lot.

On the increasingly rare occasions he was with Hannah in his flat, making love, watching television or sharing a takeaway, he would have the momentary illusion that nothing else mattered but their love, that they had managed to escape the merciless economic dictates of society, but when they were apart all the anxieties of his precarious existence returned with a vengeance. At such moments, he completely identified with Edward H's attack on the wasteful decadence and futility of consumer capitalism.

Franz turned wearily away from the tramp and the beautiful French girls, only to see Daniela flirting with a young man at the counter. He tried to console himself with the fact the stranger had a big nose. But he could not ignore his slim physique, his height or his thick black hair. The man was holding loosely in his left hand an umbrella, which he leant against the front of the counter when he reached into his jacket to get his wallet. Daniela was laughing at something he had just said and seemed reluctant to move away to the espresso machine.

Franz watched the man make his way with his coffee and umbrella to a window table on the other side of the entrance door. His clothes were casual but expensive-looking; his jacket bore the brand of an upmarket Japanese clothing chain. Franz felt sick with envy. He looked over at Daniela, taking in the harmony of her plump lower lip and round chin, but he noticed she was still looking at the young man and concluded bitterly that he had the kind of confidence that could only come with a well-paid job. Franz found a petty satisfaction in thinking about Daniela's crooked teeth. She wasn't self-conscious about them, but they made him feel that she was less desirable, forgetting that when he had first met her they had made her seem more attainable.

★

Josef set his coffee down, spilling frothy milk on to the saucer, and no sooner did he lean his umbrella against the table than it slid along the edge, to fall with a loud crack against the window. After laying it flat on the windowsill, he took off his jacket, draped it over the back of the chair and sat down, looking furtively about him. He was convinced that the barista had been laughing at him. Dropping the umbrella had only served to compound his embarrassment and make him feel that everyone was watching him.

The estate agent was late, although, to be fair, Josef had been late for their previous three meetings. The sale of the flat had progressed very quickly, but Josef was disappointed that the exchange of contracts had been delayed by two weeks. The vendors had agreed to take the property off the market not long after he had made his offer. Josef's solicitor had expressed her surprise at their readiness to do so and had grown suspicious about the sale. She had advised Josef's father to arrange a comprehensive survey and now she was querying the terms of the maintenance charge.

Josef himself suspected that his CEO, Chris, had intervened in some way, because everything had started to move very quickly after Josef mentioned to Chris in passing that he had made an offer on the flat.

Now, despite his solicitor's continued prevarications, the vendors had readily allowed him access to the flat to measure up the rooms and to plan their future layout. Josef reckoned that the cost of furnishing the place would be more than covered by the substantial bonus he had earned for his part in reducing the council's administrative costs. But he felt very guilty that his legal groundwork had led to considerable reductions in the redundancy packages offered to many of the workers.

On emerging from his reverie, he found himself gazing at the windows of the art gallery across the way. On one side of the entrance were displayed some oil paintings of fishing villages in a naïve style: multicoloured cottages; curving stone harbours; whitecaps and trawlers scattered without perspective on the thick blue impasto of the sea. On the other side, there were ultra-realist paintings of half-naked women in erotic poses.

At the corner beyond the gallery, he saw a young blonde woman bending into the doorway of a car to kiss the driver. It was only when she straightened up and pulled together her jacket lapels that he recognised her as his estate agent, Milena. The car pulled away, and as she approached the cafe entrance her face still retained the happy smile reserved for her lover. It bore no resemblance to the stiff dental display with which she responded to Josef's greeting when she arrived at his table. He stood up, wiping his mouth on his napkin, and offered to buy her a coffee and cake. She looked back at the entrance as if she were eager to get on.

'It's the least I can do for dragging you out on a wet Saturday morning,' he added, in a pleading tone that betrayed his insecurity.

She sat opposite Josef and covered her mouth with her hand when she took bites of her cake. In between mouthfuls, she responded to his questions by telling him something of her childhood. It transpired that she had been raised in a village on the Bohemian Coast, close to the one where Josef's parents had habitually rented a cottage in the summer. He wondered if their paths might have crossed on any occasion, but only a few vivid memories survived from that time, in none of which could Josef catch a glimpse of the shy young girl that Milena described.

The rain was heavier when they left the cafe half an hour later, so Josef held his umbrella over Milena. Not wanting to walk too close to her, he felt the cold rainwater running inside his jacket collar. An awkward silence descended on them, which Josef found hard to break. She eventually commented on the rainfall, such a regular feature of the city, and asked him why he had moved from the Capital, where she understood the weather was a lot better. After a moment, he replied that he had been drawn by V's proximity to the seaside that he had so loved as a child.

When they reached the apartment block, a slim, bearded young man entered the building ahead of them, and they ended up in the same lift. The stranger said nothing to them and kept his eyes slightly averted the whole way up. Josef noticed that he was heading to the seventh floor. His skin was a uniform brown and he had a scar on his left cheek. His thick, long eyelashes imparted a feminine quality to his eyes which formed an odd contrast to the tension evident in his face. Milena and Josef remained quiet, and Josef wondered if the estate agent shared his sense of the young man's implacable hostility.

As they walked along the corridor to the apartment, Josef said, 'Death to the infidels.'

'Yes, wasn't he creepy? I don't know why we allow them into our country.'

'Oh, I was only joking. He was probably just having a bad day. I'm sure we can all look that angry some of the time.' Josef almost immediately regretted saying so much. He was usually very good at hiding his true feelings, but Milena had badly marred his romantic notion of her.

He recalled his last year as an undergraduate, when he had taken part in the demonstrations that swept the country in a futile bid to prevent the war. He became aware not only of the gulf that separated him from Milena, but also of the gulf separating him from his younger self.

Perhaps sensing that she had overstepped the mark, Milena tried to distance herself from her statement by adding that she had merely been referring to the extremists and not the entire population. Then she bent to unlock the door to the apartment.

While Josef went through the unheated rooms, sketching layouts and measurements on the floor plan he had printed off from the estate agency's website, Milena remained in the living room with her arms crossed, looking through the window at the mist-enshrouded cliffs opposite. She was still standing there when Josef returned to the living room, but she was now typing a message on her mobile phone.

Josef did not want to appear as if he was trying to see what she was typing, and so he paused in a different part of the room to look at the view through the window. It occurred to him that the terrace of multi-coloured houses visible through the mist was like the rows of cottages represented on the paintings in the art gallery. He could not see the villa on the clifftop and, after glancing along the river, he resumed his task.

Milena continued to focus on her phone while he finished up his measurements in the living area, planning out the future arrangement of a dining table, settee, armchair, television stand and bookshelves. Her preoccupation with the phone made Josef feel the full weight of his loneliness.

Since he had moved to the city, his social circle had been restricted to his manager – Daria, head of the personnel department – and the five departmental heads appointed by the CEO. The remaining members of the former workforce clearly associated Josef with the new regime. They had nothing to do with him outside the interactions strictly required to carry out their jobs.

Of the small group that formed his circle, Josef socialised with Daria on a more regular basis. The other departmental heads were married natives of the city, but, like him, Daria had moved to the city to take up the job. Josef would meet up with her every two to three weeks for a drink or a meal – assignations that Daria insisted he keep secret from anyone else at work. She did not want people to talk, although she had made clear to him from the outset that she had no interest in a sexual relationship with him. Despite his initial impression of Daria at his job interview, Josef had subsequently felt little attraction to her. Yet he had been hurt by her firm disavowal of any desire for him, especially when she made him the confidant of her own troubled relationship with the CEO.

Chris had a wife and three children back in the States. No one aside from Josef knew he had set Daria up in a loft apartment in a converted stone-built warehouse on the river front. It gradually occurred to Josef that Chris knew he was socialising with Daria; that, far from being a secret, it was common knowledge in the office; that Josef's continued silence about it only served to enhance the illusion that he and Daria were an item.

Whatever was the case, Josef found those meetings to be frustrating, unsatisfactory occasions. Daria would constantly refer to her smartphone, frequently typing messages on it. When she spoke to him, she would pick his brains about her job, which was well beyond her experience and ability. She would complain about Chris's wife's refusal to grant him a divorce. She would speak admiringly of Chris's patient acceptance of his wife's moods, and of the sacrifices he made for the sake of his family; of his love for his children and his fear of losing them. Daria would dwell with thoughtless self-regard on the intensity of Chris's love and desire for her. On other occasions, without any apparent awareness of the contradictions, she would berate Chris for his cowardice and his inability to stand up to his wife.

'He's a selfish bastard,' Daria would say, her lips forming a thin, determined line. 'He's treating me like a fucking prostitute.' Uncertain of what was expected, Josef's unfledged mind would follow its own errant path, grappling with images from half-remembered films as he tried to discern the reality underlying her words. And he would become increasingly aware of her physical presence – of the light shimmers in her oily brown hair; of the lines of kohl around her eyes and the violet shadow on their lowered lids; of the way she crossed her legs under the table; of the glimpses of her bra and cleavage in the opening of her blouse – and despite her unpleasant character traits and her indifference to his feelings he would find himself wondering what it would be like to have sex with her.

Now, as he surreptitiously glanced at Milena, bent over the screen of her phone, he tried to imagine the unknown women he might invite to the apartment after he moved in, and he experienced the same sense of anticipation and wonder he used to feel as a child when reading a favourite anthology of fairy tales from the Bohemian Coast. He still had the book and on occasion he would look nostalgically at its brightly coloured illustrations: a beautiful princess in a diaphanous dress bound to a rock and menaced by a sea monster; a horseman riding along a clifftop path on a moonlit night; a zigzag of lightning illuminating a storm-tossed sailing ship; a handsome prince welcoming his bride into a firelit castle chamber.

Milena looked up and smiled. 'All done now?'

They parted with a handshake on the main road opposite the corner cafe and art gallery. He watched her make her way to the car parked a little way down the street, glanced over at the abstract paintings displayed in the window of the art gallery, and then headed home.

Josef was struck anew by the disparity between his current apartment block and the building to which he would shortly be moving. The lift was undergoing emergency repairs and so Josef had to mount the urine-stained concrete steps in the stairwell above the wheelie bins. The refuse collection was due the next day, and a faint stench from the open lid of one of the bins followed him up.

Dim energy-saving bulbs illuminated the corridor on his floor, reducing everything to the ominous half-light of his worst nightmares. The couple who lived two doors along from him were standing outside their flat, having a furious argument about money, while a small girl looked on, weeping. Josef was a reluctant auditor of several private details about a pay-day loan before the couple became aware of his presence and fell silent. The woman then took the little girl's hand and strode towards Josef with a forced smile dimpling her care-worn face. He nodded and greeted her, pretending he had witnessed nothing out of the ordinary, while a calculating inner voice revelled in her unhappiness, her tight jeans, the sexy gap between her front teeth, and her auburn hair, as if they were keys to a treasure locked away in a tower.

*

Adam F watched his wife and daughter Helena make their way past the young neighbour. Adam was humiliated by the way they must have appeared to him, arguing in the doorway like that, and conscious too of the way Katryn regarded the young man, as having all the qualities that he, Adam, so clearly lacked.

'Sorry about the noise,' he said to Josef in passing, once Katryn and Helena were out of earshot.

'No problem,' replied Josef.

'Women,' added Adam, with a smile and a shrug.

'Sure,' said Josef from his doorway, with only an awkward smile to indicate his discomfort or ignorance.

Adam looked in his son's room. Helena's favourite princess doll was bound to a chair leg, menaced by a band of painted plastic pirates. The scale was all wrong; the doll towered over the pirates. Anchored nearby on the blue pile of the rug, the pirate ship was smaller still. Several palm trees from Kris's toy zoo sufficed to suggest the flora of a treasure island. Adam rescued the princess and followed the sounds of the television to their source.

Kris was playing a computer game. The barrel of a machine gun moved forwards over a desert terrain reminiscent of the recent war, bursting into life at the press of a button when enemy soldiers appeared at the windows of half-demolished houses or from behind smouldering tanks.

'You mustn't play with Helena's dolls,' said Adam.

Kris grunted and shot another soldier.

Adam reflected on the fact that he was still paying for the game console and took the doll into Helena's room. He clipped it on to its stand beside the others on her dressing table. He looked around the neat and tidy room, such a contrast to the perpetual chaos of Kris's room. All her toys and books were so carefully arranged that Adam sat down on the bed and began to weep at the thought of his daughter's private cosmos being threatened by his irresponsible actions.

Despite having no memory of hiring the beautiful prostitute, or having sex with her, Adam had reluctantly paid his debt to Karl for fear that his friend would share the incriminating photograph with Katryn. Consequently, he had taken out a pay-day loan, thinking to cover it with his first quarter's bonus. However, a man had cancelled the life insurance policy that Adam had sold to the man's wife in March, thereby reducing Adam's sales sufficiently to disqualify him for the bonus and throwing him into a frenzy of anxiety about how he would cover the shortfall.

Katryn had only learned of the loan earlier that week, when she had opened the bank statement while he was at work. With no time to think of a plausible story, he had told her that he and Karl had ended up in a casino on their night out in April and that he had come close to winning 120 thalers on the roulette wheel before getting caught up in a losing streak. He included the specific sum of 120 thalers, which he had won in the bet on the football match, as if it would extend its portion of truth to the rest of his tale.

However, he had completely forgotten what he had told Katryn when he had returned home still drunk on the morning after the night with the prostitute. Faced with the numerous inconsistencies and contradictions between his stories, his wife became convinced he was hiding a sexual liaison of some kind and she had exiled him to the sofa, insisting that he had to get up before the children so that they would remain unaware of the rift.

The uncomfortable sofa did little to assuage Adam's insomnia, which had grown worse in recent months owing to increasing pressures at work. A new, more aggressive manager had been brought in to motivate the sales team. He instituted the practice, adopted by his former company, of recording all the reps' sales calls. During the monthly sales meetings, a random selection of these recordings would be exposed to critiques that bordered on insult and ridicule.

There had always been a graph mounted on a wall in the office to represent the reps' sales figures. The new manager now used small photographs of each rep's face, laminated on cardboard discs and fixed with Blu Tac, to compare their sales. Adam, whose sales were consistently the lowest of the team, had been taken aside on two occasions and berated for his poor performance. The main outcome of these tongue lashings had been to disturb Adam's sleep with horrific work-related dreams, which left him permanently tired and anxious.

Since he had failed to get his bonus, Adam had become uncomfortably aware of the desperation that had crept into his sales' pitches, which he was convinced was putting off potential customers. Karl had agreed that that was probably the case and had advised Adam he ought to get his shit together, because he had heard rumours that something big was going down.

'We're selling insurance, for Christ's sake, not fighting a fucking war!' replied Adam in a sudden rage.

'Jeez, calm down, man! I'm only telling you what I heard. Don't shoot the fucking messenger!'

At the meeting on the Friday just gone, the manager had spoken of the stiff competition coming from Indian call centres and of the changing role of the sales reps in the current market, before concluding that it was more important than ever that they improve their performance.

Adam had tried to tell himself that it was all just a ploy to get them to work harder, but now, sitting on his daughter's bed, with the noise of gunfire, shouts and screams coming from the living room, he wondered if his manager's words indicated that there was a real threat to his job.

He took one more look around his daughter's room before wandering through to the bathroom to wash his face. His eyes still looked red in the cabinet mirror, so he massaged some of Katryn's eye cream into the puffy skin. Then he headed to the kitchen to make beans on toast for lunch.

Kris was still playing the computer game, moving his thumbs rapidly over the controls and launching a barrage of gunfire at a building peppered with bullet holes. Adam thought of the children caught up in the recent war; thought of their rooms full of fragile treasures.

'It's time for lunch, Kris,' he said. There followed the usual rigmarole of trying to get Kris to stop playing the game. Kris clutched the handset firmly, continuing to press the firing button, compressing his lips, frowning, and fixing his gaze on the screen. Adam's stress and anxiety very quickly turned to anger. 'Give me the fucking handset!' he shouted, grabbing it so forcibly out of Kris's hands that the plug flew out of the console. At first Kris thought that his father had broken the cable, and he burst into heart-breaking sobs. Adam was profoundly relieved when he had plugged in the headset and was able to show Kris that it was working perfectly.

After lunch, Kris returned to his game. The boy was putting on weight and Katryn had told Adam that he should take him for a walk in the park while she was at her mother's. But Adam felt too weary to go through another battle with his son. He slumped on the couch; picked up the colour supplement of his Saturday newspaper; flicked through the opening column about a journalist's ongoing family tribulations, the shopping guide with its must-have gadgets and fashion tips; paused to read an interview with the hot actress of the moment; tried to imagine what it would be like to have such wealth and celebrity; tried to imagine the feel of her long, tanned legs.

Then he started to read an article about Edward H, whose book *All-Consuming Passions* had become an unexpected bestseller in the US and won a cover story in *Time*, in which the usual author portrait had been replaced by a large red question mark under the author's name, because nobody, not even the author's agent, knew who Edward H was.

The book had originally been published by a small publisher based in the Capital who specialised in Arabic literature, although there had been nothing in the book to indicate that it had been translated. A glowing endorsement by the *New York Review of Books* led to it being picked up by a US publisher, who had put out an English translation two years ago. The mysterious Edward H supported the publication with interviews in the *New York Times* and the *Washington Post*, which were organised through the author's agent and conducted by sending preprepared questionnaires to a Hotmail account that had since been closed. Royalties were paid into a numbered Swiss bank account. The recent surge in sales had sparked a frenzy of media speculation about Edward H's identity, but so far no one had been able to penetrate his mask.

Having got this far, Adam was about to give up on the article, when he was drawn to read an extended quotation from one of the interviews:

> The citizens of a state in thrall to the consumer capitalist system are so focused on the satisfaction of their immediate material desires that they fail to notice their bondage to the unattainable targets upon which the system depends. It matters not in what these

targets subsist: a spur towards ever-increasing sales; an optimum percentage of patients cured; the attainment of educational standards; the quota of weapons sold; the number of enemy slain; it matters merely that the targets are endlessly updated, to approach an ideal that keeps receding before them.

The system is, in fact, a grotesque parody of religious faith: those ever-receding targets represent a secular travesty of the search for the elusive Godhead; the material rewards ape the benediction of divine grace.

However, there is no morality in the system. It is a blindly functioning machine: material desires that can never be satiated; endless targets, never attained. No thought is given to the consequences – the environmental devastation, the inevitable economic losers, the innocent lives destroyed – so long as the machine keeps functioning, and the profits keep growing.

Under such circumstances, the citizens lose their humanity, becoming mere soulless commodities.

So perfectly did this sum up Adam's recent feelings about his job that he was filled with a strange excitement, as if the elucidation of his professional and financial difficulties had somehow raised him above them. He thought he might take Kris to the bookshop in town, to buy the book.

However, Adam didn't finish reading the article and so missed the journalist's argument that Edward H had let slip his alarming belief that the citizens of a consumer capitalist state are somehow less than human. Neither did he learn of the popularity of the book among evangelical Christians in the States, who found so much support in Edward H's arguments for their own radical Christian faith. One highly regarded preacher, reviewing the book on an American evangelical website, praised it for 'advocating the spiritual life' and said that, while he personally had no problem with the notion of working hard to make a healthy profit, 'such could only be tolerated within the context of the Christian values of faith, love, virtue and charity'. The cynical journalist concluded the article by noting the royalties flooding into that Swiss bank account and the wealth of the American TV evangelists, allowing her readers to draw the obvious conclusion.

'Why do you enjoy playing that game so much?' Adam said, but Kris did not answer. 'Do you want to go to the bookshop? I'll let you choose a book.' Still his son did not respond. 'Suit yourself.' Adam still felt guilty about the violence of his recent outburst, so he did not persist.

'Daddy's going to watch a DVD in his bedroom, so I'll be there if you need anything.' Kris shuffled round so that he had his back turned to his father. There was no let-up in the on-screen mayhem. 'I'm sorry for losing my temper, son. You know that I still love you.'

He selected a DVD from the shelves by the television, *Vivre sa vie*, in which Anna Karina had the starring role. Kris kept his eyes glued to the screen. Adam paused in the doorway, took in his son's spiked blond hair and exposed nape, which aroused in him a sudden over-whelming feeling of helpless love.

There had been a time when Adam had hoped to work in the film industry. He had studied film and screenwriting at a prestigious film school in the Capital, having gained a place largely on the strength of a short film that he had shot using his grandfather's 16 mm movie camera. Adam still had a copy of the film saved in a digital file on a memory stick, but he had not watched it for years.

After graduating, he had worked on a couple of film productions as a runner. The second film took him to V. While there he met Kat-ryn, who had taken a part-time job in a cafe to pay her way through art school. He could scarcely remember now the impassioned conver-sations they used to have then about art and film, or their nights of lovemaking.

He would go to her flat after running errands for up to twelve hours: for the actors; for the sound man; for the self-important director – often menial tasks, fetching coffee or collecting film stock from the carrier's office. On one occasion, he picked up a pair of prescription contact lenses for the short-sighted lead actress, who greeted him at the door of her Winnebago unselfconsciously dressed in her charac-ter's nineteenth-century undergarments.

For fear of disturbing Katryn's flatmate, Adam would throw a hand-ful of gravel on to Katryn's bedroom window, which looked on to a side alley less than three kilometres from where they were currently living. Then they would run hand in hand up the stairs, trying to sup-press the giggles that inevitably threatened to overwhelm them.

Unlike Adam, Katryn still looked the same as she did then. She had never liked the mousy brown colour of her hair, which she still dyed auburn. She still had that sexy gap between her front teeth, and her face still dimpled when she smiled, but she seldom smiled at him now.

Adam started to watch the DVD on his work laptop, which he positioned on the end of the bed. He had not had chance to watch a film for a while. Katryn tended to be so dismissive of the films he liked that he wondered if she had always felt that way and had merely pre-tended to enjoy the films they had gone to see together at the begin-ning of their relationship.

When the film started, he felt a sudden rush of nostalgic longing. It was a film that he had first seen in a class at film school on a poor-quality VHS with appallingly translated subtitles. At that time, Adam hadn't learned to hide his enthusiasms from his cooler and more knowing classmates. During the discussion following the screening, he had extravagantly praised the novelty of Godard's approach, the talent of the lead actress, the background glimpses of real-life Paris.

He no longer precisely recalled the scathing criticism he had suffered from the intimidatingly intelligent woman in the class, who had said he was an idiot and who had accused Godard of being a misogynist because he treated Anna Karina like a chattel. All Adam could remember now was the exciting novelty of discussing films with interesting young women and the feeling he had had then that a new life was opening before him.

When he met Katryn, it had seemed that she embodied that new life. He had felt no doubts about setting aside his film ambitions so that they could live together in V. Even when she subsequently became pregnant with Kris, he had felt no qualms about taking a better-paid job in sales. However, Katryn had said some painful things during their recent arguments, which suggested she had not shared Adam's happiness at that time; that she had found his friends intimidating and his film tastes oppressive; that she had felt trapped by the pregnancy and dissatisfied with their financial hardships.

Now, as he watched Anna Karina in the film, in her role as a sales assistant in a record shop, he was struck by her resemblance to the prostitute he had seen briefly in the Radion Hotel, caught in the wedge of light falling through the open bathroom door. The resemblance added a poignancy to the ending of the film, when Anna Karina's character, drawn into prostitution by a gangster, accidently dies during a gangland shoot-out. While at film school, he had concluded an essay he had written on this film by highlighting the way that Godard mixed a kind of documentary realism with the cliché melodrama of American film noir to unsettling effect.

Adam reflected on the way that he had stumbled out of the domestic world of his unravelling marriage into the frightening netherworld inhabited by the foreign prostitute, and, like a character in a fairy tale, drawn by a beautiful nymph into the labyrinth of a dark forest, he wasn't sure if he would ever find his way back.

After putting the DVD away in its case, he headed to the sitting room. The game console was switched off and the TV was signalling the fact that no video input could be detected. Adam set the TV back to the smart box supplied gratis by the service provider, reflecting as he did so on their twenty-five-thaler monthly charge. Adam wondered why the hell they paid for those 120 TV stations with their minor variations on a handful of tired programme formats and their endless cloying adverts. He watched a buxom chef adding chopped tomatoes and garlic to the onions already sizzling in a frying pan and then switched it off.

He tracked Kris to his bedroom, to find him making whooping noises and moving his toy pirates in a circle around Helena's half-naked doll.

'Jesus, Kris, I told you not to play with Helena's toys!' He managed to restrain his temper as he picked up the doll and pulled the bodice of its pink dress back over its plastic breasts. Then he wandered back into the sitting room, pushing in the metal poppers that held the dress in place. It was gone six. Adam wondered where Katryn and Helena were. He had expected them back before now.

The sky was overcast, so the living room was darker than usual for this time of the day. He switched on the standard lamp that stood in one corner with an upturned cone-shaped plastic shade coated on the inside with dust and dead insects. Thankfully, the princess doll and its dress appeared unharmed by its recent ordeal. Adam once again returned it to its place in Helena's bedroom. Then he went back to the sitting room.

'I'm hungry, Daddy,' Kris called from behind his closed door.

After searching for some five minutes with increasing impatience and muttered expletives, Adam located his phone under the TV guide on the coffee table. He was about to ring his mother-in-law's number, when he noticed he had received a text from Katryn:

Helena and I are staying over at Mum's. I'm having a night out with Eva. Mum thought it would do me good. Be sure and feed Kris. K.

Adam read the message again, trying to work himself up into a sense of outrage at Katryn's lack of consideration for Kris. He told himself that she had always favoured Helena over her son. He told himself that her mother had never approved of their marriage. He feared what Katryn and Eva would get up to while they were out. He remembered the photograph on Karl's phone of the prostitute gripping his penis. He remembered kissing Katryn's friend Eva in the kitchen at a party while Katryn was slow dancing in the lounge with Eva's former husband, Klaus. The kiss was never repeated, but Adam always feared that Eva might have told Katryn about it.

Adam's mother-in-law lived in a luxurious two-bedroom apartment in Selonaskala, near the bridge over the river gorge. Eva and Katryn would no doubt go out to one of the nearby wine bars that catered for the wealthy locals. Adam did not know whether he should worry more about the expense of the night out or about the fact that some handsome stranger might pay for Katryn's drinks. He looked around the room at their shared belongings and experienced a sudden feeling of claustrophobia that set his heart racing and filled him with panic.

His stomach twisted with regret and a longing to return to those early days of his relationship with Katryn: when his belly was firm and muscular; when Katryn would get so carried away by the passion of their lovemaking that she would continue to squeeze him with her thighs after she had come, stroking his lower back and buttocks, running her fingers through his thick brown hair, alternately kissing him and whispering how much she loved him, with the inevitable result that he would recover his potency and they would resume their lovemaking to the point of satiated exhaustion.

Now, more than anything else, he wanted to go out in search of Katryn; to find the words to make everything right between them; to bring her home; but he couldn't leave Kris alone in the apartment and he had to prepare their dinner. He opened the window and breathed in the cool, damp air. The spring scents calmed him a little. What, after all, was there to worry about? Next week, he might make some big sales that would transform their fortunes and allow him to pay off his loan.

He saw a couple further up the hill, approaching a street lamp whose light glistened on the wall bordering the park opposite. The woman laughed suddenly. From that distance, he couldn't make out the details of her face, but that only served to enhance the illusion of her unattainable beauty, and he experienced a crushing feeling of envy for her companion, who was putting down his umbrella and shaking it over the gutter. She took hold of his left arm with both hands and whispered something in his ear. It pained Adam to watch them walking down the hill and to realise that he would never know what she had said. He imagined it was something that not even Katryn had ever said to him, something that might redeem all the wrong turns he had taken in life.

★

Hannah felt Stefan stiffen slightly when she grasped his arm with both hands and inadvertently pulled it against her breast. She reckoned that he feared being seen with her, because he was married, and the thought added a frisson to the contact with his muscular biceps. He moved his arm sufficiently to settle his bag on his shoulder without dislodging her hold.

'So where are you taking me?' she whispered.

'That's for me to know and for you to find out.' He held the dripping umbrella away from him and seemed to relax when he fell into step beside her. She still was not sure why she had agreed to go out with him.

After she had sold him *The Journey to Varnak*, she had seen him browsing in the shop on several occasions, but he had shown no signs of noticing her. She had perceived an expression of uncertainty in his large blue eyes and boyish features that she found appealing, as if he were quite unaware of his good looks and muscular body. And then they had chanced to meet in the bookshop cafe on Monday. It had been busy and he had asked her if he could share her table. It was only when she moved her handbag off the chair that he had assumed an expression of surprised recognition, which did not altogether convince her. After setting down his coffee and cake and taking out a leather notebook and a pen, he settled into the chair and between sips and bites he wrote something in his notebook, read it and scored it out.

Hannah could no longer concentrate on her reading. She put her book down, lifted her cup with both hands and looked at him over the rim. When she returned the cup to the saucer she said, 'Did you enjoy *The Journey to Varnak*?'

He put on a clumsy pretence of surprise and confusion before saying, 'Yes, I thought it a brilliant novel.'

She and Stefan then began to feel more at ease with one another, and Hannah enjoyed discussing the book in a relaxed manner quite unlike the tense conversations she now had with Franz, which were poisoned by his unspoken fears and paranoia. With Stefan she soon fell into a kind of teasing banter. Just before the end of her tea break, she asked him why he was not at work.

'Me? I don't have to work.'

'Is that because you're so rich that you don't need to work?' she said in an ironical manner.

'Yes, as a matter of fact, that's exactly why I don't need to work.'

She was about to tell him to stop joking around, but she realised he was being quite serious.

'It's not at all how I imagined it would be, when I used to think about being rich. I suppose you imagine a world where you always get what you want, and yet, when the money is there, it isn't like that at all. You realise very quickly that you have no idea what you want.' Hannah thought of several scathing replies, but she said nothing, and he tentatively added, 'Would you like to go out with me on Saturday evening?'

'How would your wife feel about that?'

'Oh, she's away working in the Capital. Some kind of conference. My wealth has done little to help our relationship.'

He had looked at her with an unreadable expression. She had noticed that his hands were compulsively folding his cafe receipt.

'Sure, yes, why not? You can pick me up outside the bookshop at 6.15.'

Stefan felt unusually calm as they made their way down Castle Hill. He thought it unlikely that anyone he knew would see them. Since he had sold his company, he seldom saw anyone apart from his wife, his daughter and now their au pair, Nina. There was the man who came twice a week to work on the garden, and the cleaners, but Stefan thought it very unlikely that they would dine in the waterfront restaurant where he had booked a table. He had not met his broker, Anton, for nearly a year now. Out of all the money men he had encountered, Anton was the only person he would class as a friend.

His wife Elena had had a close friend from university who had married someone from V, and the two couples used to meet up regularly. They had even gone on holiday together, to a villa in Tuscany, but the friend had divorced her husband, taken a job in Stockholm, and Elena seldom heard from her now.

Elena certainly had a social life in the Capital, but Stefan had not met any of her new friends or business associates. He told himself she would not care less even if she happened to be in town and saw him walking arm in arm with Hannah, although he realised full well that this was spurious reasoning, little more than self-justification. But, at this moment, he felt as if his entire past life was an irrelevance.

There was only the empty street and Hannah walking beside him. He did not know what she was saying. He was aware of her downward-slanted eyes periodically turning towards him; of the pale curve of her cheek catching the light of first one lamp post and then another; of her musky scent; of her breast brushing against his arm that she was loosely gripping near his armpit and at the crook of his elbow as they moved in step on the glistening pavement; of the fresh spring breeze sweeping up the gorge from the sea; of the terrace of old houses beside them.

After all the time he had skulked in the bookshop, surreptitiously looking at Hannah, after his uncharacteristic advances in the cafe when he had finally overcome his fear of rejection, he could scarcely believe that he was here now with this woman.

'Doesn't it remind you of the scene in the novel when Bela and Anya escape her chaperone during the Martyrs' Procession and end up walking towards the river together?'

When these words drew him from his reverie, Stefan felt a sudden rush of desire, for he quite clearly recalled that scene, which prefaced one of the most highly charged episodes in the novel – the one in which Bela and Anya finally have sex up against a damp wall in a stinking alleyway between two warehouses.

At the foot of the hill, they passed a roundabout and joined the avenue running parallel to the waterfront. Hannah looked at the impressive stone-built warehouse opposite, which had been converted into luxury apartments by the ubiquitous ANH Corporation. A figure was standing at the panoramic window of one of the loft apartments, in which cones of soft light illuminated a blue vase and a stereo player on a shelf, one end of a red couch, and a patch of lemon paint on a wall. She could not tell if the figure was a man or a woman. Only the building's stone walls recalled the city of the past.

The view beyond the warehouse was now dominated by an apartment block with pale render between rows of windows giving on to balconies. Adjacent to it was a chain hotel and beyond that the museum of science. The restaurant was on the square behind the museum.

As the waiter led Stefan and Hannah to the tastefully furnished conservatory it occurred to her that Stefan would normally eat in far more exclusive restaurants, and she wrongly concluded that he was trying to avoid his usual circle of friends. When he took his seat opposite her, she noticed how his white linen shirt was shaped by his muscular torso, but her pleasure was marred by the notion that he had calculated precisely how much he was willing to spend in order to seduce her. For all the manifest pretensions of the table service, she could not help but see the place as an unflattering reflection of her own sexual worth.

Stefan was aware of her change of mood, but he could not figure out the cause. He was further surprised when she took out her phone without looking at the menu that the waiter placed in front of her.

'Would you like a drink?'

'Sure, anything you'd like.' She did not look up from the images through which she was scrolling. Stefan ordered an Australian dry white wine and an expensive French red.

Hannah was beginning to think that the entire date was a hideous mistake. At that moment, she received a message from her flatmate Daniela:

Franz came to cafe. He gave me your brooch. X

As usual, Hannah noted the abrupt tone and incongruous kiss. She was relieved about the brooch, but then she wondered why the hell Franz had given it to Daniela. Despite being on a date with another man, she jealously wondered how Franz had discovered where Daniela worked.

'Would you like to go somewhere else?' said Stefan.

'What, my place or yours?'

'No – what? – no. I was just wondering if you would rather eat somewhere else.'

'Oh.'

'You don't appear to like this place.'

'No, not at all. It's fine. I'm sorry.'

'What did you mean about your place or mine?'

'It was nothing, really. I was just distracted by a message from my flatmate. I wasn't thinking.'

'Would you rather go home?'

'Oh no, it's nothing serious. I'm sorry, the restaurant is great. It was just a misunderstanding with my flatmate. Everything is fine now.'

Stefan knew that her mood had changed before she had looked at her phone, but he decided to take her at her word. After a couple of glasses of wine, they began to converse more freely. He looked out of the window at the water features on the square: two granite-faced blocks with water streaming down into shallow triangular pools. The large glass panels of the conservatory could be removed, and in the summer it would revert to an ordinary terrace.

'I don't dine out very often, so I wasn't sure where I should take you. In fact, I don't go out very much at all. I mainly stay at home with my daughter.'

'You have a daughter?'

'Yes.'

'And who is looking after her?'

'Nina.'

'Who's Nina?'

'The au pair, of course.'

'Of course.' She laughed. 'You really take the biscuit.'

'What do you mean?'

'If you are so wealthy, why does your wife work?'

'Why indeed?'

'Well, why do you think she works?'

'I think she was dissatisfied – with me primarily, but I think also with her life. It's odd; my depression just annoyed her, and yet I think she found her own life to be equally meaningless.'

'God, my flatmate has got two jobs, which pay dreadfully, and she sends money to her family in Poland. Most people don't have the luxury of finding life meaningless.'

'Believe me, I know what it's like to be poor. I used to be a bookseller. At one time, I wanted to be a writer.'

Hannah ate her vegetarian option of linguine with mushrooms and special pesto sauce. She was sure that there was minced veal in Stefan's cannelloni. The whole thing was absurd. Outside of the novel, they had nothing in common, and yet she found him attractive. It was not his money. She was quite certain of that. However, the thought of his daughter made her feel uneasy.

As the waiter helped her into her coat at the end of the meal, she was preparing an excuse as to why she had to go home early. So she was nonplussed when, at the restaurant entrance, he thanked her for a lovely evening and leaned in to give her a peck on the cheek.

'I'd love to go out again,' he said. 'Perhaps you could give me your number?'

'Why don't you give me your mobile, and I can text you my number when my new contract is sorted out next week?'

'Sure.' He tore a page out of a notebook from his bag. Then, having given her his number and restored everything to its place in the bag, he shook her hand and thanked her again for the evening.

★

The job was not perfect, but it was the best that Nina had had since leaving Poland four years earlier. She had a suite of three rooms in the attic next to Natalia's bedroom and bathroom. When she had moved in six months earlier, Stefan had told her that she was to treat the rooms as her own. After three months, she had even been allowed to entertain her fiancé there, until he cheated on her with a young Estonian woman he had met in the book distribution warehouse where he worked.

The suite consisted of a bedroom, a cosy sitting room (complete with a flat-screen TV and music system) and a shower room with a toilet; all accommodated within the villa's mansard roof space. After her probation period, she had also been allowed to use the main sitting room while Stefan and Elena were out, and they ensured that they bought in supplies of food and drink that she liked.

In addition to her role as nanny, she was responsible for supervising the gardener and the cleaners. Stefan had also recently offered her extra money to provide Natalia and him with meals when Elena was away.

Nina loved Natalia, and she was reasonably sure that Natalia loved her. The child had certainly grown a lot closer to Nina since her mother had started working in the Capital. All in all, Nina's life here was a world away from the poverty her family had endured in Warsaw. She did not mind having her meals with Natalia in the kitchen, where Stefan would join them in Elena's absence. She would have had no complaints about the job at all but for the fact that when Elena was home she expected Nina to serve Stefan and her their meals in the dining room.

Elena loved cooking, and made all the meals when she was there, but she enjoyed the luxury of being waited upon and of having the kitchen cleaned afterwards. Those were the only occasions that Nina felt the humiliating inferiority of her situation. Stefan, who was more sensitive to Nina's feelings than his wife, arranged for a supplement to be paid to Nina's wages out of one of his many accounts. However, he asked Nina not to mention the payments to Elena, thereby drawing Nina into a collusion that she rather enjoyed and that went some way towards compensating her for the humiliation.

Of more concern to Nina was the fact that she would only have the job until Natalia's seventh birthday. At the outset, Elena had been quite clear that she was looking for someone to work until then. They had gone through several nannies before Natalia turned three, and Natalia had always had emotional problems when each one left. Consequently, Elena wanted Nina to work for forty-four months and, after her probation period, Nina had signed a binding contract to that effect. When Natalia turned seven, Elena planned to hire a native-born woman as governess. She would have the necessary education to provide extra-curricular tuition for Natalia, and the playroom would be converted into a schoolroom.

Nina was standing at the window of her sitting room, drinking a glass of wine and looking at the spectacular view over the city. The sky was cloudy and there was a fine mist, so the river was only visible through the glints of reflected light from the waterfront development. A string of orange bulbs illuminated the famous suspension bridge, which extended beyond the foliage on her right to the dark mass of hills on the south side of the gorge. Beyond those hills lay the fabled Bohemian Coast that had so captured her imagination when she was a child.

Her father had told Nina and her sister such marvellous tales when they were children, but, as she grew older, Nina became increasingly aware of his heavy drinking, depression, and antagonism towards everything that conflicted with his world view. He was a film director, who had fallen foul of the communist regime and lost his livelihood. Her mother had had to do various menial jobs to feed and clothe the family. Even after the fall of communism, her father could not get funding for his film projects.

Nina still harboured fond memories of the gatherings at their cramped flat in Warsaw, when artists, writers and film-makers who, like her father, had failed to find success under the new regime would converse and argue into the small hours about their respective art forms. Through the crack of her bedroom door, Nina would peer at those glamorous visitors sitting in a fug of cigarette smoke round the dining table, cluttered with beer bottles and bowls of salted snacks, and eagerly take in their mysterious and passionate arguments, feigning sleep whenever her mother put her head round the door to check on her and her sister.

Those times had been on her mind for a couple of days now, because of the DVD that her mother had sent her. It was a film – made recently by a young director, centring on a doomed love affair between two Polish writers during the last months of communism – on which her mother and father had both worked as advisors. Nina had not yet had the opportunity to watch it, but she was planning to do so that evening, while Stefan was out, on the large-screen TV in the downstairs sitting room.

It had taken half an hour to get Natalia to go to sleep. She tended to be more anxious when her mother was away. Then Nina had had a shower, changed into her pyjamas and opened a bottle of wine.

She took one last look at the varicoloured city lights climbing the slopes of Castle Hill and spreading out across the river to the southeast. She could see her pale reflection superimposed upon the view: nursing her wine glass in one hand while rubbing her bare arm to ward off the chill coming through the ventilator. A feeling of self-loathing took hold at the sight of her face with its broad cheekbones and the rather pointed chin beneath her puffy lips. No matter how often her fiancé had told her how beautiful and feline her face was, she could never believe what he said, and of course his actions had proved her right. She looked critically at her threadbare pyjamas. Elena's expensive and tastefully chosen clothes had brought home to Nina just how tawdry her own clothes were. An unpleasant shiver ran down her spine as she crossed the room to unhook the white terry-towelling bathrobe hanging from the shower room door.

She slipped the DVD under her arm and picked up the wine glass and bottle. With some difficulty, by putting glass and bottle down on one of the steps and tucking the DVD under the belt of her bathrobe, she unlocked and relocked the stair gate.

Just before settling down to watch the film, she remembered the baby monitor that she had left in her room, so her second journey down through the villa was accompanied by the soft sound of Natalia breathing in her sleep.

On her way along the first-floor landing, Nina succumbed to the temptation she had resisted earlier of looking into Elena's bedroom. She was not forbidden to enter any of the bedrooms. In fact, she had to enter all of them to check that the cleaners were doing their jobs. But it was tacitly understood that she wouldn't enter Stefan or Elena's bedrooms except strictly as required by her job.

Elena had recently had her room redecorated by a trendy designer, who had changed it from the sleek modern bedroom that Nina had loved, into a room of fashionable simplicity that the designer had modelled on his own odd notion of a Scandinavian homestead: an iron bed with an anachronistic memory-foam mattress underneath its quilt; a dressing table of distressed pine; an oak chest at the foot of the bed; a bleached deer skull on the wall; a thick, patterned rug set on reclaimed oak floorboards fitted at great expense on to the existing beams; walls plastered to give the uneven surface of an imagined cottage; a framed sampler over the chest of drawers; a nineteenth-century copy of a Caspar David Friedrich interior with a woman at a window, mounted between the doors to the en-suite and the walk-in wardrobe; a traditional Finnish rug hanging on the wall over the bed; an oak rocking chair in one corner.

Nina thought it inexplicable that anyone with money would furnish a room like that. She only found pleasure now in Elena's extravagant walk-in wardrobe and the slate-tiled en suite wet room with its gleaming wraparound shower.

She looked at Elena's dresses and suits in their polythene shrouds; at her blouses, her lingerie drawers, her neatly folded sweaters, her jewellery – everything protected from dust, arranged and classified and scented with sachets of dried lavender.

Nina found it impossible to understand Elena. She could not fathom why anyone would abandon such a beautiful villa to take on a stressful job in the Capital. Neither could she understand Elena's attitude to Stefan. So far as Nina was concerned, there was something of the magician about him. She was completely awestruck by the way he had been able to conjure such fabulous wealth out of the unpromising life of a bookseller as he had described to her.

It pained Nina that someone as ungrateful as Elena should be given this life on a plate, only so that she could turn her back on it. There was, too, the added insult of the phone call that Nina had overheard some six weeks earlier. Elena had accidently switched her phone to loudspeaker and Nina had heard a man's deep voice say something intimate. She had not been able to hear precisely what he had said, and her command of the language wasn't good enough to have picked up the subtleties of meaning anyway, but she had certainly detected the intimate and affectionate tone of the speaker.

She opened a drawer and looked at the expensive multicoloured undergarments. She wondered what it would be like always to have something so fresh and new next to your skin; never to wear anything old; never to have to mend a favourite item of clothing to extend its life.

Nina was still watching the film, curled up on the couch with her fourth glass of wine, when Stefan got home. He surprised her, because he had had the taxi drop him off outside the grounds. He took in the tastefully lit naked bodies moving on-screen and the unsubtitled Polish whispers. Nina looked around at him with a guilty expression and paused the film on an unfortunately explicit scene.

'Don't let me interrupt you, Nina. Please finish watching your film.' She was aware of his gaze skittering over her cleavage. 'I'll just make us a coffee, if you would like one?' They both looked at the screen and hastily looked away.

'I can make it if you like,' she said.

'No, not at all, Nina. Just you relax and watch your film.'

'A coffee would be very nice, thank you.'

★

Hannah got off the bus a short distance around the corner from her flat. It was not the worst area in the city. There was a small art gallery on the corner opposite and a vegetarian cafe next door. There was an artisan bakery across the main road. But just a short distance down from the baker's there was a massage parlour. Hannah was sure there was a brothel above it. She had seen a dark-haired woman with an olive complexion and high cheekbones come out on a couple of occasions and climb into a black car with a singularly handsome and thuggish-looking individual. Hannah could not imagine such a beautiful woman staying there of her own free will. She often saw men furtively making for the entrance. She did not know how they could live with themselves.

Hannah's flat was on the second floor of a three-storey building. The shop on the ground floor was currently empty – totally bare, except for the pile of mail – visible through the window – that was addressed to the former shop owner. There was a hole in the plasterboard on one wall near the window, where it had obviously been kicked hard. When passing the shop during the day, she sometimes imagined the desperate owner venting her frustration at the steadily mounting debts. Hannah would find herself imagining how to repair the wall – wondering about the various types of filler and sandpaper that might be required.

Hannah's front door was not very robust, with flaking green paint and a large panel of stippled glass, which was needed on the frequent occasions, like tonight, the bulb had failed in the hallway. She had to mount the stairs carefully, guided by the orange light of the nearest street lamp.

The flat entrance opened into a short passageway with doors to left and right that gave on to Daniela's bedroom and the bathroom. The third door opened into a large kitchen-cum-sitting-room that provided the only shared living space. Hannah's bedroom, which overlooked the backyard, had once served as the kitchen. A plumber with perhaps more imagination than ability had swapped the rooms around to turn the place into a two-bedroom rental.

Hannah's bedroom was considerably larger than Daniela's. At her own expense, Hannah had had metal bars fitted on the outside of the window for added security. Drug-addled tramps were apt to defecate in a corner of the yard. Sometimes they did not wait until nightfall.

She found Daniela, sitting at the dining table, crying.

'Oh, Hannah!' Then she spoke incomprehensibly in her own language – something she tended to do when she was upset – before adding, 'I have lost it. I have lost your brooch.'

It was a real blow. The brooch had been left to Hannah by her grandmother, but she tried hard to hide how upset she was.

'Don't worry, love. It's not your fault. It was that cretin, Franz. I don't know why he gave it to you.'

'I tell him. I tell him you are at shop. I tell him. He say he can't see you there.' Tenses forgotten in the storm of the moment.

'One time he came in to see me, when my manager was there, one time, and now he makes out that I don't want him to come to the shop. He's a complete fuckwit. Please don't upset yourself, Daniela.'

Chapter 3

Yasmin did not like going to work on the day of the Martyrs' Procession. In recent years, it had become something of a national obsession, but she could still remember the carnivalesque atmosphere that used to characterise the festival, when there would be stalls selling multicultural foods and crafts and she would feel as if she was wandering through the bazaar in her home city.

Her father used to take her to the bazaar. He was a gentle writer who had achieved fame within their country for his humorous tales of the hapless Mustafa. Mustafa would always succeed in making money in the most improbable manner and despite the ineptitude of his schemes. There were those who saw a dangerous satire in Mustafa's main antagonist, the moustachioed moneylender who ruled with an implacable iron grip the neighbourhood where all the stories were set, but who always ended up being outwitted by Mustafa.

If the Dictator noticed any similarity between the moneylender and himself, he did not let on. Perhaps because he knew that any action against the author would open himself to ridicule. However, a poem that Yasmin's father had written for his group of friends somehow found its way into the hands of the authorities. The poem characterised the Dictator as an evil clown whose taste for torture arose from his sexual inadequacy and whose absurd appearance and bellicose posturing only served to make him the laughing stock of the world. The poem compared his lustrous black moustache to a centipede and drew attention to the slight squint about which he was particularly sensitive. Yasmin would never learn which of her father's friends had betrayed him.

Without warning, four members of the Dictator's secret police burst into their house one day while Salazar and Yasmin were at school. The police repeatedly raped their mother in front of their father, before beating him insensible and dragging him off to the regime's notorious prison. Their mother never fully recovered from the ordeal. Their father's publisher helped her to flee the country with her son and daughter.

The family settled in the city of V because for many years Yasmin's father had had the foresight to transfer a proportion of his royalties to a bank account there that had been set up in her mother's name. He had chosen that city because his favourite uncle had once had a business there specialising in the import of spices, incense and lapis lazuli.

Yasmin's father had told her that, for as long as he could remember, V had held a fascination for him. As a child, he would fill sketchbooks with imagined plans of the city and drawings of invented buildings inspired by a framed engraving, given to his mother by his uncle, of the ancient castle of V. Yasmin always regretted leaving that engraving behind when they fled the country, all three of them hidden in the publisher's lorry behind a load of Qur'ans that were being delivered to Aleppo.

They did not see their father again until he appeared, much changed, on the television news some ten months after their arrival in V. He was on trial in their homeland for being part of a terrorist cell accused of killing some US military advisors who were helping the Dictator to conduct a brutal war against a neighbouring Islamist state.

The trial affected Salazar the most. He grew to hate the Americans for accepting the travesty of justice exemplified by the judicial proceedings, and for doing nothing to prevent their father's execution, despite concerns about the trial raised by Amnesty International. It was clearly obvious to Salazar that his father had suffered such extreme torture that he believed he had taken part in the attack despite being in prison when it occurred. Salazar found solace in a more radical Islamic tradition that, as head of the household, he tried to compel Yasmin to follow.

Until she befriended Akilah, another immigrant at school, Yasmin found no solace in V, an alien city that bore no resemblance to her father's beautiful inventions, where her family were living in much reduced circumstances. Akilah was the daughter of a communist who had abandoned his religion long before fleeing their country. It was she who took Yasmin to her first Martyrs' Procession. As they wandered hand in hand between the colourful stalls set out on Vandrhaf Square, the sunlight reflecting off the bright yellow crane that stretched above the construction site of the future Radion Hotel, Yasmin recalled those visits to the bazaar with her father, who would make up stories on the spot about the jewellery, decorated boxes, dolls and silk dresses that he would buy for her as a treat.

Yasmin found it extremely painful to witness the changes to the Martyrs' Procession in recent years since it had been appropriated by an extreme right-wing group. The Brotherhood of the Martyrs had taken the festival back to its nationalist roots and now bulked out the religious procession with rank upon rank of its black-shirted members following the banner it had adopted: the black crow with spread wings borne on the heraldic shield of King Corvus set against the red cross of the national flag.

The foundation myth of the twelve martyrs celebrated by the procession was key to the kingdom and was bound up with the nation's privileged place in the former Habsburg Empire. The story went that in 1705, when the future King Corvus landed on the Bohemian Coast with an army of foreign mercenaries, six monks and six nuns were held hostage by the Ottomans, together with two thousand of their countrymen, with the understanding that everyone would be spared if Corvus would only re-embark and sail away. Corvus remained and all the hostages ended up dead. The monks and nuns were singled out by their captors for particularly savage and ingenious executions, which were carried out over the course of a fortnight, before the massacre of the other hostages in an orgy of impalings and crucifixions that only served to unite the entire populace behind Corvus.

In the procession the martyrdoms were represented symbolically on twelve banners by images of the torture instruments employed in each instance. The sainted martyrs were also present in twelve bejewelled and gilded reliquaries, each containing one of their bones. Twelve nuns and twelve monks were responsible for bearing the reliquaries and the banners at the head of the procession. They were followed by two novices of each sex carrying crosses on their shoulders and then by the bishops of the realm bearing lances. A phalanx of choirboys sang hymns, accompanied by the mournful drumbeats of the Brotherhood, which brought up the rear in serried ranks with flags waving.

This was the sight that greeted Yasmin as she made her way to work along the crowded pavement in front of the council offices on Castle Hill. As she wove her way through the crowds her headscarf drew more and more looks and more and more comments. Her round gentle face seemed particularly to excite the fury of the mob. She was jeered at by leering thugs wearing T-shirts and cherry red DMs, jostled by screaming women waving plastic flags, insulted by skinny boys with blue eyes and soft hair shaved to a dark fuzz.

It was only the intervention of a disabled soldier near the main entrance to the museum that saved Yasmin from violence. He positioned himself in an aggressive stance between her and the mob, his prosthetic limb (legacy of a faulty American cluster bomb) marking him as a veteran of the recent war. Then he held up his hand and shouted, 'What the hell do you fuckers think you are doing?'

A corridor through the cowed onlookers opened for the weeping Yasmin, and she walked unhindered to the museum's staff entrance. She was grateful that Salazar had not come with her, as he had said he might. He would only have made the situation much worse.

Salazar was at that moment standing outside a lock-up in one of the archways of a railway viaduct to the north of the city centre. He was looking on as another bearded man, with a scar on his left cheek, was checking the contents of the lock-up and writing numbers in a notebook. There was nothing written on the page to indicate what the numbers meant.

There were eight large oil drums, rusted in places where the paint had peeled off; a quantity of large plastic containers with the labels removed, marked with black triangles and stacked in rows; and large mounds of screws, nails and metal parts of varied origin – door handles, padlocks, engine components – piled haphazardly around the edges of the space.

'You are certain that no one suspects, not even your family?' said the scarred man, looking up from his task.

'Yes.'

'You are making the purchases from a wide variety of suppliers, as instructed?'

'Of course I am. You have no need to doubt me. Has the date been confirmed?'

'As to that, there has been an unforeseen delay.'

'Why?'

'It is not your place to question God's will. It is his will that the shipment has been delayed. Who are we to question his plan?'

'When will I ...'

'Enough. The less you know the better. Just remain calm and enjoy the gifts that God has seen fit to bestow. All will become clear in time. Do not draw attention to yourself.'

★

It was a life size model of a woman in skimpy underwear, suspenders and stockings, kneeling on all fours and supporting a smoked glass tabletop on her back. Chips here and there on her unnaturally pink-coloured flesh and garish red and black undergarments revealed her powdery plaster innards and in places exposed the dun metal of her armature. Scattered on the tabletop were some porn magazines from the 1960s and 1970s.

Beyond the tasteless object was a stand containing vintage film posters and shelves of collectable toys – James Bond model cars, Captain Scarlet and Thunderbirds vehicles, Star Wars figures. The owner of the stall was sitting in a beat-up leather armchair in the corner – a man of about fifty with a bald pate, long grey hair, a goatee, a Whitesnake

T-shirt straining against his belly, and a pair of tan cowboy boots over skinny jeans.

'See anything you like, darling?' he said, smiling and flaunting his crotch.

Hannah could not bring herself to answer and merely shook her head.

'Your loss,' he added, and resumed reading his pulp paperback, the yellowing pages of which were folded over the back cover. His fingers glittered with chunky silver rings. A poster stuck to the end shelf at the stall's entrance advertised a burlesque show.

Hannah moved hastily on to the next stall, where an old woman with overdone eye make-up and piled-up hair sat in front of a free-standing metal frame that could barely accommodate the numerous coats, vintage dresses and fur stoles that were hanging from it. A glass cabinet filled with antique jewellery drew Hannah's eyes. She searched vainly among the elaborate gold rings, strings of pearls, and jet neck-laces for a replica of her lost brooch.

She came to a third stall that was principally devoted to antique model soldiers. The stall's owner sat at the back of the small space. He was wearing a tight, mustard-coloured cardigan, the sleeves of which were far too short. The model soldiers were set out as if on parade on shelves all around him. On the top shelf on the left a model of the royal carriage was displayed with its escort of guardsmen mounted on white horses. On the shelf below were models of King Corvus and his mercenary soldiers in their sky blue uniforms. Above the shelves on the wall behind the stall owner was an old coloured engraving of the legendary monarch mounted on his horse with his sabre raised – one of those clumsily executed, mass-produced images that had been so popular in the nineteenth century.

Hannah looked at the excited expressions on the faces of the people crowding around the king; at the conventional mountain landscape in the background, with the tiny figure of a dying martyr strung up on a distant hilltop; at the bodies of the Ottoman soldiers lying beneath the hooves of the king's horse. She felt as if she was trapped in that absurd nationalist fairy tale. There seemed to be no getting away from it. She looked back at the dazzle of sunshine in the broad entranceway to the antiques market.

It occurred to her that the success of *The Journey to Varnak* repre-sented a reaction by the liberal intelligentsia to the all-pervasive na-tionalism that was sweeping the country, and not only this country, if the news reports were to be believed. Certainly, the novel had been ridiculed in the right-wing tabloids, not only for its assault on family values and its pornographic scenes, but also for its radical reappraisal of the story of King Corvus.

Hannah was less interested in that aspect of the novel. For her, King Corvus was a straw-filled dummy stitched together from a variety of national legends to give a semblance of unity to the divided realm. She had loved the novel for its twinned female characters. The sorceress, Malastrina, of *The City by the Sea* – the novel within the novel – who either predicts or brings about the ancient city's ruin, and her mirror image, Anya, in the framing travelogue, who first abandons her family and then abandons the Hungarian protagonist, to disappear through a winding path between trees towards the mauve sky and snowy peaks of the Tarent Mountains.

Hannah had particularly liked the way the author or translator had described those mountains in such a way as to render their complex reality while at the same time suggesting a fantastical quality about them, as if Anya was in some manner returning to the world of *The City by the Sea* to be as one with Malastrina.

After Anya's disappearance, the narrative takes an abrupt turn. A silk merchant travelling from the Tarent Mountains to Varnak glimpses, through the window of a country inn, the Hungarian traveller reading *The City by the Sea* by the light of an oil lamp. The merchant decides to stop at the inn, perhaps drawn by that glimpse of the stranger reading in his cosy chamber. He turns in his saddle to instruct his escort, and *The Journey to Varnak* ends in a maddeningly precise description of the onyx brooch decorating his hat: the words following the curlicues and branches of its elaborate silver setting, until the reader is hopelessly lost among the numerous bright threads of its filigree. As Hannah stepped out on to the street, she recalled the sense of liberation she had felt on reading that strange, inconclusive ending, and imagining the possibilities expanding infinitely beyond the limits of the page.

It was hot and humid. The sky was clear blue with hazy white patches and was divided in two by the vapour trail of an aeroplane. Hannah took off her cardigan and draped it over her left arm after pulling the strap of her bag back on to her right shoulder. She was wearing a pale green dress and a pair of white leather pumps. She was not sure what to do now. She had arranged to meet Stefan that evening at a wine bar in Selonaskala not far from the suspension bridge, for a meal and a drink, but that was not for three hours yet and money was tight until the end of the month. She had just paid the deposit for a fortnight's stay at a chalet in the Tarent Mountains with an old friend from school. She had only agreed to the date with Stefan on condition that he paid her taxi fare home.

On an ordinary Saturday, she would have gone to the museum for an hour, but this was no ordinary Saturday. An alliance of left-wing and anti-fascist groups was planning a peaceful demonstration against the Martyrs' Procession, which had provoked a planned counter-demonstration by some extremist right-wing groups. The police had recommended that all the businesses and visitor attractions along the route of the procession should close and where possible pull down their shutters in the expectation of trouble.

In the end, she decided to go to the cafe on the waterfront where Daniela worked. She could read her book there over a leisurely coffee and, if she timed her journey well, she would arrive at the rendezvous in the wine bar without seeing anything of the Martyrs' Procession.

The first intimation she had that something was terribly wrong was when she realised that the cars, vans and buses on the road beside her were completely stationary. Most drivers had switched off their engines and some had even got out of their vehicles and were straining to see the cause of the hold-up.

Hannah continued walking towards the city centre, but when she was still some distance from the end of the road, she saw that the pedestrians were crammed into a tight, impassable mass that was beginning to spread out between the stationary vehicles on the carriageway.

She was gradually becoming aware of a sound like a roar, which broke up into its constituent parts when she got closer to the crowd. The excited chattering among the nearer pedestrians was barely audible against the background of aggressive chants, shouts and screams. From her position on the gentle slope of the street, Hannah could see the helmets of the ranks of policemen drawn out across the road, facing the roundabout beyond, from where the chants and shouts were coming. Above the policemen, a modern apartment block bridged the road on enormous yellow girders stretching between concrete supports covered in graffiti. A cola bottle with a burning rag stuffed into its neck appeared suddenly in the air beyond the police lines. It struck a raised riot shield, across which it spread a lick of flame.

A group of people parted at Hannah's approach to reveal a policeman with a bloodied face who was sitting on the kerb next to his shield and upturned helmet. An Asian man in a long grey robe and black embroidered skullcap was offering him a bottle of mineral water.

'Bloody anarchists, that's what they are,' muttered an old man, whose shining lower lip was visibly trembling. A skinny Russian woman with a long bony face and a slant to her eyes was shouting at her son and gripping his hand hard. The boy, who was straining to get free and holding the handlebar of a silver scooter, could hardly contain his excitement about the mysterious goings-on beyond the bodies crammed in front of him.

Since she could see no safe way through, Hannah decided to go home. She would send Stefan a text to cancel their date. However, when she was no more than a hundred metres along the road, she looked back and saw a sudden surge deforming the ranks of policeman separating the crowd from what was happening at the roundabout beyond. The terror-stricken people in front of them turned and began to run towards her. Some fell and were crushed underfoot in the panic. Without thinking, Hannah took a left off the main road and ran up a narrow street between small engineering works and student accommodation blocks. It was a neighbourhood she had never ventured into before.

She turned right in the hope of returning to her flat by a more circuitous route, but soon found herself in a labyrinth of back streets and dead ends that ultimately led her to a road bordered on the opposite side by a railway viaduct. She knew that a railway bridge crossed the main road out of the city a kilometre or so north of where the road passed by her flat.

The arches of the viaduct were being used as lock-ups. She noticed a bearded, brown-skinned man standing by while another bearded man with a white robe under his jacket was pulling down the corrugated iron shutter of one of the lock-ups. They regarded her with such hostility that she hastily averted her gaze and headed down the hill in the direction that she was sure would take her home.

She was footsore and tired, gripped by the fear that the entire city was descending into anarchy and violence; a fear that was only confirmed when she reached the junction with the main road and witnessed a group of four policemen beating a young man repeatedly with their truncheons as he crouched, screaming, with his arms crossed over his head. Some men with scarves over their faces ran past, pursued by other policemen. Scattered groups, wearing different colours according to their affiliations, were clashing with each other or with the police. A man in an apron was desperately trying to dowse a burning car with a fire extinguisher before the flames spread to the petrol tank. Shop windows along the road were smashed, and in one a man in a black hoodie was helping himself to a flat-screen television.

Hannah looked on, paralysed by panic and confusion, until it occurred to her that if she walked back up the hill and turned left at the top, she might pass by the university. Then she could arrive at the rendezvous with Stefan from another direction that might avoid the procession.

In fact, Hannah had only a vague notion of how to reach the university from where she was. She discovered that the layout of the streets did not always permit her to take the most direct route. She brought up a map on her phone which provided a dotted route to her destination, but when she looked at the street names at the first junction she realised that the small blue circle representing her position was in the wrong place. It moved after a moment, but still she could not get the network of streets on the map to tally with those she could see around her, and so she resorted to guesswork once again. She passed terraces of substantial town houses with neo-gothic arched windows and doors, and three-storey terraces of cream stucco from an earlier era. At one point, she passed through a labyrinth of paths linking together an unusual 1970s council estate of small brick houses with only a few tiny windows visible and compact gardens hidden behind wooden fence panels. The few people she encountered were quietly going about their business. They appeared oblivious of the violence taking place in other parts of the city, which now only registered in the distant sounds of sirens.

Eventually, she passed close enough to the hospital to find her way to the nearby university, and after another ten minutes she emerged on to an arterial road about a kilometre beyond the summit of Castle Hill. From there, she took a wide curve past the university student union to climb to Selonaskala, where she was able finally to sit down in a chain cafe and enjoy a latte before her date with Stefan.

The violent scenes she had witnessed appeared insubstantial and dreamlike in comparison with the quietly chatting customers around her. She looked at the familiar coffee cup and swirl of steam on the sign above the counter; the houndstooth pattern of the upholstery on the chairs; the framed photographs of Italian street scenes; the orderly queue of people waiting to be served. She thought of the network of similar cafes stretching across the country and beyond. It reassured her. She would have a civilised meal with Stefan, and by the time she got her taxi home the broken windows would be boarded up, the streets would be cleared, and order would be restored.

The comforting flavours of the pain aux raisins and coffee contributed to her sense of well-being. She relaxed into her chair and looked around at the other customers. Most of them were elderly and well dressed, offering a stark contrast to the swarthy beggar woman visible through the window. One grey-haired man sat alone in a black polo neck, looking at his phone and muttering to himself. There was a group of four people around Hannah's age sitting at the back, all gazing at their phones. One of them, a handsome man with black gleaming hair fashioned into a quiff, suddenly raised his voice and began to rant about the fucking fascists. The woman on the banquette next to him turned in evident anger and said, 'Why shout at us, Vacha? We all agree with you.'

The man in the polo neck stared at them with an enraged expression but said nothing. One of the baristas told them from the counter to keep it down or he would have to ask them to leave. Hannah's sympathies were all with the young man. She could not understand where the Brotherhood of the Martyrs and other groups like them had sprung from, with their rabid nationalism and xenophobia. Only a few years earlier, similar neo-fascist groups had been regarded as pariahs. Now, the Brotherhood was an officially sanctioned component of the National Festival, with seats in parliament. Hannah recalled her last sight of that neo-gothic extravaganza on the north bank of the Voltava, during a visit to the Capital with Franz. She recalled his endless monologue about its bizarre rituals and protocols.

★

When Stefan met her outside the wine bar, Hannah immediately burst into tears. At first, he didn't know how to respond, and then he gave her a hug, holding one hand lightly against the back of her head. Feeling mortified, she pressed her face into his jacket. She didn't move for what seemed like an age, before at last she freed herself from his embrace, searched through her bag for her tissues and said, 'Sorry.' He stood beside her in awkward silence. Then she spoke in a confused rush about the riot, about her terror and about the difficulties of her journey. She described the events as they occurred to her without regard to chronology, but the images unfolding in her head seemed scarcely credible now.

'You don't believe me, do you?' she said, finally, tears welling up again. She switched on her phone and feverishly scrolled through some videos of the riots, before showing them to Stefan.

'Look, we're here now,' he said. 'We might as well have something to eat. Hopefully, it will all be over before you go home. Worst case scenario, I can always give you money for a hotel.'

Hannah avoided everyone's eyes when they entered the wine bar. As soon as they were shown to their table, she went to the lavatory to restore her appearance. Just as in the cafe earlier, she was lulled into a sense of security by the barman polishing a glass behind the bar, by the crowded tables, by the soft piano music. Feeling calmer and less self-conscious after rejoining Stefan, she noticed how ill at ease he was as he ordered his meal from the waitress. She realised that he had been speaking truthfully on their first date when he had told her that he didn't get out much. He was wearing a checked shirt with the sleeves rolled up. She liked the way that the braided leather bracelet on his left wrist showed off his well-toned forearm. The wealthy tourists who were sitting at the adjacent tables were all talking with animation and excitement about the day's events.

'I had completely forgotten the Martyrs' Procession was happening today,' Stefan said after the waitress left. Then he fell silent, still trying to process the violent videos he had seen on Hannah's phone.

'Are you serious?'

'I was trying to fix a chair in my daughter's tree house. She's been off with me since her mother started work. I think she blames me. Anyway, I thought it would bring us closer. She spends most of her time with Nina.'

'Nina? Oh yes, the au pair.' She reckoned from the way his sentences were jumping about that he regretted bringing his daughter into the conversation and that his remarks about his wife and Nina represented a belated attempt both to explain why he was dating Hannah and to show himself to be a good father.

'I suppose the whole city could go up in flames and you would scarcely notice in your clifftop retreat.' She looked in the direction of the framed print on the wall by their table – a black and white woodcut of the famous bridge. Her eyes appeared to glaze over and she added in a quieter voice, 'It was horrible. I don't know why they were fighting in my part of town – so far from the procession.'

'I have no idea. I avoid watching the news. The problems of the world are so complicated and ... insoluble. The endless violence and cruelty depresses me.'

'But you have the wealth to make a difference.'

'You say that. At one time, I tried to fund a hospital in Somalia, during the civil war there. I sent the first instalment of 100,000 thalers through my contacts in Africa. I was sent photographs of the progress. A proposed visit was postponed due to the unstable conditions. They kept putting off the visit. Eventually, someone from Médecins Sans Frontières told me that the money had ended up in the pockets of a local warlord. Do you remember the media frenzy about the nerve gas attack that wiped out an entire village? I felt partly responsible for that attack. That was when I stopped watching the news. I now set aside an annual sum for Médecins Sans Frontières and Amnesty International and I try not to think about what goes on in the world.'

'I'm sorry. I'm hardly one to criticise. I used to do a lot of charity work at university, but I haven't done any for years. My career seemed to take over my life. Then I left my job in the council and now I can't spare anything for charity.'

'Where did you study?' he said. Realising she was perplexed by the sudden change of subject, he added, 'Where did you go to university?'

She named the famous university in the spa town of N in the foothills of the Tarent Mountains. 'I studied comparative literature.'

'You must know the famous mineral water from that town. Do you remember the old label with the cafe scene?'

Hannah shook her head. 'I don't remember that label.'

'There was a cafe with silhouettes of people in old-fashioned clothes. When I was young, I used to love the profile of one of the women. I felt something similar the first time we met.'

'How about your wife? Didn't you feel the same about her, or any number of women?'

'Elena was different. We worked together. We both thought we were just friends. That all changed one evening, during a bookselling course in the Capital, when someone tried to mug us on our way back to the hotel.'

Their starters arrived at that moment, and Hannah took the opportunity to change the subject. She started speaking about the book she was currently reading. She had been feeling increasingly uncomfortable at the turn the conversation had taken after his innocuous question about where she had gone to university. She was unsure of what Stefan was expecting of this second date, and of her own reasons for agreeing to it. It was thus with a sense of relief that she began to talk about the novel, *Ravel*, by Jean Echenoz that had recently been published in translation by a small press.

'I've never heard of Jean Echenoz,' he said.

'It didn't get any review coverage.'

She began to relax now that they were discussing a novel. She spoke of its style – the way Echenoz described the surface details of Ravel's life without offering any implausible psychological insights and yet still managed to convey the horror of the composer's gradual descent into dementia. Stefan agreed that he liked that approach, but he wondered if part of its appeal lay in the way that it set life at one remove.

As the conversation moved on to other writers whom they both admired, Hannah forgot her distress at the day's events; forgot too about Stefan's wife and daughter. Her fractious relationship with Franz appeared increasingly irrelevant. She felt at ease with Stefan in a way she had not experienced for years. The stomach-clenching anxiety about money that accompanied her like a dull ache had quite disappeared. They finished their meal, and after Stefan had paid he suggested that they go to a nearby bar for a couple of drinks before calling a taxi.

It was dark outside. A cloud had covered the moon. There was a fresh, cool breeze. As they passed under a street lamp, Stefan noticed the moving shadows between her toes that were left uncovered by her white leather pumps. He took her hand and Hannah was surprised by how natural that felt. She was not sure if it was the quantity of wine she had consumed, but she felt unusually optimistic when they entered the bar.

The place was quiet: low lighting, natural wooden floor, leather easy chairs round some of the tables, heavily bearded barman, a diminutive waitress with a tattoo of an art nouveau floral pattern stretching from shoulder to wrist, a few couples speaking softly across flickering candles, two young men bending over a chessboard, complex Cuban rhythms playing at low volume, late night snacks on the menu – smashed avocado on sourdough toast, home-baked beans in chilli sauce with chorizo and potato chunks. Stefan ordered a bottle of dry white wine to share.

When the time approached midnight, Hannah began to feel anxious. She thought she should not have had that final glass of wine. She no longer felt totally in control of her actions and she had lost her sense of well-being. Just as she was beginning to doubt Stefan's motives, however, he looked at his watch and said, 'I best call you that taxi. What's your address again?' He scribbled it down on the reverse side of his restaurant receipt.

Two taxi numbers were stored on his phone. Hannah watched him tap the screen, put the phone to his ear and, after a short interval, give the name of the bar and the destination. She could hear the quiet buzz of the reply coming from his phone speaker. Then Stefan said, 'What, none at all? Are you sure? Right, thanks.' He tapped and swiped the screen. Then he tried again.

Finally, he went to the bar to ask for another taxi number. When he returned to the table, he said, 'No taxis are running this evening. The police have cordoned off part of the city. No one is allowed in or out.' He contacted the two hotels in the area. Both were full, because of the procession.

'What am I going to do?' Hannah said, trying to control her panic, wondering if this was all an elaborate ruse to get her into his bed.

Stefan looked as if he was trying to solve an intractable puzzle. Then he smiled suddenly. 'I know where you can stay.'

'Where?'

'There is an outbuilding by the villa, where I put my library.'

'A library?' she said.

'Yes, converted from the former stables. There's a kind of office next to the library, where I used to go to write; a man cave, if you like. You'll be perfectly safe there, even from me.'

'And no one will know I'm there?'

*

They walked downhill between semi-detached houses. Then they passed individual villas, set in their own gardens, before following another road with a stone wall stretching along the opposite side.

'Look, Stefan, are you absolutely sure no one will know I am there?'

'Well, there are CCTV monitors, but Nina won't look at those unless the alarm is triggered. The main difficulty will be sneaking you out again tomorrow.'

'When is your wife getting home?'

'Not until next weekend.' He turned to look at the garden of the villa they were passing. Steps and paths descended a steep slope where terraces, planted with shrubs and flowers, were bolstered by stone walls. An artificial waterfall, reflecting fragments of moonlight, fed a pool bordered by reeds and flat stones. 'You know, I think she is having an affair.'

'So, this is your way of getting back at her, is it?'

'What would be the point in that?'

'According to you, there's no point in anything.'

'You sound just like Elena.'

He read surprise and annoyance in her expression. Fearing that he had ruined everything, he kissed her desperately. She tensed up for a moment, as if she were going to push him away, but instead she returned his kiss with a soft moan, pressing her hand to his nape. From her bedroom in the villa, a young girl, woken by night terrors, peered out at them over the windowsill, shivering in a thin nightie drenched in cold sweat. Still caught up in the coils of her nightmare, she imagined that the man was eating the beautiful woman's face.

After walking some two hundred metres, Stefan led Hannah across the road to a door set in the wall beside the left-hand stone pillar of an impressive gateway. It was only when he began to key numbers into the keypad by the door that Hannah realised that the wall that had been accompanying their walk bordered the grounds of Stefan's villa.

'What happens if you key the wrong number?'

'Nothing, so long as you don't interfere with the lock.'

When they entered the grounds, soft blue lights flickered on along the length of the footpath that ran alongside the driveway towards the villa. Another cloud had drifted across the moon, so little was visible of the extensive grounds beyond the trees on either side. The few lighted windows of the villa illuminated a raised terrace bordered by a stone balustrade that stretched its shadow across a lawn set with garden furniture. Stefan could just make out the shape of Nina's cardigan draped over one of the chairs.

The path turned abruptly to the left away from the driveway to skirt the lawn. A short distance beyond the lawn, he led Hannah on to a side path that snaked between trees and shrubs towards a dark L-shaped building behind the villa. It housed a garage with space for four cars and Stefan's library. In a room giving on to the library was the office where Stefan had attempted to write his novel. In addition to the blue swivel chair and the desk, with its laptop, pens, notebooks, dictionary and manual typewriter, there was an espresso machine, a sofa bed and a sleeping bag rolled up in its pouch by the standard lamp in the corner. Stefan had thought to sleep there when he was inspired to write late into the night, so that he did not disturb Elena by returning to the bedroom they used to share then.

Hannah could see the shelves of books stretching into the darkness beyond the open doorway and the gleam of lamplight on the parquet floor. She was nervous. Even though Stefan had carefully closed the blinds before switching on the light, she was sure that a thin band of light would still be visible from the villa. She wandered over to look at the typewriter on the desk, placing her bag beside it as she did so.

'Do you still use this?'

Stefan was in the process of unfolding the frame and mattress of the bed settee. The metal support swung down to the floor in one smooth movement. Then he sat on the end of the mattress and looked over to see what she was talking about.

'Oh, the typewriter; I haven't touched that in months. I had the stupid notion of writing a novel on an old-fashioned typewriter.'

'Why stupid?' she said, hanging her cardigan carefully over the back of the chair. She approached him, swaying from her waist with her hands clasped behind her back.

'I really don't think I have the talent or discipline necessary to be a writer, and I couldn't type to save myself.'

She drew her fingers gently along the line of his raised jaw. The sofa bed creaked when she sat down beside him, but it was well sprung and had a reasonably thick mattress. There is nothing cheap or shoddy here, she thought, and for some reason she pictured the peeling purple façade of the massage parlour near her flat.

'The sheets are clean, and there's the sleeping bag if you get cold.'

She was relieved that Stefan had not presumed he would be sharing the bed, but she could not repress a perverse feeling of disappointment that he wasn't carried away by desire. The contradiction troubled her.

They both fell silent. Hannah was sitting with her hands spread flat on either side. Stefan's gaze took in her face in profile, moving from the sweep of her lashes and the contracting pupil of her right eye, down over the bump on her nose to her chin cleft. Then looked at the red skin on her shoulder.

'You've caught the sun,' he said, stroking it gently. 'Does it hurt?'

'No.'

Whereupon he began to caress her shoulder and neck with his fingernails. It was so ticklish that Hannah pressed her cheek to his knuckles, and her hair fell in waves around his wrist and forearm. She nestled in under his arm as he ran his hand around her nape and along her left shoulder. He grasped the thin strap of her dress between thumb and forefinger and idly began to draw it up and down her arm, noting with mounting excitement the answering movement of her bodice disclosing and concealing the lacy edge of her bra.

Hannah, resting her head against his chest, could hear the dull rhythm of his increasing heart rate, and soon her body was beginning to respond with symptoms of excitement and arousal over which she had no control. It struck her that there was little physical difference between her current sexual arousal and the terror she had felt in the afternoon when the crowd had panicked – or, more disturbingly, the confusion of anguish, fear and excitement she had experienced at the sight of the policemen beating up the young man. The varied images of the afternoon now became confused with memories of her lovemaking with Franz, the physical security she felt at the contact with Stefan's muscular chest, the sensation of his penis pressing through his clothes against her hip, and the motions described by his fingers over her shoulder and arm as they circled ever closer to her breast.

She turned and drew up to kiss him. The pressure of his erection shifted to her thigh as she did so, and the movement took his hand to the small of her back. When they kissed, he gripped her tongue gently between his teeth. Hannah felt as if she was on the edge of a precipice, ready to plunge down into the threatening void, but she pulled herself back at the last moment, looked into his eyes and said, 'I'm sorry, Stefan. I'm just not ready yet.'

'Of course; I understand, Hannah. It's me who should apologise.' The tremor in his voice belied the cool rationality of his words, hinting at the violent tumult of disappointment with which he was wrestling.

As he made his way to the back entrance of the villa, he could not repress his feeling of utter rejection, which made him reflect on the chronic failure of his marriage. During his twenties, he had been almost arrogantly self-assured. It was absurd that now, after having experienced so much success in his life, he should be suffering such doubts about his attractiveness to women.

He could no longer remember when he had lost his certainty of Elena's love, but he believed that in many ways the responsibility lay with him. He had taken her for granted. After his unforeseen financial success, he had flirted with several beautiful women who wouldn't have looked at him twice when he was poor.

The belated realisation that Elena, alone, loved him for himself had helped to revive their marriage and they had decided that they would try to conceive a child. But he was sure now that he had lost Elena's love irrevocably. Although he had not been able to pluck up the courage to discuss their relationship with her, he couldn't rid himself of the suspicion she had somehow found out about his infidelity with the prostitute.

The rear entrance took him into the utility room. After carefully locking the door, he made his way into the kitchen. He was too wound up to sleep, so he put on the kettle to make a cup of tea. He thought he might watch a DVD before going to bed.

Just as the kettle boiled, one of Natalia's toys started up in the playroom. A strange, fluffy, spider-like creature, with a faulty mechanism that Stefan had tried to fix earlier in the week; it danced on its shelf, singing softly. The routine lasted less than a minute. The toy landed on the floor with a muffled thud and gave no further signs of life when Stefan went through to pick it up. Its round, fluffy body lay on one side. One of its articulated plastic legs was broken and the rest were partially extended. The eyes bore a perpetual expression of surprise and shock, which Stefan considered had finally found their meaning as he located the off switch. He stood up and tried to reattach the toy's leg.

When he saw Nina in the archway to the kitchen he let out an embarrassing, high-pitched cry. 'You gave me the fright of my life.'

'I'm sorry.'

'There's no need to apologise.' He glanced at her angular face and found himself comparing it unfavourably with Hannah's.

'Natalia will be so sad,' Nina said, looking at the broken toy he was holding.

'I don't think I can get another one. It's been discontinued.' Only now did he realise that Nina's eyes were red and puffy from crying. 'Are you alright, Nina?' he said, after an uncomfortable pause. He had the absurd notion that she was upset because she had seen him in the garden with Hannah.

'My mother is ill. The doctor says it is cancer.'

'Oh, Nina, I'm so sorry. Do you want to go home to visit her?'

'No, oh no. They have discovered it in time. My father, he needs me to work, otherwise ...' She suddenly began to sob.

Stefan reckoned he must still be drunk, because, without thinking, he dropped the toy and its leg on to the beanbag, hugged Nina to him and began to stroke her hair. She immediately relaxed into his embrace and clasped her hands behind his back. It struck him as odd that for months he had been fantasising about such intimate contact with Nina and yet now he could not stop thinking about Hannah.

The scent of Nina's hair was different from Hannah's, but, even so, it excited him. He imagined that she was fresh out of the bath or shower and he could feel that she was naked under her bathrobe. He was scarcely aware of the reassurances he was murmuring, and part of him was mortified by the stirrings of desire that he was sure she must feel. Afterwards, he could not have said how long they had remained like that, Nina with her head pressed to his chest; but eventually and, it seemed to Stefan, almost reluctantly, she freed herself from his embrace.

'I should go to bed,' she said.

Stefan did not know what to say and merely nodded as she pulled the lapels of her bathrobe back together and turned to go. He watched her make her way through the archway into the kitchen, and then he said, 'You don't have to worry about your mother, Nina. I'm happy to help with the cost of treatment.'

She half-turned towards him. 'No, Mr J, my father would never agree to that. He's a proud man. Thank you, but I cannot accept your money.'

Stefan could not concentrate on the DVD of *In the Mood for Love* that he had chosen to watch. It only served to increase his agitation by making him reflect on Elena's possible infidelities. Even now, he felt sick to his stomach when he thought of her having sex with someone else. He began to feel sorry for himself, wallowing in the notion that he was the victim, but he was brought up short by the memories of his own infidelity with the prostitute in the Capital. No matter how he tried to justify himself, he could not help but feel that he had shamelessly exploited the prostitute's vulnerability. The realisation completely undermined the image of himself that he was trying to impress upon Hannah.

He switched off the television and DVD player, put his tea mug in the sink, activated the burglar alarm and headed up to bed. His bedroom was situated in the corner of the house above the kitchen. Nina's bedroom and part of her sitting room occupied the roof space immediately above him. As he stood at the window, surveying the river and the city, he could hear Nina moving about in her bedroom. He wondered what would happen if he went upstairs and knocked on her door, but then he thought of Natalia sleeping in her own room along the corridor.

He pressed his forehead to the cool glass. No light was visible at his office window in the building below. The sounds of sirens could still be heard, getting louder and fading as they moved across the city. Parts of the city were darker than usual. Plumes of smoke rose here and there. The pattern of streetlights was different, but Stefan had no idea of how he knew this to be the case. The waterfront development seemed unaffected by events, however. Reflections of the orange street lamps there rippled on the surface of the water. He could detect no change in the pattern of lights to the south of the river.

★

Josef was sitting on his slate grey sofa with a cold bottle of beer on the coffee table in front of him. The seventh episode of a science fiction serial had just finished, and his streaming service was counting down the seconds to the next episode. His dirty dinner plate was still on the table with an empty yoghurt pot, a fork, knife, teaspoon and crumpled section of kitchen roll. Next to the plate was an onyx ashtray containing a brooch that he had found on a side street near his flat a few weeks earlier. Josef did not smoke. The ashtray was a house-warming present from Daria.

He had not left the flat all day; he had just been sitting, watching the serial about a rural community in America menaced by a creature from a parallel universe. He had not even thought of going to the Martyrs' Procession, reasoning that he would feel lonelier in a crowd, especially one composed of people who were so alien to his sensibilities.

And so he had allowed himself to get sucked into the horrific tale. At least, he thought, he had managed to have a shower, eat lunch and prepare his dinner. The serial was competently written and absorbing. It had successfully taken him out of himself. Now, the final episode was about to start and he was eager to see what would happen. But he decided to hold off watching it until he had cleaned his lunch and dinner dishes.

When he switched off the streaming service, the TV box reverted to one of the main channels and he caught a glimpse of a stand-up comic doing a routine about a disastrous one-night stand, before he switched the TV off.

He stepped out on to the balcony. It was the first breath of fresh air that he had had all day, and he drew it deep into his lungs. He looked along the river. The short section of road he could see at the foot of the cliff seemed unusually quiet for a Saturday night. When he looked in the other direction towards the city, he was surprised to see several plumes of smoke rising into the clear sky and drifting away on the gentle westerly breeze. A couple of sirens followed one another in quick succession. A police helicopter flew overhead, and he saw a shadowy figure below slipping into the car park entrance. Josef had a momentary anxiety about his brand new Audi, which had been delivered by the lease company the previous week, but he knew that who-ever it was would never get past the security gates without knowing the code.

80

It took Josef twenty minutes to wash his dishes and wipe the tops. Then he locked the balcony door, checked that the entrance door was secure, peered through the spyhole at the empty corridor and returned to the settee.

As he leaned over to pick up his beer he noticed the brooch in the ashtray. There was something teasingly familiar about it that he could not pin down. An ovoid hemisphere of fine silver filigree enclosed a piece of amber shaped like a double helix. Holding the brooch between thumb and forefinger, he looked at it from various angles before returning it to the ashtray, still none the wiser.

When he switched on the television and prepared to click on the streaming service, the evening news was showing film, shot on a mobile phone, of a crowd involved in violent clashes with riot police. A car was on fire. The camera moved over some broken shop windows, before focusing on the fighting going on between different factions within the crowd. It took Josef a moment to register the fact that the film had been shot less than five kilometres from his flat. The images became blurred for a short interval. Someone started yelling. Then the camera zoomed in on a man with a national flag draped over his shoulder being ejected from the entrance of a building with a purple façade by a man whom Josef recognised. There were no windows on the façade, but a neon sign advertising it as a massage parlour was hanging by the entrance from a plastic-coated electrical cable.

★

Anna emerged from behind the rattan screen, rubbing her crotch vigorously with a towel. She lifted the used condom from the floor and deposited it in the bin. Then she made the bed with the brisk efficiency of a nurse. She had had two clients that afternoon. The first had bragged that he would fuck her harder than she had ever been fucked. He had hairy shoulders, a broad muscular chest, a beer belly and a curious penis that resembled a doorknob even when erect. She had had trouble fitting the condom and he came after only two thrusts without achieving penetration. The second client wept.

She put on her bra, suspenders, stockings, knickers and a short black dress. Then she sat down in the room's only chair, crossed her legs and waited. The room was kept as clean as possible by Alika, the maid with the scarred face, but Anna had grown to hate its cheap pine-veneer furniture and worn carpet. There was also the gap between skirting board and floor, which affected her badly. She once had a dream in which a loathsome, maggot-like creature emerged from the gap. She was paralysed with fear as it crawled slowly towards the bed, and she woke, screaming, when she realised that it bore her sister's face.

She remembered her sister, Sofia, as a baby. She remembered the hard wood furniture in her parents' house, which had been passed down through generations, heritage of her great-grandfather's wealth. She remembered the company men in suits who had sold her father the seeds they claimed would transform his life. She remembered them returning the next year to tell her father that they had patented the seeds; that he could not plant the ones he had saved without making the necessary payment. She remembered the strange fungal disease that spread through the crop, which proved more devastating than the insects the seeds had been designed to repel. She remembered her first sight of Gyorgy, who had moved into the village shortly after the disastrous harvest: the way he fanned himself with his discoloured white hat, the sweat glistening on his fat, moustachioed face, the small gold duelling pistol decorating his tie clip. She remembered her father's face in the glass window of his coffin.

Recalling the family's increasing desperation in the weeks preceding her departure with Sergei, Anna hoped that her mother had managed to clear her debt to Georgiy and keep the furniture. But she knew nothing of her family's current circumstances, beyond what Sergei told her, and the little he did tell was calculated solely to keep her in line. She was their 'cash cow', as Sergei liked to remind her, rolling the foreign phrase around in his mouth as if it was a sweet morsel, and she couldn't begin to estimate how much money she had made for him, or Dimitrios, or the faceless power broker that stood behind them.

What would have happened if Sergei had not come along? At one stage, she had been promised to the son of Bagarian – that obese teenager with the baby face. She recalled his high-pitched voice, the pale down wetly glistening on his upper lip, his addiction to Turkish delight. His mother was Norwegian. Would things have been any different with him rolling about on top of her?

However, Bagarian had lost his fortune at the same time as her father, and his land, too, had been swallowed up by the same agri-industrial concern that had consumed her father's land. Perhaps she had been doomed all along to a life in a brothel.

She thought of the client weeping on her shoulder that afternoon: the tale he had told through his tears – the conspiracy against him in the office, his wife's indifference, his belief that she was having an affair, his son's contempt. Justification, she thought, for the unpleasant and demeaning things he had requested of her.

There was a knock on the door. Anna stood up, smoothed down her dress, took a deep breath and said, 'Come in.'

Lola, the Brazilian girl, stood in the doorway. 'What is happening?'

'What do you mean?'

'No one has come. Have you heard the sirens? I waited, but nobody has come.'

Anna shrugged her shoulders. 'I haven't heard anything.'

'My room is at the front,' said Lola, 'but, even so, you must have heard the sirens?'

They headed downstairs. Kemel was standing behind the bar, in a space that could barely accommodate his bouncer's build. Natasha was sitting in one corner, blowing on her nails. Anna's last client was sitting on the red velvet plush of a sofa, with a glass of wine on the table in front of him, chewing on the cuticle of his left pinkie. He blushed when he saw Anna. She was surprised that he was still there and she made little effort to hide her contempt.

Suddenly, a man burst through the door leading from the massage parlour on the ground floor. He was swearing and shouting, but his thick accent made it impossible to understand what he was saying. His face bore an expression of exultation and rage, which put Anna in mind of a rabid dog she had in her childhood seen being shot, by the normally amiable Kristoff, who kept goats and made cheese from their milk.

In the moment it took that image to flash through her mind, Kemel emerged from behind the bar with a dexterity and purpose he seldom had occasion to display. He delivered a karate blow to the man's kidney, which sent him stumbling towards Sergei, who was running through the room's other doorway, bearing a cattle prod. It was only when the man fell back, stunned by the jolt of electricity to his chest, that Anna noticed the national flag tied around his throat and draped ludicrously over his shoulders like a cape.

While Sergei pushed him through the doorway and sent him tumbling down the short stairway to the massage parlour, Anna looked at the framed photographs, used to advertise the girls, that were set around the red-painted walls of the bar. Below each picture was the name given the girl by Sergei; cliché sobriquets inspired by each girl's racial type or nationality. Anna found it impossible to identify with the young woman wearing a floral top in her photograph, with her head tilted back and the spotlight's shimmer in her black hair, or to recall what the photographer had said or done to make her smile like that.

Chapter 4

JULY

WEDNESDAY

The idea for the novel came to me during a visit to V two years ago, when I was attending a conference on the future of literature in the age of the internet. It was only the second time that I had been to V. My wife and I had spent a week in the city ten years earlier, after visiting the Tarent Mountains on our honeymoon. Indeed, it was nostalgia for that first visit which had prompted me to accept the invitation to the conference, the subject of which struck me as being completely irrelevant to my work as a writer.

The delegates at the conference had been invited to a meal by the city council, in a restaurant in the waterfront development, and I took the opportunity after the meal of going to a bar that my wife and I had visited together during our honeymoon. It was near that bar that the incident occurred.

As I sat, reminiscing over a cold lager, two men asked if they could sit at my table. Both wore black shirts, but at that time I was unaware that the small, shield-shaped badges sewn on to their collars, each bearing the image of a crow with spread wings, identified them as members of 'The Brotherhood of the Martyrs'. However, I could sense their immediate antagonism when they heard my accent.

Now, while I have a reasonable command of your written language, my understanding of the spoken language was not good enough to follow their whispered dialogue, even had I desired to do so, but their strident tones and the hostile glances they darted at me from time to time made me feel distinctly uneasy.

Nothing, however, prepared me for what happened afterwards. As I turned down a side street towards Vandrhaf Square I became aware that the two men were following me. I do not want to dwell on the painful humiliation of the attack that followed, or upon the collusion of the police officer who allowed it to continue because I was a foreigner and therefore suspect. Suffice it to say that, during the following months, I became obsessed with the reasons behind the attack. I wanted to understand what had happened to change the open, friendly city that my wife and I had visited ten years previously.

Don't get me wrong. I am well aware of the rise of the far right in my own country. However, for we Hungarians, your country has always had a fabulous quality, perhaps because of your famous tales from the Bohemian Coast. My young wife and I certainly felt that on our honeymoon – as if we had stepped into a magical land – and now, now your country seems to have lost that quality.

My research into 'The Brotherhood of the Martyrs' made me think about the tales of King Corvus and the story of the Martyrs. You may not know about the recent research into that story. It has yet to find a publisher in your country. But it is possible that King Corvus himself organised the martyrdoms and the subsequent massacre, to stir up the populace against the Ottomans.

And then there is the tale of Princess Erzsébet, the evil femme fatale from Moravia, who married King Vaclav and who brought about the catastrophic destruction of V when it was the capital of that fabled kingdom by the sea. Her dreadful death has been watered down in the children's versions of that old tale, but she remains a figure of profound evil in the minds of your people. I discovered that in the original tale she was an innocent, a martyr if you like, made a scapegoat by the king to hide his own responsibility for the debacle.

Of course, as soon as I started to work on *The Journey to Varnak*, the novel took on a life of its own. In writing it, I left behind my obsession with the attack, which anyway was as much a product of my grieving for my wife. So, the finished novel is less about explaining the rise of fascism in your country, and more about restoring the fabulous shimmer that my wife and I discovered on our honeymoon, in your beautiful land.

Hannah put the newspaper down on the dining table and looked over at the coffee pot heating on the hob. It was an old electric hob that took ages to heat up, and cost a fortune to run, but the landlord was not paying the electricity bill, so what did he care?

The article she had been reading was in the weekend review section of the *Čuvar* newspaper and had been written by Gyula K, author of *The Journey to Varnak*. It was clearly based on an interview with the author, but it had been edited in such a way as to make it appear like an essay. Hannah wondered if the journalist had been too frightened of the consequences of attaching his or her name to such a controversial article.

In recent months, there had been a sharp rise in the number of violent acts carried out by right-wing extremists, and people were becoming much warier of the rabid threats made by internet trolls, or so Hannah believed.

The coffee pot began to spit. After lifting the lid carefully to check the coffee was ready, she poured out two mugs and topped them up with milk heated in the microwave. She took one of the mugs through to Daniela in her bedroom. There was a framed print on her easel.

'So you managed to replace the glass?' They both looked at the print.

'Yes, I went yesterday during my break,' said Daniela. 'Thank you so much,' she added when Hannah handed her the mug.

'Are you taking it over today?' said Hannah.

'Yes, later this morning.'

'Why don't we have lunch there? My treat.'

'Are you sure?'

'Of course I am. You had to pay to get the frame fixed.'

'That was my fault, Hannah. It had nothing to do with you.'

'I know, but I am flush this month. And I'm at a loose end today.'

'Did you finish with Franz at the weekend?'

'He didn't take it very well. Said he had seen me with another man. Started shouting. I just walked away.'

Holding the mug with both hands, Daniela took a sip of coffee.

'That's nice, just what I needed,' she said, looking at her print again. She had designed it on her laptop, using a scan of an old engraving of her hometown of Krakow, and photographs she had taken around V, mixing elements of both cities in such a way as to create a plausible cityscape out of the resulting collage. Then she had printed the finished picture on parchment paper and had it framed.

It was to form the first piece in an exhibition she was putting on in an art centre and cafe that had recently opened in a trendy part of Selonaskala near the suspension bridge. The glass of the frame had broken in transit to the gallery and Daniela had had to take it back to the framer.

The private view was due to take place that Friday evening. Daniela had to buy twenty bottles of wine and six cartons of orange juice, all supplied at wholesale discount by the gallery owner. He would provide the glasses and would get fifty per cent of the value of every print sold. A heavily bearded man in his mid-thirties who had made a fortune as a corporate lawyer, he had wanted to get out of the rat race and do something of more cultural significance with his money and time, so he told Daniela when she had shown him her work a couple of months ago.

'I need to have a shower,' said Daniela. She was still wearing her pyjamas – a purple and black checked cotton top and a pair of loose-fitting purple trousers. Hannah noticed her long, slim toes with their glossy black nail varnish.

'There's no hurry. I haven't got any plans. We can go when you're ready.'

Hannah went through to the living room to drink her coffee and to finish reading the review section of her newspaper. Daniela tapped one of her front teeth. Feeling nothing, she recalled the terrible agony it had given her three months earlier. She feared the nerve was dead. Trying not to think about it, she picked up her phone and clicked on the social media site where she had advertised her exhibition with a jpeg of the cityscape. So far, twenty people had liked it and three had disliked it. She worried about those three as she began to scroll through other images uploaded by her steadily proliferating connections. Photographs and videos succeeded one another in quick succession – an old man with shoulder-length, greasy hair and a hangdog expression, standing in front of a wooden fence beside two pretty blonde girls – a parrot walking around a room, making a repetitive slapping noise with its feet – a beautiful teenage girl with long hair, dyed blue, holding her manicured fingers spread in front of her mouth – a tiny puppy with a short, dark muzzle sucking bottled milk through a rubber teat – a young man wearing a black hoodie, sitting on a red couch while a girl in a white hoodie and black leggings lay on her back in front of him moving her legs in a pedalling motion – another pretty teenager with long pink hair, false eyelashes and strange white contacts covering her irises – an old and a young woman embracing against a background of sun-shot greenery – a baby with a fuzz of dark hair and a blond man sleeping next to one another on a bed with a green sheet – a video of a man skydiving – a beautiful model advertising a dress with a pentangle of straps over her clavicles and shoulders – a cheetah making a curious sibilant sound as if it were singing – a young woman wearing a black top that exposed her tanned cleavage and belly – a handsome young man with high cheekbones and eyeliner, shot in moody black and white – an advert for a phone manufacturer with thousands of coloured balloons floating over a city – a photograph of a corridor in a derelict institutional building with ochre paint-peeling walls and a floor scattered with filth and detritus.

Daniela was not sure where the hour had gone when she finally went through to the bathroom, which was filled with stippled sunlight. The mouldy shower curtain was decorated with coloured images of fish and sea plants. She drew both hands through her hair, closed her eyes and raised her face to the powerful spray.

★

Hannah folded up the newspaper and put it to one side. As she drank the last of her coffee she thought about the disappointing trendy novels that had been selected for review. She wondered how the authors and publishers managed to get those books on to the market while they were still topical, and she found herself comparing them unfavourably with *The Journey to Varnak*. She thought she might reread that novel in the light of the author's article.

She took her coffee mug over to the sink and washed it and her breakfast dishes. Since Daniela still had not emerged from her room, Hannah went to the bathroom and put on her make-up using the mirror on the cabinet door. As usual, she was dissatisfied with her appearance. The cleft on her chin annoyed her, and she did not like her nose. Despite all that Franz and her previous boyfriends had said, she still wished that it were straighter and slimmer. She was only happy with her eyes and she devoted particular care to them.

Whenever she had to work on a Saturday, Hannah preferred to have Wednesdays off. Out of habit, though, she would still wake up at the same time, and it would take her an hour or so to stop thinking about the various tasks and problems in the bookshop. Only now, as she tidied away her mascara, eyeliner, lipstick and foundation, did she appreciate that she was free to do what she wanted for the next hour or so, until Daniela was ready to go out.

Back in the main room, she opened the curtains. The window looked on to the yard behind the charity shop on the corner. There was something deeply satisfying in the way the sun etched the shadow of their building on to the orange brickwork of the wall across the yard. The charity shop van was carefully reversing along the narrow access driveway. Two volunteers in matching blue T-shirts were chatting in the back doorway to the shop. A black and grey pigeon with a white head nodded and walked about in the path of the van, almost getting caught under its wheel, before flying clumsily on to a windowsill on the building opposite.

A warm feeling of pleasure spread through Hannah's stomach as she went through to her bedroom to retrieve her copy of *The Journey to Varnak*. When she came back through with it, she looked at Daniela's painting on the wall above the radiator – a stylised, almost abstract rendition of the garden of Daniela's childhood home in Krakow, with her mother stroking the head of their dog.

In the aftermath of the Martyrs' Procession, Hannah had felt scared and vulnerable in the flat and had begun to think that she and Daniela should seek an apartment in a safer part of town. When she had broached the possibility with Daniela, however, her flatmate thought that Hannah intended to move out. Daniela had hidden how upset she was, thinking it would be selfish to show her feelings, imagining that Hannah might be moving in with the new man in her life. But then the husband of Halina, an old friend from Poland, was beaten to death in a hate crime in the Capital. Halina was desperate to move out of the flat they had shared, so Daniela offered her Hannah's room. It was only when Daniela told her of the offer that Hannah realised that her friend had misunderstood her intentions. Hannah's suggestion had taken on a momentum of its own, which it was not possible to stop, and she realised how much she would miss her life here with Daniela.

She sat down on the couch with her book, but she found it difficult to concentrate on her reading. An acid spurt of anxiety reminded her that she still had to find a place to live. She had answered an advert for a rented room in an apartment in the waterfront development, and she had an appointment to view it that evening, but she feared that the rent would be well beyond her limited budget, and time was running out.

★

Hannah followed Daniela into the art centre and was immediately struck by the gallery running around three of the walls. It was difficult to tell what function the building had served in the past. The gallery with its wooden banister suggested it had been the chapel of some obscure Christian sect. Hannah was put in mind of the atrium of the old City Hall where she used to work. She took a seat at a table in the cafe, from where she could see Daniela up in the gallery with the bearded owner, hanging the print of the cityscape. The gallery would not be open to the public until Saturday morning, when visitors would be directed up the stairway closest to the main entrance. The cityscape would be the first artwork they would see.

It would set the scene for the subsequent collages, all of which worked as individual images, but in combination they narrated a nightmarish tale in which a young couple were pursued through a variety of street scenes by shadowy evil figures. The story was inspired by the tragic deaths of Daniela's great-grandparents during the Second

World War. Shortly after handing their only daughter into the safe keeping of well-wishers, they had been arrested by the Gestapo and gassed at Auschwitz with a train load of Jews and political prisoners sent by the compliant government of Hannah's country. It was Daniela's hope that the exhibition would highlight the dangers and horrors of fascism.

When she had seen some of the individual prints on Daniela's laptop, Hannah had thought that the narrative elements were too subtly embedded in them to be detected by the casual viewer, but she believed that the resulting ambiguity only made the exhibition more satisfying on an artistic level. In her opinion, the best way to oppose fascism through art or literature was to render the world in all its complexity and uncertainty. She believed that the violence and hate of extremist groups like the Brotherhood of the Martyrs arose from their fear of anything that lay beyond the crass certainties of their nationalist dogmas.

She did not share these thoughts when Daniela asked her opinion of the exhibition on the tram there that morning. She merely pointed out that even if the viewer did not perceive the overall narrative the individual prints would still leave them with a sense of the nameless dread underlying the crowded city scenes.

A couple of weeks earlier, when they had been discussing the exhibition, Hannah had said, 'You know, I think it is fear that is the root cause of fascism. The members of the Brotherhood are terrified of anything that is different from them.'

'Fear! Fear! How you say that? said Daniela in sudden anger. 'For years, my country is crushed by Germany and then Russia. They show no fear of Poland, or remorse. You don't know what you are talking of! Your country sacrificed your Jews and communists to the Nazis so that you could live without fear in your stupid fairy tale country.'

Only then had Daniela told Hannah that Halina's husband had been murdered the previous week. He had been so savagely beaten that his wife could only identify him by his clothes and wedding ring. According to Halina, the police were making little effort to pursue the investigation, even though her husband had received a death threat on a social media site shortly before the attack, a threat marked with the sign of the Black Hand – an ultra-violent right-wing group composed of former soldiers. Halina's husband had posted a mild criticism of the profusion of national flags decorating the houses in the Tarent Mountains where they had gone for their Easter holidays. The police inspector had observed to Halina that this had been a dangerous provocation in these troubled times.

Daniela had burst into tears, and Hannah, too, started crying. They apologised and hugged each other. Hannah explained that she had intended to move out with Daniela and not away from her, but that now the important thing was to provide Halina with a safe refuge in V, before the Black Hand targeted her as well.

When Daniela reflected on the argument afterwards, she wondered if her friend was being completely honest with her. It occurred to her that, in the light of recent events, Hannah might now be afraid to share a flat with an immigrant – a notion that was only confirmed by her eagerness to surrender her room to Halina.

Certain aspects of their disagreement still rankled with Hannah, too, while she sat in the art centre cafe two weeks later, waiting for Daniela to finish hanging the print. She had been hurt by Daniela's reference to the shameful wartime history of Hannah's country. Hannah had always found fascism abhorrent and she loved the cultural diversity that immigrants had brought to her home town. She could see no reason for dredging up the old enmities of the Second World War. After all, there were now just as many far-right groups in Poland, and Hannah thought there was little difference between them and the Brotherhood or the Black Hand.

To Hannah, ambiguity was essential in art. If art had a purpose, it was to make the viewer question the world, not to provide answers. But as she scanned the menu she realised that her insistence on ambiguity in art could be regarded as demanding a quality in art as absolute and necessary as the national and racial purity demanded by the far right. The thought made her anxious, and the anxiety brought further self-doubts and self-questionings in its wake. She concluded that Daniela was right: such weakness and confusion had no chance of combatting the wave of nationalism sweeping the country.

'Are you okay?' said Daniela, interrupting Hannah's reverie.

'Sure, I'm fine.'

Daniela placed her bag on one of the spare chairs at the table. 'It's just that you looked so sad.'

'I was thinking about the way I treated Franz.'

Daniela sat opposite Hannah and took her hand between hers. 'You did the right thing, Hannah. Better that you break up with him now than to let him think that everything is okay.'

'I know, but to skulk about going on secret dates with a married man – it's all so tawdry and cliché. I should have made a clean break with Franz before dating someone else.'

'But you haven't slept with this man, and it is not as if you were engaged to Franz,' said Daniela, although she was shocked to learn that the man was married.

They ate smashed avocado on sourdough toast, washed down with

French cider. Daniela worried how much this would be costing Hannah. They had salted caramel cheesecake with crème fraiche for dessert. The place was now full, everyone talking excitedly. A cup was dropped with a crash behind the counter. A baby, with startled blue eyes and a fuzz of spiked hair on top of its head, vomited milk down its mother's back. And Franz strolled into the bookshop at the far end of the room. It took Hannah a moment to recognise him, because she saw him from behind and his hair was cut much shorter than usual, but when he turned around, his weak chin and the missing button on his old suede jacket gave him away. With a sinking heart, she recalled him saying that he had moved into the area.

Franz was now renting a room in a nearby flat, which he shared with the owner – an elderly woman who regarded her new tenant as an unofficial carer. Franz thought this a small sacrifice to make to live in such a prestigious area, although he would have done well to consider those seemingly light burdens that gradually become monstrous the longer you have to carry them.

He had ordered a collection of essays on Edward H's *All-Consuming Passions* from this gallery bookshop because he hadn't wanted to risk running into Hannah at her work, and yet there she was, looking stunning and self-contained, with her flatmate. He tried to appear unconcerned, by nodding in their direction and then becoming overtly interested in a book displayed on the table, which he was horrified to realise was entitled *The Vagina Dentata*.

'Something to get your teeth into, eh?' said the slim, shaven-haired woman standing beside him, who laughed at his red-faced confusion as he headed to the counter.

Franz found it difficult to cope with the swirl of emotions aroused by the sight of Hannah in the cafe. Principally, there was the dreadful knowledge that he, alone of all the men there, was denied even the possibility of having sex with her. Every time he and Hannah had made love he had always had the fear that it would be the last time, but nothing had prepared him for the anguish he had felt when he saw her there and knew with a certainty that he would never again feel the touch of her skin.

His stomach knotted and his heart raced as he headed past a small tree-lined park towards Castle Hill with no clear idea of why he was heading in that direction. Since Hannah had finished with him, he had felt as if he had come unfettered from life. There was his research and his PhD dissertation. There were the weekly phone calls from his mother. There was the job he had in the wine bar four evenings a week. There were the porn websites that he had begun to frequent. There were the numberless videos, writings and adverts that he encountered when surfing the internet. But in the absence of human touch, it all seemed increasingly spurious to Franz, as if there was no difference between the actual occurrences in his life and the varied images on his phone or laptop screen.

Four women walked past him on the way to Castle Hill. He thought one of them was extraordinarily beautiful. When he saw her approach, his mind conjured scenes from the pornographic videos he had recently watched. The breeze carried the scents of her perfume and shampoo. Before looking away, he surreptitiously took in the colour of her eyes, the shimmer of her long blond hair, and the shape of her figure, but when she had passed out of sight he wondered if she had any more substance than a video image or a character in a book.

He thought about Edward H. What did all the words he had read or written about the man really amount to? The name was invented. Did the words of *All-Consuming Passions* really give any form to the person who had written them?

It appeared to Franz that the only occasions he had ever come close to experiencing reality in the true sense were in those brief moments when Hannah had held his penis gripped within the smooth walls of her vagina. As he gazed up at the clear blue sky visible between the buildings descending the slopes on either side, it struck him that in Hannah's absence he was of no more significance than the lateral shading applied to the letters of Edward H's name on the cover of *All-Consuming Passions* to make them appear as if they existed in three dimensions.

The streets became more crowded after he passed the multi-storey car park and neared the museum and City Hall. People of all ages were walking along the pavement in both directions, each pursuing his or her own mysterious goal. Franz had nothing to do until the start of his shift in the wine bar at seven o'clock that evening. His panic had reached an almost unbearable limit and its passing now left him with a feeling of hopeless lassitude. No option seemed better than any other. He abruptly stopped in confusion on the summit of Castle Hill, to the intense annoyance of a man behind him, wearing a hoodie, sweatpants and scuffed trainers, who swore at him harshly and gave him the finger. Franz made abject apologies and walked quickly away in the direction of the bookshop where Hannah worked. He realised that his stomach was empty. Although he couldn't think of what to eat, he could rest a while in the bookshop cafe, safe in the knowledge that Hannah wasn't working that day.

The cafe offered two different kinds of soup in clear plastic tubs – creamy chicken or tomato with basil. Franz reckoned his stomach could cope with the chicken. The plump young woman serving behind the counter gave him the same meaningless smile that he gave to his customers in the wine bar. He declined her offer of a hot drink, saying he would have a coffee after his soup. She smiled more genuinely at the absurdity of his uncalled-for explanation, took his money and placed the tub of soup in the microwave behind the counter. There were humorous or flirtatious men who could invest such transactions with genuine warmth, but Franz was not one of them, and the encounter did little to alleviate his sense of isolation.

He took the wooden block displaying his order number and found in the middle of the crowded cafe a recently vacated table with two abandoned cups and saucers. A napkin in one of the saucers was stained brown by spilled coffee. A torn fragment of notepaper on the table beside it bore part of a word written in Arabic script. Although he could read the language, the ink was smudged and he could not identify the word.

After eating his soup and bread, Franz was able to take his coffee and a paper cup of water to a table in a corner. Once settled on the faux leather banquette, he took out the book of essays he had bought, his notebook and the pencil case in which he kept a variety of pens with different-coloured inks.

Franz's tutor had warned him about the risks of selecting a current book as the subject for his PhD dissertation, because of the possibility that some commentator might pre-empt Franz's argument. However, Franz had been adamant that he wanted to research a contemporary subject, to help him establish his chosen career as a diplomat. The sudden success of *All-Consuming Passions* had come as something of a shock, and he now feared that his tutor might have been right after all.

Franz had still been deciding between two or three approaches to Edward H's book when he saw the publisher's advertisement for the collection of essays he had bought that morning, so it was with some trepidation that he now scanned through the contents page of *Consumerism, Desire and Faith: Edward H and the Crisis of Secularism* (edited by Theodore Hamilton III, Emeritus Professor of Philosophy at Jackson College Georgia).

Most of the essays proved to be of little interest to Franz – Christian interpretations that pointed to the evangelical organisation that had funded the book. However, one essay caught his attention: 'Attar's *Colloquy of the Birds* and the Question of Influence on *All-Consuming Passions*' by Javad Shirazi, an Iranian émigré lecturer in Columbia's philosophy department.

The title *Colloquy of the Birds* began to resonate in Franz's head, distracting him from his thoughts about Hannah. He knew the passage in *All-Consuming Passions* in which Edward H referred to the poem, but Franz only now discovered that it was written by the Sufi poet Farid ud-Din Attar. He paused for a moment, as if lost in thought, looking at two Japanese girls sitting nearby. Their legs in contrasting pale and dark tights were almost touching under the table. He reached into his bag for his battered copy of H's book and skimmed through the pages until he found the passage:

> The poem tells of how the Simug – the king of the birds – dropped one of his divine feathers in the middle of China. The birds decide to abandon their differences and join in a quest to find it. It is known that 'Simurg' means 'thirty birds', and that the royal palace stands on the Kaf, the circular mountain that surrounds the Earth. After journeying across seven valleys and seven seas, only thirty birds remain of all those that set out. Beyond the seas of Vertigo and Annihilation they arrive at the mountain that surrounds the Earth, where they come to the realisation that they are the Simurg and that the Simurg is each one of them and all of them.

In his book, Edward H inverts the conceit of the poem to criticise consumer capitalism. He argues that in advertising one of its products any company

> invariably presents it to the consumer as if it contains the spark of divinity, but that the motive of the company is purely one of greed for profit.
>
> When seeking out the product, the consumer in turn imagines himself on a quest for something that will uplift him spiritually, but which in fact only infects him with the same insatiable greed that prompted the company to manufacture the product in the first place.

Franz had made a note in the margin indicating H's sole use of the male pronoun, and questioning whether it was deliberate, but up until now he had taken no further interest in Attar's poem. He wondered how many other oversights there were in his research.

In his essay, Shirazi pointed out the odd coincidence that the Sufi poem had also been used to not dissimilar ends some forty years earlier by an anonymous Marxist thinker of Middle Eastern origin, who wrote under the pseudonym of 'Zarathustra'. In a collection of essays published by a clandestine press, funded by the Soviets, in Teheran in the late 1970s, 'Zarathustra' had cited *The Colloquy of the Birds* in connection with his argument that once the revolution had wrested control of the oil wells from their imperialist American owners the revenues would be shared equally among all citizens and the citizens would merge so completely with the communist government that all differences would be effaced.

Shirazi acknowledged that the spirituality of Edward H's book was totally at odds with the Marxism espoused by 'Zarathustra', but he wondered if the coincidence pointed to the direct influence of the earlier essay on Edward H's argument, even going so far as to speculate that Edward H might be a lapsed communist.

However, Shirazi did not pursue the idea of Edward H's communism any further. The main thrust of his argument was not that Edward H had been influenced by the communist thinker, but that the different slant he had given to the argument of 'Zarathustra' was yet another indication of Edward H's profound disenchantment with the secular world:

> In a sense, Edward H's identity is irrelevant. The power of *All-Consuming Passions* lies not in its parts, or in the identity of its author, but in the burning revelation that led its author to become Edward H and to write the book. Like Saul's epiphany on the road to Damascus, it made the author reassess everything he had thought about the world, and offer us a spiritual truth that might yet destroy the web of transient and trivial desires which currently gives meaning to our lives.

Franz was now totally absorbed by the essay, which he did not think was particularly well argued. He was not sure that it provided any concrete support for the notion of Edward H's epiphany, although Franz knew there were many indications of it in *All-Consuming Passions*. The vague poetic language of the essay's closing sentence also annoyed him. He favoured clarity and succinctness and he loathed that metaphorical web. More than anything else, he disagreed with the notion that Edward H's identity was irrelevant.

In fact, Franz experienced his own epiphany when he realised something that should have occurred to him long before: that if he could discover Edward H's identity then not only would he guarantee the success of his dissertation but he might also attract the interest of a major publisher.

In the excitement of the moment, he quite forgot about his despair over Hannah. His mind was buzzing with half-formed ideas about his research and vague fantasies of the rich rewards it might bring him. He imagined winning one of the major literary prizes and going to the award's ceremony with Hannah. He pictured her wearing the black dress he had seen only once before in a photograph, taken during a university summer ball. He pictured her lovely cleft chin.

The Japanese girls had now been replaced by a woman of about fifty in a white turtleneck angora sweater. She was reading a book that he recognised as one that Hannah had been reading recently. He asked her if she would mind keeping an eye on his stuff while he went to buy another coffee, and she acquiesced with a smile. When he returned to the table with his coffee, the woman looked up from her reading and smiled again, and he responded with what he hoped was an appropriate expression of gratitude. Then he made room on his table to set up his laptop.

His online search for *The Colloquy of the Birds* drew repeated citations of a story by Borges called 'The Approach to Al Mu'tasmin'. One website provided an extensive quotation from the story which revealed it to be the source of Edward H's description of the poem. Franz wrote the title of the story and the collection from which it was taken on a fresh page of his notebook and then logged off his laptop. He wondered if 'Zarathustra' too had taken his description from Borges; he wrote the title of the Iranian essay collection next to Borges's title. On his way out, he bought a copy of Borges's *Fictions*. The young man who served Franz looked at him with an odd expression, and Franz wondered if he too had had an affair with Hannah. Franz had seen her one evening on the waterfront with a wealthy-looking and handsome man, who didn't strike him as being her type, but the sight of them had made him wonder if Hannah had cheated on him with other men. He feared now that she had split up with him in order to go out with that wealthy man.

A tram was passing outside when he left the bookshop. He tried to see if Hannah was among the passengers. It was a beautiful, warm evening. He did not want to go home. Undecided about what to do, he collided with a young man who had just stepped on to the pavement. As happened so often in V, Franz thought that he recognised the man's slight build, thick black hair and large nose. Judging by his designer suit, he was one of those well-paid young professionals who made Franz question his wisdom in pursuing a PhD.

★

It had been a trivial incident. The stranger had apologised for bumping into him, so Josef could not understand why he felt so worked up. He had taken in the man's red hair, weak chin and scuffed suede jacket – not someone he recognised from work. There could have been no deliberation in the act. It took a few moments for Josef's heartbeat to settle down and he had already passed the traffic lights when he remembered he had planned to buy a ready meal that evening. A woman had answered the advert he had placed in the city newspaper and she was coming to look at his spare room at seven that evening.

The supermarket, situated just beyond the summit of Castle Hill, was part of an upmarket chain that stocked a range of gourmet ready meals offering the best of world cuisine. As Josef stood in the cool, brightly lit aisle he was tempted by a vegetable curry recipe from Kerala but, knowing that someone was coming to view his flat, he didn't want to fill the place with the smell, and so he bought an innocuous dish of sausage and mashed potatoes, calculated to appeal to expatriates from the UK, who for some reason found the city of V congenial.

Josef had fitted out the spare room like a bedsit, with an expensive sofa bed and a small armchair. Along one wall, he had managed to fit a wardrobe, a shoe rack, a chest of drawers and an audio-visual unit, all in oak wood, leaving space for a dressing table and mirror on the short wall by the door. In this way, he had sought to contain his imagined lodger in a separate sphere that would leave Josef free to enjoy the remaining living space with a degree of privacy.

Those were the orderly thoughts on which he tried to keep his mind focused as he joined the queue for the self-service tills: the oak wood furniture; the cosy space he had created in his spare bedroom. But even as he left the shop the tension started building again and he was overwhelmed by his many anxieties about work: the unremitting hostility of most of his colleagues; the legal intricacies of the new part-time contracts; the monthly meeting that had taken place earlier in the afternoon.

All the department heads had been there, including Josef's superior, Daria. Josef could tell from her fixed expression that she was uneasy about the meeting. Chris, displaying his usual mix of charm and menace, was spouting some nonsense about 'the dynamism of the administration and of its adaptability to the dramatic changes transforming society'. It was all bullshit as far as Josef was concerned, designed to sugar-coat the brutal benefits cuts that had been enacted by the government. Tougher criteria had been put in place to reduce the number of claimants. There were also to be new rules governing all benefit claims. Those still due benefits who failed to comply with the stricter regulations would have their payments cut or suspended. Chris pointed out that the administration could reap big financial rewards if they could reduce the city's welfare costs. Consequently, the staff administering the claims would be set targets for the number of claimants refused and for the punitive measures taken.

'I'm not sure that you can set targets for that – from a legal standpoint, I mean,' said Josef suddenly, drawing a looked of shocked surprise from Daria.

'What exactly do you mean?' said Chris.

Josef did not know why he had spoken up. When he saw Chris's expression, he immediately regretted it.

'Well, either a claimant will meet the new criteria laid down by the government, in which case they will be due the benefit, or they won't, but our staff have no control over the decision, since they haven't set the criteria.' Josef looked around the table for support, but everyone avoided his eye, so he continued with less conviction: 'The same is true of the regulations relating to the punitive measures.'

'Obviously, the targets are not about fudging the facts.' Chris's command of the language was normally so good that he could almost pass for a native speaker. But, in his barely contained rage, his American accent became so prominent that Josef found it difficult to follow what he was saying. 'They are simply there to focus the minds of the staff assessing the claims. As to the new regulations for administering the benefits, the government merely judges that welfare payments should be treated the same as the wages given for paid employment. I mean, Josef, if you were repeatedly late for work, it would be judged fair to dock your pay by the number of hours you missed, unless it was due to sickness, of course. The targets are merely there to ensure that the regulations are applied to the letter. Otherwise, how can the clients ever be prepared for the conditions of the workplace?'

As Josef made his way home he kept going over the meeting in his head. He could no longer remember exactly what he or Chris had said, but Chris's self-evident anger made him feel frightened and insecure. Most of Josef's workmates treated him with ill-concealed contempt. Daria was the only person he could count as a friend in the company. It struck him that Chris was incapable of any genuine human feeling and Josef now realised how utterly dependent he was on the CEO's goodwill.

★

As Hannah waited for the lift to arrive she wondered why she had come. Just by the look of the place, she figured the rent would be well beyond her limited budget. Also, there was something odd about the flat owner's voice when he answered the buzzer to let her in. Anyone sounded robotic and tinny through those speakers, but it seemed to Hannah as if he were trying to mask an excited tremor in his voice.

There were already two people in the lift when the door slid open: a stunningly attractive woman with long black hair and olive skin, wearing a tight black dress with shiny red high heels, and a handsome man in a well-cut black suit and white shirt buttoned up to the collar and worn without a tie. There was an odd bulge under his jacket near the left armpit which made Hannah imagine a wallet stuffed with banknotes. Dark stubble emphasised the hollows of his cheeks, his lips were unusually thick, and Hannah caught a glint of a gold tooth when he smiled and ushered her into the lift. He was lounging against the mirror behind and slightly to the woman's right. Hannah turned her back on him, but she felt her nape prickle as if he were staring at her the whole way up. She was grateful they did not get out at her floor.

She walked the wrong way along the corridor. After checking the numbers on a couple of doors, she managed to locate the one she was after. It was opened by a young man whose slim face looked vaguely familiar. He directed her along the hallway, accidently touching her arm as he did so. He withdrew his hand so abruptly and apologised so profusely that she laughed in perplexity and said that it wasn't a problem.

'I've just put some coffee on, if you would like a cup,' he said, blushing.

As he prepared the coffee she hung her bag over one of the chairs at the dining table and looked through the panoramic window at the river flowing through the gorge towards the west. A tourist boat sailed by, crowded with sightseers. She took in the evening traffic snaking along the foot of the cliff. A young woman was running along the waterfront in a bright yellow sports top. Hannah could just make out the rhythmic side-to-side sweep of her ponytail as she ran. Then her gaze travelled over the multicoloured terrace on top of the hill opposite, towards a clump of trees on the clifftop some three kilometres to the west, among which she could make out a villa that she realised with a sudden shock was Stefan's.

Josef had recognised Hannah as soon as he opened the door, and now, as he prepared the coffee, he was doing all in his power to calm himself down, but the specific details of her beauty confounded him: her sexy chin cleft, the curves of her cheeks, the haunting downward slant of her eyes, her clear blue irises. The very slight bump and hook of her nose only added to her allure. She had said nothing when she looked around the living area and she was now gazing out of the window towards the west. He feared that she was unimpressed by his interior decoration.

'How do you take your coffee?'

'White, no sugar,' she replied, turning towards him. She took a seat on the couch and crossed her legs.

He brought over the coffees on a tray with a plate of chocolate biscuits, which he placed on the coffee table next to the ashtray. As they both looked at the brooch in the ashtray, Josef realised why it was familiar to him and he experienced a warm inner glow of satisfaction and relief.

'My brooch,' she said, without thinking.

'I found it about a month ago. I should have realised …'

'I thought I had lost it for good!' In her excitement she did not take in what Josef had said, and he made no effort to repeat it. 'It's like something out of a movie,' she added. 'Something you could never imagine happening in reality.'

'It's uncanny.' He was thinking of the complex of miniature chambers exposed within a broken shell. 'As if it was fated.'

'I thought I would never see it again. I can't believe it. You have no idea how happy this makes me.'

As they drank their coffee Josef decided not to mention the fact that he had seen her wearing the brooch all those months ago. He would tell her that he was working for the local administration; of course he would. He just would not tell her when he had started.

After they had finished their coffee, he showed her the spare bedroom. She noticed that the sofa bed was the same as the one in Stefan's office. He showed her the bathroom with its modern suite and constellation of LED spotlights. She ran her finger over the curving glass shower door, took in the slate tiles, looked at the mirror cabinet on the wall.

'I don't have a bath very often, so this bathroom will effectively be yours. I have a shower in my en-suite.'

Finally, he took her through his bedroom, which he had carefully tidied and aired, and out on to the balcony. A round ironwork table was set out there with four matching chairs. Josef invited her to join him in a glass of sparkling wine that he had brought out earlier and left in an ice bucket. Hannah accepted his offer, but was concerned about the preparations, assumptions and intentions that lay behind it.

'This is a beautiful flat, Josef, but I should tell you, there is no way I could afford the rent for a place like this.'

Josef wondered if this was just her way of saying she did not want to live there. He was flustered, unsure of himself. 'The rent is not so important to me. It is more important that I should find a lodger that I can …' He paused, distressed by Hannah's suspicious expression. 'It's just more important to me to have a lodger I can get on with. I would want 300 thalers a month with a month's deposit.'

Hannah turned to look over the balcony at the apartment block opposite. The varied sounds of the city formed a humming background, pierced by a distant siren. The rent he was asking was ridiculously low, only 25 thalers more than she was currently paying. Her gaze travelled up Castle Hill to the crenellations of City Hall. Its metal roof was bathed in orange sunlight. She still was not sure about Josef's motives, but she knew she would never find another flat like this in her price range, and he had found her brooch.

'Can I think it over and let you know tomorrow?'

'Sure. You've got my mobile number.'

She smiled, finished her wine and took one last look at the view along the river. He followed the direction of her gaze to the villa that was visible among trees on the clifftop to the west. Gradually, he became aware of the music coming from above – distinctively Middle Eastern music with a woman's voice singing in what he took to be Arabic.

★

As before, the woman admitted Sergei and Anna to the apartment without speaking. Ben F was sitting at the table on the decking in the roof garden, but this time it was set out with large platters of food. He stood up and spread his arms wide when Sergei approached. Middle Eastern music was playing on a CD mini-system in the garden – a woman singing in Arabic, accompanied by the plaintive sound of a violin. Brief outbursts of applause and laughter indicated that it was the recording of a live performance and that the song was humorous. That was as much as Anna could take in before the woman pulled her unceremoniously towards Ben F's bedroom, speaking Arabic in a harsh undertone as she did so.

In the bedroom, there was a chair at a foldaway table on which had been laid a selection of exotic dishes, a carafe of water and a glass. The woman pushed Anna into the chair and signed to her to eat. Anna watched her go over to the chest of drawers to light an incense stick in a copper holder incised with an elaborate pattern. Then she said something forcibly, accompanied by a gesture that clearly instructed Anna to remain quiet, before she left the room and locked the door behind her.

The food was delicious, but Anna was too anxious to enjoy it. After eating two small triangular pastries filled with cheese and spinach, and some grilled lamb cubes with red pepper slices on a skewer, she started to wander around the room, looking at its sparse furnishings. She remembered the framed photograph from her last visit. It was on the dresser, leaning at an angle on its stand between two candlesticks, and showed a man and woman with three children – two girls and a boy. They were standing in dappled light in front of a wall of blue decorated tiles. It took Anna a moment to recognise Ben F's slim raptor's face. He was wearing a Western-style caramel-coloured sports jacket with cream trousers. The woman and children were also wearing Western clothes – the woman a startling red floral dress that contrasted with the wall.

Six objects were arranged on the dresser in front of the photograph: an elaborate filigree necklace that had partially melted into a series of elongated drops to which fragments of blackened cloth adhered; a china doll's head with singed curls and gaping eye sockets; a die-cast model of a Boeing 747 with a melted tail fin and broken undercarriage; a shiny object, impossible to identify, composed of a cluster of tiny spheres resembling petrified bubbles of boiling tar; a toy lion made of metal, the back legs of which had melted and merged with a gloopy mass with protruding antelope horns; the blackened nib of a fountain pen.

The sight of the objects made Anna feel queasy, as if she had glimpsed another, more nightmarish world than the one in which she was trapped. She imagined that some cataclysm had overtaken Ben F's family. However, her sympathy was tempered by the thought that she was not much older than the girls pictured in the photograph and yet Ben had not thought twice about possessing her body while she lay shrouded in her dress.

She found herself gazing into the empty eye sockets of the doll's head and recalling the doll that, in a rare moment of generosity, her father had given her for her tenth birthday: a cheap copy of a Barbie doll that he had picked up in the village market. The short pink dress with which it had been clothed had outraged her mother, who, like all the other women in the village, habitually wore a long black dress with thick black tights. Had her father been sober, he would no doubt have shared her outrage at the doll's naked thighs, but he was drunk and his fury at having his actions questioned by her mother far outweighed the dubious morals of the doll. He slapped her mother hard on the cheek and the violence and sound of that slap remained forever attached to that doll, with which her father compelled her henceforth to play, as a reminder to her mother of who was in charge of the household.

As if she were back in the brothel, Anna walked over to Ben F's bed, sat down and crossed her legs. She pulled down the hem of her dress in a futile bid to cover her thighs, reflecting as she did so on the countless men for whom she had waited just as she was waiting now.

However, it was not Ben F but the woman who appeared after an interval that Anna had no way of measuring. The woman expressed a sigh of annoyance at the sight of the uneaten food and proceeded to clear away everything, including the table and chair, in four laborious journeys, locking the door behind her each time she went out. She did not acknowledge Anna's presence in any way, so that Anna had the strange feeling of observing a domestic drama that had been staged purely for her benefit.

More time passed. Anna was used to waiting. She realised that the music, which she had only been able to hear very faintly, had stopped and she wondered when that had happened.

The woman returned with some black cloth draped over her arm which looked to be the same material as her robe. Anna was surprised to see that she was now wearing a veil over her face. Only her eyes were visible, but they clearly expressed her terror. She pointed at Anna's shoes and started pulling at her dress. Anna was about to protest, when the woman, in self-evident panic, whispered her first words in Anna's language.

'Please, don't speak, for me, too, I ...'

Anna was unsure what she was trying to say, but, impressed by the woman's fear, she fell silent and took off her shoes and dress before putting on the black robe, hood and veil she was offered.

Angry voices, shouting in Arabic, could now be heard through the door. Anna barely recognised Ben F's voice, so enraged did it sound, but there was something chilling about the other voice which convinced Anna that its bearer was the source of the woman's terror. Anna had no idea what they were saying. She watched the woman pushing the red shoes and dress under Ben F's bed, and then they sat side by side – the woman hunched forward, covering her eyes with her hands, rocking back and forth and trembling.

★

If Daria M hadn't been so upset when she arrived at the entrance to Josef's apartment block, she might have paid more attention to the bearded man with the scarred cheek who exited the building just as Josef pressed the buzzer to unlock the door. As it was, she did not notice the man climbing into the passenger seat of a white van with the name of a plumbing firm printed on the side. The driver, another brown-skinned, heavily bearded man, put the van into gear and made a U-turn on the road, before pulling away.

Daria could not believe what Chris was asking of her now. All her rationalisations about her beautiful loft apartment and her well-paid job had failed to make her feel any better and she was in tears when Josef opened the door to his flat. Josef had never imagined that he would see Daria cry. He felt embarrassed for her as he followed her into the living room.

Lines of mascara were running down her cheeks. Her thick brown hair had been cut to shoulder length and layered. She wiped her face and eyes with a paper tissue, before putting her bag on the dining table and taking off her jacket. Josef was surprised by the black top she was wearing under it, which was low cut at front and back with thin straps. In the short interval before she turned around, his gaze travelled from her exposed shoulder blades over the zip fastener on her mini skirt to her naked legs and back again. There was no sign of her phone.

'You've had company,' she said when she noticed the wine bottle and two used glasses on the breakfast bar.

'Oh, not really. Someone came to look at the spare room earlier. Would you like a glass?'

'Have you got anything stronger?'

'There's some Scotch whisky, schnapps and a bottle of ouzo my mum brought me from Greece.'

'Whisky, please – with ice if you have any.' So saying, she took out her make-up bag and went to the bathroom to restore her mask.

They sat side by side on the couch, drinking glass after glass of whisky, while soft piano music played on the stereo. Daria did not tell him what Chris had done to upset her so much, and he did not ask. She talked to Josef for the first time about her family and about her father – a high-ranking officer in the army, whom she hated. A strict disciplinarian with puritanical attitudes, he had once used his belt on her when he caught her kissing one of her boyfriends. At that time, Daria also despised her mother for always taking her father's side.

When Daria was seventeen, her father was forced to resign from the army because of his role in helping to set up the fascist organisation known as the Black Hand. Her mother left him shortly afterwards, taking Hannah with her, to the house in the Tarent Mountains that she had inherited from her parents. It was only then that Daria learned of the terror and depression the poor woman had suffered throughout her marriage.

After their reconciliation, Daria and her mother only enjoyed their close and loving relationship for three years. Her mother was murdered in her bedroom during a bungled break-in while Daria was in her second year at university in the Capital. As she spoke of her mother's senseless killing, Daria's face lost all composure, as if, after holding herself in check for years, she had suddenly let go. In a voice broken by sobs, she went on to tell Josef about the numerous online conspiracy theorists who blamed the Black Hand for her mother's murder, but, bad as her father was, Daria couldn't believe that he would be party to such an act, especially since he had helped her mother out financially after she left him. The mix of whisky and wine made Josef less self-conscious and more emotional than usual and so he did not hesitate to offer comfort by putting his arm around her.

He felt guilty. He had been too distracted by her cleavage and naked thighs to take in everything she had said, and he was struggling to piece together the story leading to the murder. He was also mystified by her making such intimate disclosures now, after all the times they had been out together.

The combination of her revealing outfit and unprecedented vulnerability overwhelmed him with a feeling of intense desire that he fought hard to repress but which was now exacerbated by their close physical contact. She settled into his embrace, putting her arm around his stomach, pushing off her shoes and curling her legs under her. With her head pressed against his chest, Josef realised that she must be all too aware of the frantic beating of his heart.

Had he been more experienced, he might have comprehended that they were going to end up in bed. But he had had only one girlfriend during his years at university, and she had split up with him after three months when she realised she would never want to have sex with him. He had gone further with one girl in his last year at school, and he recalled those heavy petting sessions in her darkened bedroom with a mixture of regret and retrospective excitement. At the time, everything had been too overwhelming for him to appreciate fully what was going on.

Now, he could not figure out how Daria ended up in bed with him, or who had initiated their lovemaking. All he knew for certain was that the pleasure he felt when he entered her eclipsed anything he had experienced before. As he watched her heading to the en-suite with her bra and pants trailing from her right hand, he realised that he had absolutely no idea whether she had shared his pleasure. He suspected that he had come too quickly to satisfy her, but he had also been aware of a greater inhibition on her part, as if she had had to overcome some inner scruple before permitting him to have full intercourse with her.

Initially, he thought the constraint was caused by her guilt at betraying Chris, but as he gradually succumbed to a feeling of postcoital malaise he began to wonder if she had been repulsed by his naked body.

Some ten minutes later, she emerged from the en-suite in her bra and pants and switched off the light. Then she climbed into bed with her back to him. She did not make any move to push him away when he put his arm around her waist and moulded his body to hers, but neither did she respond in any way to his touch.

It took him some time to fall asleep. When he did, he was prey to vague, disturbing nightmares which he forgot the instant he was woken by his bladder. His bedside alarm clock read 3:25. A small red dot beside the lower cursive of the '3' indicated that it was 'a.m.' He was not aware until he came back from the toilet that Daria was gone.

★

A loud cry drew Anna abruptly from a deep sleep. Her oppressive, repetitive dream faded away almost immediately as she looked around the darkened bedroom and tried to figure out where she was. Ben F was sobbing on the bed beside her. The digital alarm read 3:28. The pulsing red colon between the '3' and the '2' marked the passing seconds.

Anna did not know how to respond to the man's tears. She lay with her left cheek cupped in her hand, looking at his shadowy face. He turned his back to her when he realised that she was awake.

'I am sorry,' he said. After a while, he turned around and added, 'You know, I watched a television documentary last week, about a small boy from a village near the city of B who was badly injured by an American cluster bomb during the war.' Anna wondered why men always assumed that you could follow their chain of thought; always assumed that you were interested in what they had to say. 'Do you know what a cluster bomb is?'

'No, I don't.'

'It is a projectile that scatters over a wide area numerous small bombs that are designed to explode at waist height to inflict the most physical damage on enemy soldiers. Mark that: not to kill them, but to cause the most damage, because gravely wounded soldiers are more of a burden than dead ones. It is an indiscriminate weapon, Anna, that inflicted devastating and irreparable damage to that small boy's face.

'Well, this country took pity on that particular victim of its foreign policy and brought the boy over here so that the top plastic surgeons could recreate a semblance of a human face for him. The documentary showed the progress of his treatment. The boy was given toys, by way of a gift from a contrite nation; toys that were no doubt donated by companies eager to advertise their products – selling them in the same way as the government had previously sold the war to the reluctant electorate. Do you know how they sold the war, Anna?'

'No, I was still living in my family home in my own country at that time.'

'Well, Anna, through their supposedly unbiased news service the government told their people that the Coalition would be using pre-cision missiles so accurate that they could select an individual window in a building, to take out a military target without killing innocent civilians. Can you believe that? They claimed that they could destroy

107

a restaurant, say, where a comic-book dictator was dining with his henchmen, and leave the neighbours unhurt.'

'Why did you cry out?' said Anna. The silence after she spoke was so prolonged that she began to regret asking the question, fearing that Ben would convey his annoyance to Sergei.

'A nightmare,' he said, finally, 'about my family.'

Anna felt his hand on her leg. She had fallen asleep after they had had sex and was still wearing the burqa over her stockings.

'You know,' he said, 'before my wife fled from the theocracy that took over our country, she used to wear suspenders and stockings under her burqa. It was her way of rebelling against the morality police. Once she joined her relatives in B, she had no need to rebel in this manner and she never wore stockings again. She told me this after we were married. At that time, I was a communist. You understand, I could not admit being a communist, because of the dictatorship, but I was a communist, nevertheless. I believed in the equality of women, so I could not ask my wife to wear anything demeaning to her. I could never bring myself to tell her while she was alive, but in fantasies I often imagined that she was wearing such an outfit.' His hand had moved up Anna's leg to her naked thigh.

'Is that why you gave me the veil to wear this evening?'

'No, not all. That was for your protection, in case you were seen by the man I was arguing with earlier.'

'Who is the woman, and why was she so scared?'

'She has good reason to fear that man. Now, please turn away. I cannot bear you to look at me in such shameful circumstances. I am sorry. I am a weak man, but I imagine that, around you, all men are weak.'

'A man with a gun never appears weak to those who have no weapons,' she said as she turned on to her front, lay her head in the crook of her crossed arms and closed her eyes.

Friday morning, 11.30 a.m.: Josef K returned to his office with a mug of coffee. He told himself that there was only an afternoon to get through before the weekend, but he knew that emails could still reach him at home, and Chris was apt to show his disapproval if Josef did not reply quickly. Josef believed that the CEO deliberately waited to email him on Saturday or Sunday as a way of exerting his authority. Whatever Chris's motives, the emails made it difficult for Josef to escape his anxieties about work, which, if anything, were growing worse the longer he was in the job.

Hannah had arranged a final viewing of his flat that Sunday morning, and Josef was toying with the idea of inviting her out for lunch if she took the room. He couldn't imagine that there was any possibility of a sexual relationship with her and he was trying to convince himself he was merely excited about the prospect of having a friend outside of work.

He closed the door behind him, sat down at his desk and looked briefly out of the window at the dirty brickwork and black flaking downpipe of the university building across the alleyway. There was an email from Daria in his inbox. She made no reference to Wednesday evening, merely asking a routine question about the contract of one of the new employees. Josef was stunned by her casual tone. He felt crushed. He realised that she had felt none of the ecstasy that had overwhelmed him in that moment of penetration. Although he could not envisage having a serious relationship with her, he could barely control his excitement at the thought of having sex with her again. He also took pleasure in the notion that they were deceiving Chris. Josef considered it to be fitting revenge for the humiliations he had suffered at the monthly meeting earlier that week.

He tried not to think about Daria's body as he sipped his coffee. But images from the previous evening kept running through his head. His heart raced and he became uncomfortably erect as he scrolled through his inbox. Several emails had come in relating to the contracts of the cleaning staff in the museum. Josef's penis softened as he read them.

The janitor had recently been made redundant, and his job had been divided between three cleaners. They had been given an increased hourly rate, but simultaneously they had been forced to accept changes to their terms of employment which meant that they no longer had a guaranteed number of hours; 'job flexibility' was the euphemism by which they had been sold the new contracts. Now, a job review, using a new piece of computer software, had shown that the museum could be cleaned more efficiently; the resulting cut in staff hours meant that from the beginning of the following month even the cleaners with the increased hourly rate would take home less money.

Josef had been given the task of ensuring that all the changes adhered strictly to the rules laid down by recent employment legislation, but nevertheless he wondered what would happen to Yasmin S, whose beautiful name conjured images of *The Thousand and One Nights* and an atrociously dubbed film version of *Sinbad the Sailor* that he had caught on the television the previous weekend.

Another email contained a pdf of a new information leaflet outlining the new benefit rules. A family was pictured, smiling, in a clean and airy apartment that would have been well beyond the means of anyone claiming benefit. It was supposed to represent the kind of lifestyle to which the benefit claimants could aspire if they applied for one of the low-paid jobs the government was now subsidising with a variable credit allowance. Josef wasn't sure why he had been copied into that email and wondered if it had come to him in error.

There were some three thousand older emails in his inbox which he seldom opened but which he had kept, partly as an insurance policy against the toxic blame culture that permeated the office, partly because he found it difficult to throw anything away. In his bedroom at home, there was a yellow mug full of leather bookmarks printed in flaking gold with scenes of towns, cities and tourist attractions and there were boxes filled with painted plastic soldiers representing the armies of King Corvus and of the Ottoman Empire.

Josef thought about that bedroom, where he had spent most of his free time during his teenage years; alone, reading SF and fantasy novels or painting his model soldiers. It was an oddly shaped room, with a sloping ceiling and a dormer window, that occupied the roof space of a neo-gothic villa on the outskirts of the Capital where his mother still lived.

She had inherited it from her mother, and the family had moved in when Josef was ten years old. He still had dreams about the semi-detached house where he had spent the first years of his life, and about the small neighbourhood in which it was situated: the school behind his house, the streets around it, the local shops beyond the school, and the small area of woodland that formed the outer limit of his compact and secure world.

Even before she died, he had feared his grandmother and her strange villa, and after they moved in he lived in terror of meeting her ghost outside her room when he had to go to the bathroom at night. Rather than take her room, he had insisted on sleeping in the attic room that had formerly been occupied by the housekeeper, who had died in the same month as his grandmother. Josef had never previously seen that attic room, and so it had no bad associations for him. Once it had been painted a shade of light blue and furnished with his books, his model soldiers and his grandmother's television set, it became his sole refuge from the fearful asymmetries of the rest of the house and from the threatening world beyond.

Josef's father died of bowel cancer four years after they moved to the villa. A successful lawyer, he had left his family well provided for, and his mother was able to raise Josef and his two sisters without having to work. His father had always been a distant character who was frequently away on business, so his death made little impact on Josef's life. Yet he began to fear that his father's ghost might also start to roam the corridors of the house, appearing as he did in Josef's dreams, shuffling along in his dressing gown with a hand pressed to his belly, his chalky skin stretched tightly over his cheekbones, and his fearful eyes peering from the depths of their sockets.

At that moment, Josef's reverie was interrupted by the bright tone of his computer announcing a new email. When he saw Chris's name, in bold Calibri, he felt immediately guilty, as if he had been caught out in an embarrassing misdeed. He wondered how long he had been sitting there, lost in his memories. The email had no subject, which only added to Josef's anxiety about its contents. He began to sweat.

In an instant of blinding clarity, he realised that his flat, his car and the expensive clothes he had bought since taking the job were little more than lures to draw him further into the trap that had been sprung by Chris all those months ago when Josef first came to V for his interview. It struck him that there was now no way out.

When he finally plucked up the courage to open the email, he was confronted by a command that was stark in its simplicity but which opened his mind to a multitude of dire speculations.

'Come to my office now.'

There were tales from the Bohemian Coast which Josef had read as a child, and still periodically reread, in the de luxe illustrated edition that children in this country still received as a matter of course on their fifth birthday. These tales were widely read to children around the world and conspired with the heroic epic of King Corvus to establish the image of the nation as a fairy tale realm in the minds of most foreigners.

The first story in the collection began with a poor young man setting out on a journey; it was accompanied by a colour illustration, on the frontispiece, of a winding forest path dappled with sunlight. The young man did not know where the journey would take him. He believed that he was only going to the market in the nearest village to sell eggs and cheese from his parents' farm. He had no idea that he would end up rescuing a princess from an evil demon and that he would thereby win himself a kingdom by the sea. Josef was thinking of the illustration of that sun-shot forest path as he passed through the call centre towards the brushed steel doors of the executive lift. One of the men in the call centre cast a disdainful look at him as he made his way past. All the staff there wore headsets, and most were talking into the slender microphones and tapping their keyboards. Since the benefit changes had come into effect, the phone lines had been jammed with the calls of desperate claimants.

Two young women from the finance department, who were chatting by the water cooler, fell silent at Josef's approach. He had the absurd feeling that everyone else knew why he had been summoned to Chris's office.

The head of the education department was already in the lift when the doors slid open. She was wearing a rust-coloured skirt suit, with cafe-au-lait tights and high heels that matched the suit. She did not look at Josef when he entered the lift and stood beside her. She tilted one foot back on its heel and began peering at the point of her shoe as if something there had caught her attention. After exiting the lift, Josef stood for a moment, watching her walking down the corridor, before he turned and headed off in the opposite direction towards Chris's office.

The carpets were thicker on the executive level. There were abstract paintings by Vasily K on the walls of the corridor. The office doors were made of varnished oak. Josef grew more apprehensive when he looked at the brass panel on the door at the end of the corridor, which was engraved with Chris's name and position. After he pressed the buzzer and spoke his name into the small speakerphone above the keypad, the door opened smoothly with a quiet whirring sound.

Chris's new secretary looked up from her computer screen, which had a curving metal stand. A large diary lay open on the desk next to it, with a fountain pen slanting across its cream-coloured pages, and there was a telephone switchboard of the same metal as the computer stand. Between the inverted triangles supporting the desk, Josef could see the secretary's crossed legs and the point of her right shoe tracing an arc above the floor as she swivelled her chair towards him. The intense blue of her eyes made him wonder if she was wearing coloured lenses. He smiled and said, 'Hello,' but her face remained impassive as she observed his approach. He marvelled at her flawless skin as he took in her prominent cheekbones and slender neck. A small gold crucifix on a chain glittered between her clavicles in the opening of her blouse. When she tilted her head towards the intercom to announce Josef's arrival, her hair uncovered her small, lobeless ear. After a moment,

Chris's voice came through the speaker, asking Ildiko to send Josef in. Whereupon she stood up, smoothed down her skirt, opened the door to Chris's office and gestured to Josef to enter.

Chris was standing, looking out of the window, with his hands behind his back and his legs slightly parted, rocking gently on his heels. He heard the door closing behind Josef, but he neither looked round nor spoke for what seemed like an eternity. It struck Josef, while he waited with mounting trepidation, that all Chris's postures and actions were calculated to impress, yet he did not believe that any were natural expressions of the CEO's personality. Josef suspected that Chris had picked them up from a variety of people he had encountered during his career. He wondered if there was anything behind them at all. He feared that he was being sucked into that void.

The tinted glass of the window cast everything outside in an amber light. Josef could see his apartment block. From this height, it was possible to see, stretching to right and left, the roof gardens of the two penthouse apartments. Two figures were standing close together in the right-hand garden. He wondered if Chris was looking in that direction.

'Ah Josef, what are we to do with you?' said Chris finally, and turned to look at him. The CEO's expression was that of a patient teacher disappointed by the behaviour of a favourite pupil. He directed Josef to sit in the chair that had been placed in the front of the desk. Then he sat behind the desk and picked up a sheet of writing paper, on which Josef could see that something had been written in blue ink.

Chris put the paper down, rested his elbows on the desk on either side of it and pressed the tips of his fingers together in front of his chin.

'A serious allegation has been made against you, Josef, by your department head, Daria.'

'Daria?' said Josef, visibly blanching.

'She claims that during a recent visit to your apartment you got her drunk and then raped her.'

'But that's not how it happened at all,' said Josef.

'So, you don't deny that she came to your apartment and that you had sex with her?'

Josef looked away. He felt as if someone had delivered a sharp blow to his stomach. His heart was pounding and he found it difficult to breathe.

'I'm not saying that I believe what she says, but if she decides to act, it will be very difficult to clear your name. Mud sticks, I'm afraid, Josef. In that eventuality, we would have to let you go.'

Josef's initial shock and outrage were now giving way to uncertainty and self-doubt. He recalled the strange restraint that Daria had displayed when he was trying to penetrate her. He began to question his memory of their lovemaking.

Chris sat back in his chair with his hands clasped over his belly. He was wearing a charcoal grey pinstriped waistcoat and a pale blue shirt. His cufflinks were in the form of alphas and omegas linked through the buttonholes by golden rods. His tie was deep red with navy diagonal stripes.

'I think the best thing is to get you out of Personnel and away from Daria. I have an opening in the tenders department, for which you are ideally suited. Your specialist knowledge will make you very useful to us there. Let us get you into that job. We can show you the ropes, give you an idea of what is expected of you, and then I can deal with Daria.'

'You're not going to sack her, are you?

'Nothing so drastic, Josef. I know exactly what makes Daria tick. If you prove your worth to me, I can make her forget the whole thing. Sexual relationships are fraught with misunderstandings.' After a pause, he continued in his own language. 'Maybe in future you can avoid taking a dump in your own backyard.' So saying, Chris pressed a buzzer, nodded, and gestured towards the door that Ildiko was already opening.

*

When he left work that evening, Josef saw Daria on the street outside the bookshop. He hoped that she would not notice him standing at the crossing, waiting for the lights to change, although part of him desperately wanted to demand an explanation from her. However, just as she reached the bookshop entrance she turned to look in his direction. It was as if she had sensed his presence, but he only caught a brief glimpse of her face before a tram blocked his view. He thought she looked angry, but by the time the tram had moved on she had disappeared. He wondered why she had gone into the bookshop, because he could not imagine her ever reading a book. He had the absurd fear that she might tell Hannah he was a rapist.

The enormity of the accusation hit him again, filling him with the panic that had swept through him repeatedly since his meeting with Chris. Everything around him began to appear unreal, as if his relationship to the world had been knocked out of kilter.

When he had crossed the road and turned to head down the hill, he tried to put things in perspective. After all, Chris had said that he did not believe the accusation. Josef thought about the job change that the CEO had proposed. Perhaps he ought to accept the opening in the tenders department, even if he had the impression he was being blackmailed into taking it.

He briefly wondered if Daria had made the accusation at all. He was not sure that she had seen him at the crossing, and his glimpse of her expression had been too fleeting to give any real idea of her feelings. Her email that morning had given no indication that anything was wrong. But in that case he could think of no reason why she should confess her infidelity to Chris. Moreover, it was Chris who had given him the job, and he could just as easily take it away from him, no matter what Daria had said or done.

Another acid spurt of anxiety undermined all his rationalisations, leaving him confused and fearful about the future. He began seeing signs of suspicion and ridicule on the faces of passers-by, which put him in mind of the paranoia he had suffered throughout school and university. He recalled his difficulties in accommodating himself to other people and his complete inability to talk to girls. The one girl he had gone out with in his last year at school had used her non-identical twin sister as an intermediary to ask him out. Josef had thought the whole thing was a cruel joke, and it had taken him nearly a month to pluck up the courage to kiss her. He still vividly remembered her expression of discomfort and distress the first time he had tried to take their relationship to the next level.

His sense of alienation began to expand. He started to see all human interactions in a negative light. Even his own sexual desires struck him as being evil and sadistic. In fact, all sexual relations appeared to be no more than a futile, endlessly repeated struggle for domination. He thought of the complex of chambers within a broken shell. The expressive faces of those around him now seemed like crude masks, calculated to hide their owners' depraved or violent urges. The buzzing of thoughts in his head was becoming unbearable. At first, he barely registered the lips on the face in front of him as they moved and widened in a smile.

'Hi, don't you remember me?'

It took Josef a moment to recognise the receding hairline and fleshy face of his former neighbour. He clearly remembered the man's wife's dimpled cheeks and the sexy gap between her front teeth.

'Sure, I remember you,' said Josef. 'How's it going?'

'Not so bad,' he said. 'I'm working in an out-of-town call centre now. My company had to rationalise. It's tough in sales, but things could be worse.'

Josef thought he seemed nervous; too eager to continue the conversation. They hardly knew each other, and Josef wondered if he would have remembered him at all, had it not been for his wife.

'You know, I don't think we ever properly introduced ourselves,' said Josef.

'I'm Adam, Adam F.'

'I'm Josef K.' They shook hands belatedly.

'Where are you living now, Josef?'

'I bought a new apartment on the waterfront.'

'Oh.'

'I rather overstretched myself, so I'm having to take in a lodger,' he said, because Adam looked so crestfallen on hearing Josef had bought an apartment.

'I suppose I should be heading home. My wife will have my dinner ready by now. I'm sure you remember Katryn.'

Josef merely smiled, not knowing what answer was expected of him.

'Yes, I'm pretty eager to get home myself. A bad day at the office.'

'Onwards and upwards.' The cliché rang false, and Josef wondered if Adam was being ironical.

★

Adam stood for a moment, watching Josef make his way down the hill. It was unbearably hot. The air was hazy and close. A thunderstorm was forecast for later that evening, but, for now, the young women passing in their scanty clothes only made Adam more aware of his age and of the hopelessness of his situation. How different it must be for Josef with his apartment, his designer suit, his well-paid job and his youth? Adam told himself that Josef's nose was quite large and his eyes were too close together, but it was small consolation.

Adam remembered the evenings he had spent when he was at university, conversing in bars with like-minded individuals about films, books and art. He imagined having such an evening with Josef – talking about Godard; about the screenplay with which he had tinkered for years, before abandoning it finally after Helena was born. He wondered if young people still had evenings like that. They were always bent over their smartphones now.

He started walking over the brow of the hill, past the City Hall, the museum and the triangle of buildings that stood at the fork of the road. The tramlines glittered in the sun. Unlike the trams elsewhere on the continent, the trams in V had been imported from the States and were like the ones used on the hills of San Francisco. When he had first come to the city, they had reminded Adam of Hitchcock's *Vertigo* and of *Bullitt*. He had felt then as if he were entering a cinematic world far removed from his childhood home in the provinces, but he could scarcely imagine that world now, caught up as he was in the implacable logic of his pay-day loan and the figures that kept multiplying in his head.

He recalled the television advert for the loan, but only now did he reflect on the fact that its makers had gone through the same processes as any other film-maker. There had been three animated characters with skin made of felt; caricatures, really, of old people: two elderly ladies – one with bouffant hair, one with a tight perm – and a bald old man wearing a yellow sleeveless cardigan. The women had offered sound advice, fruit of their age and experience, while the man had been quite clearly an old buffoon. The loan company took its name from a slang term for money. Their pretence of sound advice was belied by the 1529% APR printed in tiny letters at the foot of the screen. The three old codgers had started to sing, and Adam, in desperation, had gambled on the expectation of his bonus.

Things had gone from bad to worse. When the sales team had relocated to a call centre on the outskirts of V, Adam had had to reapply for his job. He had only been successful because one of the other applicants had pulled out at the last minute, or so his sales manager had told him. He had had to take a cut in salary, offset by an increase in commission, but the commission was calculated on sales targets that were almost impossible to meet. Moreover, he now had to pay nearly 100 thalers per month in tram fares to and from the call centre. So he had never been able to clear the debt.

He estimated that it was costing him four thalers eighteen pfennigs every day for each thaler borrowed. The trouble was that he could not work out how many thalers of the debt he paid off in any one month. He began to think of those thalers as individual enemy soldiers in one of Kris's computer games, moving through an arid landscape reminiscent of the recent war. Each soldier taken out meant a reduction of the debt, but more and more kept coming, accruing interest at the rate of four thalers eighteen pfennigs per day.

Ominous calculations would permeate his dreams, waking him in panic in the night. Adam could not remember when he had last had a full night's sleep. It occurred to him now, as he peered into the stairwell of his apartment block, that his poor sleep pattern pre-dated the pay-day loan, and he wondered if he was suffering from more deeply rooted psychological problems. Whatever the case, since he took out the loan he had felt hopelessly trapped. He often found himself contemplating suicide, even going so far as to weigh up the pros and cons of various methods.

One of his near neighbours was putting some rubbish in one of the wheelie bins by the foot of the stairs – Adelka, a woman of indeterminate age, with dyed black hair, large eyes and a skeletal face. She was wearing a short-sleeved top that uncovered her midriff, with very tight black jeans slashed at the knees. She lived with her daughter three doors down from Adam and, during the past months, had had affairs with at least three men, all shady characters, one of whom had threatened her with a knife. Adam was terrified of getting drawn into the chaos and nonsense of her life.

'The bins are always minging at this time of year,' she said, and fell into step beside him. As they made their way upstairs together, he took in the mingled scents of freshly laundered clothes and musky perfume. She asked him how Helena was getting on at primary school; said how much her daughter, Irma, missed going there now she was in secondary school; reminisced about an end-of-year show in which Irma had sung a solo rendition of 'I Will Survive'. Adam tried to hide his ignorance of his own children's lives behind an increasingly strained smile.

When he finally arrived home, he found Katryn dressed to go out. She was wearing a tight-fitting blue dress that she had not worn since her sister's wedding, and she was applying lipstick at the mirror in the hallway. Adam placed his keys in a Japanese lacquer ashtray kept for that purpose near the front door on a tall oak table that doubled as an umbrella stand.

'You're late,' she said, without looking at him.

'I missed my stop.' He was about to tell her that he had bumped into Josef, but he thought better of it, fearing she might say something that would betray her desire for their former neighbour.

'The kids have been fed and your dinner is in the microwave.'

'You're going out?'

'I'm going to a private view with Eva.'

'A private view?'

'Do you even remember that I was at art school when we met?'

'Of course I remember. I just can't recall you mentioning a private view.'

'I'll be late if I don't go now,' she said, putting her lipstick in her bag. She disappeared into their bedroom while Adam hung his jacket up and checked the emails on his phone. He heard his daughter singing in her room and the sounds of gunfire from the sitting room. Katryn reappeared wearing a white cardigan over her dress. She popped her head round Helena's door, told her that Daddy was home and said goodbye, before repeating the process with Kris in the sitting room.

Adam had the distinct impression that Katryn shrank away from him as they passed each other in the hallway, but after he saw himself in the mirror he thought it perfectly understandable. His thinning hair was shiny with grease. There were sweat stains on his shirt, and his hairy paunch was visible where a button had come undone beneath his tie.

'It looks as if it's going to thunder later. Maybe you should take a raincoat,' he said, but she was already closing the door behind her.

He found Helena happily playing with her dolls on her bed. She held up her favourite to him and he greeted it as if it were a real person. As he took in his daughter's neat brown hair and thin arms his stomach twisted at the thought of how fragile and vulnerable she was. When he put his head round the door of the sitting room, Kris was playing a zombie shoot-em-up, to judge by the on-screen corpse dragging itself along the veranda of a Wild West saloon bar. Since his son was so absorbed in the game, Adam thought he could risk having a shower before reheating his dinner.

A great weariness descended on him as he made his way across the threadbare carpet in the hallway, past the bedrooms to the bathroom. There were traces of auburn hair dye around the sink. Kris had recently dropped the heavy wooden seat on the toilet and there was now a crack inside the bowl, above the water level. Adam knew it was only a matter of time before the crack worked its way down to the water and he would have to find the money to replace the toilet. As he took off his clothes, he looked at the mould spreading across the Artex ceiling. The extractor fan was making its familiar rattle and hum. Everything seemed squalid and second-rate. He well understood why Katryn would want to get away, but he could not bear the thought of her leaving him.

He sought reassurance in the fact that she had recently allowed him back into the marriage bed, but this change of heart was itself a cause of concern: even though they slept side by side every night, an invisible barrier remained between them that he didn't dare cross. More than anything else, he feared that she was having an affair, and the sight of his naked body in the mirrored doors of the wall cabinet did nothing to allay his fear.

He tried desperately to lose himself in the sensation of the high-pressure spray on his scalp, shoulders and back, but he could not stop thinking about what Katryn might be getting up to at the private view. If anything, the needlepoints of water on his skin only brought home to him how long it had been since he had last had any physical contact with his wife. He dragged his fingers through his hair and tilted his head forward to rinse the soap from his nape.

When he turned off the shower, he became aware of the sounds of shouts and screams coming from somewhere in the flat, but the noise of the fan made it difficult to hear what was going on and lent the sounds an elusive, nightmarish quality. He quickly towelled himself and pulled his pants on with difficulty over his damp thighs.

By the time he emerged from the bathroom with his trousers clinging to his legs and the towel draped over his shoulders, he could hear Kris shouting at Helena to keep quiet. She was sobbing and voicing incomprehensible laments that twisted Adam's stomach with helpless anguish.

'What the hell have you done to your sister now?' he shouted, and broke into a run.

He heard Kris's voice say in rising panic, 'I told you to keep quiet, Helifant. Now see what's happened!'

The towel had slipped off by the time Adam reached the open doorway to his daughter's bedroom. She was kneeling on her bed, weeping inconsolably, holding her favourite doll in one hand. It took Adam a moment to realise that the length of pink plastic she was holding in her other hand was one of the doll's legs. Kris stood nearby with his hands behind his back and his head on one side. He kept avoiding his father's furious gaze. Helena fell into shocked silence at the sight of Adam, standing half naked in the doorway with droplets of water glistening among his chest hair.

Adam could find no adequate outlet for the hopelessness and rage he now felt. He knew that he would never hit his son, but he grabbed the boy's arm and yelled at him so loudly that Helena started crying again. Kris, too, burst into tears, and the next-door neighbour began banging on the wall. Adam threatened to chuck his son's games console in the bin, and he set off towards the sitting room, with Kris in pursuit, pulling at his leg, sobbing, and begging him not to do it.

Adam raised the console over his head with both hands, stretching taut the cable that connected it to the television.

'I'll get her a new doll, Daddy. Please don't …'

Of course, Adam could no more damage the console than he could hit his son. After a moment, he put it back in its place. He felt utterly crushed by his inability to fix the situation.

He imagined another man who in his place would find a way to mend the doll's leg; a muscular, well-paid man, careful with money, sensitive to the needs of his children.

Adam sat on the couch with his shoulders hunched, his back bent and his paunch on full display. Much to Kris's astonishment, he began to cry. The boy looked at him open-mouthed. Helena, who was standing in the doorway, walked over to him in her usual precise manner, began gently to pat his head, and said, 'There, there,' in the same tone that Katryn's mother used when trying to console the children.

*

Daniela and Hannah arrived at the art centre half an hour before the opening of the exhibition. Daniela, anxious that something had been overlooked, went up to the gallery. First, she checked that the prints were straight and that they had the correct labels mounted beside them. In order to justify the high prices that Janos, the gallery owner, had suggested she charge for them, she had made only five copies of each print, which she had numbered and signed before deleting the images permanently from her laptop and memory stick in the presence of Janos, his solicitor and Hannah.

Daniela made sure that the circular red sticker was affixed to the first print in the exhibition, of which Janos had bought one of the edition. Even after taking off his commission, he had paid her ten times the amount she owed him for the drinks.

She checked the catalogue listing of prices, copies of which were piled on a table near the top of the entrance stairway, next to a packet of red stickers. There was also a two-tiered cardboard counter display, borrowed from the cafe bookshop, in which she had arranged some of her older prints to sell in beige-coloured card mounts or in the form of greetings cards and postcards.

Finally, she checked the drinks table near the top of the exit stairway, which was supervised by a young, painfully thin Estonian woman in a white blouse and black skirt. Daniela smiled, glanced at the woman's prominent reddish knuckles and bitten nails and rejoined Hannah, who was talking to Janos by the bar downstairs.

'Would you like a drink, Daniela?' he said. 'We've recently imported a very fine craft beer from Poland. I'm offering it at a special price during your exhibition.' Daniela nodded and thanked him. After the barman filled her glass, Janos added, 'Don't worry, Daniela. Everything is going to be fine. Even our millionaire recluse has said he will be here. You are honoured. It is the first time he has deigned to answer any of my invitations.'

'Who's that?' said Daniela.

'Stefan J. I did some work for him when he was selling his online business a few years back, although, to be fair, he may not remember me.'

Hannah spluttered, and covered her mouth with her hand.

'Are you alright, Hannah?' said Daniela.

'I'm fine. My drink went down the wrong way, that's all.'

A Billie Holliday song began to play through hidden speakers a quarter of an hour before the exhibition was due to open. By then, about twenty people were gathered near the bar, drinking and chatting. Janos took Daniela by the elbow and gently led her to a tall, slim man who had shaved his balding head. He was wearing a pair of red half-framed glasses that magnified his blue eyes and exposed his dark, elegantly shaped eyebrows.

'This is Valdemar V,' said Janos, but Daniela had already recognised the famous owner of the arts journal *Konundrum*.

Hannah felt extremely uncomfortable among the wealthy cosmo-politans Janos had invited to the private view. She slipped away through the crowd to an unoccupied table. From there, she observed Valdemar's predatory expression as he spoke to Daniela. Hannah hoped that he would give the exhibition a positive review in his jour-nal, because her friend desperately needed to sell her prints, although Hannah also worried about the publicity it might bring Daniela.

Valdemar loved to bait the right-wing press with the controversial articles he published in *Konundrum*, but Hannah doubted his motives. A petrol bomb attack on the journal's offices – attributed to the Black Hand and permanently scarring a young editorial assistant – had tripled its circulation among the liberal intelligentsia. But the *Čuvar* had recently implicated Valdemar in an insider trading scandal. He had invested heavily in Dynamic Systems, an arms manufacturer, shortly before its takeover by the ANH Corporation led to a twenty-fold increase in its share value. The accusation only served to confirm Hannah's long-held suspicion that Valdemar was deliberately using *Konundrum* to dis-credit the liberal cultural values ostensibly espoused by the journal.

Two women came over to speak to Daniela after she left Valdemar – one tall, with spiked grey hair shaved at the back and sides, wearing a purple silk top, black pedal pushers and high heels; the other of me-dium height, with dark wavy hair, wearing a vintage floral dress. Even from where she was sitting, Hannah could see that Daniela was torn between the conflicting needs to be polite and to join Janos for the formal opening of the exhibition, but the women were insistent, con-scious of their importance, determined that Daniela appreciate the in-terest they were taking in her, or so it appeared to Hannah.

By now, Janos was standing on the second step of the entrance stairway to the gallery, holding a microphone. A bright yellow rope suspended between the banisters behind him offered a notional barrier. The crowd, now swollen to thirty-five chattering people, gathered in a rough semicircle in front of him.

Daniela smiled awkwardly, told the women that she really ought to be going and promised to resume their conversation later. While Janos began to strike his glass with a spoon, Daniela eased her way through the crush to join him on the step. Unnoticed by anyone but Hannah, a young blonde woman, wearing a white blouse, black skirt and a pair of black tights, crossed the room from behind the bookshop counter to climb the exit stairway to the gallery. As she made her way she periodically pressed a hand to her stomach and grimaced, as if she were in pain.

Another group of people were streaming through the main en-trance as Janos began his speech. Hannah saw Stefan entering behind them, looking cool and collected in a fashionable suit, accompanied by a petite woman with a platinum bob, glasses and bright red lipstick. Hannah was stunned by the intense feeling of jealousy she experienced at the sight of her. She wondered if she should just make her excuses and leave before Stefan noticed she was there.

Janos was still speaking. Daniela looked very nervous. Hannah knew how much she had laboured over her short speech. She had gone through it with Hannah to check her pronunciation and grammar. She was terrified of appearing stupid. Realising that she could not abandon her friend now, Hannah breathed slowly and deeply to calm herself down.

'Do you mind if I sit here?' The woman who had spoken was wearing a grey pinstriped skirt suit, a dove grey blouse and honey-coloured tights. A small black brooch in the shape of a crow with spread wings was pinned at her collar. Her thickly lashed round eyes and small upturned nose gave her a curious doll-like appearance. It took Hannah a moment to recognise her as the candidate for the Party of the Brotherhood in the upcoming by-election. 'You are a friend of the artist?'

'What makes you think I'm not an invited guest?' said Hannah, bristling at the woman's presumption.

'This is hardly your milieu, is it?' The woman looked over at Janos, who was still speaking, his amplified voice echoing off the high ceiling. 'They don't really care about your friend, you know. It is what she represents that appeals to them. They see an authenticity in her alien culture that is sorely lacking in their own shallow lives. She is like an exotic flower, to be put on show until its petals wilt. Then they will move on to something else.'

'So long as they buy the prints, my friend doesn't much care what happens after that.' There was a burst of applause and Hannah saw Janos handing the microphone to Daniela. 'Excuse me,' she said, making no effort to hide her irritation. The woman merely smiled, nodded, and raised her glass.

Daniela delivered her speech with only a slight tremor in her voice. After the applause had subsided, Janos ceremoniously pulled aside the rope barrier before he and Daniela led the way upstairs to the gallery.

Hannah decided she would go up to the exhibition after the crowd had begun to disperse. Stefan found her sitting alone in one of the cosy booths situated beneath the gallery. His wife was nowhere to be seen.

'I didn't expect to see you here,' he said.

'That's blatantly obvious.'

'It was my wife who wanted to come. Her boss heard that one of their prospective clients would be here. I didn't realise the artist was your flatmate.' Stefan looked around nervously as he spoke.

'She won't be for long.'

'Oh, have you found a new place?'

'I think I'm going to take that room on the waterfront.'

Hannah noticed two women making their way upstairs to the gallery. One of them was wearing a white cardigan over a blue dress. Hannah reckoned her auburn hair was dyed. Unlike her companion, she looked self-conscious and out of place among the other women who were there. It took Hannah a moment to realise that her dress, which had been fashionable two or three years earlier, did not fit with the informal styles and vintage clothes now favoured by the elite of V.

'You know, I could easily set you up in an apartment of your own.'

'Are you kidding? How many times do I have to tell you that I'm not for sale? My cunt's not a commodity, for Christ's sake.'

Stefan looked about in panic, to make sure nobody had overheard. 'Of course not,' he replied in a strained, pleading whisper. 'I wouldn't expect ... There would be no strings ... Please don't ...' Hannah thought he was about to cry, but after a moment he said, 'I'm sorry. I have to go. I'll call you soon.' Then he walked away.

By the time he reached the gallery, Stefan's agitation was turning to anger at Hannah's unjustified outburst. He could not understand how she could misjudge his motives so completely. He was glad he had not told her about his infidelity with the prostitute. God knows what she would have made of that. He looked around at the people now gathered in groups, drinking wine and making small talk. Some were still looking at the artworks, pausing in between to read the information cards.

Stefan wandered over to the first print and lost himself for a moment in the cityscape, noting the almost seamless merging of the old engraving of Krakow with the photographic images of V.

As he moved on to the next print, someone touched his arm. His first thought was that it was Hannah, come to apologise, and his surprise must have been all too apparent when he turned to see his wife Elena.

'Stefan,' she said, 'I'm really sorry. Tomas is here, from the office.' Stefan was sure he had heard that name before, and he looked with interest at Elena's handsome colleague. He was standing nearby with a grey-haired man and a young blonde woman in a scarlet dress with a tight strapless bodice and a flared skirt printed with blue flowers. Tomas raised his glass to Stefan and smiled. 'Things are moving much faster than we anticipated. We are taking them to dinner. It looks as if we can close the deal this evening.'

'What are you saying, Elena?'

'I'm sorry, Stefan. Tomas is going to drive me back to the Capital tonight, so that we can get the ball rolling tomorrow. It's the only way we can secure the contract.'

'And what about Natalia?'

'I know. I know it's a big ask, but can't you do something with Nina? Go somewhere, the three of you – the zoo or the beach? Please try to understand why this is important to me.'

'Why is it important?'

'Christ, Stefan! Look, I haven't got time for this now. I'll see you on Sunday.'

Stefan watched her heading towards the exit stairway with Tomas, the grey-haired man and the woman in the red floral dress. On the way, the grey-haired man stopped to speak to a woman in a grey pin-striped skirt suit. Stefan took in her familiar doll-like face and realised she was Drita N, the candidate for the Party of the Brotherhood in the forthcoming by-election. He wondered why the hell she had been invited to the exhibition of a Polish artist. The grey-haired man in-troduced Elena and Tomas to Drita, and the four exchanged pleasant-ries and smiles, while the woman in red waited by the top of the stairs, looking bored.

After they had gone, Stefan looked around in despair at the people scattered in groups around the gallery. It never ceased to surprise him that his wealth could offer no palliative to his recurring sense of anguish and confusion. If anything, his money had only served to drive Hannah away, and it certainly had not prevented him from alienating his wife. He told himself that what really upset him now was the way Elena had strayed so far from her youthful ideals as to socialise with a neo-fascist to close a business deal, but the truth was that he was jealous of Tomas.

Stefan imagined his daughter's disappointment when she woke the next morning to discover her mother gone. He thought about travel-ling to the Bohemian Coast with Nina and Natalia. With a shiver of vengeful desire, he remembered embracing Nina in the kitchen on the night of the Martyrs' Procession.

He would have left the private view then had his attention not been caught by a detail on the third print in the exhibition. It was a figure in one of the archways giving on to the tree-lined boulevard that formed the focus of the print: just a pale face with shadow-filled sock-ets, whose body could only be discerned as a deeper black against the shadows around it. Stefan was not sure why that figure caught his at-tention, but it led him to look at the first two prints again and to make a careful study of each subsequent print. Thus it was that he noticed a young couple in sepia walking hand in hand along the boulevard in the third print.

He took in the crowded streets of the city that Daniela had

painstakingly constructed from engravings and photographs. When he noticed the recurrence of the couple in successive prints, he realised that the artist had further manipulated the images on her computer. He had the impression that a narrative thread ran through the exhibition. Other shadowy figures that kept appearing suggested a conspiracy of some kind. But, as in Bruegel's paintings, the scenes were so crowded with events and people that Stefan began to wonder if he was just imagining things.

He was reminded of the crowded streets of V on the day that he met Hannah for the first time; and of the novel, *The Journey to Varnak*, that had brought them together. He thought of the upsetting things she had said earlier in the evening and he desperately wished that they were sitting in the bar, discussing the exhibition – those shadowy figures, the recurring image of the couple. He wanted to tell Hannah that he loved her. But he could not suppress the nagging suspicion that she had been right about him; that, for all his romantic avowals, he was driven purely by the desire to possess her body. His thoughts were interrupted by someone tapping him on the shoulder.

'I don't know if you remember me, Stefan. It's Janos. I helped you to sell your company in my former life.' Stefan looked at him with a blank expression, until it gradually dawned on him why the name on the invitation had seemed so familiar.

'I'm sorry. It seems so long ago now. As you say, it was a former life.'

'I'd like to introduce you to the artist, Daniela, and also to Katryn and Eva.'

Stefan shook each of their hands in turn. Katryn's hand felt damp and she appeared ill at ease.

'What do you think of the exhibition?' said Janos.

Stefan found himself suddenly lost for words; quite incapable of conveying the excitement he had felt when looking at the prints.

'You should not ask such a question, Janos. And certainly not in front of the artist,' said Daniela, but her eyes betrayed her eagerness to hear his opinion.

'Not at all,' said Stefan. 'I'm just finding it difficult to put my impressions into words. I think your work is extraordinary. In fact, I would like to buy two of the prints.'

'Now you really are embarrassing me,' said Daniela, laughing.

Stefan wondered if he had really intended to buy the prints, but her self-evident pleasure filled him with a sense of well-being that went some way towards restoring his self-esteem after his bruising encounter with Hannah.

'Which two?' said Daniela, taking his arm. The pressure of her breast on his elbow reminded him of his first date with Hannah. He looked around guiltily to see if Hannah had come up to the gallery. 'Are you sure you want to buy the prints?' said Daniela.

'Oh, I'm quite certain. I love the exhibition. There is a young couple that appear in several of the prints, including the ones that caught my interest.'

'I'm glad you noticed them. My flatmate thought that people would not notice them. They are my great-grandparents. I scanned that image from the only photograph of them that I have. They were murdered in Auschwitz. The exhibition tells their story and is dedicated to them.'

'That's really dreadful,' he said.

'Is this one that interests you?'

'Yes, and also the third one.'

'I'll be back in a moment,' she said, letting go of his arm and heading towards the gallery exit.

Stefan took a closer look at the print. The couple were in a small square bordered by shops and cafes on three sides and with a baroque church on the fourth. Three men were standing in a huddle by a crowded cafe terrace, wearing black suits reminiscent of those favoured by the Brotherhood.

Stefan straightened up and looked over at Janos, who was talking to Katryn and Eva, although it was obvious that he was paying more attention to Katryn. Her dress suited her, but Stefan thought it was probably out of fashion. He remembered that his wife had a similar one that she had not worn for years.

When she returned, Daniela gently pressed his arm to attract his attention. 'So, you are quite sure that you want this one?'

'Absolutely.'

'It is Stefan J, isn't it?' she said. He took in the motions of her slender fingers as she removed a red sticker from its backing and attached it to the frame.

'Both prints are in a limited edition of five,' she said. 'Would you like me to arrange delivery?'

'That would be perfect.'

Daniela drew an order form from under her catalogue listing, looked at it and said, 'It might be easier to fill this out at the sales desk in the shop.' She carefully slipped the form under the pen and stickers and on top of the catalogue listing, all of which she was holding in place with her left hand. Stefan watched her complete the awkward task and then his gaze lingered on her breasts, before moving up to her emerald eyes.

'And which was the other one?' Her smile revealed a reddish lipstick stain on her uneven teeth, one of which was slightly discoloured.

He rested his hand on the small of her back as he led her to the print. Looking again at its tree-lined boulevard, with its mix of characters from an old engraving of Krakow and from Daniela's photographs of V, he saw three young men with shorn heads, wearing black shirts, and there was the shadowy figure in the archway observing the sepia image of Daniela's great-grandparents. Then Stefan noticed that her great-grandfather was partially hidden by some kind of tradesman who had a tray suspended from a strap around his neck. It was impossible to identify the tiny objects displayed on his tray.

★

Hannah was still sitting at the table beneath the gallery. Rather unwisely, she had consumed two double gin and tonics in quick succession, so she was feeling sorry for herself even before she saw Stefan and Daniela crossing the room towards the bookshop. They were deep in conversation. Stefan seemed totally enthralled by Daniela's beautiful green eyes. Just as when she had seen Stefan with his wife earlier, Hannah felt a surge of bitter jealousy at the sight of them. But then she observed Daniela talking to the sales assistant in the bookshop while Stefan slipped a credit card out of his wallet, and the realisation that he was buying a print brought home to her the absurdity of her fears. She could not face being with either of them now, so she took the opportunity to go up to the gallery while they were preoccupied with the transaction.

There were few people still around when she reached the top of the stairs. The young woman in the white blouse and black skirt was tidying the prints and cards. The painfully thin Estonian woman was gathering up the empty glasses. The two women who had spoken to Daniela earlier were having an animated discussion in front of one of the prints. Janos was talking to the woman in the blue dress and her companion by the wooden banister that stretched around the gallery.

Hannah did not want to speak to him and was grateful that he did not notice her walking over to the first print. Red stickers on the frame indicated that three of the five copies had been sold. Hannah did not know how much of the sale price Janos would take in commission, but she understood that he had agreed to advance Daniela the money to cover the framing of each print that she sold. Daniela had been heartbroken when she had dropped this print two weeks earlier and smashed the glass in the frame, because she had hardly been able to afford the cost of replacement. It made Hannah angry to think of Stefan's ridiculous neuroses when she considered her friend's precarious financial situation and the real dangers posed to Daniela by the xenophobia sweeping through the nation. She resented the way that Stefan's wealth protected him from the harsh realities of life. So far as she was concerned, he was like all the other rich liberals at the private view who could be heard discussing the rise of the far right, the proliferation of hate crimes, and other deplorable events that scarcely affected their comfortable lifestyles.

When she finally turned her attention to the print, she was so annoyed that she only gradually fell under its spell. As in all the art that Hannah loved, there was no attempt to mask the artificial quality of the piece. Daniela had no intention of holding a mirror up to nature. As with those medieval painters who rendered their religious images with odd distortions of scale and perspective, there was a real sense of transcending time and place, so that the printed image was both Krakow and V; past and present. And Hannah felt as if she was entering that timeless space. Even the agitations besetting the characters in that pictured city were like so many facets cut into the surface of a jewel to make it sparkle with light.

Hannah had seen some of the prints before, but this was her first opportunity to see them all together, so she looked closely at each one before moving on to the next. She completely forgot about her surroundings, and about Stefan, as she became immersed in the unfolding narrative she had previously been sceptical about. The oblique manner with which Daniela approached the story of her great-grandparents and linked it to current events reminded Hannah of *The Journey to Varnak*.

When she finally turned away from the last print, only the young Estonian woman remained on the gallery, putting glasses into boxes on the table by the exit stairway. Hannah walked over to the banister and looked down at the bar and the bookshop. There was no sign of Stefan. Daniela was standing by the counter in the bookshop, talking to Janos and one of the booksellers. The woman in the blue dress was standing at the bar with her friend. Hannah recognised some other visitors to the private view still gathered nearby, drinking and chatting, but they were now outnumbered by the bar's regular clients. She made her way down the entrance stairway and was just unhooking the rope barrier that was once more in place, when a terrifying eruption of shouts and screams echoed through the room.

*

Katryn realised that she shouldn't have come to the private view. She had felt out of place as soon as she arrived.

'Let me see your hand,' said Janos. When he raised her arm, she winced and looked away, focusing on an amethyst pyramid on his desk to distract her from the pain. The recent events still crowded her mind with senseless violent images. She could still hear the horrible crunching sound of the knuckleduster striking the face of the man standing at the bar next to her, but she had absolutely no recollection of the members of the Brotherhood entering the bar; she had only become aware of them when she heard the shouted insults.

After the man who had been punched crumpled in a heap on the floor, she had been pushed roughly aside. That was when the man's broken glass had pierced the palm of her right hand. Initially, she had scarcely felt it, and so she had been shocked by the amount of blood.

Janos had then appeared, as if by magic, and as he had led her away to his office she had looked back at the three men in black and seen them confronted by a woman with a familiar, doll-like face, whose fragile presence had made the men's self-evident terror so shockingly inexplicable.

Janos held her hand cupped in his large palm while he scrutinised the wound. Very carefully, he gripped between his finger and thumb the glittering shard that he saw there and drew it slowly out. The sensation of the glass sliding against her torn flesh set her teeth on edge but did not hurt as much as she had feared it would.

'Let me just clean the wound, so that I can see if there are any other fragments.' She watched him take out the white handkerchief folded in his jacket pocket. 'Unused,' he said, reaching over for a bottle of cask-strength single malt that was standing on a shelf near the desk. He pressed the bunched handkerchief to the opening of the bottle and soaked it in whisky. Then he began dabbing gently at the blood around the wound. 'Is that okay?'

'I've known worse,' she said. 'It's imagination that makes cowards of us all.'

'Who was it that said that?' he asked, without looking up from his task.

'I don't know. I read it somewhere a long time ago and it stuck in my mind.'

She experienced a wave of nausea and thought she was going to be sick, but the feeling passed. Her legs were crossed away from Janos. She recalled a psychologist on a TV reality show saying that crossing your legs like that indicated a lack of sexual interest. Her heart was still pounding from shock and fear and she had no idea why she should remember that bizarre piece of cod psychology, now of all times.

Her gaze moved to the hem of her dress and the dark mesh covering her exposed thighs. She wondered why she had worn that minidress. Another mistake. Some of the men at the private view had looked at her brazenly, as if she were a whore, and yet everyone had been wearing that style only three years earlier. She reflected on the hypocritical morality currently being espoused by the tabloids, and that led her by association to the misogynistic threats that were increasingly being directed by internet trolls at female celebrities and prominent feminists.

'What the hell is happening?' she said suddenly, forgetting that Janos was not privy to her train of thought.

'I'm pretty sure it's all over now,' he said, and continued dabbing at the wound with the alcohol-soaked handkerchief. She noted the care he was taking to avoid hurting her more than was necessary, and she wondered what Adam would have done in his place. Given how angry her husband had been about her going out with Eva that evening, she imagined that his first reaction would have been to blame her for what had happened. No doubt he would have flown into a rage and would have been quite incapable of dealing with the situation.

★

The taxi driver flashed a look in the mirror when Stefan asked to stop at the entrance gates to the villa – a questioning, suspicious look, or so Stefan thought, because surely the owner of such a place would have his own chauffeur-driven car, or, at the very least, he would activate the gates using some kind of radio-controlled device. Why, after all, would a man of such wealth risk getting caught in the threatening downpour? Why would he approach his own house like a thief in the night?

As he keyed in the number of the side gate, Stefan experienced an odd sense of unreality. He imagined that he was merely dreaming his life of unlimited wealth; that he might wake up the next morning to find himself in some menial job, perhaps in sales, battling constantly with rising debts and unreasonable targets.

When the gate had closed behind him, he looked up at the dense clouds piled overhead and then he followed the lights on the path. Everything was still. The calm before the storm. How easily the clichés came to mind. How difficult it was to pin down the truth. He wondered if the artist, Daniela, had been flirting with him. It struck him that Hannah had not told her anything about him, but then again what was there to tell? What did their relationship amount to?

It was absurd really to feel this way about Hannah, but Stefan was overwhelmed by despair. He felt lost and alone. He reasoned that it was only his fears about his wife's infidelity that made him desire Hannah so intensely. He pictured Elena in the arms of her handsome colleague Tomas or kneeling to unzip the fly of the grey-haired client she had met at the exhibition.

A light was on in the library. He must have forgotten to switch it off earlier. He was tempted to go to his office there, to write or to attempt to write. He could sleep on the sofa bed. Perhaps his sleeping bag would still retain the scent of Hannah's perfume. The thought set his mind revolving again around their distressing encounter earlier in the evening. He tried to convince himself that there was no point in attempting to have a relationship with Hannah; that it would in no way change his life for the better, or assuage his despair, but still he ached to possess her. When they were apart, he was perpetually agitated, constantly ruminating on ways that he might bring about a meeting, constantly tempted to phone her or to go to the bookshop where she worked.

Light from the kitchen windows stretched long rectangles across the gravel path that crunched beneath his feet, outlining each small, cream-coloured stone with a crescent of shadow. He took in the brightly illuminated interior: the oak-panelled cupboard doors; the silver fridge-freezer with its array of magnets; the hanging copper pots; the archway to the playroom beyond.

And then Nina appeared in her terry-towelling bathrobe. Stefan stood mesmerised by the contrast between her thick black hair and her pale slender neck. She crossed the length of one window, disappeared, and reappeared in the next window. Then she turned her back to him and busied herself with something at the hidden worktop. When she turned to go back she was holding a glass of red wine.

Everything within the frame of the window appeared so clear under the LED spotlights that, for a moment, Stefan had a real sense of Nina as a living and breathing person, existing completely independently of him in four dimensions. In comparison, his confused memories of Daniela's private view had no more reality than the invisible flicker of a film reel, or the illusion of a passing moment frozen on a painted canvas.

When he entered the house, Stefan was greeted by the familiar smell of home, and the kitchen, visible through the utility room doorway, resumed its normal, somewhat jaded appearance. He locked the door behind him, draped his jacket over one of the chairs at the dining table and poured himself a glass of wine from the bottle on the worktop.

As he stood in the doorway to the living room it was clear that Nina was still unaware of his presence, absorbed as she was in the crime drama unfolding on the television. A young woman was looking through her kitchen window at a snowman illuminated on the lawn by the lights from the house. Clearly disturbed by what was happening on-screen, when Nina finally noticed Stefan she nearly spilled her wine and let out a strangled cry.

'You frightened me.'

'I'm sorry, Nina. Do you mind if I join you in a glass of wine?'

'Is Elena not with you?'

'She had to go to the Capital, I'm afraid. An important client she met at the private view.'

Nina seemed to think about this for a moment, before saying, 'Of course you can join me, Stefan. The film has just started, but if you don't want to watch it I can always go up to my room.'

'I'd be happy to watch it with you,' said Stefan, joining her on the couch. 'I'm glad of the company.'

After filling Stefan in on what had happened so far, Nina fell silent and then they sat side by side, watching what proved to be an unpleasant and violent thriller. Stefan found it difficult to concentrate on the film, since his mind kept raking over the evening's events. He wondered what Hannah had done after he left. He wondered where his wife was and with whom. The film that had offered him a ready excuse to join Nina now felt like an obstacle preventing him from talking to her, and so he sat rather stiffly, trying to avoid brushing against her, enveloped in the alluring scents of her soap, shampoo and body lotion.

He was relieved when he was able to refill their glasses at the first commercial break, but he was only able to ask Nina if she had had any trouble getting Natalia to sleep, before the film restarted.

The wine finally began to relax him, and as the film progressed he found it difficult to keep his eyes open. He was scarcely aware of putting his empty glass on the floor. He woke suddenly with no clear idea where he was, but then he became aware of the soft material cushioning his cheek, and when he awkwardly turned his head he could see Nina's smiling face looking down at him.

'The film has just finished,' she said. His left hand was resting on her thigh, and her hand was on his shoulder.

'Oh, I'm really sorry, Nina,' he said. 'You should have just pushed me off.'

She merely smiled and shook her head. He raised himself with his left arm, realised that his right arm had gone to sleep, and nearly fell back. Nina, laughing, helped him to sit upright. His dangling arm felt as if it was three times its normal size and was beginning to tingle excruciatingly with the renewed blood flow.

'I'm really sorry, Nina. I hope I didn't spoil the film for you.'

'Not at all.'

He looked at the column of names scrolling up the television screen and drew his fingers through his hair. The digital clock on the DVD player read 11:15.

'Elena suggested that I drive Natalia and you to the beach tomorrow if the weather's good. Would you like that?'

'Oh, that would be lovely, Stefan.'

'You know, I was having the most pleasant dream,' he said, 'but I forgot it completely as soon as I opened my eyes.'

★

Adam had not enjoyed the film at all. He stood up and paused for a moment, unsure what to do. There was still no sign of Katryn. Helena's doll lay on the coffee table with its leg beside it. He did not think he could fix it, but, thankfully, Helena and Kris were now sleeping soundly.

He went through to the kitchen and was pouring himself a glass of Pilsner when a flash illuminated the window and there was a sudden deafening thunderclap. Rain began pelting the glass.

'Jesus!' he said, and returned to the sitting room with his lager.

All evening, he had been growing more anxious about Katryn, and now, after watching that stupid film, he was close to panic. He tried to reassure himself that she was safe with Eva, but, if anything, that only served to increase his worries. There was another thunderclap and a sudden gust drove the rain against the window. He pulled aside the curtains and peered out.

A Mercedes was turning on the street below. It came to a halt by the near pavement and, after a moment, an umbrella unfurled in the opening of the front passenger door. The Mercedes pulled away, trailing its wavering tail lights. Just before the entrance to the block, the umbrella was blown inside out, revealing Katryn turning round to drag its broken struts and flapping material through the doorway after her.

Chapter 5

AUGUST

The heat and the humidity were unbearable. Yasmin longed for the cool rooms of their family home in B. She looked at her brother nervously from the doorway to their mother's bedroom. Salazar was watching a news report on the television about air strikes in the Middle East. The presenter was asking the Defence Minister why two of our jet fighters had been sent to the aid of the Americans. It was, she contended, a ludicrously inadequate yet expensive gesture. The minister merely smiled and voiced a series of platitudes about freedom and democracy, which effectively sidestepped the question. Yasmin could not understand why Salazar was so enamoured of the vicious extremists who held sway in that mountainous region, but she could sense his rage at the events unfolding on the television.

'Would you like some coffee?' she said, but he gave no indication of having heard the question. She took in his tense, angry expression, his shining beard, the sweep of his eyelashes, and wondered what had happened to the happy, inventive boy who could conjure adventures from the most unpromising household materials: the den he had constructed from a clothes horse and some blankets; the beautiful, intricate palace he had made for her from their father's index cards and subject dividers.

Yet, for all that she missed their homeland, it occurred to Yasmin that they had been lucky to have fled the country before the first war. The years up to the second war had apparently been bad enough, but now there seemed to be no end to the cycle of violence that was spreading through the Middle East.

She wanted to tell Salazar that nothing good could ever come from hatred, but she herself was no longer sure she believed that. She reflected on the violent crowd that had threatened her on the day of the Martyrs' Procession, the snide comments that Vladik had started making since she rejected his clumsy advances earlier in the week, and his subsequent refusal to let her near the model city because he claimed she was cleaning it carelessly. The needless cruelty and injustice made her seethe with unexpressed anger and resentment, but still she feared what would become of the family if Salazar lost control of his temper.

She sat on the settee, completely unaware of the wringing motions of her hands, which continued with stubborn disregard of their cliché nature, as if misfortune had so thoroughly drained her of individuality that she had become a mere cypher, or a symbol of something or other.

She thought of her friend Akilah who had followed her communist father to England, where he had been offered a job as a politics lecturer in the University of Bristol. In her most recent letter to Yasmin, she had expressed her disappointment with Bristol. 'It was', she had written, 'just the same as V.' She cited the horrible murder of an immigrant from the Middle East who had been accused of paedophilia by a racist neighbour because he had photographed children vandalising his hanging baskets.

Yasmin thought of the troubles at work. Her hours had been cut. Increasingly, she was doing unpaid overtime because the job simply could not be done in the time allocated by the computer. Her relationships with the other cleaners were constantly undermined by the way they were forced to compete for the limited available hours. And now she feared that Vladik might have her sacked.

She already missed the job of cleaning the model city, which she vowed to visit in her spare time. She found some correlation between it and the few bright memories she retained from childhood. Like the model, those memories seemed to recreate a self-contained, highly detailed world that was immune to the ravages of time and history.

Salazar began to rant about the evils of their adopted country, cursing the fate that had brought them there, swearing revenge on the infidels. Yasmin could only sit in silence, wishing he would stop, casting around for anything she could offer from her own experience, any vague hope of improvement to their situation, but there was nothing, and she found herself gazing vacantly at the pudgy face of a dark-haired woman which had appeared on the television to illustrate the next news item.

Stefan recognised the young woman as soon as her face appeared on the television: Radomira D. He wondered if there would have been such an outcry if her name had not been so evidently Bulgarian. He was about to say something to Elena, but his wife had already nodded off.

It was unusual for Elena to come home midweek. She told Stefan that her office had been hit by a computer virus, which had destroyed many valuable files, so she had driven through the worst of the rush hour traffic to retrieve some memory sticks on which she had saved her most important documents. Her explanation sounded so convoluted that Stefan wondered if she suspected his affair with Nina, but he was reassured by the evening news report that a cyber-attack, believed to have originated in North Korea, had struck businesses across the country and paralysed several hospitals in the Capital.

Elena was stretched out on the other settee. It suited Stefan to believe that he had lost her love long before he had started to fantasise about Nina or fallen for Hannah. In fact, he liked to think that she had ceased to be attracted to him even before he slept with the prostitute. As he gazed at his wife's sleeping form, and observed the brown hair edging her parting, he was filled with an almost painful longing to return to the early months of their relationship, or to that period of shared anticipation and hope which had culminated in the birth of Natalia. He could not bear the idea that by his own actions he had destroyed the relationship that was most precious to him.

On the television, there was now a panel discussion about the case of Radomira D, involving the programme's main presenter, another younger woman with a black bob, carefully shaped eyebrows and bright lipstick, who was introduced as a media expert, and an older classicist famed for her book on the Roman settlement in V. Stefan recognised the only man present as Gyula K from his photograph on the back cover of *The Journey to Varnak*.

It had been Hannah who had told Stefan the story of Radomira D when they had dined together earlier that month in a Czech restaurant. It had been their first meeting since Daniela's private view. Hannah had chosen the restaurant partly because it had been the focus of a recent attack by far-right thugs, partly because the owner had fled Czechoslovakia in the 1960s and the psychedelic posters on the walls of films and bands from that era attracted the young booksellers in her shop. The brick vaults and candlelit tables combined with the protest songs and experimental electronic music to create an atmosphere suggestive of that radical period.

During the evening, Stefan and she had fallen back into the easygoing conversation that had characterised their early meetings. Hannah was completely unaware that since their argument at the private view Stefan had slept with Nina three times, and so she had no idea why he was so much calmer and more at ease in her company.

Hannah was talking about her upcoming holiday in the Tarent Mountains with her friend Angelika when she got sidetracked by the story Angelika had told her about Radomira. Angelika worked as an editor for a prestigious publisher based in the Capital. She had recently finished editing Radomira's collection of feminist reworkings of *The Tales of the Bohemian Coast* and of the less-known *Tales of the Tarent Mountains*. After all her hard work, Angelika was outraged by the move that the government made to ban the book.

A scandal had broken out when a post that Radomira had put up on a social media site had somehow leaked into the public domain and gone viral. She had referred to the famous story of the king, later identified with King Corvus, who, following the death of his wife, falls in love with a young maid serving in the castle of the sea lord – the Mareduche, as he was known in the ancient language of the region.

There was hardly a child in the country who didn't know the famous illustration, made by Dagomar N, of the king riding his white stallion along a windswept clifftop, cape flying, beneath a full moon partially obscured by ragged clouds.

Radomira hinted in her post that the king in her tale would lack the potency of his traditional counterpart. She confessed that she had struggled for a long time to find an alternative ending to the misogynistic tragedy of the original.

Subsequently, a member of the Brotherhood – employed by DigiGrafix, the company that was printing the book – had sent a screenshot of one of its controversial illustrations to *Iron Fist*, a murky online magazine with links to the Black Hand. The image showed the king with his tights around his ankles and his buttocks exposed to the viewer, while the maid, covering herself with her torn dress, was laughing at him.

Radomira had gone into hiding after a skull and a black hand was stencilled on her apartment door. The government claimed they were banning the book 'purely to prevent its publication from deepening the political divisions that threatened the very fabric of the nation'.

Stefan had rather upset Hannah by saying how much he liked Dagomar's illustrations of *The Adventures of King Corvus*, which only added to the growing irritation she felt at his coolness and distance. A large part of her annoyance was directed at herself. It depressed her to think that she was not fully in control of her feelings, and she was appalled by the way Stefan's indifference stimulated her desire for him. Her gaze travelled from the sweep of blond hair falling across his forehead, over his well-shaped lips, to the outline of his pectoral muscles showing around the pockets on his maroon shirt. She recalled the reassuringly solid feel of his chest when they had embraced on the night of the Martyrs' Procession. For the first time, she was afraid that she might lose him. So she relished his look of distress when she told him that her flatmate, Josef, was joining Angelika and her on their holiday; that he had agreed to collect Angelika from her flat and to drive them all to the holiday chalet in the mountains.

Stefan remembered the tight hug that Hannah had given him outside the restaurant. The entrance was situated at the foot of a stone stairway that joined the main road on Castle Hill to the lower road that passed beneath it. A red neon sign, advertising the restaurant, illuminated the gleaming pavement beside them. Two figures were huddled in conversation in the underpass, rendered almost invisible by their black paramilitary clothing.

The Tarent Mountains used to terrify Stefan as a child. His father, who hated the tourists who crowded the Bohemian Coast during the holiday season, had bought one of those basic wooden chalets in the mountains, formerly used by farmers when they took their cows to the high summer pastures. Stefan remembered the night terrors that used to haunt him in the bare room, which his father had built on to the chalet, that Stefan used to share with his sister.

His mind then followed an odd chain of associations: the gleaming eye of an ogre in a cave from a fearful engraving in a book of folklore that he had chanced upon in his grandmother's house; a breakfast of pancakes and eggs, taken with Elena in a guest house, during their first holiday together; a panic-stricken search the previous summer when Natalia had wandered away from their picnic table into the forest; the jerky monochrome image of a horse and carriage approaching a castle on a painted mountain in a silent film.

On emerging from his reverie, Stefan was surprised to realise that only six minutes had passed and the television discussion about Radomira was still in mid-flow. He did not know what Gyula K had said to annoy the young media expert, but she was staring daggers at him and arguing that the internet had effectively made novelists redundant.

'Young people are now fully engaged with the stimulating narratives of their own lives which they record and share online,' she said. 'If Radomira had merely published her stories in a book, there would have been no scandal and we wouldn't be wasting your time by discussing her now. But she made her statement on a social media site.'

'I am not engaged in a popularity contest,' said Gyula. 'I cannot speak for Radomira, but, for me, well, as soon as I complete a novel, I cease to think about its fate.'

'But no one is threatening your life. No one is burning your book. Surely that should convince you that the novel is a spent force.'

'I wrote it in Hungarian. In Hungary all the critics praised it for its style, and while my country has its own pressing problems with the ideology of the far right, it does not concern itself with your nationalist fantasies, and neither do I. It is surely one of the greatest ironies of our time that the surfeit of information created by the internet should have reduced humanity to a collection of warring tribes and solipsistic wankers, and I am using that word literally in this instance.'

Elena woke up at that moment, making a face as if she had just tasted something unpleasant. The rough texture of the settee cushion had reproduced itself in red and white on her right cheek.

'I should have gone to bed hours ago,' she said. 'I have an early start tomorrow.'

'You're going back then?'

'They need my files right away, and I can't send them by email because of the virus. Apparently, the new client is making a stink.'

'You realise he is a fascist?'

'Nonsense; you don't know him at all, Stefan. Why would you say that?'

'I saw you all talking to the Brotherhood candidate at the private view.'

'No businessman can afford to ignore what is happening. Of course he spoke to her. It doesn't mean he agrees with her policies. As usual, you don't know what you are talking about, Stefan. Anyway, I'm surprised you noticed me at all that night. You were so busy ogling the artist.'

She collected the empty wine bottle and their glasses and headed with them to the kitchen, calling 'Goodnight' as she passed the doorway on her way to the stairs. Stefan nodded and resumed staring at the now blank screen. He did not know what to do. He did not love Nina. He felt guilty about having sex with her, and there was something alarming about the eagerness of her lovemaking, but now his remembered images of her body were causing warm sliding sensations around his groin and he recalled the sleepy warmth with which she had welcomed him into her bed the previous week, encircling him with all her limbs.

Despite his growing lust, however, his thoughts kept returning to Hannah. He could not understand why she had gone on holiday with Josef so soon after moving into his flat. Stefan had liked to think that she was using the poor sap.

He waited until he heard Elena crossing the landing to her bedroom. When he was quite certain she was in bed, he called Hannah on his mobile. It took what seemed like an age before he heard the reassuring old-fashioned sound of a ringing phone.

'Hello Stefan.' Hannah's voice sounded annoyed, but almost immediately it was drowned by static.

'Hello, can you hear me?' he said.

'It's a bad …' She was interrupted by more static. Then there was a burst of laughter in the background and his phone went dead.

★

Josef woke much later than usual that Friday morning, from a nightmare about Daria that he forgot immediately on waking. He then experienced a moment of panic when he thought that it was a normal workday. It was only when he looked around his darkened bedroom and saw the thin line of light coming between the curtains that he remembered he was on holiday for two weeks and that he had told Chris that there was no Wi-Fi coverage where he would be staying. Josef was determined not to think about work at all during the holiday. He would try to live entirely in the moment without worrying about the future. He now felt the kind of euphoria he used to experience during the long summer holidays from school.

He crossed the room in his underpants and pulled aside the curtain to see what the weather was like. The sky was clear blue. Diamonds of sunlight were dancing on the river. A tourist boat, full of early morning sightseers, chugged towards the gorge. He was surprised to see Hannah in a loose black T-shirt and leggings sitting at the iron-work table further along the balcony. She had gathered her long hair over one shoulder. It glimmered with bronze highlights in the sunshine. She was reading a book as usual and unconsciously running a fingertip over her chin cleft. Steam rose from the white mug on the table next to her sunglasses, her closed notebook and her pen.

Josef let the curtains fall back into place before she noticed him. Then he had a quick shower in his en-suite, although there was no hurry to get ready. They would not be leaving until the early afternoon. Hannah reckoned that it would take no more than two hours to reach the Capital.

His suitcase was already packed. He only had to put his toiletries and his book into the bag he had set aside for their overnight stay in Angelika's flat. Hannah had given him the novel *The Journey to Varnak*. It was lying at an angle on his bedside table, next to his watch and his phone. There was something about the painting of the woman on the dust wrapper that reminded him of Hannah, but he was not sure what it was. He was not enjoying the book. He had only managed to read some five pages in the past week. He had blamed pressures of work for his slow reading when she had asked him how he was getting on with it.

Josef read mainly fantasy and science fiction, much of it in English – obscure and rare American titles that he ordered online. When he saw the kinds of books that Hannah read, he feared that she would think his tastes were immature. It was only when she had been living in the flat for a week that she asked him about the carefully arranged book-shelves in his bedroom and he was compelled to confess to his tastes. He was surprised to learn that she had studied a module on science fiction at university and had read some of his favourite authors, although she did not say whether she liked them or not. She gave him the copy of *The Journey to Varnak* by way of a thank you for finding her brooch, saying that she thought he would enjoy its fantastical elements.

He could not remember when she had first spoken about the difficulties that she and her friend Angelika were having with their holiday transport. A long-running dispute between railway management and train drivers had resulted in several one-day strikes being organised for August; but then all the drivers walked out at the beginning of the month, after one of their number had been sacked on what the union considered to be trumped-up charges.

Hannah was reluctantly considering cancelling the holiday, because their train tickets had been refunded and the bus service was fully booked. He could tell how disappointed she was when she told him about the three-bedroom chalet that belonged to a friend of Angelika's mother. Normally, it would be fully booked for the entire summer, so they were unlikely to get another chance to stay in such a lovely place at a price they could afford.

Josef had already had a couple of beers that evening, otherwise he would never have plucked up the courage to suggest that he could be given the third bedroom. He would happily drive them to and from the chalet. He had never been to the Tarent Mountains and he was certain he could find lots to do if they wanted to have time to themselves. They could then split the living expenses and the petrol three ways, which would make the holiday cheaper for them all.

As he put on the clothes he had carefully selected for the journey, his only disappointment was that he would have to read *The Journey to Varnak* instead of the fantasy novel that had arrived in the post that week, which, like many such novels, started with the hero leaving the security of his castle home to go on a quest into the unknown. On reflection, he thought he would bring that book as well.

After getting dressed, Josef took his breakfast out to the balcony, where Hannah was starting on a second mug of coffee. The cool westerly breeze, carrying scents from the sea, reminded Josef of happy childhood holidays on the Bohemian Coast, but the slight uneasiness he still felt in Hannah's company prevented him from sharing his happiness with her. His anxieties about driving to the Capital also made it hard for him fully to recapture the irresponsible joy of those childhood summers. But he did make Hannah smile when he told her of the time his father had set out to drive to their holiday cottage in his slippers, only realising his error when they stopped for petrol. Josef clearly pictured the blue and grey dashboard of his father's car, with its narrow rectangular speedometer, its adjustable air vents and its numerous round knobs.

Hannah did not finish packing until lunchtime. By then she was dressed in a sleeveless purple T-shirt and a pair of frayed black shorts that she had made by cutting down an old pair of jeans. She had gathered her hair at the back of her neck with a black scrunchie. Josef was always almost preternaturally conscious of what she was wearing. They had cheese sandwiches with lattes to use up the last of the milk. After washing and clearing away the dishes, they took their luggage down to the car in two journeys. Josef had to go back to the flat to reassure himself that everything was switched off. He returned a second and third time, to convince himself he had locked the door, before calling the lift. As he descended to the underground car park he felt an acute sense of excitement, mingled with terror. It was his first long-distance drive and he dreaded the complicated and crowded road network of the Capital, even though he would not be going anywhere near the narrow, twisted streets of the Gothic Quarter.

Josef did not look directly at Hannah while he was switching on the satnav, but he caught glimpses of her on the periphery of his vision, and he was completely enveloped in her perfume which vied with the new car smell.

After a moment, the screen of the satnav reproduced a map of the immediate vicinity, with a red arrow indicating the position of the car between the nearest road and the blue expanse of the river, which, beyond the basins and quays of V, would be reduced at that time to a modest stream running between mudbanks, awaiting the swell of the incoming tide.

He keyed in Angelika's address and pressed the start button, and the map expanded to reveal the entire route between V and the Capital. That sudden upward zoom reminded Josef of the only part of *The Journey to Varnak* that he had actually enjoyed – the short prologue, in which the viewpoint of a migrating bird takes in the glittering curve of the River Amira between the hills to the east and south of Varnak, before swooping down to observe a horse-drawn carriage travelling along the main road from the Capital towards the outskirts of the city.

It was nearly impossible to imagine the old narrow road that used to join the Capital to the real city of V, passing through rolling hills chequered with fields and woodland, swallowed up as it now was by a six-lane highway, rumbling with the noise of juggernauts and sparkling with the chrome and metallic paintwork of hundreds of speeding cars, along which Josef was driving in a state of concentrated anguish, gripping his steering wheel so hard that his knuckles turned white. He scarcely comprehended what Hannah said, answering her with non-committal grunts, and was grateful when she fell asleep with her head on a cushion pressed up against the passenger window.

The Capital announced itself with out-of-town shopping centres, light industrial units and modern housing developments. Some of the shopping centres dated from the 1980s – malls decorated with gothic details in brick or concrete. Those of more recent construction were generic, hastily fabricated buildings whose rectangular forms were masked behind reassuringly domestic shopfronts. Further in, there were suburbs built in the 1930s, interspersed with high-rise flats and office blocks sporting the names of international corporations. Billboards advertised imported cars and American movies. The satnav was now leading Josef through a terrifying labyrinth in which he tried to take note of every road sign and lane indicator. The other drivers were impatient and aggressive. He was dripping with sweat despite the air conditioning. Finally, he took a left turn into a small estate of art nouveau tenements, each block slightly different from the next, all with gothic arched windows and other details harking back to a quite fictitious past.

Hannah woke up and smiled. She directed him to park in one of the free spaces outside the block beside which he was idling.

'Angelika will give you a permit to park here tonight,' she said. 'It's quite safe.'

She sent a text to her friend, announcing their arrival, while Josef parked the car. By the time they emerged from the relative cool of the air conditioning into the muggy heat outside, Angelika had appeared at a nearby entrance in a loose-fitting floral dress and sandals.

Josef took in her blond wavy hair, her large eyes, red lipstick and the glimmers of perspiration on her exposed clavicles. A void seemed to open in the pit of his stomach as he watched Hannah rushing over to give her a hug.

'It's so hot,' Angelika said. 'And you must be Josef?' She approached him, shook his outstretched hand and gave him the permit.

To hide the blush spreading over his face, he immediately walked back to the car, placed the permit on his dashboard and collected their overnight bags. He wondered what was wrong with him – and with sickening slidings of dread he recalled Daria's rape allegation. He had heard nothing more about it after his move to the tenders department, but on the few occasions he had since encountered Daria at work she had neither acknowledged his greetings nor given any indication that she knew him.

Josef now found it impossible to recall exactly what had occurred between them that night. There were vivid images of their lovemaking and of the conversation that preceded it, but there were so many gaps in his memory that he could no longer construct a coherent narrative of events, untainted by imagination, guilt or self-justification.

This troubling and inconclusive episode very much complicated his relationship with Hannah. He felt ashamed of his desire for her, which he feared reduced their deepening friendship to little more than a means of seduction, and his immediate physical attraction to Angelika only served to confuse him further. He carried the bags up to the flat, keeping his eyes on the steps, trying not to look at Angelika and Hannah ascending in front of him, their voices and laughter echoing in the stairwell. On the fourth landing, Josef followed them along the right-hand corridor, just in time to see them disappearing into a doorway on the left.

He was surprised to find himself in a short, gloomy hallway. An alcove on the right contained a wooden shoe rack and coats and jackets hanging from hooks. A wedge of light fell through the only other doorway, which opened on to the bed-sitting room. The first thing Josef noticed on entering was the large gothic window giving on to the balcony, where Hannah was leaning on the balustrade. Angelika poked her head round the archway in the opposite corner and asked him what he would like to drink.

'What are you having?'

'White wine and soda, but I also have lager and cider if you'd prefer.'

'Lager would be great, thanks.'

'Just leave Hannah's bag by the futon. I've made your bed behind the screen for privacy.'

Josef looked at the futon that currently served as a sofa. He put Hannah's bag by the wicker basket next to it and went over to the rattan screen. It was folded into an L-shape, with one panel some sixty centimetres from the bookshelves on the wall opposite the entrance, and three panels stopping short of the wall opposite the balcony. An inflatable bed, made up with a sheet and duvet, stretched beside the bookshelves in the space bordered by the screen. There was a wooden box beside the pillow with a reading lamp on it.

He put his bag by the foot of the bed and joined Hannah on the balcony. The curved balustrade was made from a sinuous network of wrought iron branches and leaves. Angelika brought out the drinks. She talked incessantly – about the salad she had prepared for tea, listing its ingredients for Josef in case he didn't like any of them or had food allergies; about their holiday; about her work – the whole forming a breathless monologue that spared Josef and Hannah the need to make conversation. While Angelika spoke, he gazed at the spectacular view of the Capital caught in the golden evening sunlight – the glittering windows of the skyscrapers across the river, and the numerous spires and towers of the Gothic Quarter. He breathed in the scents of the flowers in the hanging baskets, which mingled with the various perfumes and creams worn by Angelika and Hannah, and for the first time since moving to V he experienced a sense of unalloyed happiness, bordering on rapture.

After he finished his lager, Josef said that he would just freshen up before they ate. Angelika followed him, still nursing her drink, and watched him unpack his toiletries bag, his books and a fresh T-shirt.

'I hope it's not too stuffy for you?' she said.

'No, it's great, thanks.'

'Did Hannah give you *The Journey to Varnak*?'

'Yes, how did you know?'

'She's always going on about that novel.'

'Have you read it?'

'Yes, she bought it for me, too.'

'What did you think of it?'

'I loved the first part, but I'm not sure about the second part. I thought most of the sex scenes were unnecessary and self-indulgent.'

'I've only just started it,' he said.

'Oh, don't mind me. You'll probably love it.'

'Don't spoil it for him,' said Hannah, peering around Angelika's shoulder.

'I'll finish making the dinner,' said Angelika, draining the last of her drink.

Hannah briefly scanned the bookshelves and then followed her to the kitchenette.

After their meal, taken at the round dining table near the kitchenette, Josef helped Angelika with the dishes. The three of them spent the rest of the evening drinking, chatting and listening to music. Josef sat on the armchair, while Angelika and Hannah shared the futon. A cool breeze started after nightfall. The standard lamp in the corner cast a cone of warm light on the edge of the rug, leaving the rest of the room in shadow. Josef felt at ease in their company in a way he had not experienced since his early childhood before his family moved into his grandmother's villa.

He had a distant, almost dreamlike memory of a theatrical performance put on for the younger children by the teenagers of the neighbourhood, in a garage across the road from his house. He could recall nothing of the performance itself, only that he had had a crush on one of the teenage girls taking part. This evening with Hannah and Angelika seemed to have the same magical quality as that forgotten performance. The conversation flowed so easily. Neither of the women looked at their phones once. The music Angelika selected was serene and otherworldly. Towards the end of the evening, Angelika recounted some eerie tales from the Tarent Mountains that made Josef shiver with pleasurable fear. He did not want the evening to end, but

Hannah finally broke the spell by saying they had an early start in the morning and ought to turn in.

Lying on the overinflated mattress, separated from the women by the screen, Josef felt an unpleasant sense of exclusion as he heard them making up the futon for the night. He tried to concentrate on reading *The Journey to Varnak* and did begin to find something hypnotic about its catalogue of sights, customs and bizarre tales of the fictitious city. When he could not keep his eyes open any longer, he closed the book and switched off the reading lamp. He heard the women whispering and laughing for a short time, before he drifted off.

He had a nightmare in which he was lost in a strange city cobbled together from odds and ends of his past life. Just before waking at 4.00 a.m., he was attempting to manoeuvre his car in a narrow alleyway, which was at the same time a corridor in his grandmother's villa where the emaciated figure of his father stood in his ill-fitting bathrobe. He had a vague recollection of leaving the girl he had gone out with at school, who was living with him in a derelict house that used to terrify him as a child. He was driving to work in the dream and, despite the logical inconsistencies that followed, he had the anguished feeling that he had spent the rest of the dream trying to get back to her. At one point, his boss, Chris, was standing beside him, next to the old model of V, pointing to a tiny car that Josef was simultaneously driving through its streets. Chris's new secretary, Ildiko, was standing naked on the other side of the model, but when she looked at Josef she had Hannah's features. Josef's miniscule double climbed out of the car, and he suddenly found himself in a lift with his estate agent and a dark-skinned, bearded man with a scarred face, who was pulling something out of a canvas holdall that had flaking plastic handles. Entangled in the duvet, drenched in sweat, Josef could see orange glimmers catching in the pattern of the rattan screen. He imagined all kinds of problems and dangers arising on their journey to the mountains, and then his thoughts began to revolve around his numerous anxieties about work. He was scarcely aware of going back to sleep an hour later, before he woke in sudden terror, to find Angelika kneeling by his bed, tapping him gently on the shoulder with her glossy red fingernails.

'Sorry to give you such a fright, but breakfast is ready,' she said, smiling at his confusion.

'Rise and shine.' She was wearing a red T-shirt and a pair of jeans with ragged holes at the knees. When she stood up and headed round the screen, he noticed the matching red varnish on her toenails. He looked at the multicoloured spines of the books on the shelves next to him, still unsure of where he was.

He dressed quickly and joined Angelika at the dining table, just as

Hannah emerged from the bathroom in a borrowed dressing gown with her hair wrapped in a towel.

'You're up then,' she said as she sat down at the table.

There were croissants with butter, and coffee. Josef noticed an additional layer of pastry forming a familiar shape between the horns of each croissant.

'That's not King Corvus's crow, is it?'

'I'm afraid so,' said Angelika. 'All the bakeries have started adding them to their croissants; even the ones owned by immigrants. 'And this is a present for you. I meant to give it to you yesterday.'

'For me?' said Josef.

'Yes, for saving our holiday.'

It was a book, *Tales of the Sea and Mountains* by Radomira D.

'The stories I told last night are from this book. It's a real rarity.'

'The government ordered Angelika's publisher to pulp the entire print run,' said Hannah, spreading honey on her second croissant and licking her fingers, one by one.

'I don't know what to say,' said Josef.

Angelika helped to navigate Josef out of the city and on to the northbound motorway. She had been advised not to use a satnav to locate their holiday chalet. Periodically, Josef would catch sight of Hannah in the rear-view mirror – her neck twisting as she looked out of the window, the orange glow of sunshine on her face, the sweep of her eyeliner, the downward slant of her canthus, her sleeveless purple dress with a pattern of black tulips.

They stopped for a coffee at some services. The cafe-bar occupied a bridge that stretched over the motorway. A coachload of men in the black uniforms of the Brotherhood noisily crowded the tables around them, no doubt travelling to their training camp in the mountains. A couple of the younger members made salacious comments about Hannah and Angelika, for which they were severely rebuked by the officer in charge. He apologised profusely for the insult, assuring the women that such behaviour was totally at odds with the values of the Brotherhood. Hannah's sarcastic reply only served to make Josef feel more humiliated by the fearful silence he maintained throughout.

When they resumed their journey, Angelika joined Hannah on the back seat. They encountered two traffic jams caused by accidents in the congested industrial heartland of the country, between the cities of A and O, where several connecting motorways branched off to east and west. Time stretched to breaking point. The grass on the verges was parched and yellow.

Further north, the motorway became quieter, the grass greener and the countryside hillier. Josef began to relax and enjoy the drive. They passed through a broad river valley. Cows grazed in the fields. There were scattered farms, villages and clumps of birch trees. Sunlight reflected off the onion domes of the churches. The houses bore the distinctive yellow stucco and steeply pitched roofs of the region. Goats dotted the higher slopes. On the hills, regularly shaped plantations of firs had replaced the ancient forest felled in the distant past for the navy of some Ottoman despot.

Up ahead, an ominous black cloud kept appearing, sometimes on the right, sometimes on the left. After following a curve round the shoulder of a steep hillside, Josef found himself driving through a torrential thunderstorm. Lightning flashed. The windscreen wipers could barely cope with the downpour, and water streaming across the carriageway would make the car swerve unexpectedly. They emerged from the storm as suddenly as they had entered it. Trembling water droplets glistened and gleamed on the bonnet. Blinding sunlight reflected off the wet asphalt. A rainbow arched over the motorway, and then, in a gap between two hills, they had their first sight of the snow-capped peaks of the Tarent Mountains. A band of cloud made it appear as if they were suspended in the sky.

By mid-afternoon, they were an hour's drive short of the mountains. They had a late lunch at an upmarket service stop. The building housing the restaurant and shop was faced with orange stucco decorated in the traditional manner with painted vines and leaves. It overlooked an artificial pond. Ducks and geese swam on the glinting water, and children ran and played on the grassy slope beyond.

The restaurant offered a range of national dishes made from local farm produce. Hannah and Angelika were restricted to vegetarian burgers. Josef rather sheepishly opted for mutton stew and dumplings. They sat at a table by a window overlooking the pond. Before leaving, Josef thought it best to have a strong coffee to keep him awake for the final and most difficult part of the journey. When he was just finishing up the last dregs, a caffeine-induced anxiety prompted him to twist round in his chair to check the car, which was parked on the other side of the pond. He saw a man with untidy grey hair and a beard supervising his daughters, who were throwing bread to the birds.

Then Josef noticed a newspaper abandoned on the table behind him. It was a rabid right-wing tabloid that he hated on principle, but he was intrigued by the headline: 'Islamist Outrage in V'. Beneath it were pictured in heroic mode the faces of three members of the Brotherhood whose bodies had been discovered by a dog walker in the early hours of the previous morning, mutilated and beheaded, in Castle Hill Park in V. Drita N, the newly elected parliamentary representative for V, laid the blame fairly and squarely on the government 'for the criminal laxity of an immigration policy that had allowed all manner of dangerous elements into the country'.

'I'm sure those were the three men who attacked Daniela's private view last month,' said Hannah.

'They can't possibly know who was responsible,' said Angelika.

Josef threw the paper down in disgust.

'Hanging's too good for them,' said a passing pensioner holding a tray, mistaking the target of Josef's anger. He made no attempt to contradict her.

'I suppose we should be going now,' he said.

No doubt it was the caffeine that filled Josef with such trembling excitement when Angelika climbed into the front passenger seat beside him to help navigate the final leg of the journey. She sat with a road atlas draped over her thighs, tracing the route with a glossy red fingernail.

Hannah was jolted awake by Josef making an emergency stop. They were on the exit slip road of the last junction before the tunnel, that extravagant feat of engineering that had finally provided the country with a fast transport link through the Tarent Mountains to the northern province of Bijela. Josef had been caught up in a discussion with Angelika about the recent developments in that province, where a separatist party had gained a majority in the provincial parliament and were calling for a referendum on independence.

'It was my fault,' said Angelika, looking back at Hannah. 'I was distracting Josef.'

They headed eastwards along the old Roman road, skirting the foothills of the Tarent Mountains, which were hidden by the remnants of the ancient forest. The view opened up for a stretch around the town of S, which was founded by Saxon miners in the eleventh century. Its timber-framed houses rose into the sunlight on their left, with glimpses of sheer cliffs visible between the swathes of cloud beyond.

Not long afterwards, they joined the main road to the Kalimi Pass, which at one time had offered the only route through the mountains to the north. Angelika directed Josef to turn off some eight kilometres short of the pass.

'Another left turn,' she said, 'just like a labyrinth.'

Finally, they started to climb into the mountains proper, in a series of hairpin bends. The land fell away from the very edge of the road, descending through trees in precipitous slopes littered with boulders and scree. Tendrils of mist swirled between the trees. Angelika was too frightened to look out of the passenger window and, as the road narrowed, Josef grew increasingly anxious about the possibility of encountering an oncoming vehicle.

They came at length to a small town situated on an upland plateau. There was a police station, a town hall with a classical pediment supported by Corinthian columns, three hotels, some olde worlde taverns, various shops catering for tourists and a quaint railway terminus, whose beige and white façade put Hannah in mind of a gingerbread house. Everywhere they looked, there were national flags – draped around flagpoles, hanging from windows, stickered on cars and vans. Many of the flags bore the shield of King Corvus with its stylised crow.

'You take the second turning on the left after we leave the town,' said Angelika.

A brown sign at the first turn-off indicated the way to Karlstein Castle. Nearly a kilometre further on, Josef turned on to the narrow, tree-lined track that led to the chalet. A light over the door was triggered by their approach.

'I'll make the dinner,' said Hannah, 'since I've done nothing but sleep for most of the journey.'

Angelika keyed in the code to unlock the door, and they unloaded the car while the sun steadily sank behind a distant spur.

'This place is fucking brilliant,' said Josef, taking in the varnished wooden walls and elegant furnishings. The living space and kitchen occupied an open area that rose to the sharp angle of the roof, with large picture windows facing east and west and three smaller windows, above and on either side of the door, looking on to the veranda. The entrance to the bathroom was at one end and the entrance to the first bedroom at the other. Stairs led up to a gallery giving on to the other two bedrooms.

While Angelika had a shower, Josef put away the groceries and poured beers for Hannah and himself.

'Do you want any help?' he said.

'No, you just relax now. You must be tired after the drive.'

He wandered over to the west-facing window. The trees on the left formed a solid black mass. Above the meadow the snow-covered peaks and ridges on the right now glowed in the moonlight which outlined their shadow-filled gullies with almost heartbreaking precision. Nothing could be seen of Karlstein Castle on its rocky outcrop. It was wrapped in mist and darkness. Not a glimmer of light hinted at its presence. While Hannah hummed a popular tune and fried the onions, Josef went to his bedroom on the ground floor and unpacked his belongings. A small, atmospheric engraving of Karlstein Castle was mounted in a frame on the wall next to his bed.

On Monday morning, they had to take their ID cards to the police station in town to register their stay. Previously, this requirement had only applied to foreign visitors, but the government had extended it to its own citizens as part of a raft of measures to combat illegal immigration. The policeman on duty was wearing the familiar sky blue shirt, the colour of which had been inspired by the uniform of King Corvus's mercenaries. However, there was the novelty addition of a badge embroidered on the left breast pocket, representing a crow with spread wings on a white background in the shape of a shield. The policeman noted the direction of Josef's gaze.

'A splendid symbol, don't you agree?' he said in a low, caressive tone. There was a framed photograph of the police headquarters in N on the wall behind him. After carefully appraising their ID cards, he gave them a warm smile. 'It is one of the consolations of these troubled times that our compatriots are finally waking up to the beauties of this wonderful region.' So saying, he entered their names and accommodation details on his computer.

He gave each of them a slight nod as he handed them back their ID cards. 'I wish you a pleasant stay in Bijeli Vuk.'

Josef looked at Hannah with the panicked expression of a student confronting an unexpected exam question.

'You seem confused by the name,' the policeman added. 'As a southerner, you no doubt only know the province by its current name, Z. But for us it will always be Bijeli Vuk, which means "White Wolf" in our dialect, after our ancient prince who defeated the King of Bijela and drove him back over the Tarent Mountains. With the people of Bijela threatening independence, we northerners and southerners must stand together. But, even so, my innocent stripling, it would be foolish to forget that you are staying in the land of the White Wolf. You will be quite isolated up there near Karlstein Castle, but, never fear, my men shall be looking after you. It might interest you to know that King Corvus named the castle after his Austrian general, but hereabouts it will always be Vucja Jazbina, the Wolf's Lair.'

Josef was relieved to get out into the fresh air. Although the temperature was noticeably lower than in the Capital, the sun had already burned off the morning mist. The breeze barely ruffled the flag on the town hall. Further along the main street, they passed a telecom truck with a hydraulic lift, parked by a shining metal pole. A man in grey overalls was tinkering with a CCTV camera, while the driver of the truck gazed at him with a malign expression, drumming his fingers on the steering wheel. A young boy, in a blue and white striped T-shirt and red shorts that were gradually slipping down, ran past with a rustic loaf held awkwardly under his arm. A crow cawed harshly from its perch on a telegraph pole.

'Do you think the policeman sent that crow to spy on us?' said Josef.

A thin old lady in a turquoise twinset turned to look at him as if stung, muttered something under her breath and made an odd gesture in front of her face.

'I reckon she's warding off the evil eye,' Angelika whispered.

'You don't think she'll report me?' Almost immediately, he regretted saying something that so clearly betrayed his anxiety.

'I'm sure she didn't understand a word you said,' replied Hannah. 'She probably thinks you're a foreigner.'

They paused outside a gift shop while Josef selected postcards for his mother and sisters from a squeaky card spinner. Most of the postcards represented the castle in a variety of styles: nineteenth-century hand-tinted prints; Kodachrome photographs taken in the sixties, with old-fashioned cars parked on the approach road; recent black and white images playing up its gothic appearance; other well-composed shots with sunset skies or full moons. There were also postcards of the town and mountains, from which Josef made his selection, since he had not yet seen the castle emerge from its shroud of mist.

After that, they had a coffee at a table outside one of the inns. The waiter was not friendly. The apron hanging over his trousers was none too clean. He wiped the table with a cloth smelling of bleach, which he stuffed into his apron pocket. Then he stood nearby, holding a pencil stub over his pad, with an angry expression on his jowly, unshaven face.

The coffee and cakes were better than expected. Angelika spoke about some novels she had worked on, and Hannah gave her opinion of them, but nothing of what they said made much sense to Josef. He found it hard to speak about the books that he liked, or to explain why he liked them. If pushed to say something, he might have described them as a refuge of some kind, which was odd because they usually involved adventures in unreal places or distant galaxies. His thoughts continued to wander. He felt excluded from their conversation, as he had done on the previous evening, after he had gone to bed, when he heard their laughter drifting down from one of their rooms.

The scarcely acknowledged desire he felt for both women focused suddenly on Angelika's eyes. Their green, yellow-flecked irises caught the light in unexpected ways that lent them a liquid sheen and drew his gaze to the unnerving depths of her pupils. He wondered how he appeared to her – and then he realised that both she and Hannah were looking at him expectantly.

'I'm sorry,' he said. 'I was miles away.'

'I just asked you how you're enjoying *The Journey to Varnak*,' said Hannah.

'I am actually finding it really compelling.'

'The opening section is quite demanding, although I love the strange lists the narrator makes, but wait until you get to part two; that's when it starts to get really interesting.'

'And erotic,' said Angelika.

In the grocer's afterwards, the elderly proprietor took their order at the counter. Wheezing and breathing heavily, she insisted on collecting the items herself, bagging the fruit and vegetables with a dexterous twist before they could inspect them. An old man, with wrinkles showing white against his tan, winked at Hannah and Angelika, keeping up an incessant and incomprehensible chatter while he patiently waited his turn. The shopkeeper rolled her eyes and muttered something under her breath, which set off a hacking cough.

Outside, a group of chatting women fell silent when Josef, Angelika and Hannah walked past laden with bags. These grew heavier as they neared the car park on the outskirts of town. Mechanical diggers were shifting earth in a neighbouring field where concrete-filled trenches measured out the dimensions of a future supermarket.

★

Hannah woke early on Tuesday morning from a troubled sleep. She felt incredibly tired and, although she could remember little of her dream, she had the unpleasant feeling of having been betrayed by a loved one, which recalled her minor disagreement with Angelika on the previous evening. They had been talking in Angelika's room after Josef had gone to bed. It had been a silly argument about *The Journey to Varnak*. If she was honest with herself, Hannah realised that it had arisen from her unspoken anxieties about Josef.

She did not like the way that Angelika was flirting with him. During the few weeks she had known Josef, she had come to regard him as a fragile, romantically inclined person. Hannah recognised soon after she moved into his flat that he had feelings for her, and, without wanting to hurt him, she had made clear her lack of interest in him, or so she believed.

She was very conscious of the fact that Angelika had made no mention to Josef of her boyfriend, Pavel, and that she appeared to be enjoying Josef's evident attraction to her. Hannah did not want Josef to get hurt. She knew that he would not understand the limits of a holiday fling, and she could not imagine that Angelika was interested in anything more serious.

Unable to get back to sleep, she decided to take a walk in the woods. The air would be cold and fresh at this time in the morning, the light beautiful. Through her window, she could see the tiled gothic roof of the castle emerging from the mist. She pulled on a pair of jeans and a fleece and tried not to make any noise when she put on her hiking boots and headed out.

The forest descended the slopes towards the east, skirting the high summer pastures around the town before spreading out over the broad lower reaches of the Kalimi Pass. Much of it had been planted with a variety of trees during the past ten years by a charity set up to recreate the ancient forest of the region, which still clung on among the foot-hills of the Tarent Mountains. Nature was gradually reasserting itself alongside the winding paths that had been laid out among the trees with different-coloured arrows to indicate the ways. A scandal had been brewing in parliament for several months regarding the role an international hotel conglomerate had played in setting up the charity. Questions were being asked about why the same conglomerate was now making a bid to buy Karlstein Castle from the cash-strapped government.

The morning was as beautiful as Hannah had anticipated. The or-ange sunlight slanting through the trees sparkled on the dew-laden leaves. Mist still snaked between the tree trunks, filling the hollows and dells. She felt her unjustified rancour dissipate as she breathed in the fresh, pine-scented air. But she was surprised, after taking a turn through some thick shrubbery, to discover a group of men in high-viz jackets and black overalls carrying out various incomprehensible tasks among the trees, under the indolent supervision of a soldier who was leaning against an ash tree and smoking.

When he caught sight of Hannah, he swung his machine gun on to his back, approached her smiling and held out a packet of cigarettes. Taking in his handsome features and friendly expression, she said, 'Thanks a lot, but I don't smoke.'

'It's a filthy habit,' he said, stubbing out his cigarette on a branch. He checked it was completely extinguished before flicking it into the undergrowth. Hannah followed its trajectory with her eyes, frowned and looked over at the men.

'What are they doing?'

'That, I can't tell you, but what brings you to this godforsaken place?'

'I'm on holiday with friends. And anyway it's beautiful here, when people don't litter it with cigarettes and electronic gewgaws.'

He shrugged his shoulders and said, 'There's not much in the way of nightlife.' He looked at the men. Some were crouching; one was bending over an object with a tiny screwdriver; another was unrolling a spool of cable. 'I'm not sure what they are doing, truth be told. Strictly hush-hush, national security and all that bollocks.'

'And you on your lonesome, protecting them.'

'My mate will be back shortly.'

'Well, there's clearly nothing I can do here. And you're very well armed if anything should come along – a deer, a goat or, heaven forbid, a bear.'

'I do get leave at the weekends. If you want some time away from your friends, you could meet me for a drink in town.'

She smiled and shook her head. 'How can you be so sure you'll survive until then?'

At that moment, another soldier appeared – a tall man with a thin neck. As her soldier turned to greet the newcomer, Hannah noticed on the butt of the machine gun a small circle containing an upward-pointing arrowhead and the words 'Dynamic Systems' in relief. She walked away along the path she had come by, without looking back.

When she arrived at the chalet, Josef was cooking a vegetarian fry-up for breakfast; Angelika was relaxing on the couch, reading a leaflet. She looked up and smiled when Hannah entered, showing no sign of awkwardness about their recent argument. Josef, too, greeted her and smiled in his usual self-conscious manner.

'Where have you been?' he said.

'I didn't sleep well, so I went for a walk to clear my head. It was really odd. There was a group of men working in the woods, under the supervision of a soldier.'

'What were they doing?' said Angelika.

'The soldier didn't know, or if he did he certainly wasn't telling.'

Angelika seemed to consider this for a moment, and then said, 'Do you fancy going to S today. Josef said he's happy to drive us.'

★

That night, Angelika had a dream. She was eating lunch with Hannah and Josef at the table outside the cafe in S. The cafe was in a small square of half-timbered buildings. There was a postcard beside her plate showing a narrow street of houses faced with orange stucco, leading up to the church on the hill. She was trying to prevent the filling in her pasty from sliding out on to her right hand, while her left hand rested on Josef's thigh under the table. There was a tiny detail in a doorway near the top of the street in the postcard, but, no matter how hard she tried, she couldn't make it out. She suddenly found herself in her office in the Capital, correcting a proof page from Radomira's *Tales of the Sea and Mountains* and weeping inconsolably.

★

The weather on Wednesday was glorious. They decided to go for a picnic. After taking a shower, Josef emerged from the bathroom in one of the white terry-towelling bathrobes that came with the chalet. Angelika was arranging sandwiches, crisps, biscuits and wine in a cool bag, and Hannah came over to show him the plastic picnic set she had just found in one of the kitchen cupboards. It came strapped into its own wicker basket.

They followed the gentle incline of the meadow towards the steeper slopes, where a winding path led them between sparse, wind-distorted pines, through asters and asphodels, to the sheer cliff face that towered behind their chalet. From the base of the cliff, they could see the roofs and sun-glittering windows of the town, and the forest stretching down to the Kalimi Pass.

They discovered a pleasant grassy spot, sheltered by rocks from the cool easterly breeze, where they ate their lunch and slowly worked their way through the wine. The late afternoon sun found them still there. Hannah was lying on her side, cheek cupped in hand, support-ing her head on her right elbow, while Angelika lay on her back, gaz-ing at the sky, with her head resting on Hannah's waist. Josef lay stretched out on the other side of the picnic rug with his hands behind his head. A grasshopper chirred nearby and high above them a jet trail thinned as it spread across the clear blue sky.

Josef twisted his neck to look at the women and tried to fool himself into thinking that he wanted nothing more than this. Then his thoughts drifted to his job, which he had almost entirely forgotten during the past few days. It came back to him now with stomach-churning intimations of dread.

*

They were sitting around the coffee table in the living area after their evening meal, drinking wine and talking by candlelight, when Han-nah's phone started ringing. She looked annoyed as she crossed the room to silence it. At the sight of Stefan's name on the screen, she swore under her breath and only reluctantly accepted the call.

'Hello Stefan.'

After a short interval of static, he said, 'Hello, can you hear me?' in a distant, ghostly voice.

'It's a bad ...' was all she was able to say before being cut off again, but a single bar appeared on the signal indicator when she moved closer to the coffee table. Josef laughed at something Angelika said, and Hannah ended the call before attempting to say anything else. Then she switched off the phone.

'I don't know why I got this bloody thing,' she said. 'I hate it.'

On Thursday, Josef drove them to H, a town situated to the east of the Kalimi Pass which was famous for its second-hand bookshops. They had decided to go there that morning because rain was forecast. The journey in a sudden downpour proved to be the most dangerous he had yet undertaken, and he was relieved when they finally arrived at the car park in H. Damp scents coming from the trees and ferns beyond the boundary wall reminded him of rainy summer days on the Bohemian Coast.

As they retrieved their jackets and bags from the car boot, Josef looked up at the dark cloud overhead, but the rain had stopped for the time being. Hannah suggested that they go their separate ways for the morning and meet up later for lunch. Josef noted Angelika's reluctance to accept the plan. It was the first time he had been aware of any friction between the two women, but in the event it was Angelika who left them first, heading down a narrow cobbled street towards a favourite shop specialising in poetry books.

'Follow me,' said Hannah, and with a sudden swell of excitement Josef thought that she had deliberately arranged things so they could have time alone together. She led him through several turns, before stopping in front of a shop and saying, 'Here we are.' Italic lettering above the window in faded yellow paint spelled out the words 'Dark They Were and Golden Eyed'. It was a shop specialising in science fiction and fantasy books. 'I found this place on my phone this morning when I managed to get online. I wanted to surprise you.' Then, after confirming the arrangement to meet back in the car park at one, she headed back up the street.

Josef watched her go with a mixture of disappointment and anticipation. A middle-aged woman sat behind the sales desk in the shop. Her smile revealed her uneven teeth, and she shook her head when Josef asked her if he should leave his bag with her. He reflected that he would not have been able to indulge his pleasure in browsing if Angelika and Hannah had come with him, and there was still the certainty that he would be having lunch with them. A handwritten sign directed him to a room full of English-language paperbacks, which he approached slowly, savouring his expectation of marvels.

★

Angelika looked closely at the binding and then flicked through the pages to check their condition. The typeface was elegant and clear and was printed on cream wove paper. It was a bilingual edition of Sylvia

Plath's collected poems which had been published in the 1970s. She had recently read an article about the poet which cited it as being by far the best translation of her work, but the prices being asked by online sellers were well beyond Angelika's means. This copy lacked a dust wrapper and had library stamps but was otherwise in good condition and was priced at only ninety-five thalers. It was still an extravagant sum, and she owed a lot on her Visa card, so she was finding it hard to justify the purchase. There were also rumours at work of possible redundancies in the editorial department, following the recent takeover. Nevertheless, she gave in to temptation. The sheer pleasure of buying the book helped mitigate her annoyance with Hannah.

When she left the musty shop and breathed in the fresh, damp air, she realised how absurd it was to imagine that her friend was trying to keep her away from Josef. Three weeks earlier, she had found a strange message on her boyfriend's phone. She had discovered it quite by chance while unplugging the charger. It was from a woman Angelika didn't know. The message referred to a meeting and sought to clear up a misunderstanding about an email. There was nothing in the words themselves to indicate any intimacy, but what was left out of the message suggested the kind of shorthand that arises from a close relationship. She did not feel that she could confront Pavel about it, however, for fear that he would think she was spying on him. Now she realised that since the discovery the tormenting doubts she had about him were tainting all her relationships, making her paranoid and suspicious of her friends and work colleagues. She had not yet discussed the message with Hannah.

Angelika made her way carefully over the wet cobblestones in her low heels. There were rows of cottages on either side. The smooth stonework around the windows and doors was painted in a variety of bright colours. Four people were grouped beside a doorway up ahead: an elderly couple, a middle-aged woman and a teenage boy in a black uniform, who was pointing at the red and black badge sewn on to his left sleeve above two white chevrons. The old man was chuckling and rubbing the boy's shaven head, while the old lady was speaking excitedly in a high-pitched voice. They all fell silent when Angelika approached and they seemed reluctant to make way for her. As she squeezed between them, the old man's tangled eyebrows formed a V as he regarded her unbuttoned jacket and whorish dress with an expression of mingled bafflement and outrage.

★

Josef woke early the following morning, before it was light, from a repetitive and oppressive work dream. After half an hour of fretting in the dark, he gave up trying to get back to sleep and switched on his bedside lamp. He lay on his side, contemplating the print of Karlstein Castle in its warm halo of varnished pine. He reflected on the fact that it was Friday already. There was still another week to go, but time was passing too quickly. In a desperate bid to avoid thinking about his inevitable return to V, he started to read *The Journey to Varnak*. He was nearing the conclusion of the first part.

The Hungarian traveller had found lodging in the town house of a powerful nobleman keen to secure a diplomatic position in Budapest for his younger son. He welcomed the traveller into his home by laying on an evening of entertainment attended by the cream of Varnak society. A pianist, a violinist and a cellist performed a Schubert piano trio. Then there was a recital by the city's poet laureate of a turgid nationalistic ode.

When the traveller finally made his way to his room, guided by the flame of a cheap candle, he was surprised to find a young woman waiting in the darkness outside his door. The traveller was excited by her flagrant disregard of Varnak's rigid social conventions and by her candlelit décolletage. It struck him that he had not noticed her at the gathering earlier, and he wondered if her beauty was merely a product of the poor lighting and her impropriety. In the event, all she did was to hand him a leather-bound book.

He took it in his left hand and inclined the candle flame towards the gold lettering on the spine. He was still unable to read the language with any fluency, and he laboriously translated it into Hungarian in his head – A város a tenger mellet – before saying 'The City Beside the Sea' in a questioning tone.

'The City by the Sea,' she said. 'I wanted to show you the best of our literature. Not all our writers produce barrack-room doggerel for armchair soldiers like my father. I hope you find it stimulating?'

'Not, surely, as stimulating as your company,' he said, or thought he said.

'I do hope you aren't going to disappoint me, Béla Sassy.'

'In Hungary, the names are ...' he paused '... ordered in reverse and your name I have not.'

'You're not in Hungary now, Sassy Béla, and my name is Anya.'

'Only Anya?'

'It is all I have to call my own, pitiful as you may find it, sir.

My mother gave it to me. All the rest belongs to my father. Now, let me wish you a good night.' So saying, she walked away along the corridor, and he watched the last traces of candlelight shimmering on the emerald silk of her dress.

As he entered his room, placed the book next to the candle on his bedside table and regarded the pathetic remains of blackened wood glowing in the grate, he wondered why the count had not introduced him to this daughter.

Nothing in the novel so far had prepared Josef for this narrative turn. He looked at the two books he had bought on the previous day, with their creased spines and yellowing pages. Only an aficionado like Josef would appreciate their rarity and value. They were stacked on top of the fantasy novel he had brought with him and the fairy tale collection given to him by Angelika. All had been momentarily eclipsed by the description of the young woman caught by candlelight outside the traveller's room.

Josef slipped his marker between the pages and closed the book. Then he climbed out of bed, crept over to the window and parted the curtains to look at Karlstein Castle. There was no mist this morning. Beneath the massive keep, Josef could see a cluster of smaller buildings and towers, and the curtain wall circling the rocky outcrop and descending towards the forest below. Only the keep and the pointed roof of a circular tower emerged into the early morning sunlight which picked out all their details with the bright intensity of one of Dagomar's famous illustrations. It seemed to Josef that even at that distance he could make out every gleaming slate and shadow-lined irregularity in the stonework.

He recalled the coloured image of a clifftop castle, framed by nested vermilion lines, and the words on the cream-coloured paper of the facing page, describing the beautiful maiden imprisoned in its dungeon, hapless victim of the king's lust, doomed to suffer the vengeance of the jealous Mareduche. He thought of the other heroines from *The Tales of the Bohemian Coast*; of the pneumatic and docile women populating his pulp science fiction novels; of his succession of schoolboy crushes; of the awkward and unsatisfactory reality of his only two relationships to date. He thought of his one night stand with Daria and reflected upon Angelika and Hannah sleeping in their bedrooms above. He had no idea how long his reverie lasted, but he noticed that orange sunlight now coated the roof of a long, low building that rose directly from the wall of Karlstein Castle.

He had the odd feeling that the castle had been eluding him in some profound manner during the entire course of that week, as if the perpetual mist in which it had been shrouded had been deliberately placed there by a malign entity and that he might win Hannah's love if he could only get her to the castle, but then he found himself picturing Angelika's eyes and he became confused and despondent when he considered the ludicrous turn his thoughts had taken.

While they were eating breakfast later that morning, Josef broached the possibility of going to Karlstein Castle.

Angelika looked at Hannah, who said, 'Actually, we were wondering if you would mind driving us to N. One of our old university friends messaged Angelika yesterday and asked if we could meet him for lunch.'

'We can go to Karlstein Castle tomorrow,' said Angelika.

'And, of course, we'll pay for the petrol,' said Hannah.

'I'd be happy to,' said Josef, smiling stiffly, trying to hide his irritation and disappointment.

'Have you ever been to N?' said Angelika.

'No, never. The Tarent Mountains frightened my mother,' he said, pushing the toast crumbs on his plate into a circle and then a square.

'You'll love it,' said Hannah. 'It's a really beautiful town. And lunch will be on us.'

When they returned from N that evening, they ate a light meal and opened two bottles of wine. As Josef became inebriated, he alluded to the stresses, disappointments and resentments of the day in such an oblique and ironical manner that neither Angelika nor Hannah, themselves fairly drunk, had any idea of what he was trying to say.

At midnight, the women went upstairs together to get ready for bed. Josef heard them laughing in Angelika's room. He heard successive flushing of the toilet in the en-suite. He heard the murmur of resumed conversation. A great weariness descended on him. With enormous effort, he went to the downstairs bathroom to relieve himself and brush his teeth.

But when he finally lay down in bed he could not get to sleep. Images of the day began to run pell-mell through his mind. The long, tortuous drive through the winding forest road behind a labouring tractor with a trailer full of hay bales. The first sight of the grey spires of N. The patchwork lapdog lost and shivering in the shadows of a cobbled alley while its elderly owner stood near a cafe entrance around the corner, staring in perplexity at the broken collar trailing from her lead. The pub terrace by the river where they ate lunch with the old university friend, whose calm self-assurance gave no hint of his precarious job situation – the St Christopher medallion glinting in the opening of his skirt; his barbed comments about Josef; the hidden history behind every gesture and phrase. The brash skinhead, with his tin and his cluster of small flags, demanding with menace five thalers for a wounded soldiers' charity. The twisting columns by the entrance to a church. The pub terrace. The anguish. The shivering lapdog. The skinhead. The belching smokestack of the tractor. The glinting medallion. The broken collar. The green, yellow-flecked irises of Angelika's eyes. The framed print of the castle, barely visible on the wall. Hannah's smiling face fading into the darkness.

★

Angelika woke at seven o'clock on Saturday morning from a disturbing erotic dream about Andel, with whom they had had lunch in N on the previous day – disturbing because she had realised during the lunch that he had lost none of the deluded arrogance that had made her split up with him in the first place. Josef's presence had only served to put all Andel's faults into bold relief.

She pulled on her dressing gown and went down to the kitchen, where she switched on the coffee machine. While waiting for the water to heat, she collected her duvet and took it out to the wooden recliner on the veranda. Stirring the milk into her coffee, she reflected on the fact that Josef had not wanted to drive to N. It had been Hannah who had wanted to go there and to meet Andel for lunch. Angelika had more or less decided to decline the invitation, until she had got caught up in Hannah's enthusiastic plan to revisit their old university haunts.

Angelika had cringed inwardly when her friend had proposed the trip to Josef at breakfast. His ready agreement only confirmed Angelika's suspicion that Hannah was shamelessly exploiting his infatuation.

So she reasoned, trying to set out her thoughts in a logical manner, ironing out the inconsistencies – the burst of excitement she had felt when Andel's invitation had come through on the intermittent Wi-Fi connection; her desire for Josef, which was becoming more insistent and fuelling her jealousy of Hannah. Or was it that message to Pavel from the mysterious woman that perturbed her and kept her in a permanent state of agitation?

She settled down under her duvet on the veranda, sipped her coffee and tried to lose herself in the calm contemplation of the meadow descending towards the trees, but her heart was pounding and there were fluttering sensations in her stomach that filled her with a frustrated desire for some kind of violent activity.

'It's so beautiful. I wish we could stay here for ever.' Josef blushed when she turned at the sound of his voice. 'I mean … well, I don't really know what I mean.'

'I could happily live here,' she said, 'if it wasn't for work.'

'Yes, work.' He was wearing a white T-shirt, jeans and an old pair of sneakers. His hair was dishevelled. Angelika did not think they had much in common, and she didn't think he was particularly attractive, so she found it hard to explain her growing feelings for him. She did not know what precisely he did for a living. Hannah had told her that he had recently transferred from Personnel to another department in V's city council, but he had been unwilling to talk about his new role. Angelika reckoned he was only about twenty-one or twenty-two. There could be no future in a relationship, and she thought his reading tastes were, frankly, ridiculous, but her stomach took a sudden dip as she regarded him now and imagined the disorder of his recently vacated bed.

'So, we'll visit the castle today?' she said. Her mouth was dry. She looked at the coffee dregs in her mug.

'Oh, only if you and Hannah want to go. I'm not sure why the place fascinates me so much.'

'It's your holiday too, Josef. You don't have to drive us everywhere. Do you fancy a coffee? I'm just going to make some fresh.'

It was nearly three o'clock in the afternoon by the time they reached the castle. The car park was empty, which Josef thought unusual, given that it was a Saturday in August. He slowed to a halt in front of a row of traffic cones that formed a barrier across the main gateway. The cobbled courtyard beyond terminated in a long, three-storey building, which was itself pierced by a wide inner gateway. A cluster of buildings climbed the slope visible above its pantiled roof towards the imposing keep on the summit.

A heftily built security guard approached the car. The red and black insignia on his uniform identified him as an employee of the controversial private security firm recently implicated in a massacre of civilians in the Middle East. Josef wound down the window and the guard bent to peer in at him, before turning his attention to Angelika and Hannah, who were both sitting on the back seat. He allowed his gaze to linger on their bare legs and then he winked at them.

'Did you not see the sign?' he said, directing the question at Josef in a contemptuous tone.

'No, where was the sign?'

Giving no indication that he had heard him, the guard continued, 'The castle is now under private ownership and is no longer open to the public.' His boots creaked as he straightened up. He inclined his head, cupped a hand over his mouth and spoke into the walkie-talkie strapped to his shoulder. The only word Josef could make out was 'tourists'.

'Fascist pig,' said Hannah, under her breath.

The guard remained impassive, fixing Josef with his cold stare, before saying, 'You all have a good day, now,' and turning on his heel.

As he prepared to drive off, Josef saw a tall woman crossing the castle courtyard in a dark pinstriped suit with an extremely short skirt and a pair of honey-coloured tights. She was walking carefully on the cobblestones in her high heels, but nevertheless appeared unflustered and poised. Light shimmered in her long black hair as she emerged into angled sunlight. It was only when she turned to look over her shoulder that he realised she was Chris's secretary, Ildiko, and then he experienced a sudden rush of helpless panic when his CEO entered his field of vision in an expensive designer suit. Chris let his hand rest for a moment on Ildiko's bottom, before moving it to the small of her back and guiding her gently towards the inner gateway.

Josef accelerated away in a spray of gravel, driving dangerously down the twisting forest road.

'What's wrong?' said Angelika, gripping the back of the passenger seat, and only then did he slow down.

Hannah cooked the meal that evening, and Angelika and Josef washed and cleared away the dishes. Afterwards, they drank wine and talked by candlelight, but Josef no longer experienced the euphoric sense of communion he had felt at the start of the holiday. He was aware of the increasing tension between the women, although he did not know what was causing it.

Angelika asked him about his CEO. Primarily, she wondered if Josef knew why Chris was at the castle, but she was also seeking an explanation for Josef's odd behaviour that afternoon. Josef blushed, stumbled over his words and avoided her eyes, giving the impression that he knew more than he was letting on. His reticence perplexed and upset her.

Josef did not like talking about work. He was afraid that Hannah would discover that he had been responsible for the reduction of her redundancy package from the city council. It was only the fact that she had taken voluntary redundancy that had prevented their meeting at the time her job was under review.

Meanwhile he had realised that the new job he was doing for Chris in the tenders department was illegal. Josef was using his legal knowledge to hide corruption in the granting of contracts, and he was sure that Chris was using him as a fall guy, should this practice ever come to light. But he could not tell Angelika and Hannah anything about it. It would be impossible to explain how Chris had blackmailed him into the job without mentioning the rape allegation, and he lived in perpetual fear that Hannah might hear about that from one of her former colleagues.

Hannah wished that Angelika would spend less time thinking about Josef. All those bloody questions about his CEO! Hannah remembered when Chris had visited her department in the city council. She had reckoned then that he was an utter bastard. He had been completely mystified as to why the council was funding health information, expressing the opinion to Hannah's then manager that all individuals should be responsible for their own health. Hannah could well understand why someone like Josef would find it stressful working for such a monster.

She had hoped that she and Angelika would have more time to themselves on this holiday. She had wanted to ask her friend's advice about Stefan. Hannah could not understand why her thoughts kept returning to him. She had never imagined herself falling for a married man, and one with a daughter as well. It was absurd. She had always considered herself to be in control of her feelings, and here she was, acting like a lovesick teenager. She reckoned that Angelika took Pavel for granted. Her friend did not realise how lucky she was to have such a good relationship.

Thus their thoughts hummed and buzzed against the uncertain rhythm of the conversation, heedless of the numberless complex workings of their bodies, while they kept subtly shifting their positions in relation to each other on the chair and settee and worked their way steadily through their last three bottles of wine. Josef was wearing a yellow T-shirt with terracotta shorts, while Angelika and Hannah wore loose-fitting floral print dresses. The left strap of Angelika's dress had slipped off her shoulder.

Hannah drifted off to sleep, her head sliding from her supporting elbow on to Angelika's thigh. Angelika appeared to be lost in thought. She began quietly singing a lullaby and stroking Hannah's hair. Josef said nothing. As he looked at them in the candlelight, the frustrations and resentments of the past days gradually evaporated, leaving him with a sense of profound contentment.

This perfect moment was brutally shattered, however, by the sudden illumination of the security light. Angelika let out a cry which woke Hannah up.

'Fucking hell!' said Josef as he hurried to the nearest window, overlooking the front of the chalet. The light imparted an eerie precision to everything within its range, as if a meticulous artist had inked in the shadow of each blade of grass, but everything beyond was cast into deeper darkness. Josef could see nothing that might have triggered the light.

'A deer?' he said in an uncertain, questioning tone. Hannah was still looking around in confusion.

'Yes,' said Angelika. 'It was probably a deer.'

He locked and bolted the door and then carefully closed the blinds on every window.

'Maybe we should go to bed,' said Angelika, collecting the empty glasses. Hannah followed her to the kitchen area with the empty bottles.

Despite his many anxieties, Josef fell into a drunken stupor as soon as his head hit the pillow. He dreamed of the tender on which he had been working during the week before the holiday. It had been for a council contract to supply the police force in V with guns, but it was transformed by the dream into the vision of thousands of police hats spreading over the courtyard of Karlstein Castle. Josef was attempting to cross the courtyard without either stepping on any of the hats or being seen by the heftily built security guard, who was having sex with Ildiko against the castle wall between a corner turret and one of the gate towers. Chris was pacing nearby and speaking on his mobile.

Josef had in his pocket an entrance ticket to the castle with Daria's name written on the reverse. Chris had told him that this was the name ascribed to the company that was to be granted the contract. Josef's task was to use his legal expertise to hide anything that linked this company to the actual beneficiary of the contract, whose name Josef could just make out, tattooed in black ink on Ildiko's naked thigh.

Then, in a sudden dream shift, Josef found himself in the labyrinthine corridors of the castle, running hand in hand with Ildiko, who was still naked. No matter how many right-angle turns they took, or how many doors they passed through, they constantly encountered the same portly man, wearing the bowler hat, pinstriped cutaway jacket and grey trousers of an old-fashioned English bureaucrat, who would bow and raise his hat to Ildiko before drawing a sheet of cream-coloured paper from his briefcase. Josef desperately tried to hide the name on Ildiko's thigh with a ragged facecloth that was quite inadequate to the task, while she kept slapping his hand away and complaining that he had abducted her.

He woke thinking of Daria: her selfishness; her coldness and beauty; her unexplained tears when she had arrived at his flat on the night they had sex. And then he recalled what she had told him of her mother's murder and of her father's involvement with the Black Hand, and the incident with the security light took on a sudden terrifying significance. Inevitably, his thoughts turned to his job.

He reflected on the many crooked byways that linked all the successful tenders he had overseen to the ANH Corporation, and now that corporation merged in his imagination with the Black Hand to form a single entity, like the alien creature in one of his favourite tales of cosmic horror, extending its slimy tentacles into every aspect of his life.

Josef lay in the dark, trying to get back to sleep, but he could hear his heart thumping when he lay on his left side, and every time he closed his eyes his thoughts kept revolving obsessively around his job and the untold number of emails that would be awaiting his return to work. In the end, he clambered out of bed and scrabbled around in the dark for his jeans and T-shirt, before padding into the living room in his bare feet.

He was surprised to find Angelika stretched out on the settee, reading a book by the light of a clip-on reading lamp.

'I'm really sorry, Josef. I tried to be as quiet as possible.' She spoke in a whisper, casting anxious glances towards Hannah's bedroom door.

'Oh, it wasn't you that woke me up. I had a nightmare. Do you fancy some juice?' He headed over to the kitchen area.

'Yes, please.' She sat up, unclipped the reading lamp and switched on the light on the small table by the settee.

When he sat down on the chair opposite her, he became suddenly conscious of his bare feet, which he considered to be unpleasant and ugly – narrow, flat and with simian toes. He pulled them as far under the chair as he could and took a long draught of juice, before saying, 'What were you reading?'

When she held up the book, he realised that it was a copy of the same book as she had given to him.

'There are only twenty-five copies in existence,' she said. 'They will be worth a fortune one day – if people still read books in the future, which I grant you is very unlikely.' They were both speaking in exaggerated whispers, as if fearful of waking a sleeping ogre.

'I was rereading the story that caused all the scandal,' she said, in the same quiet voice. Josef, using the ready excuse offered, put down his empty glass and joined her on the settee to look at the book.

'I wasn't aware of the scandal,' he whispered, taking in the fleshy whorls of her ear between the strands of hair. He was close enough to detect the subtle trace of perfume on her neck and to see the intricate floral pattern of her pyjama top in the opening of her bathrobe. The plastic of the buttons mimicked mother-of-pearl. After a moment, he turned his attention to the book, which was lying open in her lap halfway through 'The Story of the King and the Chambermaid'.

'You know the story of the Mareduche?' she said.

'Oddly enough, I was thinking of that very story yesterday. The castle in the morning sunlight made me think of Dagomar's illustration.'

'Yes, and there's the other one of the king riding along the clifftop, having been duped by the Mareduche.' She looked Josef in the eye and added, 'Why are we whispering like this?'

'I have no idea. We're like children doing something naughty in the night, fearful of waking our parents.'

'"Naughty",' she said, laughing. '"Naughty" – who even uses that word?' She fell silent, holding her glass in both hands and looking down at the patterned rug as if lost in thought.

Josef followed her gaze to the curious shapes stretching in lines across the rug, divided by different-coloured stripes. Angelika's legs were crossed just below the hems of her pyjama trousers. There was chipped red varnish on her toenails. A delicate blue vein forked on her right foot. The edge of her shoe had left a curving line of paler skin across her toes.

'Have you ever read the original tale of the Mareduche?' she said suddenly.

'No, I don't believe I have.'

'In it, the chambermaid was quite clearly raped by the king, and she suffered a similar fate at the hands of the steward before being hurled over the clifftop on the orders of the Mareduche.'

'None of that was in the version I read.'

'At the end of the nineteenth century, *The Tales of the Bohemian Coast* were rewritten in a form acceptable to the sensibilities of the middle classes. Dagomar, who had just finished illustrating *The Adventures of King Corvus*, was commissioned to provide the illustrations and was largely responsible for the association of the king in this story with King Corvus.' Josef wondered where she was going with this conversation and began to feel out of his depth. 'Even in its sanitised version, it is an unsettling, misogynistic story: the ugliness of Ruzena, the Mareduche's daughter; the way the chambermaid is killed for having sex with the king, as if she had deliberately lured him away from Ruzena. It panders to the idea that female sexuality is evil, and it portrays women as mere adjuncts to men. Radomira found this story the hardest to rewrite. In the end, she hit upon the idea of merging it with that other misogynistic story about the princess rescued from the sea monster by the valiant knight.'

Josef felt uneasy about the turn the conversation had taken, not least because during his early teens he had been sexually aroused by the story of the beautiful princess chained to the rock beside the sea. Even now, he would frequently return to Dagomar's illustration of the scene, with its rendering of the raven-haired princess in her diaphanous gown.

Angelika put down her empty glass and turned towards Josef, tucking her legs under her, before continuing: 'In Radomira's version, the king is unmanned by the chambermaid's laughter when he attempts to rape her, and, utterly humiliated by his impotence, he fails to go through with the assault. Rejected by her, and yet completely in her thrall, he readily accepts the Mareduche's lie that she has fled the castle, and he sets out on his famous midnight ride along the clifftop. Then, instead of taking his revenge by hurling the chambermaid over the cliff, the Mareduche has her chained to a rock by the sea to await her death by drowning at high tide. It is the princess – whom the king encounters on his ride – who rescues the chambermaid, rather than marrying the king as she does in the original tale. In Radomira's story, the princess is unimpressed by the king's romanticised version of events and decides to find out for herself what has happened. So she finds the chambermaid before she is drowned by the incoming tide.'

Angelika fell silent. Josef looked at her lips, but his desire to kiss her now seemed monstrously inappropriate. He feared that she would think he was no better than the rapacious king in the story. He even began to question his teenage reveries about the princess chained to the rock. He had always pictured himself as the knight coming to her rescue and being rewarded with her love, but now he wondered if he wasn't more excited by the idea of her being chained and vulnerable, unable to fend off his advances.

'I'm sorry,' Angelika said. 'I got carried away with my narrative. I have spoiled the ending for you.' She knew that she had said too much. She always talked too much when she was nervous. She had been so certain that Josef had meant to kiss her when he joined her on the settee. She had been unsettled by his failure to do so, and now she was convinced that she had scared him off with all her talk. Perhaps it was for the best. Perhaps, after all, she had read too much into the message on Pavel's phone.

'What are you two conspiring about down there?' The sound of Hannah's voice made them both jump.

'Neither of us could sleep,' said Angelika.

'I hope we didn't wake you,' said Josef.

'No, I had a dreadful nightmare about werewolves, of all things, wearing the tattered black uniforms of the Brotherhood. It must have been something to do with the security light. It's put us all on edge.'

★

After parking the car at the summit of the Kalimi Pass, Josef gazed at the hills of Bijela extending in waves towards the north, losing their definition as they gradually disappeared into the haze, and he experienced an unexpected sense of exhilaration. Unexpected because the holiday was nearly over and because he had felt since his night-time conversation with Angelika that his relationships with both women had changed irrevocably. He had come to realise over the previous few days that he had missed an opportunity with Angelika, without fully understanding its nature. Hannah clearly suspected that something had happened that night, but Josef could think of no way to tell her that she was mistaken.

Now, he stood on the edge of the viewpoint, some distance from Hannah and Angelika, looking at the road coiling in a series of hairpin bends before straightening out further down the valley and running towards the town on the other side of the border which they had decided to visit that day. None of them had ever been north of the Tarent Mountains or crossed the border into Bijela, and this was their last chance to visit the ancient kingdom before heading home. Only a church steeple and some gleaming black roofs were visible among the conifers and pines that clustered around the town.

The fresh northern breeze seemed to carry a promise of freedom and possibility that made Josef feel as if he might be able to extricate himself after all from the dreadful entanglements of V. But the euphoria gradually dissipated on the journey down the valley. The sharp turns and sudden drop in pressure made him feel queasy, and the conversation between Angelika and Hannah was so peppered with unknown names and obscure references that it might as well have been taking place in another world. When they crossed the border they noticed that some construction work was going on.

'It looks as if they are preparing for Bijela's independence,' said Angelika.

Two soldiers who were standing near a portacabin looked at the car as it passed. One was drawing on a cigarette. A billboard decorated with the flag of Bijela welcomed travellers in the words of its former language.

The town of G, built from the hard brown stone of the region, looked drear beneath the dark clouds that had sailed in from the north. After having lunch together in a bakery, with a clientele largely composed of friendly old ladies in hand-knitted cardigans and thick woollen skirts, Josef wandered off by himself. Angelika asked him with a worried expression if he was alright. Smiling weakly, he answered that he was okay; that he just wanted to give them some time to themselves.

He wandered around a local museum, looking at old farm machinery, a blackened fragment of an Iron Age sword, the cheek guard of a Roman legionary's helmet, a pair of leather buskins rescued from a nearby peat bog together with some pieces of checked cloth, a gleaming Ottoman scimitar from the collection of a local dignitary, and an iron buckler and a flintlock musket from the time of the conquest by King Corvus.

Afterwards, he started to feel sorry for himself, realising full well the self-destructive element in his nature that had deprived him of the women's company. He was approaching an old coaching inn, with an archway through to a cobbled courtyard, and wondering whether he could risk a small bottle of lager, when he saw Angelika and Hannah up ahead. Hannah smiled and raised her hand and Angelika turned to look at him, pulling some strands of wind-blown hair away from her face. He waved back, smiled, and glanced into a window of the inn. A handsome dark-haired man with unusually full lips was sitting at the window table inside. Josef could not think for the life of him why he recognised the man, who turned away at that moment to greet someone.

★

Sergei ordered a glass of white wine for the young woman without asking her what she wanted. She sat opposite him and looked out of the window at Josef's retreating back. Then she put her handbag on the table and opened its clasp.

'So, you like your new position?' Sergei said.

'Does it really matter to you whether I do or don't?'

'No, but your life is surely better than before.' Sergei took a drink of lager, wiped his mouth with the back of his hand and looked around the room, which was quiet at this time of day – just three locals, standing by a one-armed bandit near the bar, hardened drinkers by all appearances. 'What is he like, then, this American?' he said. She had been looking intently into her bag while they were talking, her long black hair swaying gently on either side of her throat.

'You've met him. You know as much as I do.'

'Men always give themselves away when they fuck.'

'You, of all people, believe that?'

'Tell me what you know.' There was a chilling edge to his voice, but, showing no fear, she began to shuffle things about in her bag, as if looking for something. Sergei remembered the similar movements of his mother's hand when she used to search for something in her handbag.

'He enjoys humiliating and hurting me and he never lets me see him come. Does that answer your question?'

'I'm just surprised that he has sent you with the instructions when you are so close to him. It is careless, and he doesn't strike me as a careless man, so I just wonder about his motives.'

'I really haven't got time for this. I have to meet him at the lodge in an hour.'

'So you have learned nothing?'

'He has told me that I am part of a deal, but not anything else about the deal. Judging by the jobs he has given me, everything that he does

172

he does to advance the interests of the corporation, and his own position within it, but you surely knew that before you bartered me.'

The light from the window was reflected on her glass. A bluebottle made a series of jerky back and forth movements on the table as it explored an arc of stickiness missed by an indolent waiter.

'Listen carefully to me,' Sergei said. 'Everyone has a weak spot, and I know where to lay my hands on yours. There is a point where his interests diverge from those of the corporation. You must use all your many charms to find that point. Now give me the instructions.'

She handed him a white envelope with a wax seal on which was impressed an alpha and omega. He checked the seal, then broke it and opened the envelope. Within the envelope was another (gummed) envelope and within that was a till receipt. Most of the letters and numbers had been blacked out with a marker pen.

'The message is given from right to left and from top to bottom,' she said, deliberately destroying the broken seal with her fingernails. 'The first six letters and numbers are an address code. Six kilometres north of this address there is a lay-by on the west side of the main road. Be there at one o'clock precisely tomorrow morning. The next eight numbers and letters form the registration number of the lorry that you should find parked there. You must give the driver the code formed by the remaining letters and numbers. That is all Chris has told me.'

The three drunkards turned in unison to ogle her as she made her way towards the exit on her clicking heels.

The satnav took Sergei to a service station some fifty kilometres north of the Kalimi Pass. He filled the tank of his BMW and parked up at the all-night diner. He had an hour to kill. It stretched out like the awful, empty steppe of his distant childhood, where his father worked as a mechanic on a collective farm – numbing his mind with vodka, periodically raping Sergei's mother and meting out regular beatings to Sergei and his siblings.

Sergei looked at the chef pressing a burger on the griddle with his spatula and at the pretty waitress in her yellow tunic. He whiled away the time calculating how much he could make from her over a three-month period in V. He thought about the takings lost following the riot in June, and the repair costs.

At five to one, he pulled out of the services and roared along the straight road to the north. The moorland climbed in gentle gradients towards the hills on either side. A plantation of firs formed a dark rectangle on the right-hand side of the road ahead, and some fifteen kilometres beyond rose another range of hills. The moon was hanging in the sky on his left, with only a sliver of shadow on one side to indicate that it was waning. Sergei focused on the catseyes and white lines illuminated by his headlamps. Three minutes later, they picked out the reflective tail lights of an articulated lorry parked in a lay-by on the left.

When he pulled in behind the lorry, an enormous man wearing a vest and jeans emerged from the cab and climbed slowly down. Sergei checked the number plate before switching off his engine and getting out of the car. The lorry driver stood with his folded arms resting on his belly, staring at him until Sergei recited the code, whereupon the driver lowered the tailgate of the lorry and pushed one end of a long wooden crate towards him. Similar crates were stacked, barely visible, in the darkness beyond. The driver helped Sergei lift the crate into the boot of his car. Two words stencilled on top of the crate had been crudely painted over. The terminal letter 'c' of the first word was still visible. The driver then bolted and locked the tailgate and climbed back into the cab without saying a thing.

When he got back into his car, Sergei washed down a pill with bottled water. Shortly afterwards, he felt a surge of excitement as he sped southwards along the road, foot pressed to the floor, utterly entranced by the broken white lines and twinkling catseyes unspooling on the tarmac.

The sun was still hidden behind Castle Hill when he drove through Vandrhaf Square early the next morning. He parked around the corner from the coffee shop on the waterfront and waited for some ten minutes. A white van, with the name of a plumbing firm printed on the side, slowed as it passed him, and Sergei pulled out behind it. He followed it through the gorge out of the city and on to the motorway that led to the Bohemian Coast.

Sergei had made it clear that if anything happened to him, then the authorities would be informed of Ben F's role in purchasing several automatic assault rifles plus ammunition, but he was still afraid of being led into a trap.

At the third junction the van led him off the motorway, and after several kilometres it turned down a narrow side road and stopped finally by a gate to a field shrouded in mist. A dark-skinned, bearded man with a scar on his left cheek climbed out of the passenger side of the van. He shook Sergei's hand and his mouth shifted into a smile, but his expression remained cold and there was something implacable in his dark brown eyes. It struck Sergei that he had never had dealings with anyone whose motives were so hard to read. The van driver, who was wearing overalls, gazed at them through the open doorway. Sergei was certain that he was armed.

Sergei opened his car boot, and the bearded man set to the lid of the crate with a chisel that he had fetched from the van. The four automatic assault weapons were not the latest models. Neither the scarred man nor Sergei knew that they had been part of a shipment originally intended for a warlord in S and had no marks or serial numbers to identify their manufacturer.

The scarred man then counted the spare magazines, and only after Sergei helped him carry the crate to the van did he hand Sergei the thick manila envelope containing the payment. Aside from the glistening spiderweb in the hedgerow, the confused tyre tracks in the reddish soil by the gate, and the lowing of cattle, the transaction was little different from the many in which Sergei had been involved over the years. And yet this one filled him with a strange disquiet and he was grateful to drive away from the scarred man and his curious invocations of God.

★

It was nearly noon when Franz stepped out of the shower and opened wide the bathroom window. He looked disparagingly at the green walls and ancient bathroom fittings. The only concession to the modern world was the chrome circular shower rail and the wall clip that he had fitted for the snaking rubber hose and spray so that he could take a shower without flooding the house.

As the condensation cleared from the cabinet mirror, the sight of his reflection filled him with self-loathing. His gaze moved from the bedroom farce of his genitals, over his bloated torso, to the weak chin bequeathed to him by his mother's brother, a reclusive, overweight misanthrope who had lived and died alone. Franz sometimes feared that he had inherited his uncle's fate together with his chin.

The few friends he had made during his undergraduate years had moved away to study in other universities. They seldom wrote and during their infrequent visits to V they tended to fit Franz in after seeing other, closer friends in the town. It was to one of those friends that he owed his meeting with Hannah, at a party in the previous year.

In retrospect, his tormented relationship with Hannah had all the splendour and glamour of a screen romance, but he felt now as if he was doomed to spend the rest of his days among the decaying props and faded dainties of his landlady's world.

As he made his way back to his room, with his clothes clinging in places to his damp body, he realised that his only hope of escape lay in his PhD on Edward H; but he had reached an impasse. With only the coincidence of a metaphor and the Persian poet Farid ud-Din Attar linking two pieces of writing, he saw no alternative but to embark on a desperate online search for the elusive essay writer, 'Zarathustra'.

There was no rhyme or reason that Franz could see in the order imposed by the search engine on his laptop. He knew that Nietzsche would figure prominently, as would the historical Zarathustra or Zoroaster, but when he entered other terms in a bid to refine the search, it merely expanded it in unpredictable ways. He resigned himself reluctantly to ploughing through pages and pages of Zarathustras. Not for the first time, he longed for the clarity and logic of the alphabetic system.

He found a transgender poet who styled themself 'Zarathustra' and who wrote desperate poems in blank verse expressing their passionate desire for someone called Morgana. Franz assumed that that, too, was a pseudonym. He found a black and white kitten named Zarathustra, with oversized ears and eyes, patting a curled hedgehog with one of its forepaws and fleeing in pain and fright. He found a photograph, taken by someone named Izzy Zarathustra, of a beautifully arranged bento meal in a restaurant in Kyoto. He found a video of an American youth who called himself 'Zarathustra', wore a Batman mask and ranted in a deep voice, edged with panic, about a conspiracy that was positioning all the furniture retailers in one part of his town for some ill-defined but sinister purpose. He found a leopard gecko, named Zarathustra, being dressed up by its owner in a pair of tiny sunglasses, a flashing collar and a pink broad-brimmed hat.

After two hours of this kind of gibberish, he stood up, pressed his hands to the base of his spine and stretched his back. He was close to giving up. His frustration and failure set his mind circling around Hannah, torturing him with unresolved doubts about her fidelity when they had been together, and imagined details of her current sex life. He went over to the window and pressed his forehead against the glass. A young woman walked by on the pavement below in jeggings and a yellow top that exposed her midriff. Two elderly women were talking outside the charity shop opposite. He saw a beggar in a pork-pie hat with a tangled white beard approaching the women. A black BMW roared past. Toying with the notion that all black objects brought luck, he returned to his worktable and clicked on the next page.

He worked through a loathsome article by a member of the Black Hand, extolling an Aryan Zarathustra and offering spurious justifications for the slaughter of immigrants; scrolled past the bedroom, cluttered with red and gold kitsch, belonging to a drag queen named Zaria Zarathustra, which momentarily distracted him from a carefully worded and cogent attack on an Islamist regime in the Middle East, written from a Marxist perspective and signed by 'Zarathustra'. It had been posted by someone called Kriss Kross, an anarchist punk, whose photograph next to the essay showed his shaved hair dyed in a green and black chequerboard. His sole purpose in uploading the essay was to condemn its Marxist author for contributing to a journal funded by the CIA. What excited Franz was the fact that the journal had been published in Arabic and English in B fourteen years before the city was comprehensively bombed in the recent war.

It was unclear where Kriss Kross had obtained his information, but he also stated that the CIA had funded the journal with the full support of the vicious dictator whose moustachioed portrait and statues then dominated the cityscapes of B and who was at that time engaged in a costly war with the Islamist regime attacked in the essay. Kriss Kross then launched into an incoherent, anti-communist rant.

Franz stopped reading. He thought it unlikely that the anti-imperialist 'Zarathustra' of the 1970s would countenance working for the CIA, but it was possible that he was unaware of their involvement in the journal. And what better way was there for the CIA to camouflage their presence than by including an essay by a Marxist? Franz decided to focus his research on events in and around B during the year the journal had been published, in the wild hope that finding 'Zarathustra' might lead him to Edward H.

Franz imagined himself a diplomat in a bespoke pinstriped suit, battling through the complexities of Middle Eastern politics as a knight of old might battle a dragon in a forest. He imagined himself living in a four-storey townhouse in the Capital with a cream stucco façade, a gleaming black door and a gold knocker. He imagined the tasteful master bedroom, with its teal and gold wallpaper, its elaborate plaster mouldings and its oak bedroom suite. He tried vainly to picture Hannah waiting for him in that bedroom, but his reverie was interrupted by a gentle knocking on his door. His heart sank when he heard the whining voice of his landlady calling his name.

He bookmarked the page on his laptop and spent the next hour trying to find a replacement bulb for her bedroom light, which she knew she had put somewhere but could not remember where. His search was accompanied by her laments about her failing eyesight, her various aches and pains, her loss of memory. He said he would go to the nearby supermarket to buy her a replacement, but she was adamant that she had one and, indeed, he did find a cache of spare light bulbs under a shawl in the hall cupboard, behind an old broken hoover and a box of cat litter that had been there since before the death of her cat, Tommy, six years earlier.

'That was my mother's shawl,' she said, close to tears. 'It was a present from Franco, no less, after her performance of *Madama Butterfly* in Madrid.'

By the time he returned to his room, Franz had lost all motivation to pursue his studies. He made himself a cheese sandwich and a mug of coffee. After he had eaten, he looked out his copy of *All-Consuming Passions*, but he could not concentrate on it. His mind was in a ferment and there was a hollow, sick feeling in his stomach. He thought about Hannah again. He could scarcely believe that they had ever had sex. Since she had split up with him, his fears of what she might be doing with other men had made him shy away from recalling what they had done together. Now he found it difficult to differentiate the reality of their shared past from the pornographic online videos that he watched in shame and despair.

He had four hours until he had to head out for work that evening. There was a new TV series offered by his streaming service – a political thriller based on an English novel, about a beautiful blonde actress recruited by Mossad to infiltrate a group of Palestinian terrorists. Franz had watched the first episode and been caught up immediately in the fate of the actress. The story appealed to his romanticised vision of work in the diplomatic services, and the cinematography created an alluring world of international intrigue that was more interesting than his tortuous, probably futile, search for 'Zarathustra'. He managed to convince himself that the TV series was relevant enough to his PhD to justify watching it.

There was little chance of further interruptions, since his landlady was expecting her gentleman friend to come for afternoon tea – a rather alarming, trimly built old man with a scar on his cheek, who sported a monocle and had a walking stick with an unusual silver wolf's-head handle. The jaws of the wolf were curled in a snarl, and its sharp teeth could easily cause an injury if you were careless in gripping the handle.

When they met for the first time, the old man had directed an insistent, searching gaze at Franz, one eye monstrously enlarged by the monocle, before saying that he had been a legionnaire in the Steel Wolves. Only later did Franz learn that this had been a paramilitary organisation of Nazi sympathisers in the 1930s, which had formed a brigade in the SS during the Second World War. Judging by his appearance, Franz reckoned the old fraud was no more than seventy years old and thus had not even been born when the war ended. It had soon become apparent that he was sponging off Franz's landlady.

The old man was making his way downstairs when Franz headed out that evening. He decided to wait on the landing until he heard the distinctive tapping of the old man's stick crossing the hallway below and the front door closing behind him. At that moment, his landlady came out of her sitting room, wearing a red silk dressing gown decorated in green and gold with the coils and scales of a Chinese dragon. When she saw Franz standing by his door, she pulled her lapels together and blushed.

He said, 'I'm late for work,' and then started down the stairs before she had a chance to say anything.

The wine bar where he worked was less than three hundred metres from the entrance to the flat. Its curved façade was situated at the corner of the next junction. Franz went to the back entrance of the wine bar, passed through the kitchen and crossed a corridor to the staff room. There was a sink at one end and a Formica worktop above a fridge. A kettle stood on the worktop beside jars of instant coffee, tea bags and sugar. Holiday postcards from staff members were stuck on the doors of a wall-mounted cupboard housing a motley collection of mugs and glasses. The staff lockers stretched along the opposite wall. A battered couch and armchair completed the furnishings.

Eleda, one of the waitresses who was working the same shift as Franz, was putting her jacket and handbag into her locker. She was wearing a black sleeveless top with a miniskirt and purple paisley tights. Franz could never fathom how she managed to do her job wearing three-inch stilettoes. She had a bat in flight tattooed on her left shoulder, monochrome save for the red drops of blood dripping from its fangs.

Franz had hoped he might have some time alone with her, but now, in her presence, he lost all self-composure. He knew that his arrival had irritated her, but he found her so attractive that he desperately wanted to say something to impress her. Casting around for a subject, he hit upon the TV series he had just been watching and he launched into a description of its unfolding plot. He sensed very soon that he was losing her in its complexities and that his explanatory digressions were only making matters worse. Eleda's irritation was turning to impatience and anger when she was rescued from this unpleasantness by the arrival of Ivan, the senior bartender.

Ivan was too clean-cut to appeal to Eleda, but she nevertheless took pleasure in the way his shirt showed off his muscular torso, and she enjoyed both his sense of humour and his confidence in expressing his opinions, even when she disagreed with them.

Franz had fallen silent when Ivan entered. He looked on as the senior bartender hugged Eleda and kissed both her cheeks; then he returned Ivan's greeting with a great show of enthusiasm before putting his canvas shoulder bag into his locker with his jacket and heading to the bar. He passed the new waitress, Olga, in the corridor, but he was too distracted and upset to pay her any attention.

By nine o'clock, the place was heaving. Ivan was mixing cocktails at the far end of the counter for a raucous group of young ladies out on the town. As always, Eleda seemed calm and collected, betraying little of her annoyance at the incompetence of the new waitress, who was struggling to cope. Franz had been in the job long enough to deal with the frenzy at the bar, but he disliked the pressure and he was beginning to resent the servile nature of his role.

He scarcely even noticed the many beautiful women there. When he had started working in the bar, he had felt as if sexual possibilities were opening up for him again, but the women were invariably accompanied by equally attractive partners, not always male. They all appeared wealthy and their arrogant self-entitlement seemed to justify all of Edward H's contempt for consumer capitalism, although Franz was too self-aware not to realise that his judgement was clouded by bitterness and envy.

He was surprised now to recognise Janos standing nonchalantly among the eager customers crowding the bar. Franz knew that Janos owned the nearby art centre, currently one of the most fashionable spots in V. He could not figure out why Janos had come here, until he noticed the auburn-haired woman with him. Her smile dimpled her cheeks and revealed the sexy gap between her front teeth, but the anxious expression in her eyes betrayed her discomfort. She lacked the self-assurance and arrogance of most of the other customers and was hanging back slightly, as if she did not want to be seen with Janos.

Franz was not sure what prompted him to take Janos's order before the customers already waiting at the counter, but, ignoring their angry looks, he opened an overpriced bottle of red wine, collected two glasses and filled bowls with olives and macadamia nuts – all charged to Janos's Platinum American Express card. As he put everything on a tray for Eleda, he watched Janos stroll over to a table occupied by a bald man and his girlfriend. The bald man was something of a dandy, in his designer clothes and trainers, but as soon as he saw Janos approaching he voluntarily surrendered his table. The two men acted like friendly acquaintances. They shook hands. The bald man introduced his girlfriend to Janos. Janos did not reciprocate by introducing the woman who was with him, but his gaze lingered on the other young woman and he held her hand for longer than was strictly necessary.

While the bald man and his girlfriend headed towards the exit, Katryn watched the young waitress returning to the bar with the empty tray and depositing Janos's generous tip in the large glass jar that the red-haired barman brought out from behind the counter. She remembered the other, more handsome barman from the last time she had come here with Eva. She tried unsuccessfully to remember his name.

She still felt out of place, despite the fashionable outfit she had bought with her mother's birthday cheque – a yellow and dark green plaid pinafore dress with a pale green top and matching leggings. It struck her that, after years of raising children, she did not know who she was or what she wanted out of life. She certainly did not know why she had accepted Janos's invitation. She looked across the table at him.

'That was Vasily K,' he said, and took a sip of wine.

'I didn't recognise him. He looks different now.'

She turned to watch Vasily following his girlfriend out of the bar. Katryn remembered the media frenzy surrounding the young artist's degree show when Charles Saatchi flew in from the UK to buy some of his controversial artworks. She remembered the commission Vasily had subsequently been given to decorate the restaurant of a famous chef in the Capital. At the time, she had been as jealous of his success as she had been contemptuous of his art, which had struck her as meaningless and trite when you stripped away the conceptual flam-flummery lapped up by the journalists.

The artist had attended parties given by the Prime Minister, together with writers and luminaries of the music world. There had been a consensus in the media that the country was undergoing a cultural renaissance.

'He's lost his hair,' said Katryn.

'And his New York gallery,' said Janos. 'He is worried now that I might change my mind about signing him up to my new gallery.'

'And will you change your mind?'

'Probably not. I have to think in the long term. He may well regain his popularity, but it is good that he is worried. What do you think of his art?'

'I never liked it.'

'Really? Why?'

'Does it matter what I think? I mean, you are signing him up.'

'I'm interested. I'd really like to know what you think.'

'Well, I thought his famous piece, the one with the stuffed vixen mirrored by her skeleton, was just a tired reworking of the symbolist cliché "Death and the Maiden".'

'I think I know what you mean, although no one has described it to me like that before. It might interest you to know that when we met to discuss his contract he described his new paintings as symbolist works. He claimed he took inspiration from cheap nineteenth-century prints of King Corvus and from the bloody melodramas of the Grand Guignol Theatre. Of course, his studio assistants have done most of the actual painting.'

'Did he show you the paintings?'

'Oh no, he is keeping them under wraps until King Corvus's Day. He is understandably nervous. There's a lot hanging on the success of his new work.' Katryn speared an olive with a cocktail stick. It was stuffed with feta and chilli. She took a drink of wine to take away the burn of the chilli. Janos looked down, rubbing his thumb with his forefinger for a moment, before adding, 'I plan to make one of his paintings the centrepiece in the opening exhibition of my new gallery, but the rest of the works will be by talented new artists. I have a large client base of contacts from my former profession. They're keen to buy artworks by undiscovered artists when there is more chance of making a large profit. It's a high-risk strategy, but my role is to reduce their risk and, so far, I've been remarkably successful at doing so.'

'Janos, why did you invite me here this evening?'

'I thought that was obvious.'

'You mentioned an "opportunity" in your email, but I have no idea what you mean by that.'

For a long interval, he said nothing. He just looked at her and smiled. His knee brushed hers under the table and withdrew. 'I want to employ you as a curator at my gallery here in V, of course. I thought I had made that clear.'

'Me?'

'Yes. I was impressed by your remarks about Daniela's prints at her private view. I need someone to assist me now that I have my new gallery.'

'But I am completely out of touch with the art world.'

'That is precisely why you are so suited to the job – that and your critical acuity. It is the combination I've been looking for.' There had been no further contact with her legs under the table. 'You're not saying anything,' he said.

'It seems too good to be true.' She was still buzzing from his brief touch, her mind lost in the labyrinth of possibilities.

'It's a genuine offer.'

She took a handful of macadamia nuts. She had not tasted them in years and had quite forgotten how much she liked them, but she stopped herself from taking more, for fear of appearing greedy.

'I'm not sure that I'm qualified for such a job.'

'Oh, there's nothing to it for someone like you, and anyway I will be with you at the start. We will visit artists' studios, degree shows and, of course, there are the submissions made by artists to the galleries. I am confident of your ability to detect the work of lasting value among the dross.' His leg brushed hers under the table again. He grinned and said, 'I'm sorry. I forgot how crowded and cramped it is here on a Saturday night.'

Katryn smiled awkwardly, drank some wine and tried to collect her thoughts.

Janos noticed a young and attractive woman sitting at a nearby table with two men. She was wearing an elegant black dress that must have cost a small fortune. Janos reckoned she was with the grey-haired man who was wearing a designer suit and a white linen shirt with a Nehru collar. The other man was young with black hair and the brutal good looks of a matinee idol. The grey-haired man leaned over and whispered something to the woman, who in evident annoyance stood up and headed to the ladies.

Sergei watched her wending her way between the tables. When she was out of earshot, he turned to Dimitrios and said, 'I could easily find you a more attractive and compliant woman.'

'But don't you see that it is Vera's wilfulness that draws me to her. I know that when she is with me she wants to be with me. You, my friend, have never had that pleasure.'

'I experienced it once, Dimitrios. It was you who showed me the impossibility of that relationship, as I recall.'

'Ah yes, I forgot. But you are my weapon, Sergei, and a weapon must not have feelings. Now, tell me about the American and the Arab. Particularly the American. What is his game? Why did he sell you the goods? What is the Arab planning?'

A group of solicitors were gathered round a nearby table. The men were all wearing pinstriped suits. The women wore formal blouses of various shades with dark skirts, sheer tights and high heels. When the waitress, Eleda, placed a single malt on the coaster by the older man at the head of the table, he asked if he might trace a certain path he had discerned in the pattern on her tights.

'You wish!' she said, avoiding his outstretched hand with a twist of her hip and making her way back to the bar.

A young man at another table interrupted his fiancée's monologue about the seating plan at their wedding to show her a video on his phone of a cute puppy – a red setter with large brown eyes, pressing its jaw and its forepaws into a fluffy blanket.

Chapter 6

SEPTEMBER

Anna had had no clients on the previous evening, and she returned from her lukewarm shower to find Alika waiting in her room. As usual, Anna tried to avoid looking at her scars. An overnight bag was lying unzipped on the bed.

'Sergei wants you to pack what you need for two days,' said Alika.

Sergei came to collect Anna before she had a chance to eat breakfast. Outside, it was grey and misty. The sharp intake of cold, damp air recalled autumn days in her home village, when the moisture carried from the Black Sea was released into the air by the morning sun. But her swell of happiness was cut short by the noise of the closing car door. With a pang of envy, Anna noticed a young, dark-haired woman crossing the road at the traffic lights with a French stick.

During the short, familiar journey, Sergei said nothing, but, just after he parked the car near the main entrance to Ben F's apartment block, he turned towards her, gripping the back of her seat, and asked her if Ben ever spoke about his life.

'He hardly speaks to me at all,' she said.

'Have you ever seen a bearded man with a scar on his cheek?'

'I don't know. He argued with a man when I was last there, but I was hidden in Ben's room. Ben didn't want him to know I was there. His woman is terrified of that man.'

'That is exactly the kind of information I require. Tell me everything you hear about Ben's life and his reasons for coming to V. Now go.' He told her the number to enter on the intercom.

'When am I to meet you?' she said.

Sergei automatically glanced at her cleavage, which was exposed when she leaned into the car. It was a weakness in himself that he deplored. 'Ben F will arrange the time.'

As Anna walked towards the entrance she reflected on what Sergei had said. She had never had such a clear impression that, for all his posturing, he was no freer than she was.

There was no sign of Ben F in the apartment. After admitting her, the woman hung Anna's coat on a hook by the door, took her bag into Ben's bedroom and then prepared a breakfast of sausages and eggs in tomato sauce with pitta bread, which she served at the breakfast bar. Anna offered to help with the dishes, but the woman refused emphatically and, after clearing everything away, she ushered Anna into her own bedroom.

There was a dressmaker's dummy there, modelling a red floral dress with a plunging neckline, which looked vaguely familiar to Anna. Speaking slowly and clearly, she asked the woman what her relationship was to Ben. She had to repeat the question several times, accompanying her words with gestures. Understanding finally dawned and the woman said a short sentence she had clearly rehearsed many times.

'He saved my life.'

Then she unzipped the dress and carefully removed it from the dummy, gesturing to Anna to take off her clothes. The dress proved to be too big. Its bodice hung down, revealing Anna's bra. The woman reached round to unhook the bra and slipped it off. Dropping the bra on the bed, she went to collect some pins from the dressing table.

She placed the pins between her lips and then pinned the dress strap above Anna's left breast. Next she raised Anna's left arm, indicating with a couple of slaps that she should keep it there while she pinned the seam under her armpit. She repeated the process on the other side and then nodded and smiled. It was the first time Anna had seen her smile. She grasped Anna's shoulder and gently turned her round, before unzipping the dress and working it down over Anna's arms, carefully, to avoid disturbing the pins.

The door opened and Ben F was about to enter the room. He stopped at the sight of Anna's naked back emerging from the dress, looked down, apologised and closed the door again.

Anna put her bra back on and reached for her dress, but the woman shook her head and offered her a towel to cover herself before leading her to one of the bathrooms. A stool had been set up in the middle of the floor. A framed photograph stood rather incongruously on the marble surface beside the sink. Next to it were a comb and a pair of scissors. Only when she sat down on the stool did Anna realise why the red floral dress material looked so familiar. It was like that of the dress worn by Ben F's wife in the photograph, which she saw now was the one of his family that had been on the dresser in his bedroom.

When the woman started to cut her hair, Anna was overwhelmed by waves of panic and horror. It was as if the woman was removing the last vestiges of Anna's real self, reducing her to nothing more than an implausible figment. She looked in despair at Ben's wife smiling in the sunlight of the past, the red of her dress contrasting with the rich blue colour of the tiles with their elaborate patterns suggestive of labyrinths or oriental gardens.

Anna did not know how long she waited in the woman's bedroom with the naked dummy. The sun was gradually setting. Through the window, she could see the river losing its orange lustre and taking on the grey gleam of the sky above while the street lamps running along the waterfront flickered on one by one. The dark outline of a villa was visible above a cluster of trees on the top of the cliff. Lights appeared in some of its windows.

The woman returned with the floral dress draped over her arm and indicated again that Anna should take off her clothes. When the woman zipped up the back of the dress, Anna looked at her reflection in the tilted mirror on the dresser. In the half-light she could almost pass for Ben F's wife. A shiver ran down her spine. She recalled a film about a mummy's curse which she had watched as a child with Bagarian's son, under the lax supervision of the boy's Norwegian mother. The mummy of an Egyptian priest was set on reincarnating his queen in the identical form of the modern English heroine.

Arabic music filtered into the room. Anna was certain it was the same female singer she had heard the last time she had been there. The woman took her to the roof garden, where Ben F was waiting in a caramel-coloured sports jacket with a floral shirt and cream trousers. Anna saw tears welling up in his eyes when he caught sight of her. A brazier stood nearby, filled with glowing coals. The music system had been set up on the coffee table brought out from the lounge. Coloured lights played upon the water in the pool. Food and drink were laid out on the table. Anna could see City Hall on Castle Hill, silhouetted like an ancient fortress against the swathe of orange sky.

She wanted to scream at Ben F that she was not his wife, but she merely stood on the decking, awkwardly shifting from foot to foot, until he came over, took her hand and led her over to the food. The woman disappeared into the apartment.

Neither Anna nor Ben had much appetite. Ben was drinking wine. He poured a glass for her.

'I'm not meant to drink wine,' he said, and indeed it seemed to have affected him already, as if he had not had alcohol for a long time. 'But I am no longer sure what I believe or whose side I am on. Deception becomes a habit that is difficult to break.' They sat down on chairs near the brazier. Its flickering light reflected off their faces and burnished the whites of their eyes.

'Your woman told me that you saved her life.'

'She is not my woman,' he said, 'and I am sure she exaggerates.'

'Why have you had me dressed in your wife's clothes and had my hair cut in her style? I can never be like her. I am nothing more than a slave.'

'Sometimes an illusion is all a man requires, but of course you are right. Then again, she and I were not so different from you, although we didn't realise it until it was too late.' He looked down and took a swig of wine. 'Have I told you that I used to be a communist?'

'Yes.'

'A faith, like any other; well, more rigid than some. When we settled down to married life in B, my wife and I both thought we would never lose that faith in the better world that was coming. But when you wear a mask for any length of time you can lose sight of who you are.'

'Why are you talking in riddles?' Anna said, showing her exasperation despite herself.

'I thought you might understand. After all, you must have to bury your own feelings very deep.'

'Me, I'm a china doll. I have no feelings.'

'Perhaps. Let me be clear: I am not foolish enough to compare the role I adopted to the one that has been forced on you. I myself thought it ludicrous, but with my skills as a journalist I became a sports writer for one of the main newspapers in B. What better way to hide yourself in plain sight? The job paid well. We were able to raise a family, live comfortably within the limits set by the dictatorship. We acquired a circle of friends. My wife wore her red floral dress on the final happy occasion of our life together – a dinner party. The children were sleeping in their rooms. The guests had all departed. We left the dishes for the morning and we made love passionately for the last time.'

'Ah,' said Anna.

'But my article had appeared the previous weekend, so our paths were already set. The Dictator's elder son had been placed in charge of sports. He had used his money and position to assemble a football team. Of course, it performed well in the league. How could it not? There were rumours that he tortured those who played badly. Asked by my editor to write an article on their league victory, I devoted all my rhetorical flourishes to the task.

'The Dictator's son invited my wife and me to the celebration party at his palace. He would brook no refusal. Ulay – let us call him by his name – coveted my beautiful wife. Two of his henchmen grabbed her when she went to the toilet. When I refused to accept the situation proposed by one of his lackeys, I was dragged away. The other guests averted their eyes. Three of Ulay's guards systematically beat me in a room specially reserved for such purposes and threw me out of the palace.

'I will spare you the details of what happened to my wife. You, I am sure, know all there is to know of men's desires. She was returned to me two days later, alive, more or less. The surgeon who treated her was threatened. They threatened my children in order to silence me. My wife never fully recovered from her ordeal. We never made love again.'

'What did you do?'

'What else can you do when you are powerless? I offered my services to those capable of hurting my enemy. And now the Dictator and both his sons are dead. But so too are my wife and children.'

Anna did not know what to say. The horrors of the world seemed endless and implacable, but, for all that Ben understood the contradictions of their relationship, like all men he continued to take advantage of her.

'Why cannot we, just for this one evening, imagine that our lives are otherwise than they are?' he said.

★

When Anna emerged from the lift two days later, she encountered a young woman approaching from the main entrance, carrying a jute tote bag advertising a supermarket chain. Some strands of wind-blown hair partially covered the cleft on the woman's chin. She was slouching slightly, as if she was self-conscious about her height. Indeed, despite her flat shoes, she was taller than Anna.

Anna realised that she had seen her in the building before, in the lift. She remembered Sergei's predatory gaze. It was a way he had of looking at all attractive young women who were not in his power. Anna believed that there was no real sexual desire in that gaze. It was a look of cold calculation.

The woman smiled at Anna in passing. Anna found it difficult to smile back, as if her facial muscles were no longer capable of a natural response. She recalled Ben F's comment about wearing a mask as she shifted her bag on to her other hand and pressed the green button to release the lock.

★

In the lift, Hannah tried to remember where she had seen the woman before, but she was too agitated to think clearly. Stefan had been so distant and self-possessed during their recent dates that she feared she was losing him. A kind of madness had taken hold of her. She could not stop thinking about him, and her money worries were compounded by recurring panic attacks. And yet she was incapable of communicating her feelings when they were together. They would talk about books, or the deplorable political situation, any number of topics, while she became desperately aware that time was slipping away and she had failed once again to find any resolution. Then it had occurred to her to invite him to the apartment for lunch; it seemed such an obvious solution that she wondered why she had not thought of it before.

At the supermarket that morning, she had been unable to find several key ingredients for the Moroccan tajine she had planned to cook. After wandering up and down the aisles in a state of anxious indecision, she had finally managed to gather the makings of an Italian meal, even going so far as to buy Parma ham and salami for Stefan.

As she exited the lift and headed to the apartment the strap of her handbag started to slide down her shoulders. It slipped off just as she reached the door. The reflex of trying to catch it made her drop the carrier bag, smashing a jar of passata. Thankfully, all the other items in the bag were canned or wrapped in plastic, but it was a messy and laborious business to wipe them clean and set them out on the worktop. She looked in vain on the jute carrier bag for any indication that it was machine washable.

There was no time now to replace the passata before Stefan arrived, so she rooted around in Josef's cupboard until she discovered a tin of tomato and basil soup. By then she was beginning to question the whole idea of the lunch date. She kept picking up her phone while she prepared the pasta sauce, but she could not bring herself to make the call. When the appointed hour approached, her stomach began to dip and tremble.

*

Stefan was lying awake in bed. It was 6.30 in the morning. He did not have to get up for anything, so it was ludicrous to wake so early after a late night. Increasingly often, his sleep was disturbed by elusive and dreadful dreams that left him with a feeling of anguish. Occasionally, as this morning, he would be woken so suddenly from a deep sleep that he would lie for untold minutes in a state of blind panic, sweat cooling on his body. He was lying on his left side, as he used to do when snuggling into Elena, and he could hear his heart pounding through the mattress. He tried to remember the dream, but the vague image of figures moving in a wood-panelled room gave no hint of what had frightened him out of his sleep.

Shortly afterwards, he heard a soft knocking on the bedroom door and Nina entered holding the baby monitor, which amplified the slow, regular breathing of his sleeping daughter.

Several weeks earlier, Nina had grown tired of waiting for his erratic and infrequent visits to her room and – on weekdays when Elena was working in the Capital – had started to come to his room before Natalia woke up. After the first such visit, he had decided to break off the relationship, but he was unable to do so because he feared how she might react, or so he reasoned. Now, she was coming three or four times a week. Stefan was convinced that he was in love with Hannah, but he was caught up with Nina in this shameful sexual liaison that increasingly felt like a trap.

Outside these visits, they never discussed what was happening, which made it seem to Stefan as if his life were splitting into two distinct parts. In one of them, Natalia, Nina and he coexisted in a daylight world of humdrum pursuits and clearly delineated relationships, while, in the other, Nina, sensing his reluctance, was driven to a desperate passion that would end up infecting him.

The sound of Natalia's breathing could be heard again, coming from the monitor on Stefan's copy of *The Journey to Varnak* on the bedside table, beside a box of paper handkerchiefs, a crumpled paper hankie and a noise-operated stainless-steel lamp, which had switched on and off several times during Stefan and Nina's lovemaking.

Stefan lay on his back with his arm around Nina's shoulder while she rested her head on his chest and clung on to him with arm and thigh. Neither spoke. Only once, in the throes of his orgasm, had Stefan said that he loved her. She was still waiting for him to say it again. As she listened to the dull thuds of his heart and pressed her crotch against his thigh she remembered the exhilaration she had felt the first time they had made love. It had seemed as if she had finally solved the intractable puzzle of her existence. But now everything appeared precarious. Her desire for him became more intense the more she feared losing him, and she dreaded what might happen if she told him.

A series of noises and sighs came from the baby monitor, before they heard Natalia's voice describing her dream in a matter-of-fact tone to her favourite soft toy – a penguin with a red and green knitted scarf. Nina reluctantly let go of Stefan. He watched her with his hands behind his head as she pulled on her pants and nightie. When she left the room, still trying to push her arm into the elusive sleeve of her dressing gown, he briefly glimpsed the mysterious woman he had so ardently desired in the first months after she moved in.

Natalia was now teaching her penguin some of the words that Nina had taught her from her new storybook. Stefan noticed that his daughter gave them a Polish pronunciation. He judged that, during the intervals between each short sentence, Natalia was holding the toy's yellow felt beak to her ear as if it were repeating the words back to her in penguin-speak.

Stefan picked up the monitor. It was unlike Nina to forget to take it with her. He toyed with the idea of going to see his daughter, but he couldn't remember the last time he had dressed her in the morning. He worried that it would alarm her if he appeared, instead of Nina, and anyway Natalia was still chatting happily to her penguin. As happened every morning, Stefan gradually let go of the idea that he had to do something. Now, he contented himself with looking at the band of light on the wall by the window, which was coloured yellow close to the frame by the reflection from the curtain material. He could scarcely remember the time in his life when this feeling was limited to the few weeks' holiday that he had in a year, but as he lay there looking at the play of light on his wall and listening to the happy prattling of Natalia through the distortions of the speaker, he began to feel sliding sensations of anxiety in his stomach, for which he could initially find no cause.

He put the monitor down and reached for his copy of *The Journey to Varnak*. He was nearing the end of his second reading and wanted to finish the book before seeing Hannah later. It distressed him that the novel, which had brought Hannah and him together, should now have become a source of discord between them. He had started to reread the novel to understand why her reading differed so much from his own.

As he slipped the receipt he was using as a bookmark into the front of the book and began reading the closing chapter, he heard Nina entering Natalia's bedroom and saying, 'Where's my maly ptak?' He heard Natalia's joyful response and then the click of the monitor being switched off.

The final chapter of *The Journey to Varnak* opens with the narrator being abandoned by Anya, just as the prince had been abandoned by the sorceress, Malastrina, shortly before the destruction of the city by the sea. Stefan understood this recurring theme as the author's anguished response to the death of his wife, whereas Hannah interpreted it in a more positive light as a celebration of the author's marriage, which had owed its success to the freedom and equality of Gyula's wife. Hannah had argued that the narrator in the novel is not a mere stand-in for the author and that it was the narrator's failure to recognise Anya as an individual beyond his selfish passion for her that led Anya to abandon him, just as the prince's attempt to bind Malastrina to him leads to the destruction of the city by the sea.

Hannah had further argued that it is in the ambiguity of Malastrina's role in the city's destruction, in the fantastical description of the mountains towards which Anya journeys after abandoning the narrator, and finally in the filigree of the merchant's brooch that she found the true greatness of Gyula's writing. Stefan had no idea what Hannah meant by this, and was none the wiser now as he read the closing words of the novel.

He realised that the background white noise that had been unconsciously irritating him for some time was coming from the baby monitor. He switched it off and closed the book. Then he lay on his back and stared at the ceiling. He had always used fictitious business meetings to hide his dates with Hannah, but since he had started having sex with Nina he had found it harder to lie to her convincingly. This was not his only anxiety about his impending lunch date, and he gradually lost himself in a labyrinth of possibilities and speculations.

★

Nina looked through the kitchen window at the small patch of blue sky above the screen of trees and bushes to the west. She was having a coffee at the breakfast bar, from where she could supervise Natalia, who was sitting very upright on the beanbag in the playroom beside her toy plastic cooker, hosting a tea party for her penguin, a plush giraffe with a floppy neck (her former favourite), a baby doll in a red and white striped pinafore and a teddy bear with a purple ribbon tied in a bow around its neck. Stefan had just left. He had not been sure how long the meeting would last. He had said he would text her.

That morning, the postman had delivered a letter and a parcel for Nina. Her mother wrote that she had been clear of cancer for two months now and that the doctors seemed optimistic. She thanked Nina for the extra money she had sent from her savings, promising to pay her back as soon as possible. It occurred to Nina that Stefan had not asked about her mother since the night she had told him of her cancer. It had been the night of the Martyrs' Procession. She recalled Stefan comforting her with a hug, which was quite out of character. She told herself that it was his unusual sensitivity that prevented him from talking about her mother's illness; that he was waiting for her to volunteer the information when she was ready to do so.

As always, her mother mentioned Nina's ex-boyfriend, Jan. She made a point of telling Nina that his car dealership was thriving. Then she closed the letter by lamenting her daughter's taste for the kind of bohemian wastrel that had bedevilled her own life. Nina recalled Jan mooning over her when he was a mechanic in his father's garage and she was sleeping with Kruk, the singer in a heavy metal band, whose real name she could no longer remember. She recalled the way her father used to shrug and wink at her during her mother's many outbursts of anger.

The parcel contained a book she had ordered. The partially burned antique plan of a fortified city was reproduced on its cover. The title, *Podróż do Warnaku*, and author's name, Gyula K, were printed on its charred and blackened upper-right quarter. Nina had noticed that Stefan was reading the Hungarian novel for the second time and she had ordered the recently published Polish translation online. Although she could speak her adopted language well and read children's books to Natalia with ease, she had decided to read *The Journey to Varnak* in Polish because she was eager to understand Stefan's fascination with the novel, as if doing so might offer an insight into the many mysteries of his life. While reading the blurb, she caught something of her grandmother's intonation at family celebrations when issuing instructions to Nina's mother and aunts as they helped to prepare meals in the steam-filled kitchen of her country cottage.

Stefan never spoke to Nina about books. He seemed to be completely unaware of the small collection of treasured novels she had brought with her from Poland. He did not know that she had studied literature and film studies at university, but then she had never talked about her studies, or the disappointing, poverty-stricken years in Warsaw following her graduation.

In truth, she seldom read books now, devoting her spare time to watching films and connecting with her Polish friends on social media. It was a source of regret that her parents did not own a computer or a smartphone. Her father refused to waste money on any of that crap. He considered that digital technology had destroyed the film industry. And so Nina would have to sit down to write a reply to her mother and then buy a stamp to post it.

She looked over at Natalia, who was completely immersed in her imaginary party. It would soon be time for the child's morning walk. Nina thought she might check the Polish translation against Stefan's copy of *The Journey to Varnak* while she finished her coffee.

'I'm just going upstairs to get something,' she said to Natalia, who looked at her and smiled. Natalia was gathering her plastic cups, saucers and plates when Nina returned to the kitchen. 'Bring them over here if you want me to wash them with the lunch dishes,' said Nina, getting into the game. 'We'll go for our morning walk when I finish my coffee.'

Nina looked at the painting reproduced on the cover of Stefan's book. She envied the looks of the woman portrayed in the emerald dress, wondering if Stefan would love her more if she resembled that woman. Then she compared the opening paragraphs. The Polish version had an archaic quality, but Nina didn't know his language well enough to judge the style of the translation in Stefan's copy. As she flicked through more pages of his book a piece of paper slid out on to the worktop.

'Here they are,' said Natalia, carefully balancing a pile of cups, saucers and plates, which tottered and fell, scattering with a succession of plastic percussions across the stone tiles.

'Oh dear!' said Nina. 'But no harm done.'

Natalia looked dismayed, tears brightening her eyes. Nina lifted her up and sat her on her lap, stroking her hair and murmuring reassurances. Only then did she notice the address written in black ink on the piece of paper. Still clasping Natalia in her left arm, she turned the paper over and saw that it was an itemised receipt for a meal for two in the Luda Brasserie, dating from the evening of the Martyrs' Procession.

★

Daniela reread the email, her initial surprise and shock giving way to feelings of distress and nausea. Her hands were trembling. Her heart pounded and her tears made it difficult to see the words on her phone screen. Janos started off by apologising profusely, but he was afraid that there would now be no room for her prints in the opening exhibition of his new gallery in the Capital. The message continued with further cloying and unconvincing regrets. He insisted that this was in no way a reflection on the quality of her work, before concluding that a fledgling gallery had to move with the times if it were to survive in the current economic climate.

Janos had abandoned his original plan for the opening exhibition back in August. He had told Daniela that its new title would be 'Founding Myths: King Corvus Re-imagined', although he had been at pains to assure her that she was free to interpret the theme in any way she wanted. She had had to set aside the prints on which she had been working and take a month off her evening supermarket job to complete two prints in time for the deadline. Janos had given her to believe that in her case the selection procedure would be a mere formality.

Both the prints were collages, but Daniela had inserted two of her own recent woodcuts into them and she had made the collages using the old-fashioned paper technique of cut and paste. In the vintage market near the flat, she had discovered two early twentieth-century hand-coloured prints of King Corvus, created by a mediocre follower of Dagomar, which portrayed the king in the style of his legendary predecessor Vaclav, ruler of the fabled kingdom by the sea.

The first showed Corvus armoured and mounted on a white horse at a tournament. His shield bore the image of a crow with spread wings and he had raised his sword to catch the sky blue garter thrown by his queen, who sat among her ladies-in-waiting on the royal stand – all rendered in the bright colours of a fairy tale illustration. In the background Daniela placed an intense colour photograph, taken from an old calendar, of the Tarent Mountains at sunset. In between these two images, and in stark contrast, she inserted her black and white woodcut of a hilltop rising above conifers, where a group of men clad in black uniforms were frozen in the act of crucifying a young Islamic woman in a torn black robe. Her face was veiled save for her eyes, which formed the focal point of the collage, creating the uneasy impression that she was staring directly at the viewer.

The hand-coloured print in the other collage owed a debt not only to Dagomar but also to several nineteenth-century English paintings of *The Death of Arthur*. The print made no effort to portray a purely medieval scene. King Corvus lay on his bier in his eighteenth-century uniform on a narrow stretch of sand at the foot of a rugged granite cliff on the Bohemian Coast. A row of maidens in medieval clothing stood with bowed heads, the colours of their dresses matching those of the country's seven provinces, including the white of recently conquered Bijela. The sea, rippling with the gold of the setting sun, curved in a broad bay to the southern headland, where another grey cliff rose from a pile of boulders, and a single-masted boat approached the coast with a woman standing in the helm. Its billowing sail bore the image of the sacred heart superimposed on a golden cross.

Daniela had pasted a woodcut of the City Hall in V on to the print so that it resembled a fortress on top of the southern cliff. King Corvus's banner was hanging above the crenellations next to a banner bearing the open pair of compasses, stylised tower, and initials of the ANH Corporation. Taking advantage of a ledge on the near cliff, Daniela had inserted a monochrome photograph, cut into an acute triangle, of Nazi SS stormtroopers, viewed obliquely from behind so that they appeared to be marching towards the fortress.

Daniela thought of the lost wages and of the fact that she had been covering Halina's rent until her friend could get a job. She tried to figure out how much was left of the money she had received for the prints sold in her July exhibition. She reckoned around two hundred thalers. She tried to reassure herself that everything would be alright. She would be starting back at the supermarket at the weekend. Halina had just found a job in the office of a plumbing firm and would soon be able to clear her debt. Daniela took several deep breaths. They would get by.

A David Bowie playlist was blasting out of her iPod dock's rather tinny speaker. It was 13:48 according to her phone. She closed the email app and the screen reverted to the home page photograph of her grandmother's pet wolfhound lying by the stove in her parents' flat. A small circular icon of a pretty smiling woman signalled that a message had come through, but Daniela did not feel like reading it.

She looked at the two battered box files on the desk, in which she kept her collection of images gleaned over a ten-year period from magazines, academic journals and old books. She remembered the be-musement of the immigration officer at the airport outside V when he opened one of those files and searched through its contents for contraband. She thought that would make a great subject for a print, and she wondered what subtle theme she might weave from the mass of partially obscured images scattered on his counter.

She thought of the months she had shared the flat with Hannah. She thought about the scarred woman from the massage parlour down the road, who had been in the bakery that morning. Only gradually did she become aware of some troubling, insistent sounds, but she had no idea of when they had started. She switched off the music and realised it was Halina calling from her room, but her words remained indistinct, with a haunting, elusive quality that reminded Daniela of a recent nightmare. Her sense of foreboding was only confirmed when Halina suddenly screamed her name. Daniela found her friend in the living room, sobbing and keying something on to her phone.

'Daniela, it is dreadful! I am calling the police. They are raping her! There is a little girl.'

Between the bars in Halina's bedroom window, Daniela saw three members of the Brotherhood struggling with a young woman in the courtyard below. Two of them were holding her down and stifling her screams, while a third clawed at her skirt and tights. A large blue wheelie bin hid them from the little blonde girl who was clutching a toy penguin and crying near the entrance to the passageway that connected with the street. Daniela instinctively drew back from the window. When she returned to the living room, Halina was giving their address to the emergency services.

'They'll be too late,' said Daniela from the doorway, before pulling on her DMs and heading downstairs to the front door.

She heard Halina shouting, 'You mustn't go. The police and ambulance are on their way.' By then Daniela was running down the stairs and out the main entrance. The door banged behind her but did not close.

The only person in sight was an elderly woman looking bewildered and terrified by the entrance to the empty shop next door. Daniela ran into the vegan cafe just around the opposite corner and began to shout incoherently. The place was crowded. The people near the entrance turned to look at her without surprise, as if such outbursts were a common occurrence.

'Don't you understand? They are raping a woman! We have to stop them!' she yelled, almost weeping with frustration. More people turned to look at her. Odd phrases stood out in the unexpected quiet.

A slim black man with delicate features stood up from his laptop and said, 'Please try to be calm. You must tell us where they are.'

A heftily built man and a woman with her hair bound in a bandana came out from behind the counter. Another man with a blue plaster on his right index finger joined them. They seemed to Daniela to be moving with agonising deliberation. She became intensely aware of a woman in the kitchen putting down her knife, walking over to the counter by the till and looking at her with a quizzical expression. Two female customers at a nearby table rose from their unfinished soup. One had a shaven head. The other, with hennaed dreadlocks, nodded at Daniela, who now turned to pull open the door.

With sudden urgency, the six of them hurtled out of the cafe and followed Daniela to the nearby passageway. Daniela picked up the little girl, who was still standing at the entrance to the courtyard, and began to run with her back towards the street.

'They're behind the wheelie bin,' she said to the heftily built man, who ran across the courtyard beside the black man, the others following close behind. From the pavement where she stopped to stroke the little girl's hair and murmur reassurances, Daniela heard a cacophony of screams, expletives and shouted threats. A gunshot rang out. There was a prolonged cry. Then two of the Brotherhood men appeared in the passageway, looking back over their shoulders and cursing, while the third fell headlong between them with his trousers uncovering his buttocks. Daniela turned and ran, bearing the girl inside the main entrance to her flat just before the three men reached the pavement. The stippled glass shivered in its frame when she forced the door closed. She saw the distorted shapes of people coming from the direction of the cafe and prayed that the men were too distracted to see where she had gone. Then Halina came downstairs and took the little girl from her.

'You can stay with us until our friends get your mummy,' said Daniela to the fearful child, who was looking at her over Halina's shoulder. 'Everything will be alright now.'

Halina sat down on the couch with her and said, 'What's your name, my little one?'

The child had stopped crying and was looking around in frank amazement through dark brown sparkling eyes.

'Natalia,' she said, after a moment.

'That's a beautiful name. And what is your penguin called?'

'Lumi.'

'Like the princess in the fairy tale. Now, you must not be afraid. Your mummy will be here soon.'

'She's not my mummy. She's Nina.' After a moment of reflection, the girl added, 'You talk just like Nina.'

Through the window in Halina's room, Daniela could see the shaven-haired woman and her companion comforting Nina, who was looking about her, sobbing, and screaming Natalia's name, with blood running down her legs. The heftily built man was lying on the ground, clutching his stomach, his face twisted into a mask of pain, while the black man knelt beside him supporting his neck. The man with the blue plaster and the woman in the bandana emerged from the passageway, shaking their heads.

Daniela opened the window and shouted: 'The little girl is safe in here with us. We have called an ambulance, and the police are on their way.'

★

Stefan looked around the room, at the oak wood furniture; at the arrangement of cosmetics, lipsticks and nail varnish bottles on the dressing table; at the framed print on the wall above the chest of drawers, which he recognised as the same as the one he had bought from the artist at the private view to which he had gone in July. He tried to remember her name as his gaze wandered over the floor where his clothes were entangled with Hannah's.

Hannah was lying on her side, naked, with her arm around his stomach and her leg across his thighs. He drew her long hair away from her face and ran his finger over her cheek and across the cleft on her chin. Only now did it strike him that the bed on which they were lying was a sofa bed, like the one he had installed in the office by his library. He wondered if she had folded it out specially for their lovemaking, or whether she kept it out permanently.

The extraordinary excitement he had felt when Hannah had kissed him suddenly after lunch had carried through their passionate fumbling with each other's clothes in her bedroom, and the slight awkwardness of their foreplay, to the stormy conclusion on the bed. Only now was the warm afterglow giving way to anxious thoughts about Nina, Elena and Natalia.

He became conscious that Hannah was embracing him exactly as Nina had done that morning, and he was troubled now by memories of his lovemaking with Nina. He had never felt the overwhelming excitement with her that he had experienced with Hannah that afternoon, but there had never been any awkwardness with Nina and he didn't have the doubts with her that he had now, about whether Hannah shared his passion or had achieved an orgasm. For all his mental handwringing, Stefan could not deny that he felt a scarcely admissible thrill at bedding two women on the same day.

'I wonder what time it is,' he said.

'So, time hasn't stopped for you. What a shame. Just as you were showing fresh signs of life.' Thinking his wife must be waiting at home, she disengaged from him brusquely and, squatting on the floor, began to gather up their clothes, tossing his haphazardly towards him as she did so. He wanted to say something, but he could think of nothing that might redeem the situation. He had to phone Nina anyway, he thought, as he reached over the side of the bed for his briefs, which were bright red with a broad blue waistband.

It was only when he retrieved his phone that he noticed the numerous missed calls. He did not recognise the number, but he had an awful sense of foreboding when he pressed the screen to return the last call, without thinking to check his voicemail.

'Ah, Mr J.' The voice was female. It sounded strained and tired. The woman made no effort to hide her annoyance. 'I have been trying to reach you for over an hour.'

'I'm sorry, but how did you get this number?'

'I haven't got time to go into that now. It is the Queen Erzsébet Hospital. Ms W is here with your daughter.'

'My daughter? What … ?'

'Your daughter is fine, Mr J. But please come right away.'

'Is Nina …'

'Really, Mr J. Please come now. If you identify yourself at reception in the obstetrics department on Level 4, you will be directed where to go.'

★

Josef was working late in the office on some particularly complex problems that had arisen from two separate tenders for the police department in V. He had already been working for over a month on a tender to supply the police force with guns.

A journalist from the *Čuvar* had been sending repeated enquiries about that tender; Josef was unsure how she had obtained his email address. Chris wanted to award the tender to Briggs Firearms, Inc., an American firm that had recently been sold off by Dynamic Systems as a cost-cutting measure following its takeover by the ANH Corporation. Briggs specialised in the manufacture of hunting rifles, military assault weapons, light machine guns, and pistols. The journalist was asking pointed questions about the sale and the new owners. Josef recalled the insider trading scandal over the takeover, which had cost the previous MP for V his seat in parliament and had cast suspicion on several prominent businessmen in the city.

The other, more controversial, tender arose from a proposal by the ruling party in parliament that private security firms should take on the anti-terror role that was currently handled by the police. The proposal was a response to two terrorist attacks in the Middle East: one on a US military base near the city of B; the other targeting the airbase used by the country's small air force for its recent bombing raid in support of the US.

Neither of the contracts had the support of the Police Commissioner in V, who thought they represented attempts by both local and central government to undermine his authority.

Chris had also indicated to Josef the company he had in mind for the second tender, impressing on him the sensitive nature of the contract and the public scrutiny it would arouse. No suspicions of illegality or corruption could be countenanced in the successful tender; it was up to Josef to ensure that there was no evidence of wrongdoing.

Josef felt isolated and trapped. There was no one he could turn to. He glanced at the reflection of his face in the window, lit by the glow of the computer screen, as he studied the details of the private security firm on the official US government database, searching – like the young man in the fairy tale – for the secret path through the forest that would lead to the demon's lair, although Josef was very conscious in this instance that he was working for the demon.

It was against the black background of that window that he now saw his office door opening to reveal the CEO. Ildiko's pale face was visible in the shadows beyond, illuminated by the emergency lighting in the empty expanse of the call centre.

'Ah, still at your desk, Josef,' said Chris. 'I imagined you had forgotten to clock off, but here you are.'

'I thought I would put in some overtime on the security tenders.'

'There was something I wanted to ask you, out of office hours. That's why Ildiko and I are here; just on the off chance that you were still at your desk.' He turned to Ildiko and added, in a louder voice, 'And here he still is.'

'I could have come to your office earlier today.'

'I have only your best interests at heart, Josef. I merely wanted to ask you if you knew why Daria hasn't been at work for the past two days, and I didn't want rumours to spread around the office.'

None of this made any sense. Chris's reasoning was absurd. Josef looked at him in unfeigned perplexity.

'I haven't had any contact with Daria for nearly two months. Surely you know why?'

'Office gossip says otherwise.'

'I can't be held responsible for the misapprehensions of others,' said Josef, an edge of panic in his voice.

'That's true, Josef. But I feel it's only fair to warn you that others think you are still involved with her. Heaven forbid that anything bad should happen to her, but if something does, it is as well to be prepared for what others might say. Now, how are things going with our private security firm?'

'It's a complicated business, and you must remember the massacre in B.'

'The company has been cleared of all charges there. You well know the lengths to which certain groups are willing to go in that region. They think nothing of sacrificing civilians to protect themselves.'

'It's more about its reputation – the fears that a similar mistake might happen here. Also, a lot of suspicion surrounds one of its major shareholders: Dimitrios Y.'

'This pessimism is not at all like you, Josef. I want you to picture the Great Pyramid in Egypt. Imagine the immense labour that went into carving each stone in that structure. Do you know that they were finished so accurately that when they were in place in the walls of the pyramid it was impossible to pass a knife blade between them? When you have finished your work on this tender, I want the regulators to have the same experience if they attempt to penetrate your metaphorical barrier. Do I make myself clear?'

So saying, Chris turned away. Josef watched him pass through the doorway to join Ildiko in the shadows. He could not see what Chris then did to make her gasp like that, but a glimmer of light caught on the CEO's teeth when he looked back and smiled at Josef.

After they left, he found it impossible to concentrate on his work. He kept going over what Chris had said about Daria. Josef's memories of his night with her were becoming ever more confused and elusive. What harm could possibly come to her? What had Chris been insinuating? Josef could reach no conclusion. His thoughts kept circling around the CEO's words, to no purpose.

He logged off his computer, put his paperwork in order and locked it up in one of his desk drawers. Then he put on his jacket, switched off the light and headed out. He paused at the desk of one of the young women in the call centre. Several small plastic animals formed a semicircle beside her computer monitor, all creatures from Japanese anime films. The nearest emergency light stretched their shadows in front of them. The framed photograph of her girlfriend stood behind them, but the image was lost in the shadows. The young woman was so beautiful, and her sexuality so baffling to Josef, that he could never look at her directly. He doubted that anyone would ever place his photograph on their desk.

He said goodnight to the security guard, Igor, who was flicking through a porno magazine at the main reception desk. Igor looked up at him and made an obscene reference to Chris and his secretary. Josef smiled awkwardly and Igor went on to describe the things he would like to do to Ildiko. Josef squirmed in embarrassment, but said nothing as he walked past the plastic model of the city and clocked off by waving his identity card in front of the sensor by the main entrance – a recent innovation supplied by Alcatec Electronics.

'Poofter,' said Igor. It was a word that Josef had not heard since primary school. He consoled himself with the thought that Igor was a cretin.

He headed to the wine bar by the supermarket on the Triangle. He had not yet eaten, but he had little appetite and he had got into the habit of going there for a quick drink after work, to help him to un-wind. Occasionally he would treat himself to a meal in the steakhouse upstairs. He had almost given up eating meat at home because Hannah was a vegetarian.

The wine bar was quiet. He took a bottled lager and a packet of peanuts to one of the window tables. A candle flickered in an antique medicine bottle made of blue glass. He peered through his dim reflection at the people walking by the brightly lit shops and cafes across the road.

The barman flirted with a waitress, who had come down with a wine order from the restaurant. Her white blouse was tinged blue by the spotlights above the bar counter. Carefully balancing two bottles on her tray, she walked past two grey-haired men in pinstriped suits who were sitting, splay-legged, beside one another on a black leather couch. One of them looked over, his interest piqued by the top of her order book, which was poking out of a pocket on her apron.

A party of five women were gathered round another table. Four of them occupied two couches facing each other. The fifth sat on a higher chair at one end of the table and had to bend awkwardly to reach for her drink or to take part in the conversation. She was wearing a short skirt and black sheer tights and Josef found it hard not to stare at her legs. A young couple entered, laughing. They let go of each other's hand when they reached the bar. While the man ordered their drinks and joked with the barman, the woman looked around to see where they would sit. Her gaze travelled over Josef as if he were not there, and she sat at another window table some distance from him. Feeling lonely and unwanted, Josef quickly finished his drink and left.

When he arrived at the apartment, Hannah was sitting in the lounge watching the television. She was wearing her dressing gown and pyjamas. Her thoughts were still full of Stefan and she was ashamed of the repulsion aroused in her by the sight of Josef leaning over the breakfast bar to ask if she wanted tea or coffee. His eyes seemed too close together and his nose unpleasantly large, in comparison with Stefan's. She cringed inwardly at the abrupt way she declined his offer, and then added, 'I'm really bushed. I'm going to bed as soon as the film is finished.'

Josef filled the kettle, switched it on and put a tea bag in a mug. Music started up on the television – sweeping romantic music. He looked at the names scrolling up on the screen.

'Was it a good film?' he said.

'Nothing special; a stupid romcom. I don't know why I got caught up in it really.'

Her phone started ringing in her room. After a short interval, Josef heard her speaking through the open door.

'That's dreadful! Truly dreadful. How about Natalia? Is she okay?' After another pause, he heard her say in a surprised, questioning tone, 'Daniela?' and then she closed the door. Josef could then only hear the periodic rise and fall of her voice.

He heated up a pasta ready meal and sat down to eat it on the couch with his tea. He had drawn the blinds so that he could not see City Hall illuminated on Castle Hill, but he could not escape the ever-present hum of the city, its random night-time sounds. Hannah was still talking to her mysterious caller.

A news programme started – one that looked in detail at the top stories of the day: the flooding in France and the UK, which was being blamed on climate change; the bombings in the Middle East carried out by the US in retaliation for the recent terrorist attacks; a series of unexplained deaths in the children's hospital in the Capital; a shocking hate crime in V.

Josef strained to make out what Hannah was saying, but he did not switch off the television lest she think he was eavesdropping. Finally, she went to the bathroom and he heard the buzz of her electric toothbrush. His attention was drawn back to the news programme.

Drita N, the new MP for V, was talking to the presenter and a member of the Socialist Front. Drita's doll-like face gleamed in the studio lights as if it were made of plastic. It remained utterly expressionless when the presenter asked whether her party felt any responsibility for the rise in the number of hate crimes, and in particular for the savage rape and shooting that had been carried out in V that day by members of its paramilitary wing. Drita stated vehemently that there was no proof the rapists were members of the Brotherhood. She said that there had been many recent instances of people trying to discredit the organisation – an organisation, she added, that had the support of a sizable proportion of the electorate. She pointed out that one of the witnesses was an illegal immigrant from North Africa. The others were anarchists or animal activists. None of them could be considered reliable.

The presenter, refusing to be cowed, replied that, whatever Drita said, the fact remained that a young Polish au pair, living and working in the country quite legally, had been raped, and a chef from a local cafe had been shot, by men wearing the uniform of the Brotherhood.

Drita reiterated that there was no proof that the perpetrators were actual members. She stated that the Brotherhood would certainly be carrying out its own thorough internal investigation, and she concluded by saying that neither she nor her party condoned violence against immigrants, legal or otherwise.

The presenter then turned to the spokesperson for the Socialist Front and said, 'You can hardly blame the Brotherhood for stoking up hatred against immigrants, when your party has so clearly pandered to anti-immigrant feeling among its own working-class voters.'

At that moment, Hannah emerged from the bathroom and said wearily, 'Goodnight, Josef.' She looked and sounded upset.

'Sleep tight. Don't let the bugs bite,' Josef said with unnatural levity, eliciting an awkward smile before she disappeared. He switched off the television and put his plate, mug and cutlery in the dishwasher. They always set it last thing, to wash the day's dishes overnight. He realised, when he saw the crockery and glasses already stacked in it, that Hannah must have had a visitor for lunch or dinner.

Chapter 7

It was surprisingly warm for a Saturday morning in October. Hannah was not working, but she had woken at her usual time and could not get back to sleep. She climbed out of bed and peered between the curtains towards Stefan's villa among the trees on its clifftop perch. The storm that had been wracking the apartment for most of the night had moved inland. The sun was rising and the river was a riot of red, orange and violet reflections.

She had a headache. Josef and she had shared two bottles of wine on the previous evening. They had eaten an Indian takeaway and watched a DVD together. It was a subtitled Korean film about a triangular relationship involving a poor young man with ambitions to be a writer, a beautiful young woman from his village, and a cynical rich man who may or may not have ended up murdering the woman. She did not think Josef had enjoyed it, but he was in a strange mood. She sensed that something had happened at his work, but although they had stayed up late, talking, he did not let on that anything was bothering him. She could hardly blame him. She had said nothing about her situation with Stefan.

She had not seen Stefan since they had made love some two weeks earlier. He had phoned her that evening from the hospital to tell her that Nina, his au pair, had been raped by fascist thugs and that his daughter, Natalia, had been there when it happened. Hannah found it hard to comprehend the full horror of what he was saying, and she was completely unnerved when he told her Daniela had helped stop the rape and had accompanied Nina and Natalia to the hospital. It seemed too implausible a coincidence.

Throughout the phone call, Stefan had sounded close to tears. He kept blaming himself for what had happened. Then he grew maudlin, reassuring Hannah of her importance in his life. He told her that he had never felt about anyone the way he felt about her, but that now everything had gone to fuck. He said that it would be impossible to see her while Nina was recovering, because he had to look after Natalia. Hannah had thought he would keep in touch by phone or text, but she had heard nothing further from him.

A few days ago there had been a film report on the evening news in which a lawyer addressed journalists, paparazzi and TV reporters at the gates of Stefan's villa. The lawyer had said that Ms W utterly refuted the vile rumour that she had suffered a miscarriage. There had been more, but it was only Nina's rumoured miscarriage that stuck in Hannah's mind. A fake news report that Nina and a group of activists had staged the attack to discredit the Brotherhood had gone viral, while in a tabloid exclusive Nina's ex-fiancé had accused her of being a nymphomaniac. Hannah thought the injustice was obscene, and she could scarcely imagine the impact of the assault on Natalia, but she was desperate to hear from Stefan.

After pulling on her dressing gown, Hannah went to the loo. Then, despite her resolution not to check her phone, she collected it from her room, picked up her book and headed to the kitchen to prepare some coffee and croissants. Once settled at the dining table with her breakfast, she opened the book. It was a publisher's proof copy – given to her last week by her favourite rep – of a newly translated novel by Ann Quin, an English writer of whom Hannah had never heard. The novel was set in a seaside guest house and was written in an unusual style – short, discrete sentences; descriptive phrases and words separated by full stops – but there was an immediacy about it that vividly conveyed the seediness of the setting. It reminded Hannah of her old flat and set her mind wandering. She became nostalgic for her early morning trips to the bakery: the smell of freshly baked bread; the vibrancy and sometimes frightening diversity of the people in that part of town, a stark contrast to their neighbours in this apartment block, who seldom showed themselves.

As far as she could make out, there were no old people or children in the entire building. She occasionally shared the lift with a smartly dressed young male or female professional, who would nod or make a brief greeting, before they fell into an awkward silence. There was the anomaly of the brown-skinned, bearded man whom she had seen on several occasions. Hannah thought him both beautiful and terrifying, with his scarred cheek, large brown eyes and thick lashes. She tried to avoid getting in the lift with him, because of his hostile gaze and his manifest reluctance to make way for her. There was something implacable about him, and judgemental, as if he had looked at her intently and found her wanting. She used to feel something similar when she went to church as a child.

Then there was the mysterious dark-haired woman with the widely spaced almond-shaped eyes, and perfect lips, whom Hannah had seen on the day Stefan had come to the apartment. Only later did she associate that woman with the massage parlour near her old flat and recall her earlier encounter with the woman and her sleazy minder on the evening she had come to view the apartment. The realisation had filled Hannah with the same disquiet as she had experienced on learning that Daniela had been in the hospital with Nina and Natalia.

Reflecting on these chance meetings now, as she emptied the clean crockery and cutlery from the dishwasher, Hannah remembered a nightmare she had had during a fraught period in her childhood when her irascible and highly strung father had tried to teach her to play chess. She had been prey to night terrors until her late teens, but this nightmare had stayed with her and would still recur periodically.

In an atmosphere of nameless dread, she would step through the front entrance of her childhood home to find herself stranded on a giant gameboard. A circle of dim light, with no obvious source, illuminated the nearest rows of coloured squares, which were arranged in patterns of maddening complexity. In the shadowy zone outside the circle, she could discern dark figures moving across the board in a strange mechanical manner that filled Hannah with revulsion, as if they were following a set of rules that she could not, and never would, comprehend. She would wake screaming, with the idea that her death was the sole object of their mysterious game.

Hannah tried to cast the nightmare from her mind by focusing on the present moment. She stretched out on the couch with phone and book and looked at the black and white photograph of the young, dark-haired author on the cover. She wanted to relax and read, but she was distracted by the compulsion that had taken hold over the past two weeks to check her phone for messages from Stefan. She had not looked at the phone for three days now, but she could resist the temptation no longer. She experienced an intense rush of excitement when she saw she had received two texts. One was from a bloke who had started working in the bookshop earlier that month, asking her, for the third time, if she wanted to go out for a drink. The other one was from Daniela. Halina and she would be in the Alchemia Bar from 8.00 p.m. onwards if Hannah wanted to meet up.

The day of leisure that had seemed so expansive and full of promise suddenly lost its lustre. Everything was now coloured by her bitter disappointment. She struggled to find any motivation and idly began to scroll through the top newsfeeds on her phone: a celebrity couple from a reality TV show had split up after eight months; a pop singer was launching her own fashion brand; a soap opera star was being accused of sexual assault by a young woman who had appeared as an extra in the soap during her teens; a typhoon had killed two thousand people on an island in Indonesia, including some forty Western tourists; the rather clownish leader of the parliamentary Party of the Brotherhood had resigned following a series of financial scandals. He had been replaced by Yudek S, the shadowy leader of their paramilitary wing, who, like Drita N, had won a seat in parliament at a recent by-election. His constituency was largely formed of a poor community living in a decaying 1960s housing development in the southeast of the Capital, hemmed in on all sides by gentrification and urban renewal.

Hannah followed a link to a subtitled video in which an anti-immigration speech Yudek had made at a recent rally had been dubbed over with a sound recording from an old American cartoon of the Three Little Pigs singing in a squeaky vibrato about the Big Bad Wolf. She thought the video was hilarious, but she reckoned it would do little to undermine the insidious power of the man, or to diminish his esteem in the eyes of the electorate, and she ended up feeling dissatisfied and impotent.

She put her phone and book on the coffee table and went to open the sliding door to the balcony. It needed oiling and she worried that the scraping sound would waken Josef, but once she was outside, the mild breeze helped to clear her thoughts, and the autumnal scents carried on the air momentarily eclipsed the absurd abstractions of the political world. She looked at the traffic snaking along the road by the river and at a woman in a pink tracksuit running along the waterfront. Her ponytail swayed from side to side as she ran. A gull squawked and took flight from the rooftop opposite.

Hannah looked up at City Hall. She struggled to recall the four years she had worked there in a musty office with wood-panelled walls and rotting window frames. Nothing remained in that building of her time there. But then she remembered the model of the city which had been moved to the museum. The fact of its survival gave her a strange sense of hope.

She left the door open, to air the flat, when she went inside. Back in her room, she chose a green dress and a black lacy top. While she was rummaging in her underwear drawer, she came upon the velvet-covered jewellery box in which she now kept her brooch. Even though a jeweller had repaired the rotating mechanism that locked its pin, she had been too fearful of losing it again to wear it on her jacket. She gazed at it now against the padded faux silk, trying to understand why it meant so much to her, and gradually she lost herself in the numerous bright threads of its filigree.

About half an hour later, when Josef emerged from his bedroom, he was surprised by the sight of Hannah heading to her room from the bathroom with a towel wrapped around her. His heart leapt at the sight of her naked shoulder blades beaded with moisture, and the cluster of freckles on her right calf, but she appeared as unattainable as ever. He looked down at the carpet impressed with her damp footprints.

'Do you fancy going to the Bohemian Coast for the day?' he said suddenly, and blushed. 'I mean, if you haven't got any other plans?'

It struck Josef that he had in some sense conjured the passing scenery from his own feverish desire: the motorway bridge stretching in a giant curve over the river mouth; the rows and rows of imported cars glimpsed on the parking lot far below; and Hannah on the passenger seat beside him, in a low-cut green dress and dark lacy top, gazing out of the window at the articulated lorry he was overtaking. As the motorway climbed, it separated into two levels that had been cut into the hillside, before descending into a broad valley. Everything appeared novel to Josef. Nothing recalled the journeys he had taken with his family, on successive summers during his childhood, to the cottage his parents used to rent in a small fishing village on the Bohemian Coast.

Josef had seen a photograph of the village on his laptop that morning when he was looking for the address code of a car park for his satnav. It seemed unchanged in the twelve years since he had last been there, and he was certain he could make out the whitewashed wall of the cottage among some trees near the top of the hill above the harbour. In his mind's eye, he could still follow the journey he had taken many times with his family to the sandy cove beyond the headland, where he had once glimpsed the complex pattern of chambers within a broken shell.

Hannah asked if she could play her music and pushed her phone cable into the USB dock beneath the dashboard. She seemed preoccupied, staring vacantly at the broad sweep of the road ahead and the grassy slopes on the left as she waited for the media player to connect with her phone.

Josef was more at ease driving on motorways now. He felt a burst of excitement as he accelerated past a four-by-four. A black Labrador was pressing its nose to the opening of the rear passenger window, and the grinning face of a small boy peered around it. Josef drove under a bridge that slanted down from a low ridge on the other side of the motorway. A melancholic love song began to play, sung by a woman accompanied by a slide guitar.

Josef touched the dashboard screen to bring back the satnav map. He had not been sure which was the best junction to take for the Bohemian Coast. The old road atlas he had brought with him to V had offered several alternative routes, so he had decided with some trepidation to follow his satnav. He also wanted to find the tourist car park above the village, to avoid the precipitous narrow road to the harbour.

'When did you last go to the Bohemian Coast?' Hannah said suddenly, pulling down the hem of her dress, which had ridden up when she changed position.

'Just over twelve years ago,' said Josef, 'before my father fell ill. We had been going to the same cottage for five or six years before then. My dad disliked change. Have you really never been?'

'It's ridiculous, isn't it, after all the years I've been living in V? I was meant to go with an ex, but we split up and he ended up taking my friend.'

'Some friend.'

Josef started thinking about his job. It would creep up on him at any time, filling him with acute anxiety, as it did now. Sometimes, when he became involved in an intricate work problem, he would completely forget himself and even take pleasure in finding a solution, but then his thoughts would move beyond the problem and he would realise the impossibility of his job. The world was too complicated to predict all the eventualities. There would always be something that he failed to notice; a vulnerability that at any moment might betray the corruption in which he was mired.

Such a notion would give him a momentary sense of superiority over Chris. He would imagine that his CEO was blind to the failings of his organisation and the limits of his power. Chris would soon revert to his usual omnipotent presence in Josef's mind; an almost mythological force for evil, who could anticipate Josef's every move.

By suggesting the trip to Hannah that morning, Josef believed he had out-manoeuvred Chris. It was like one of those impulsive chess moves with which an amateur can dumbfound a grandmaster. He had left his work phone at the apartment. He had escaped and the world seemed full of exciting possibilities. He could make Hannah forget her unhappiness. They could run away together and find a new life far from V.

Josef experienced a surge of sudden joy as he accelerated up a shallow incline. A large hotel and conference centre stood halfway up the hill on the left. Hannah looked at it and then turned to Josef and smiled. A David Bowie song was now playing – 'Always Crashing in the Same Car'.

'I hope that's not tempting fate,' he said, but he did not believe they would crash.

He pictured the village towards which they were heading at 120 kilometres per hour. There would be a hotel near the waterfront. He would suggest that they stay overnight. He would pay for Hannah's room. They would have an intimate meal together at a window overlooking the harbour.

He recalled a hotel restaurant he had gone to one summer with his family: a watercolour seascape framed on the wall; the beautiful redhaired waitress ruffling his hair; the walk back to the cottage afterwards; his parents arguing as they lagged behind Josef and his sisters on the stepped alleyway that climbed the steep slope. He could still clearly visualise his mother's angry face caught in the light of an old-fashioned street lamp. He quickly suppressed the image.

At that moment, Josef noticed the thick red line edging the motorway at the top of his satnav map. He hoped that it was a mistake, but after another eight kilometres the brake lights of the cars ahead gave the first indication of the traffic jam. Ten minutes later, they were still stationary on the middle lane between a Polish lorry driver in a checked shirt and a family of six in a silver Korean people carrier.

During the three hours it took to reach the next junction, Josef's mood passed from irritation, to frustration, to futile rage, all of which he tried to hide from Hannah, who seemed to be taking everything in her stride as if it did not matter whether they reached their destination or not. About half an hour in, the female voice of the satnav cautioned them about slow-moving traffic on the motorway, which Hannah found funny and which infuriated Josef. When they finally reached the junction, they discovered the motorway was closed. It took twenty minutes to cross the bridge, and the detour route was gridlocked as far as they could see. A traffic announcement on the radio described a motorway pile-up, caused by a jack-knifing lorry, that had involved a school minibus taking pupils to a sporting event.

'Why don't we just go back to the mall at Corvi Crucis to get a bite to eat?' said Hannah. 'We are never going to get to the Bohemian Coast now.'

'Sure,' said Josef, turning on to the slip road and heading up the empty northbound side, towards the large shopping centre overlooking the motorway just west of V.

When they reached the motorway exit, Hannah, sensing his disappointment, suggested they both join Daniela and Halina that evening in the Alchemia Bar. Josef knew that Hannah's former flatmate worked in the cafe near their apartment. He was sure that she had served him several times before Hannah moved in, but he had never been introduced to her. Hannah avoided going into the cafe when Daniela was working. He had no idea who Halina was. The evening seemed suddenly full of exciting possibilities.

After parking the car in one of the enormous car parks surrounding the shopping mall, they went to a noodle bar and ate spicy tofu and noodles beneath the curving glass roof. Two children, a small girl and boy, chased each other between the tables, holding brightly coloured plastic monsters from an online children's game. The mother, in a pink tracksuit and white trainers, periodically shouted at them from a nearby table covered in takeaway boxes and empty cola cans.

A rectangular grey planter with a row of impressive green ferns divided the tables of the noodle bar from those of the neighbouring jacket potato outlet. Trying desperately not to slurp his noodles, Josef could not decide whether the ferns were real or plastic.

★

Josef spent some time after his shower trying to decide what to wear. As he walked across Vandrhaf Square with Hannah he was certain he had made the wrong choice. Hannah was wearing a tight-fitting purple dress with a PVC biker's jacket, black leggings and DMs. Josef thought that his clothes were too casual and normal, clearly advertising to all the passers-by that he was not, and never could be, part of Hannah's world.

She suggested they have a quick bite before meeting Daniela and recommended a tapas bar that was not too far out of their way. Hannah texted her friend that they would be at the Alchemia at 8.30 and they headed up a stepped alley beyond the square. The old-fashioned street lamps lighting the way recalled his childhood climbs to the holiday cottage on the Bohemian Coast. They passed a trendy pub, a Turkish barber's and a specialist DVD rental shop with a tiny cinema, before Hannah stopped at the tapas bar. Josef looked back between the walls of the alley at the multistorey office block rising behind them. Two patches of orange sky above its roof were all that remained of the sunset.

They sat facing each other by candlelight over an assortment of four tapas dishes in plain ceramic bowls, accompanied by glasses of tap water and bottles of Estrella. Hannah said the place reminded her of a favourite university haunt. Josef's attention kept drifting to the shadows flickering in the hollows around her clavicles.

When they emerged on to the alleyway afterwards, Josef was grateful that they had avoided two members of the Brotherhood who were descending the steps below, drunkenly singing a pornographic song dating from an almost forgotten war.

The Alchemia Bar occupied the corner house of an old terrace at the top of the hill, near the university. The ochre-coloured render on its walls had broken away in patches, revealing the brickwork underneath.

There was a glass canopy over the main entrance, and a metal sign reading 'Alchemia' protruded from the corner of the building.

Josef realised as soon as he entered that he did not fit in here. Everyone else looked trendy and cool. Nobody else seemed to notice the stuffed crocodile hanging over the bar.

He followed Hannah through the archway to the back room. It was lit solely by candles, which imparted warmth to the red patterned wallpaper and made the space appear cosier and more welcoming. Daniela and Halina were sitting at a table near the back, next to a wardrobe and a wall-mounted mirror with two candleholders fixed to its metal frame. Two young men, wearing eyeliner and scuffed leather jackets, were chatting them up, but they moved away when they saw Hannah approaching with Josef.

'I hope we're not interrupting anything?' said Hannah.

'Not all all,' said Daniela. 'Just boring art students. We're glad you drove them away.' Turning to Josef, she added, 'This is my flatmate, Halina. Halina, this, I assume, is Hannah's landlord, Josef.' He was slightly disconcerted by the contrast between Halina's round cheeks and small mouth.

'What would you all like to drink?' he said, blushing.

'There's no need for that, Josef,' said Halina, holding out her hand.

'No, really, it's no problem. It would be my pleasure.'

'Where did you find him, Hannah?' said Daniela, shaking Josef's hand and laughing. 'The nineteenth century?'

'In a manner of speaking,' said Hannah. 'By his own account, he was locked in the attic of an old gothic mansion before escaping to V.'

Josef had the paranoid feeling that they were referring to his old-fashioned clothes, but after he bought the drinks and joined them at the table he gradually felt less uptight and began to enjoy himself. He still avoided Daniela's gaze, fearful for no good reason that she might remember serving him in the cafe. As the evening wore on he became romantically drawn to the sadness he discerned in Halina's kohl-lined hazel eyes, but he was completely unprepared for the revelation of her husband's brutal killing.

Daniela and Hannah left them deep in conversation to go to the bar.

'I was really surprised to hear that you were in the hospital with Stefan's au pair and his daughter,' said Hannah while they waited to be served.

'Stefan is your married man?' said Daniela, clearly shocked.

'Didn't I tell you?'

'No, I had no idea.'

'Anyway, it was awful what happened to Nina.'

'I think the police thought we knew her, because she is Polish,' said Daniela. 'I volunteered to go to the hospital with Natalia. A policewoman came with us. She was the only person from the police who did not seem to think it was Nina's fault. It was disgusting, the way they treated her. It made me sick. Fucking fascists! Of course, Stefan was embarrassed to see me at the hospital. He had clearly forgotten my name.'

'Did Nina say why she was there, so far from Stefan's villa?'

'She could not say anything. She was in too much pain and shock. Halina reckoned she was miscarrying. And the poor chef! I felt dreadful about involving him. I was so relieved that he survived.' After a moment, she added, 'I cannot believe Stefan is your married man. Why did you not tell me? I was flirting with him shamelessly at my private view. I would never have done that if I had known.'

'I haven't heard from him since he phoned from the hospital. Please don't mention him to Josef.'

'Really?'

They were interrupted by the barman, who gazed at Hannah while they gave him their order and winked at her when he pressed the change into her hand.

SUNDAY

Yasmin took the opportunity to reread the letter while the men were in the main room at their midday prayers. Mother was in bed, too ill to pray, and Salazar had no idea that Yasmin had stopped praying weeks before. The faith had never been a part of their family life under the dictatorship, and the harsh form of it adopted by her brother following his accident had never appealed to Yasmin.

The letter was from Yasmin's friend Akilah in England. Akilah's father was still lecturing in Bristol University, but he was no longer a communist, and Yasmin's friend feared that the conviction had gone out of his teaching. She wrote that she was now studying politics at the London School of Economics. Yasmin felt that there was an unpleasant note of superiority in the tone of the letter which her friend had never shown before.

In Yasmin's last letter, she had written about her fascination with the model city in the museum. It had been the first time she had ever shared her feelings about it, and she was shocked by the ridicule in Akilah's response. She had particularly mocked Yasmin's notion of the women in the model city pursuing their dreams and interests, unfettered by society, as if Yasmin were too naïve to realise the truth about life in nineteenth-century V.

When she had read the letter the previous day, following Salazar's usual suspicious interrogation about who was writing to her, Yasmin had been deeply hurt by Akilah's remarks. Yasmin thought she had made it clear that the model city was the embodiment for her of a beautiful idea. She compared it to her own father's architectural fantasies inspired by his engraving of the ancient castle of V.

Now, as she reread the letter, Yasmin thought she discovered something defensive in its superior tone, as if her friend did not want to admit to the difficulties and unhappiness she was experiencing in London.

Yasmin carefully folded the letter and put it back in the envelope. She looked at the Queen's head on the stamp and contemplated the symbolism that still clung to that figurehead. She compared it with the ever-present symbols of King Corvus around V and then with the endless images of the Dictator in her home city. She remembered the thrill of seeing film footage of the Dictator's statue being pulled down by the jubilant crowds at the end of the war. The jubilation was short-lived.

Salazar called to Yasmin that it was time to prepare lunch. When she went through to the main room, he and Amit were sitting side by side on the couch. They stopped speaking when she entered.

She did not think that 'Amit' was his real name, but it was clear that Salazar was afraid of him. Shortly after her brother met him at the mosque at the end of the previous year, her brother had asked her if she would consider marrying Amit. She had said that she would sooner kill herself and had thought that Salazar was relieved by her reply, as if he had not wanted to ask her. She did not know what answer her brother had given to Amit, but the subject was never raised again.

Yasmin could not rationalise the physical revulsion that Amit had always provoked in her. Like her brother, Amit had beautiful, almost feminine features, with long eyelashes. He was very particular about the care of his beard. His face had been scarred during an Israeli air strike in his childhood, or so Salazar had said. But there was something chilling about his eyes which stifled any sympathy she might have felt for him. He would speak with an implacable authority about everything within his limited sphere of interest, but he only addressed her brother, and then with the arrogance of a superior, not as a friend.

Only once did Yasmin hear Amit refer to her – when he pointed out to Salazar that she had not covered her face. It was not so much an observation as an indictment. As Yasmin had known he would, Salazar raised the subject of her wearing a veil after Amit had left. He became consumed with impotent rage at her resolute refusal to do so.

On another occasion, she told Salazar that Amit was the kind of hypocritical zealot who would rape a Yazidi girl after slaughtering her parents in cold blood. It was the only time in the past months that she had noticed a hint of uncertainty in his expression. He had walked away without replying.

She cooked eggs with spicy lamb sausages in tomato sauce, and spat copiously into Amit's portion before taking the tray through for the men. Then she shared out the remainder and ate with her mother in her mother's bedroom.

Amit was gone when she took the dirty dishes through to the kitchen. Salazar was sitting on the armchair, lost in thought. A large parcel covered in crumpled brown paper and tied with string was on the floor beside the couch. She had not noticed it earlier. She asked Salazar what it was. She asked him if he wanted coffee. He did not reply. He rubbed his temples with both hands and stared at his scarred ankle, which was crossed over his other leg beneath his white robe.

Salazar had been working as a labourer on the construction of the waterfront apartments when the injury had occurred. He had made the mistake of complaining about the lax health and safety measures that had led to the accident. The lawyers for the ANH Corporation had bullied him into accepting a derisory pay-off, and all his subsequent job applications had met with rejection. Yasmin believed that that was why he had fallen under the influence of the Wahhabi imam who had introduced him to Amit.

MONDAY

Elena found it strange to be in her bedroom in V on a Monday morning. She sipped her coffee and looked at the glossy prospectus that was resting on the duvet, supported by her raised thighs. It was printed on high-quality art paper. The computer-generated image of the building complex, in its setting of rolling hills, was so convincingly real that she had been shocked to see the scaffolding around the ruined castle when she visited the site. The castle had once been home to the family of an Austrian adventurer who had fought alongside King Corvus.

The prospectus was Elena's brainchild, but even with the discount obtained from the printer, DigiGrafix, it was proving awfully expensive to produce and she was nervous of showing it to Dimitrios when she met him that evening. She particularly worried about the preamble she had commissioned from one of the most imaginative copywriters in the business, which described the special landmarks that distinguished the country from its more prosaic neighbours – 'the fantastical peaks of its misty mountains and the rugged, ghost-haunted cliffs of the Bohemian Coast'. She wondered if it was too fanciful a beginning to fit with the subsequent descriptions of the country's cutting-edge industries, its modern infrastructure, its international transport links and the financial centre in its ancient capital.

Once Dimitrios gave the prospectus the okay, she would place translations of it as advertising features in the weekend colour supplements of newspapers in Russia, Germany, France, the UK and the US, as well as in a government-sponsored business journal in China. These would be backed up by a targeted online campaign arranged through the biggest search engines and social media platforms.

Dimitrios had the venture capital in place, so work had already begun on the luxury hotel and conference centre due to open in the spring. It would be situated only twenty-five kilometres from both the Capital's main airport and financial centre. The main selling points for the wealthy business traveller were the transport and entertainment package that would be included in the cost of accommodation. This would provide a luxury shuttle service for the businessman or -woman, to either airport or office, and during their stay would offer them whatever their heart desired.

Elena was hoping that, when they had their meeting, Dimitrios would give her some clarification as to the nature of the entertainments on offer, because she felt that the prospectus was still too vague on that point. She had arranged to meet the copywriter in the office first thing the following morning to go through any adjustments before the prospectus was sent to the printer. She intended to drive to her flat in the Capital later that evening.

She carefully returned the prospectus to one of the protective pockets in her briefcase, and then looked around her room – at the framed sampler above the chest of drawers, the copy of the Caspar David Friedrich painting, and the deer skull. She was no longer satisfied with the room's decor and found it hard to recapture the enthusiasm she had shared with the designer.

It was harder still to recall her enthusiasm when she had met Stefan in the bookshop all those years ago. He would always talk about his writing then and she was too much in love to notice his self-obsession. It seemed ridiculous when she looked back on it. He never asked her about her own writing – such as the article that had appeared in a feminist magazine, about the predominance of male sexual desire in advertising. At that time, she would never have considered working for a PR company. Her younger self would have been appalled by the vapid lives of her wealthy clients and the triviality of many of her contracts. But she had found the work surprisingly stimulating and rewarding. Only now, having learned by email that Tomas had outmanoeuvred her for the promotion, did she question not only her job but every aspect of her life.

It was 8.15 according to her Apple watch. She slipped out of bed and pulled on her dressing gown. She would go up to see Natalia and fit in a couple of hours with her daughter before preparing for the meeting. It had been Stefan's idea to have a baby. She wondered why she had gone along with it. She loved Natalia, of course, but she had found the first months extremely hard. The feelings had not come naturally.

It had been a strange time for both Stefan and Elena – the sudden wealth coming after years of struggle; exciting in a way, until she realised that her contribution was being overlooked. She had continued working as a bookshop manager so that Stefan could study computing. The agreement had been that he would support her when he got a job, and she would do something more interesting, but then Stefan's wealth changed everything.

It was all a blur now, with excruciating bright spots, like the party in the Capital to celebrate the sale of Stefan's business. But nobody had spoken to her then. She had been regarded as little more than an appendage. Everyone had wanted to speak to the man of the moment – those beautiful women, hanging on his every word, panting after his money. It had been grotesque. She remembered thinking that her entire life had turned into one of those dreadful novels sold in airports and railway stations – chunky affairs printed on bad paper, with bright covers, embossed titles and ludicrous plots.

Natalia was so happy to see her mother coming into her bedroom that Elena felt tears welling in her eyes. She was relieved that her daughter had recovered so well from the unfortunate business with Nina. Natalia eagerly introduced her to her soft toys and showed her the drawings and paintings she had made since her mother had last been there. Elena did not understand why she could not feel simply happy with Natalia; why a nagging criticism of this or that aspect of her paintings or drawings always came to mind; why she was always at one remove from her feelings.

She picked Natalia up, told her how beautiful her pictures were, how much her mother loved her. She hoped her daughter would not notice the lack of spontaneity. She balanced Natalia's bottom on her hip and carried her over to the window.

The sky was overcast. All the colours were muted. Elena pointed to the masts of a sailing ship that was anchored near the Millenium

Bridge, in the quay beyond the science museum. As her gaze swept back over the waterfront development, she noticed two tiny figures emerging from one of the apartment blocks.

'Maly ptak,' squealed Natalia, pointing at a distant seagull. 'It means "little bird". Nina taught it me.'

★

Josef had become used to Hannah's morning moods and was content to walk beside her in silence as they made their way between the apartment blocks and passed the cafe where Daniela worked. Hannah waved at her friend through the window, but Daniela was preoccupied with serving a customer and did not notice her.

The sky was pale grey, with only some irregular darker patches to indicate the gaps between the clouds. It was cooler than it had been at the weekend, and there was a fresh westerly breeze. He thought of his conversation with Halina on Saturday evening, of the ease he had felt in her company, of how he had become aware during the evening of just how attractive she was. She had given him her mobile number while Hannah and Daniela were at the bar, but he had not plucked up the courage to phone her. He worried that he would catch her at an awkward moment, and he still clung to the hope that something might happen with Hannah.

They crossed the main road at the traffic lights beyond the science museum. Hannah walked ahead of him up the stepped alleyway, towards the grass and trees of Cathedral Green. Josef gazed at her legs through the shimmer of her tights, trying to discern the freckles on her calf. Every part of her body seemed replete with meaning and mystery. A young man in a red checked jacket, propelling a skateboard on a path through the green, embarked on a series of tricks for her benefit, cursing when he failed to complete the last one and nearly tripped over his board. Hannah paid him no attention.

Josef drew level with her as they started to climb Castle Hill.

'I'm sorry, Josef,' she said. 'I'm not angry with you. I just hate Monday mornings.'

'I know what you mean. The feeling starts halfway through Sunday for me; earlier if I have a hangover, like yesterday.'

'I love books as well. It's just all the crap that goes along with the job.'

A tram overtook them when they were halfway up the hill. A down-and-out with a matted, filthy beard bowed his head at Hannah and mumbled incomprehensibly, hands held palms out on either side, like a biblical illustration of Jesus.

After Hannah left him at the entrance to the bookshop, Josef found the last stretch of the journey almost unbearable. The roads separating him from City Hall comprised four lanes and two tramlines, controlled by two sets of traffic lights. He was nearly overwhelmed by a feeling of panic when he passed through the revolving doors, waved his card in front of the sensor and saw the white model of the city stretching out on its table in the atrium. Its bland uniformity chimed in Josef's mind with the banality of his increasingly stressful job.

He had now sent through the authorisation for both police tenders. All his recommendations to Chris about them had been made verbally, in places chosen by Chris at the last moment. No paper or electronic trail would lead to or from the CEO. Josef would invariably find that a bonus had been paid into his account after each successful tender. The bonus would be apparently above board; a legitimate financial incentive related to the efficient running of the city administration, but Josef knew it was less a reward than an incrimination.

As usual, everyone blanked him as he made his way to his office, so it was only when he saw the note propped up against his computer monitor that he knew something was terribly wrong. 'You're a lying cunt,' it read, in thickly scored capital letters that betrayed the writer's fury.

As soon as he switched on his computer he was summoned by email to Chris's office. Josef wondered at the coincidence. But now there were no coincidences, only the constant surveillance by humming machines through connected digital networks, observing and anticipating his every move and desire. Chris knew exactly when he had clocked on.

Josef was aware of furtive and brazen looks as he made his way through the call centre. The only person heading in the same direction – Andrey from Transport – stopped abruptly when he realised Josef was about to enter the lift. Two secretaries by the water cooler stopped speaking and glared at him until the doors closed behind him.

The thick carpet on the executive level absorbed every sound and seemed to impede Josef's progress as if he were struggling through tangled foliage, like the would-be assassin fleeing from the bear in the fairy tale. Beads of sweat appeared on Josef's forehead. He felt utterly defeated by the time he pressed the buzzer by the CEO's door and heard the soft whirring sound of its opening.

Chris was standing behind Ildiko with his hands on her shoulders. Josef thought that he was gripping them so tightly that it must have been uncomfortable for her. Chris let go and turned towards his office door without saying anything, expecting Josef to follow him in.

'Please sit down.' Chris took his seat behind the desk and shuffled the contents of a yellow folder. The silence extended unbearably, in a manner that Josef had begun to regard as a ritual. He gazed hopelessly through the windows at the amber-tinted sky.

'I have had some shocking news, Josef. Appalling, really. Difficult to grasp in this day and age.' Josef said nothing, lowered his head. He noticed a small toothpaste stain on his right trouser leg. 'The fact is, Josef, that Daria's body was discovered by the police at the weekend. She had been dead for a long time before one of the neighbours realised that something was wrong. Now, please answer me honestly, when did you last see her?'

'What do you mean? How ... Jesus Christ! You know why I haven't seen her in months.'

'It's not what I think that matters, Josef, as I have told you before. Look here, I have kept it all in this file: Daria's original statement; her later statement withdrawing the accusation. It is all here, none of it in the official files. There is really no reason, no reason at all, why any of this should come to the attention of the police. However, someone in the office might tell them of your involvement with her. Office tittle-tattle, you could rightly argue, but then the police might question you.' Chris waved his hand in a dismissive gesture over the papers. Josef noticed the alpha glittering on his cuff. 'I mean, from what they have said to me, they clearly believe it was suicide. But if they did question you, Josef, what would you say? After all, Daria was a very imaginative and unstable person; some might call her a fantasist and certainly that would be supported by part of this file.

'Let me just point out, it would be a shame if anything in here found its way to the acting head of personnel. You know Petrov, a regular bulldog when he gets his teeth into something, and filing systems are so prone to fail. It is the human factor. Vital documents can be lost irremediably. Things can go astray, only to reappear at the most embarrassing moments. Please try to bear all this in mind if the police should question you. We really don't want the whole thing turning into a murder investigation.'

★

Dimitrios pressed Elena's hand when she moved to open the briefcase. 'Let's not spoil the meal by talking business,' he said. 'Plenty of time for that after we have eaten.'

Elena's roots had now been dyed the same platinum blond as the rest of her hair, which had recently been cut short in a fashionable messy style. As usual, she had tried to compensate for the thinness of her lips with bright lipgloss, edged with a slightly darker shade to enhance the effect. She covered her glass when he tried to pour some wine for her.

'Honestly, I can't have any. I have to drive to my flat in the Capital after our meeting.'

'Nonsense. Where is your car?'

'Back at the villa. I was going to take a taxi there when we finished.'

'Well, that solves everything. My driver is taking me to the Capital this evening. I would be happy to have him drop you off at your flat. I insist. Let your hair down. Mix a little pleasure with business.' She reluctantly allowed him to pour wine into her glass. 'After all, it is your flat. You surely have everything there you could possibly need. I'm happy for you to charge the train and taxi fares home to my account.'

Although Elena had met Dimitrios on four previous occasions, this was the first time she had been alone with him. Despite her fears about the journey they were to take together later, she was reassured by the fact that his gaze never shifted to her body, as happened with all the other men she knew. Most of the time, he looked her directly in the eye. She began to warm to his humorous anecdotes of growing up in Greece and of his move during his early twenties to a bustling Black Sea port.

His vivid descriptions contrasted with a vagueness about what he did for a living and about the setting, so that Elena was never sure if a particular colonnade, hotel, square or harbour was in Greece, Bulgaria or Ukraine, and the images that arose in her mind were of generic white buildings with flat roofs, brilliant blue seas in the background, curving harbour walls made of cream-coloured stones, with lizards darting into shadow-filled crevices, and brightly coloured boats rocking gently at anchor with unsettling eyes painted on their prows.

She found it hard to correlate the slim, darkly handsome hero of his tales with the portly reality of Dimitrios sitting opposite, in his well-tailored jacket and dazzling white shirt, cutting his steak carefully into cubes. He had fleshy lips, multiple chins and thinning grey hair, but he happily alluded to the effects of ageing with wry self-deprecation.

She was completely relaxed and enjoying herself by the time he led her to the bar downstairs, where the business part of their meeting was to take place. She was gratified by his swift comprehension of the prospectus and by the acuity of his editorial suggestions. There was no hint of condescension in his remarks and she felt flattered that he did not hold back in his few criticisms because of her sex. She noted the changes on her laptop.

Then she asked him if he could clarify what would be offered in the entertainment package, since she thought the current wording rather vague. They were sitting side by side on a banquette at the back of the bar so they could both look at the laptop. A candle, spilling wax over an antique blue medicine bottle, flickered near Dimitrios's whisky glass, reflecting in the amber liquid.

'I'm not sure that I would want to specify what will be on offer,

Elena. Surely that would only limit the imagination of the potential customer.' He leaned in close, brushed her thigh with his knuckle and whispered, 'After all, what pleasures would you seek out if there were no limits or moral constraints.' Elena instinctively drew back, but Dimitrios had already moved away and was sipping his whisky as if nothing had happened. 'What I mean is that the entertainment package will, obviously, change according to the payment level the client opts for, but I want you to create the illusion of pleasure without limits.'

Two men swayed by them and headed towards the exit. One looked about ten years younger than the other and was clearly having difficulty walking straight. Dimitrios looked at them and then looked back at Elena and smiled. 'There, you have the reality of pleasure-seeking. I want you to sell the dream.'

*

Josef had drunk too much lager too quickly. He nearly fell over when Adam and he made their way out of the bar. Adam took his arm and told him they had to hurry. As they headed past a pedestrian crossing, Josef's gaze swept in an arc around him and he tried to figure out where he was. The lighted windows of the shops and cafes merged with the car headlights and street lamps in a blur of coloured lines that made him feel sick.

Adam, who was considerably less drunk, helped him to walk. Josef tried to focus on the pavement moving immediately in front of him, until that too made him feel ill. Closing his eyes made him feel worse. He looked at his companion, trying to remember how and why they had met. With some effort, he recaptured the image of Adam, approaching him in the bar, raising his drink and smiling.

Now, Josef embarked on a lengthy explanation of his relationship with Daria, but Adam could not understand what he was trying to say. His frustration turning quickly to anger, Josef jabbed Adam's arm with his forefinger and continued, 'It wasn't sexual ... We did not ... Jesus fucking Christ ... Only once ... It wasn't my fault ... I didn't ...'

Adam merely laughed and said he would make him a coffee when they got back to his flat but that they had to go faster or Katryn would be angry.

The fresh air did little to sober Josef up. He could not get the orange light of the street lamps to stay still, and he had no idea how long they had been walking when Adam led him into the stairwell of a familiar building. The smell coming from the large wheelie bins made Josef gag. It took all his concentration to keep himself from vomiting on the concrete steps.

When Adam opened the door to his apartment, Katryn was about to start shouting at him, but then she saw Josef swaying in the doorway. Josef stumbled in, gawping at her dimpled cheeks, slender neck, long white blouse, dark brown leggings and high heels. Adam dragged him past her, along the hallway to the living room, where he dumped him unceremoniously on the couch.

Katryn had put on a brown suede jacket when she reappeared. She looked between the curtains and saw the Mercedes pull up at the kerb below.

'Janos is here. But before I go, I should warn you that Helena had a sore tummy earlier. She took a while to go down and she may wake up again.'

'Is this really the only time you could do this?' said Adam, who was still standing beside the couch.

'I'm tired of going over this, Adam. I've told you before about this artist, Vasily K. He is a complete arsehole. He insisted on unveiling his paintings tonight. It's to do with the anniversary of King Corvus's death.'

'But there is no way that Janos will reject his work now, so close to the opening.'

'Janos is no fool, and Vasily isn't as talented as he thinks he is. Of course Janos will reject them if necessary. The reputation of his gallery is at stake.'

'But what have you got to do with it?'

'I'm being paid to go, you idiot, and it's because of you that we need the bloody money. Now, I don't know how long this fiasco is going to go on, so don't wait up. Is this numpty staying?'

'I've no idea,' he said.

She gave Adam a quick peck on the cheek and walked out. Josef's head lolled on the cushion as he tried to watch her go.

TUESDAY

Daniela was growing irritated. There was no sign of her replacement, and she was worried that she would be late for the appointment at her former gallery. There was a queue of customers, so she reluctantly started to prepare a latte and asked her colleague to put on a tuna melt when the grill was free. But Daniela was distracted and the latte was too frothy when she put it on the woman's tray.

She was relieved to see her replacement, pushing his fringe out of his eyes, as he rushed through the door. Unbuttoning his jacket and mouthing apologies to Daniela, he crossed the cafe to the staffroom.

Daniela quickly changed out of her uniform and collected her bag, portfolio and jacket from her locker. She caught a tram at the foot of Castle Hill and sat down in the last free space on one of the side seats near the driver. An old man climbed aboard just before the tram started, and Daniela offered him her seat.

'No, love, you're alright. I'm only going a couple of stops.' His frank gaze unsettled her, so she placed her portfolio and bag on her lap and turned to look through the windscreen as the tram made its way up the hill. He was still gazing at her and smiling when she looked back at him.

'I suppose you'll soon be going back to your own country now,' he said.

'What did you say?'

'I said, you'll soon be going back to your own country.' He leaned heavily on the hand strap as the tram slowed for the next stop, and handed her the folded newspaper he was holding in his other hand. It was a right-wing tabloid that she utterly detested. Unwilling to read it, she held it for a moment before unfolding it. Above a photograph of Yudek S in a double-breasted suit, with badges of King Corvus's shield sewn on to the lapels, the words 'Yudek Humiliates Premier' were printed in bold. She only got a chance to take in, 'Yudek's Private Member's Bill has unexpectedly …' before the old man took the paper back, saying, 'This is my stop, love.'

A young man wearing a grey pinstriped suit and trainers, who was following the old man off the tram, turned towards Daniela with a vicious expression and said, 'Yeah, why don't you fuck off home?'

Daniela had read about the successful vote on her phone the previous evening. The bill would require all foreign residents to be registered and categorised according to their job skills and country of origin. She had taken heart from the fact that many members of the upper house were planning to oppose it. Now, she was frightened and shocked. Everyone avoided her eye, but she had no idea if it was out of embarrassment or out of agreement with her abuser, and she was grateful when the tram arrived at her stop.

She still felt spooked when she headed down the side street to the gallery. She looked behind her periodically to see if anyone was following her. The only person to pay her any attention was a chubby young man with dyed green hair who appeared from a doorway on to the pavement ahead. He was wearing an unbuttoned leather coat, in the opening of which it was possible to see the print on his T-shirt, of a blue goat's head in a red pentangle. He gazed at her in an unsettling manner as she walked past. He was, thankfully, gone when she looked back from the entrance of the gallery.

A new intern was sitting behind the reception desk. On the bare white walls, there were some bright abstract landscapes – a series of aerial views of fields and copses, rendered in primary colours. It had been a while since Daniela had seen Lena, the gallery owner. She came through the door at the back when Daniela was only halfway across the room – a tall, slim woman in her late fifties in a simple white blouse and a pair of natural linen trousers.

'Punctual as ever, Daniela,' said Lena, and led her through to her office. 'Would you like a glass of wine?' She gestured towards the armchairs set up on opposite sides of a coffee table in the corner.

'That would be lovely, thanks.'

While Lena poured the wine, Daniela took out the artworks she wanted to show her. Firstly, the two King Corvus collages that Janos had rejected.

'These are very powerful, Daniela, but there is no way that I could display them in my gallery now.' She looked through the other artworks and sipped her wine. 'I'm sorry, Daniela, things have changed so much since I put on your last exhibition. I don't know if people are afraid, or whether they're starting to believe the nonsense they hear on the news, but there is little appetite for this kind of art.'

'Is it because I went to Janos,' said Daniela, trying to hold back her tears.

'No, Daniela, how could you think that? You had to accept his offer. I could never have given you that kind of exposure. It's just that I can't risk my livelihood. Don't get me wrong, I love my current exhibition, but it is purely decorative art. It's not going to offend anyone.'

Lena turned her attention to Daniela's latest piece – a pen, brush and ink drawing. The façade of the theatre on Vandrhaf Square rose in the background with a large poster above the main entrance advertising Wagner's opera *Tristan and Isolde*. The poster was in the medieval style fashionable in the nineteenth century. Tristan stood on the left, raising the goblet filled with the love philtre, while Isolde adopted the cliché attitude of a serpentine femme fatale. There was a framed portrait between them, presumably of King Mark, pictured bareheaded, in armour. His hair was cut in a bowl-like medieval style, but his moustache made him look like Adolf Hitler.

In the middle ground of the drawing, the audience were spilling out of the theatre after the performance. The women were all dressed to the nines, some in ballgowns and fur jackets, others in stylish coats and feathered hats. Most of the men were in dinner suits, but some wore black uniforms and peaked caps.

In the square in the foreground a copy of the *Čuvar* lay, partially sodden, on the edge of one of the decorative pools. Daniela had managed to portray on its front cover a photograph of a young, dark-haired woman beneath the headline 'Hate Crime'. A full moon, reflected in the pool, explained the eerie brilliance of the scene. The ground in front of the pool was littered with a battered shoe, a wedding ring, a silver chain purse, a pair of glasses with a cracked lens, a woman's pillbox hat and veil, a christening spoon, the gleaming crown of a tooth, and a teddy bear. A scrap of striped cloth was all there was to indicate that these objects belonged to victims of the Holocaust.

'I know someone who may be interested in this one, Daniela. If you want me to show it to her, I will only take twenty per cent commission, plus the cost of the frame. I know it's not much.'

'No, Lena, it's not your fault.'

'Here, let's have another drink to better times.'

As Daniela started to return the rejected prints to her portfolio, one of her earlier pen and ink drawings slipped out on to the table.

'What's that,' said Lena.

'I didn't realise it was in there. I made it when I first moved here. It is the Devil's Bridge. I was on holiday with my boyfriend in the Tarent Mountains.'

Lena put the glasses on the coffee table and picked up the drawing. It was a moonlit scene with the Devil's Bridge curving over a fast-flowing stream filled with broken reflections. There were dark mountains in the background, topped with gleaming snow, and fir trees covered the slopes on either side of the stream. Lena turned it over and read the title Daniela had given it: *The Stag in the Forest Runs Free*.

'Why does it have that title?'

'Look,' said Daniela, pointing to a detail in the bottom right-hand corner. The figure of a hunter, in the traditional costume inspired by King Corvus's alpine sharpshooters, was carrying a dead roe deer with hobbled legs.

Lena laughed. 'Yes, that would go very well with the other drawing. Do you mind if I show both to my customer?'

Daniela decided to walk home. The street on which the gallery was situated led almost directly to her flat; she would get there in about half an hour. She could not face catching a bus or tram, after what had happened earlier. But her anxiety about what other people might say or do led her to turn into quieter thoroughfares and involved her in so many unplanned detours that she completely lost her sense of direction. The sun was hidden by clouds, so she had to resort to the map on her phone. Moving between various scales to position both herself and her destination proved to be quite confusing, especially since adverts for various bars or shops would pop up if she pressed too heavily on this or that part of the map. She was finally able to orientate herself by the railway line, which she knew crossed the main road less than a kilometre north of her flat.

It was so spookily quiet that she feared she might have been better on a crowded street, where there was always the chance of help if something bad happened. She kept looking around her, fearful that she might encounter members of the Brotherhood on that stretch of dilapidated stucco terraces, small manufacturers, and boarded-up shops covered in tattered posters advertising gigs, exhibitions in small galleries, anti-capitalist protests, nationalist rallies, tarot readings, Pilates classes. But she saw no one, until she reached some railway arches housing small storage units, where she saw two dark-skinned, bearded men. One was wearing a pair of grey overalls and had a scar on his face. The other, in a black jacket and white robe, was bending to pull down a corrugated iron shutter. In the closing aperture, she saw a row of oil drums on a dusty concrete floor.

She looked away, and when she looked back the men were eyeing her with hostility and suspicion. They relaxed visibly when she smiled and said, 'Hello.' The man in the white robe smiled back, before resuming his blank expression as if he had forgotten himself for a moment.

Halina was not long home from work when Daniela arrived at the flat. 'Any luck, Daniela?'

At the sight of her friend's concerned, questioning expression, Daniela suddenly burst into tears. Halina hugged her, murmuring reassurances, before suggesting she make some coffee.

Daniela dried her eyes with a paper hanky. Then she hung her jacket on one of the hooks near the front door, took off her shoes and put her portfolio and bag in her room. Halina was pouring the coffee and humming a tune in the kitchen when Daniela entered the living room. Halina brought the tray through with the coffee and a couple of lemon drizzle cakes from the bakery across the road.

Daniela said, 'Have you heard anything from Josef?'

'No, nothing; but I am too old to be playing these stupid games. I thought we got on well together. I would have liked to see him again, but I won't lose any sleep over him.'

They sat, side by side, on the couch, eating their cake and drinking their coffee in silence. Daniela looked up at the framed print that Halina had brought with her from the Capital. It was a mountain landscape by Peter Schmidt. There was a dark blue mountain in the left foreground with a winding white path cut into its cliff face, and other mountains retreating on the right in a range of lighter shades, the summit of the lightest and tallest piercing the clouds in the background.

She took in the view, through the window, of the brick wall across the courtyard, with a damp patch under an overflow pipe, and then her gaze moved over the mantelpiece – where a bronze statuette of a wolf, which had belonged to Halina's husband, stood between two pewter candlesticks – to rest on the framed watercolour Daniela had painted of her mother and dog in their garden in Krakow.

'Maybe I should just make colourful, decorative art,' said Daniela.

'You should make what the fuck you want,' replied Halina, and they both started laughing.

WEDNESDAY

It was pouring with rain and Anna got surprisingly wet in the short distance from Sergei's BMW to the apartment block entrance. When she looked back through the glass doors, she saw the car was still there. She thought she could discern Sergei, staring through the side window with his arm stretched across the back of the passenger seat, but it was difficult to make out anything through the streaming rainwater. The car did not pull away until she pressed the button to call the lift.

She turned her back on the mirror, avoiding her reflection. She could not count the times that clients had praised her beauty. It made some angry. Others took a perverse delight in sullying it. Yet others enumerated its qualities in obscene ways, as if to flatter her. She no longer took account of the clients' differences; flabby or muscular, ugly or handsome, everything was dulled by repetition. Now she was away from Sergei and the brothel, she tried to live entirely in the moment: in the details of the lift; in the minor blemishes and marks of use; in the numbered buttons that lit up when pressed and switched off when the lift arrived at its destination. Anna had come to feel an affinity with the robotic female voice that warned of the closing doors and announced her arrival at the seventh floor.

The woman opened the apartment door immediately that Anna knocked, as if she had been waiting behind it. The apartment was filled with the aromatic smells of her marvellous cooking. She took Anna's wet coat and hung it on a hook by the door, then led her to one of the settees in the living area. A bowl of macadamia nuts and another of Bombay mix were set out on the coffee table with a bottle of red wine and two glasses. The woman poured her some wine.

Anna put down her bag and sat with her legs crossed, sipping the wine, picking up handfuls of Bombay mix and staring through the rain-soaked glass beyond the dining table at the bleary orange lights marking the top of the cliff. She was experiencing conflicting emotions. She felt guilty for telling Sergei that Ben had worked as a sportswriter in B and that his wife had been raped by the Dictator's son, but she had had to tell him something. Why should she protect Ben when he took advantage of her like any other client? She began to get agitated and tried to calm herself by imagining that she was here to enjoy a meal with a friend, or a loving husband, as if another way of life were possible, and she tried to forget the brutal exchange that would take place later in Ben's room.

Ben seemed more agitated than she had ever seen him when he finally made his appearance – in a blue silk shirt, open at the collar, black trousers and sand-coloured moccasins. He avoided her eye and poured a large measure of wine as if he had completely cast aside his religion. He sat opposite her, taking gulps of wine and looking at the floor, not speaking, until the woman served their meal.

Anna focused purely on savouring the food and wine, while he refilled his glass, grabbed a few mouthfuls of food and pushed his plate away. The woman approached to take the plate and he said to her, 'Go to your room!' with a concentrated fury that filled Anna with a habitual, icy dread.

After the woman was gone, Ben drank more wine and ate some more. Then he started speaking as if responding to an inner argument rather than out of any desire to communicate with Anna.

'Why does any of it matter, after all? Why go through the motions? Why does anyone do it – furnish their homes, follow their pathetic family rituals?' He drank more wine, expecting no answer. Anna was determined to continue enjoying her food, despite her inner turmoil. She resented the numerous ways in which her body betrayed her with its visceral chemical reactions. 'We create these pointless systems, Anna – you, me, everyone – all these fucking systems. We try to force everything into them – all the complexities and contradictions of the world. It is like trying to mould liquid with your bare hands. And tell me, Anna, tell me what we humans do when someone opposes these meaningless, flaccid structures!'

'I have no idea what you want me to say, Ben.'

'Let me show you, Anna. Let me show you what we fucking do.' So saying, he upended the table and dragged her by the arm towards his room. She did not struggle. She let him pull her. It was all part of the futile rigmarole that passed for her life.

He was crying by the time he slammed the door and pushed her on to his bed. He picked up his family photograph and brought it close to her face.

'It's been going on for millennia, Anna. Craftsmen sharpening metal, creating barbs and blades. Industrialists mass-producing bullets and missiles. Crazed boffins inventing bombs of ever greater magnitude, and all for what?' He paused for effect. 'To pierce fragile bodies like these. He flung the photograph aside, forced her legs apart and started tearing at her knickers, before collapsing, sobbing, on top of her. 'Why can't you love me, Anna? Why can't you love me?'

She relaxed under him and started going through the familiar motions, stroking his hair, babbling reassurances, moving her hands over his back and buttocks, while her mind was elsewhere, picturing a field of mustard, with a row of cypresses beyond, swaying wildly in a wind from the east.

THURSDAY

Janos was sitting at a table in the cafe in his arts centre, working on his laptop and drinking coffee. He was using a spreadsheet to work out the cost of opening the new gallery, with a view to offsetting the capital expenditure against his tax over the next five years. He had arranged to meet Katryn for lunch to discuss the King Corvus triptych that Vasily K had unveiled in his gallery on Monday night. Janos had decided to go ahead with making Vasily's surprisingly hagiographic and bloodthirsty artwork – representing the birth, death and apotheosis of King Corvus – the focal point of the exhibition due to open that Saturday evening in his new gallery.

Katryn had not been so sure. She had thought the space should be given to Petra L's more ironical work. Janos could see her point, but he thought that Vasily was riding the zeitgeist and that the controversy the triptych was sure to generate among leftist intellectuals would only provide more publicity for the exhibition. Also, Janos thought that the prominent position of such a nationalist artwork would serve as a guarantee of police protection for the exhibition.

Katryn arrived promptly, just minutes after Janos finished working on his spreadsheet. He watched her walking across the room in a rust-coloured polo neck and brown suede jacket, with regret that she had not worn her tight-fitting blue dress since their first meeting in July. He took in her dimples and the sexy gap between her front teeth.

She hung her bag over the chair, took off her jacket and sat down. He signalled the new waitress to come over to take their drinks order. Katryn wanted a soft drink, but, bowing to pressure from Janos, she asked for a vodka and orange. She told Janos, after the waitress had gone, that she must not get drunk, because she had to pick the children up from school at three o'clock.

They ate lunch: she, cauliflower and cheese soup with rye bread and butter; he, a lamb tagine with couscous. She knew that she would end up agreeing that Vasily K was a better proposition than Petra L, despite the mediocrity of his ideas, and that Petra would be given the space in the back room of the gallery which Janos had originally earmarked for Daniela N. He had rejected Daniela's prints out of fear of the violence they might provoke. Katryn finished her soup and then drank her coffee. Her role was not as independent as Janos had suggested it would be, but the job paid well and she consoled herself with the thought that she had chosen six of the artists in the exhibition.

When she put on her jacket to leave at half-past two, Janos said he would collect her from her flat at five o'clock the following afternoon. She had not yet told Adam that she would be staying in the Capital on both Friday and Saturday night so that she could help with the gallery opening. Her mother had agreed to pick Helena and Kris up from school and have them stay with her until Sunday morning.

On her way out, Katryn passed a young, red-haired man in a beat-up suede jacket of a similar shade to her own, who looked at her so intently that she wondered if she had met him before. But he hastily looked away, clearly mistaking her confusion for annoyance.

★

Franz had been coming to the arts centre every day since he had first seen the new waitress at the end of the previous week. Although she had shown no sign of recognition, these daily visits had provided him with a pleasurable structure to fill the empty hours between rising late and starting work at the bar in the evening. They also allowed him to escape the constant interruptions of his landlady.

On the third day, Franz had learned that the waitress was called Kata. He had seen her long brown hair in a ponytail, in plaits, and loose and falling in waves over her shoulders, but he had made no effort to say anything beyond the conventional pleasantries when giving his orders.

He had spent most of his time in the cafe reading a history of Islam, watching a video documentary about Islamic art on his laptop and consulting online encyclopedias about Islamic religion. In the process, he had begun to question his education, which had so effectively portrayed the Arabs and the Ottomans as bogeymen threatening the civilised west, confounded in their diabolical aims by Charlemagne in

France and by the Habsburgs and their allies at the gates of Vienna.

The plan that morning had been to treat himself to a late lunch and then to do some work on his PhD. When he arrived at the arts centre he was surprised to recognise a woman with auburn hair and a sexy gap between her front teeth, who was just leaving. As he tried to place her she stopped smiling. The annoyance with which she responded to his insistent gaze utterly crushed him. He could barely look at Kata when he took his seat, so convinced was he in his current mood that she could only ever regard him with contempt. His heart was still thumping when she came to take his order. He kept his eyes fixed on the menu as he made his selection.

At a neighbouring table, two old women in pale floral blouses were having cream teas. A young man with long black hair and in a baggy grandpa shirt and braces, who was sitting at another table, represented everything Franz imagined would appeal to Kata. Franz became so downcast that he struggled to motivate himself to work, tempted by any distraction offered by his laptop rather than tackle the seemingly insurmountable difficulties of his research.

Kata's male colleague came to collect Franz's empty plate and glass. The young waiter had a complicated tattoo spreading over his forearm: a woman's beautiful face emerging from red and white roses with sharp thorns that gave every appearance of piercing his flesh. Franz ordered a latte and caramel shortbread, then took out his notebook and forced himself to read his notes about the communist, 'Zarathustra', and the poet, Attar, and those he had made about the essay that he had tracked down on the internet two months earlier, signed by 'Zarathustra'. Since then, he had found no other sign of the mysterious essayist.

All he had had to go on was the place and year the essay had been published. He had sought 'Zarathustra' in B. He had searched in places linked to Zoroaster. He had tried to link the pseudonym to major events throughout the country. Now he decided to focus his search on the city of B itself. Keying it and the year into the search engine on his laptop, he accidently clicked 'images'. Among the many photographs of the city and the Dictator that came up on his screen, he noticed a couple of newspaper front pages. Upon enlarging one of them, he was able to read an article praising the Dictator's swift action in helping the inhabitants of a poor neighbourhood on the outskirts of B which had been devastated by an explosion at a chemical plant.

Franz felt as if he was being given a glimpse into everyday life in the city during the late nineties. He now searched for newspapers in B from the same year. A multitude of front pages appeared on the screen. He read about a party thrown by the Dictator to celebrate his birthday. Another article described a conspiracy organised by the neighbouring Islamist state, which had resulted in fifty-three arrests. Other articles covered the opening of a mosque, a terrorist atrocity by a breakaway group trying to establish an independent state in the north, a military parade, the construction of a hospital, an increase in welfare payments for the unemployed. All showed the Dictator in a positive light. Franz was beginning to find them boring and predictable, when he came unexpectedly upon a description of a football match.

It seemed strange to find an article about a sporting event on the front page, until he realised that the team, which had just won the League Cup, had been created by Ulay, the Dictator's elder son. The article was signed by the sports editor, Ben F. Intrigued, Franz read on.

He could barely contain his excitement when he discovered that the journalist had compared Ulay's football team to *The Colloquy of the Birds* by the Sufi poet Farid ud-Din Attar. In reference to the poem, the journalist praised the players for completely subsuming their personalities and individual skills in the team, to become the very embodiment of the beautiful game. Franz read the passage with a profound sense of release as he recalled the similar comparisons made by 'Zarathustra' and by Edward H in *All-Consuming Passions*. He reread the article to make sure that he had correctly interpreted it and bookmarked the page.

He had never felt such a sense of inner peace and contentment as he did at that moment, and he was never to feel it again. He keyed in a search for the journalist Ben F. Only one entry referring to his Ben F came up: an article in the online edition of the *Čuvar* covering Ben F's arrival in the Capital shortly after the recent war in the Middle East. The journalist wrote,

> Ben F's family had been wiped out by a US led air strike directed at the Dictator and his notorious military advisor, who were believed erroneously to be eating in a neighbouring restaurant. Sadly, it was one of our jet fighters that fired the fatal missile. The US Government is to be praised for the compensation paid to Ben F, but it is surely odd that he should be singled out, when so many of his compatriots suffered in the war. And one can only wonder why he sought refuge in our country and not in the United States.

At that moment, Kata asked Franz if he would like anything else.

He was smiling when he looked up at her. 'What's the best bottled lager that you do? Do you have any Budvar?'

'Of course,' she said, smiling in turn. 'You come here every day, don't you?'

'I work in a bar in the evening,' he said, but on realising that that explained nothing, he added, 'It's the only way I can do my work without being interrupted.'

'I hope that I didn't interrupt you.'

'You? You could never interrupt me.'

She smiled again, but with less warmth, and her expression conveyed both confusion and suspicion.

FRIDAY

10.30 a.m.

Stefan was sitting on a chair by Nina's bed while she lay, curled up in a foetal position under her duvet, with her back to him. Keeping half an ear out for Natalia's cheerful babble through the baby monitor, he uttered Nina's name several times, but she did not respond. He shifted the duvet to uncover her dark, greasy hair and gently stroked her head, but still she did not respond. 'Maybe later,' he said and strolled over to the window.

He looked out with his right palm pressed against the glass. Sunlight glittered on the river. The city spread out to the southeast, the angles and shapes of the buildings clearly delineated in patterns of shadow and light. The colours on the waterfront apartments were unusually bright. He counted the floors of one of the blocks, trying to locate Hannah's apartment on the corner, but of course she would be at work.

He wondered if he ought to phone Elena again. She had sent him a text on Tuesday evening, saying she needed to talk. For years, she had not sent him any message that went beyond a strictly utilitarian function of making, or confirming, arrangements. He had tried to phone her a couple of times, but the calls had gone straight through to message. Then she had texted him again, saying it was nothing that could not wait until the weekend.

On the previous Monday, they had argued about Nina. Elena was still angry that the au pair had taken Natalia to such a dangerous part of town. She could not understand why Nina would do that. Stefan had told her that Nina was in no condition to answer any questions, but Elena had finished by saying that they could not look after her indefinitely, that they would have to think about finding a new au pair. 'It would be by far the kindest thing for Nina,' she said, 'to give her three months' severance pay and cover her airfare back to her family in Poland.'

Stefan wandered around Nina's sitting room, pausing at the selection of books and DVDs on the shelf unit near the TV and CD player. It struck him that he had never asked Nina about the books and films that she liked, and that he knew nothing of her thoughts. He picked up a book that was lying on top of the others, took in the antique plan of a fortified city on its dust wrapper, and only then did he read the title: *Podróz do Warnaku*. Feeling suddenly queasy, he put the book back where he had found it.

11.30 a.m.

Katryn grew frantic when she was put through to Janos's voicemail for the fifth time. She had left a message an hour earlier, telling him that her mother had broken her ankle and was in the hospital. Half an hour later, she had left another message saying that she had arranged to take Kris and Helena to meet Adam in the bookshop opposite City Hall at 5.30 p.m. and that she could meet Janos at the arts centre around a quarter to six. She decided to send him a text and an email as well, adding in both messages that she was really sorry about the delay but that there was nothing she could do about it.

She reckoned that she had done all she could to get the message to him. She started to think about what she should take to the Capital. Janos had been assured by his PR company that the *Čuvar* would be doing a two-page colour spread in their weekend culture supplement, and he had asked Katryn to dress accordingly, whatever that meant. Since she had started the job in September, her sleep had been disturbed by frequent work-related nightmares, from which she would wake in fright, drenched in sweat, convinced that she was in way over her head.

On the previous evening, she had finally plucked up the courage to tell Adam that she would be staying in the Capital for two nights because of the opening of the new gallery, and had been unsettled by his apparent indifference. She had told him that Janos would be driving her there with one of the waitresses from the arts centre, who was also helping with the gallery opening, hoping that this would set his mind at ease, but Adam did not show any reaction. Even when she had texted her husband that morning about her mother's accident, he had not objected to collecting the children from the bookshop, as if it made no difference to him.

12.30 p.m.

Josef was drinking a latte and looking out of his office window at the dismal view of the brick wall and flaking downpipe. If he strained to look to the left, he could see the back wall of the museum and a black door protected by a metal gate. A pigeon was strutting around the alleyway below, oblivious of the scraggy grey cat crouching nearby, its haunches moving slowly from side to side as it prepared to pounce. The noise of a window opening two floors below startled the pigeon into clumsy flight before the cat could make its move. Alexey from Housing Benefit was having an illicit cigarette.

There was not much work for Josef now he had finished with the police tenders. However, the government was currently trying to get a bill through parliament which would greatly extend the privatisation of public services. Chris was already rubbing his hands about the slew of lucrative contracts that were in the offing.

So far, the police had not contacted Josef about Daria's suicide. He had no idea why she had done it, but he could not rid himself of the notion that he was to blame. Certainly, everyone in the council offices held him responsible. No one would speak to him. Someone had deliberately smashed his mug in the staff kitchen. He had begun buying takeaway lattes from a nearby cafe, even though he had to clock off and on each time he left the building. It was impossible for him to tell anyone of Chris's long-term relationship with Daria, and even if he did so, he was sure that no one would believe him.

His computer made two bleeps in different tones to announce that there had been no activity for three minutes outside of a scheduled break, so he returned to the spreadsheet he was putting together of all current private contracts, by department and duration, with notes indicating any limits and exceptions written into the contracts. He was not sure that Chris would approve, but Josef found a certain satisfaction in putting things in order.

He checked his emails and was grateful to see that there was only one. It was from the trade union representing the cleaning staff, which clearly had not updated its records, because it was a personnel issue, relating to the union's concerns about an innovative cleaning product, manufactured by Alcatec Industries, that contained an ingredient that had been recently linked to skin cancer.

1.30 p.m.

Daniela was sitting in her room, making a new collage from her collection of images. On her desk she had placed a reproduction of a sixteenth-century print by a Dutch artist, Philips Galle. Money was portrayed as a haughty queen, Regina Pecunia, hiding the figure of Robbery under her mantle and sitting on a chariot drawn by figures representing Fear and Danger. Behind the chariot, Folly, in the guise of a jester, gazed at Pandemia, who was pictured as a woman holding a whip, with a cornucopia over her shoulder and the world balanced on her head.

Daniela was attempting to place a brightly coloured photograph from the 1960s – of a fashion model wearing a silver minidress and plastic red boots – over the image of Queen Money without obscuring the figure representing Robbery. The task was making her squirm with frustration because parts of the Queen would keep poking out beyond the model.

A large photograph from a magazine, which Daniela had previously glued on to cream-coloured mounting board, portrayed a group of heavily armed American soldiers, in helmets and desert fatigues, patrolling a dusty road near a white, flat-roofed building, with a small boy in the background flying a kite.

Daniela planned to cut out the sixteenth-century print in such a way that when it was placed on the photograph it would appear that a contemporary Queen Money were progressing on her chariot, accompanied by her allegorical entourage, along the dusty road behind the American soldiers.

She wanted to finish the collage by four o'clock, because she was meeting Hannah at the bookshop at 5.30 to go out for a meal with her. Daniela had wanted to make the most of her day off work, since she would be working every afternoon and evening for the next seven days in the cafe and supermarket.

2.30 p.m.

Franz was browsing in the bookshop in the arts centre. He was looking through a photography book celebrating the traditions and folk festivals of the country – the guards of the Royal Palace in their uniforms dating from the time of King Corvus, a cheese-rolling competition in the hilly province north of V, a dog show in the lakes region south of the Tarent Mountains.

He had hardly slept the night before, after having made his exciting discovery. But still he wasn't certain about it. His supervisor had warned of the dangers of allowing 'a theory to impose a spurious coherence on random events'. 'It is', he had added, in the ponderous manner that grated on Franz, 'one of the problems of PhDs, which require the student to present a thesis, before they have completed their research.' The supervisor had then permitted himself a quiet chuckle at the paradox.

Franz was also worried about how to proceed if he *had* correctly identified Edward H as Ben F. He did not want his supervisor to take the credit for his discovery, but if he approached a publisher independently they might offer the truth of Edward H's identity to a well-established writer, to make a bigger impact and ensure better sales. He vaguely recalled a story about a young man being given a promissory note for a million dollars and finding it impossible to spend.

His mind was abuzz when he took his usual table in the cafe and set up his laptop, but Kata, the waitress, was nowhere in sight. The young waiter with the tattoo on his arm was serving. Franz could not pluck up the courage to ask him where she was.

3.30 p.m.

Chris called Ildiko into his office. She sat in the chair in front of his desk without being asked, while he stood with his hands clasped behind his back, looking through the tinted glass of the window without saying anything. By now, Ildiko had become accustomed to his many absurdities, and she waited patiently for him to speak. Time expanded, but it held no terrors for her. She saw right through Chris. He was a stuffed dummy stitched together from overpriced suits, mendacious cufflinks, sexual anxieties, brute fear and temper tantrums, little more than a papier mâché Devil bobbing around on the edge of a religious procession, awaiting the auto-da-fé, however much pain and humiliation he put her through to convince himself otherwise.

'I'm going out for a meeting now,' he said finally. 'I won't be back this afternoon. When you clock off at 5.30, I want you to pick up a book I have ordered – from the bookshop. You are to bring it to the apartment and wait for me in my bedroom. I'm not sure when my meeting will end.'

Saying nothing, Ildiko merely nodded and returned to her desk. There was a tiny camera in her office through which Chris could observe her whenever she was there, even from his phone. She had discovered it soon after starting the job and had taken control of it, with the help of Harun in IT, so she was able to feed to Chris images taken from the many video recordings the camera had already stored of her working in the office on different days and in various outfits. She had no intention of wasting her limited free time after work. She would have a leisurely coffee in the bookshop and collect his bloody book before she clocked off. Igor at reception would say nothing about it. She had him wrapped around her little finger.

Anna was tired. Her last, nervous client had just left – missionary position, short duration, sickening expression of gratitude. She lay still for a moment, before going through the dismal routine of throwing away the used condom, squatting on the bidet behind the rattan screen and getting dressed again.

She did not have to wait for long. Her next client appeared five minutes later, a curious man with a round red face, pug nose and pork-pie hat, which he raised when he saw her. His language was full of old-fashioned courtesies and slang words. Anna thought that his boyish smile masked the appetites of a rabid monster. He was, he said, a sales representative for a book publisher. She reminded him, he said, of a book buyer with whom he had had an appointment earlier that afternoon.

★

Wrapped in a towel, Daniela came back from the shower and deposited her pyjamas and knickers in the laundry bag at the foot of the wardrobe. She switched on the hairdryer and styled her hair in front of the mirror that was leaning against the wall near the desk.

The intricate task of cutting the figures out of the sixteenth-century print had worked out beautifully. The collage was finished and ready to mount in the frame that she had bought cheap the previous afternoon in the charity shop on the corner and had inspired her to make the collage.

★

Ildiko walked briskly through the atrium, leaving Chris to watch a perfectly timed video of her working in the office, edited from previous footage. It would seamlessly shift to the actual view at 5.30 if Harun had taught her well. She smiled warmly at Igor, who had just started his shift at the reception desk.

'Chris asked me to collect something for him,' she said. 'I'll clock off at 5.30 when I have done so.'

She headed over to the bookshop – where a bookseller was busy dismantling the display in one of the windows – to enjoy a stolen hour in the cafe. Only after she had finished her coffee and cake did she text Sergei to say that Chris had left earlier than expected.

★

Stefan was sitting outside his villa, enjoying the sunshine, drinking coffee and reading a film magazine. Natalia was playing with her soft toys in the treehouse.

'Come and see this, Daddy!' she said.

'In a minute, love.' He thought they should put her in a nursery soon, so that she could have the company of other children. She seemed to be a happy child, but Stefan wondered if she would be happier if Elena and he led more ordinary lives. He looked at his watch: quarter to five. He wondered if he had left it too late to see Hannah in the bookshop.

'Daddy! You said a minute.'

'Natalia, shall we go to the bookshop in town and find you a new storybook? Would you like that?' Her smiling face popped up at the treehouse window.

*

Adam was sitting at his desk in his company's call centre. His headset was lying beside his computer keyboard. He was reading the letter that his manager had just handed him. It was unusual, in a company missive, to read language expressing sadness and regret in such sentimental terms, but of course it was a redundancy letter.

He would receive one week's standard salary for each year he had worked for the company, which sadly could not take account of any commission he might have earnt in that time. He looked at the CEO's signature with a swelling feeling of happiness such as he had not experienced for years. Then he pulled on his jacket, loosened his tie, folded the letter and put it in his briefcase. Heading out of the office for the last time, he walked past the young trees bordering the industrial estate, towards the street of semi-detached houses, and the tram, waiting at the terminus, dappled with the shadows of the oaks in the park.

*

A white van was parked at an angle off the road, in front of one of the storage units under the railway arches. The initials of an international delivery service were printed on its side. Salazar, in a brown baseball cap, brown shirt with the same initials on the pocket, and a pair of brown trousers, was throwing cardboard boxes into the back of the van with the help of Amit. The boxes were taped shut, but they were clearly empty. A plumber's van was parked further up the street. Its bearded driver was finger-tapping the steering wheel and looking around nervously.

Amit felt his phone vibrating in his jacket pocket. The message consisted only of the name of a bar on the waterfront. He deleted it, looked in the back of the van – which now appeared to be filled with boxes – patted Salazar's back, nodded at him and locked the doors. Salazar climbed on to the driver's seat and started the engine while Amit walked up to the plumber's van.

★

Yasmin left at the usual time, but she was still angry. She could not understand why Salazar should order her not to go to work. It made no sense. Over lunch, she had told their mother that he had gone too far this time, but Yasmin had immediately regretted involving her. Their mother was ill and she hated it when Yasmin and Salazar argued. Yasmin had no one to turn to; the argument was still festering in her head when she saw City Hall appear around the shallow bend.

★

Sergei entered the bar and saw Dimitrios sitting with his back to him at a window table.

'He's not here yet?' said Sergei, taking a seat opposite Dimitrios.

'He'll be here at the appointed time.'

'The appointment in Samarra,' said Sergei, laughing.

'Don't be stupid.' Dimitrios looked at a young woman in a short skirt and matching navy blue jacket who had paused on the bridge to look out over the quay in the direction of Vandrhaf Square. He observed the light shining on her honey-coloured tights.

Sergei's phone vibrated. He took it out and read the message, before saying. 'He left early, or so she says.'

'Can we trust her?' said Dimitrios.

'Can anyone trust anyone?'

A waitress came up to the table to take Sergei's order.

★

It was late Friday afternoon in V and unseasonably warm. The sun was low in the sky to the west, filling the air with orange light, stretching out the shadows. City Hall overlooked the confluence of four main roads and three side streets. All kinds of people progressed at different speeds up and down the pavements on Castle Hill. Constant streams of individuals were passing the museum in both directions, the delicate traceries of their brains pulsing with numberless plans, hopes, fantasies

242

and emotions. Perhaps two hundred and fifty people, all told, were working and circulating within a four-hundred-foot radius of the revolving doors of City Hall: Igor, in his security guard's uniform, gazing vacantly at the white plastic model of V stretching out on its table in the atrium; students making evening plans, or joking, as they made their way to their digs; workers walking home; lovers holding hands; four pensioners in the entrance hall of the museum – two couples trying to decide where to eat, while one of the men, bored, looked up at the vintage monoplane suspended by wires from the ceiling; the young woman in the navy blue waistcoat and white blouse sitting behind the information desk; two old men, each with the brass badge of a famous regiment on their lapel, drinking wheat beer in the bar across the way; boys and girls in school uniforms milling around the tram stop; one girl, with shiny blond hair, pale eyelashes and long white knitted socks, turning to look at the approaching tram; a well-built young man with an aquiline nose and a flick of dark hair that kept falling over one eye, who was buying a rucksack in a specialist travel shop next to the bar; a beautiful dark-haired woman, eyes thickly lined with kohl, struggling with her overpacked burger in the diner near the Triangle.

★

Hannah was trying to put her window display to rights. It advertised a new photography book celebrating the country's traditions and folk festivals. The publisher had supplied several items for the display – a horse head mask for a May Day celebration, the hat worn by a guard in the Royal Palace, a martyr's banner and a papier mâché Devil. She had looked at the display from outside and realised that one of the books at the back was squeegee. So she had climbed back into the window space and reached up to right it, displacing some other books in the process.

'Fuck it!' she said.

5.24 p.m.

Daniela looked at her phone. She thought she was running late and began to hurry along the road towards City Hall.

5.25 p.m.

Two members of the Brotherhood were standing outside the bar across from the museum, arguing about who had bought the most rounds. The one standing nearest the road was able to see Hannah sorting books in the window of the bookshop further down the hill. He had stopped listening to his friend and was ogling her bottom as she bent to reach a book. A tram pulled up at the stop in front of them.

5.26 p.m.

Salazar had taken advantage of the pedestrian lights to pull out on to the main road by the museum. He had further angered the impatient driver of the Audi behind him by stopping, with two wheels on the pavement, directly in front of City Hall.

He climbed out holding a small parcel and was hurrying away from the vehicle, as if to make a delivery, when another delivery man, wearing the same uniform, asked him what the hell he was doing on his patch. Yasmin walked right past her brother without recognising him, because the peak of his cap was pulled low over his face, but he saw her.

5.27 p.m.

Somebody rang the bell for the next stop. Through the tram's windscreen, Adam could see the crenellated roof of City Hall further down the hill, and the junction at the top of the Triangle. He checked his watch, fearing that he would be late. He imagined that Helena would be waiting for him at the entrance to the bookshop. It made her feel important to keep a lookout for him when he had an arrangement to meet Katryn and the children in town.

Katryn was standing beside her trolley case in the bookshop, close to the cafe entrance. Kris had found a Star Wars notebook and was trying to persuade her to buy it for him. Helena said brightly that she would go to look out for Daddy. Her purple twinset was neat and clean. Katryn said she would hold her jacket.

'Don't go near the road,' said Katryn, before turning to Kris and saying, 'No, we can't afford that.'

'Aw Mum, but ...'

Helena walked through the door and glanced through the window at Hannah, who was at work on the display. She positioned herself where she could see her mother. Katryn anxiously returned her smile, before Helena looked away to see if her father was coming.

5.28 p.m.

Salazar pushed away the angry delivery driver and headed after Yasmin, who was already about to turn the corner by the museum. Her sad expression reminded him of the time he had made a palace for her out of their father's index cards, to make up for some childish cruelty he could no longer recall. Feeling suddenly bereft, he turned back. 'God does not want this!' he shouted, and began to run towards the van, yelling at the pedestrians streaming past City Hall to get the hell away. His cap fell off as he ran.

5.29 p.m.

The two members of the Brotherhood stopped arguing. One looked at the blonde schoolgirl who climbed on to the tram just as it was pulling away. A dark-skinned, bearded man could now be seen running on the other side of the road, past the museum, shouting and gesturing at the passers-by.

'What the fuck is that raghead doing?' said the other man, stepping towards the road.

5.30 p.m.

Stefan passed the end of the Triangle before he realised that Natalia was not with him. As soon as she saw the members of the Brotherhood, she had started running, without thinking, abjectly terrified. When Stefan turned round, she was over a hundred metres away and still running. He did not get a chance to say anything.

Epilogue

Yasmin, who was nearly at the staff entrance to the museum, was knocked off her feet by the sudden blast. The façade of City Hall buckled and collapsed. Hannah was thrown against the bookcases backing on to the window and showered with shards of glass. Katryn, flung to the floor next to Kris, was spared the sight of her daughter. Ildiko, at the sales desk downstairs, arguing with a puzzled assistant about Chris's order, saw an avalanche of books tumbling from the shelves behind her as she was spun around and hurled, relatively un-hurt, to the floor. Natalia, knocked over by the blast, started scream-ing, believing that one of the Brotherhood had shoved her and was going to drag her away, as the men had done with Nina. Adam saw the windscreen of the tram shatter and its supports buckle as the tram was derailed, pushed backwards by the force of the explosion and spat-tered with small pieces of debris. Daniela was propelled into a doorway by the initial blast and lived long enough to hear the shrapnel roaring past and striking the stonework next to her. Stefan was killed instantly, before the metal fragments reached him. Nothing recognisable re-mained of Salazar and some twenty other people on the pavement around him. Cars were reduced to fragments. Fuel explosions contrib-uted to the mayhem. One of the doors from Salazar's van became lodged between the chimney and slates of a roof some distance down Castle Hill. Hannah was still conscious, but she had never experienced such agony and shortly afterwards passed out from the shock. Katryn, hardly noticing the pain in her twisted legs, was desperately running her hands over Kris's body, asking if he was alright, while he lay whimpering next to some fallen shelves and stationery. Then she started shouting her daughter's name in mounting anguish. Josef, sprawling near the doorway of his office, his legs crushed and trapped by masonry, could see bodies scattered around the call centre. He could hear weeping and screaming. Some people were wandering around, dazed. The floor was slanting away steeply from the doors of the executive lift, towards the atrium, where one of the shattered pub-lic lifts was dangling by its wires with two figures clinging to the floor.

In its room in the museum, the table of the model city was jolted by the initial shock wave. The frames of the paintings strained against their fixtures, splintering their glass and showering the floor with dangerous fragments. Then, with a quiet hum, the lights on the model began to flicker on in the darkened room. The lighted windows in the doors of City Hall illuminated the tiny figures of two men fighting beside a horse-drawn wagon loaded with barrels. A woman in a fur-collared jacket was walking up the side street from the corner of the museum, the bright red of her ankle-length dress reflecting the light of a nearby window. A street lamp lengthened the shadow of a little girl running along a pavement on the southern edge of the Triangle.

Outside, shrapnel and debris were sucked back into the vacuum caused by the blast. Nothing could be seen of City Hall. It was wrapped in smoke, dust and flames. There was no hint of its presence.

★

Amit and Gunman 3 emerged from the plumber's van on Vandrhaf Square. Gunmen 1 and 2 had been dropped off earlier. Amit was carrying what could pass for a plumber's tool bag: a green canvas holdall with fake leather bands sewn around it near each end. The flaking brown handles betrayed the plastic of which they were made. Stroking the scar on his cheek, he stopped near the entrance to the covered walkway by the quay to allow Gunman 3 to catch up with him.

Gunman 3 was trembling with fear and excitement. His abstract hatred battling against the reality of the passers-by, he tried to stoke up the hatred by telling himself they were evil heretics and by remembering the multitudes of Arabs betrayed and murdered by the Western powers, the Palestinians routinely slaughtered by the Israelis, the perfection of the one God, the purity of his word, the only hope of salvation. Terrified by the acts he was about to commit, he tried to trace the God-willed journey that had brought him here from his university engineering course. Only Amit could offer him certainty in the whirlpool of thoughts and memories that engulfed him.

Amit looked at him intently and touched his arm to stop him when they emerged from the covered walkway along the quay and reached the abutment of the bridge. Tables were laid out in front of all the bars, crowded with workers celebrating the start of the weekend. For the space of two minutes, during which everything froze for Gunman 3, Amit's gaze travelled over the tables outside the bar ahead, before he caught sight of Sergei through the reflections of one of the windows. Amit figured that the grey-haired man sitting opposite him was Dimitrios.

Amit touched the shoulder of Gunman 3 and pointed back at the chattering crowds behind them. Then Amit placed the holdall on the ground and slowly unzipped it. It was at that moment that he took out his cellphone, checked the time, waited a moment and keyed in the number to detonate the bomb.

Gunman 3's eyes widened with fear at the sound of the blast, which shook the windows all around, and then Amit was pushing an assault rifle into his hand. Gunman 3 had two spare magazines in the deep pockets of his overall. Amit was already walking away with the other assault rifle. He fired a burst through the window at Sergei and Dimitrios, who were on their feet, engaged in furious discussion. Then he fired into the people crowding the outside tables. Some looked round, crying out in terror at the sound of the gunfire, while others were still staring in dazed silence towards the roar of the blast. They were mown down as they struggled out of their seats before they had any idea of what was happening. Once inside the bar, Amit emptied the magazine into Dimitrios's and Sergei's fallen bodies. It was pandemonium. He could see people running in panic across the bridge as he pushed a fresh magazine into the gun and, invoking God, started firing indiscriminately around the bar.

When Amit came out, Gunman 3 was weeping about what he had done. Amit shot him in the back of the head and then fired a burst at the people running along the covered walkway towards Vandrhaf Square. He walked steadily after them, firing through the bar windows as he passed. He missed a small boy sidling slowly around a pillar next to his father, who was playing dead. When Amit reached the steps to the square, he fired into a half-empty tourist boat that was about to dock. 'Evil will be defeated!' he shouted in Arabic as a heavyset woman in a paisley scarf and yellow dress fell back into the water. 'Paradise will come!'

By now, he could hear sirens racing towards City Hall. On reaching the plumber's van, he ended his own trail of death and injury with an arc of fire across Vandrhaf Square towards a bus picking up passengers by the Radion Hotel. Then he climbed into the driver's seat and headed west, towards his rented cottage on the Bohemian Coast, where two gunmen lay in wait for him in a hidden VW saloon.

★

Anna was grateful when the eccentric pervert finally left. She was sitting on the edge of the bed with her legs crossed, waiting for the next client, when the explosion rattled her window and dislodged flakes of paint from the ceiling. The shooting started shortly afterwards.

★

A black VW saloon with tinted rear windows pulled up at Josef and Hannah's apartment block soon after the explosion. Two men in black suits and black leather gloves climbed out of the car and walked to the entrance. One was carrying a black Gladstone bag. The other keyed into the keypad a number taken from a scrap of paper which he tore into shreds while the doors opened.

They entered the building just as a pretty estate agent with strawberry blond hair emerged from the lift, accompanied by a woman in a red skirt and matching jacket. They were hurrying, talking excitedly and looking through the glass entrance doors at the plume of smoke rising on Castle Hill. The blonde turned to speak to one of the men, but his expression was so intimidating that she immediately turned away. The other man pressed the button to keep the lift doors open. They waited until the women had left the building and disappeared, before taking the lift to the seventh floor.

When they reached Ben F's apartment, one of the men leaned on the wall beyond the door, while the other man placed the Gladstone bag on the floor and opened it. Two handguns with silencers were strapped on one side. He handed one to his companion and put the other in the pocket of his jacket. Then he took a stencil and a tin of black spray paint out of the bag and sprayed a black hand and a skull on the door.

He was just closing the bag when a Chinese property tycoon in an Armani suit appeared in the doorway opposite. His much younger wife, who was wearing a dove grey shantung skirt and an unbuttoned white blouse, was trying to drag him back inside, speaking to him furiously in Chinese. The property tycoon just had time to take in the black hand and skull painted on his neighbour's door and to see the man in black kneeling by the Gladstone bag, before the other man shot him and his wife dead. Then the kneeling man pushed the bag against the wall, produced a key from a jacket pocket and opened Ben F's door. No one saw them leaving the apartment block twenty minutes later.

★

Everything is quiet now. Anna lies in the dark with a hand on her stomach. In a sense, she has been waiting and planning for this moment since coming to V, but she cannot believe that it is finally here. She feels as if she is outside herself, looking on, as she struggles out of bed, retrieves from their hiding place the banknotes she has patiently gathered over the years and stuffs them together with her clothes into a bag. Then she puts on her coat and shoes. Just as she has imagined, Kemel's body is slumped over the bar, while two other members of Sergei's gang are sprawling dead on the floor.

She walks down the stairs, past the entrance to the massage parlour, with the odd feeling that she must picture every movement of her legs and then recite those movements to herself. It is dark outside. The sky is twinkling with a multitude of stars. There is no need to hurry, she thinks, as she heads towards the city centre. When she reaches the roundabout beyond the archway of apartments at the end of the road, the traffic is stopped at a red light.

A woman in a silver car opens the passenger window, leans over and says, 'Where are you going?'

'The Bohemian Coast,' says Anna. The name has always appealed to her.

'Get in,' says the woman, unlocking the door. Anna somehow knew it would happen like this. 'But you're hurt,' the woman adds when Anna climbs in.

'It's nothing,' says Anna. 'It is just a scratch.' She notices the elaborate silver brooch on the woman's jacket lapel. The lights turn green, and the traffic moves off, only to stop at the next set of lights. Anna has a severe pain in her stomach, but it will pass, she thinks. All things must pass. A figure in a black suit is visible in a lighted window overlooking the road. Anna can make out the cheap veneer furniture and rattan screen in the room beyond. The lights change and the car starts moving again. Gradually it leaves the city behind. It picks up speed.

'Not long, now,' says the woman. The car roars through the night. Anna imagines a succession of hills, fields and forests. She pulls her hand away from her stomach, and the dark liquid covering her palm sparkles with the lights of the dashboard. She has a sudden vision of the horrible sluglike creature with her sister's face, squeezing its flaccid body through the gap between skirting board and floor. She closes her eyes, and when she opens them again the full moon appears from behind a cloud.

'It's exactly how I imagined it would be,' says Anna in a dreamy voice. The dark outline of a castle is visible on a distant headland. She can see a man in a billowing cape riding a white horse along the cliff, ragged clouds edged with moonlight, the white spume of a storm-tossed sea, a row of cypresses swaying in the wind, the naked thighs of a cheap plastic doll, a hand in a black glove gripping the edge of her bedroom door to pull it closed. 'I'm so tired.'

'Just go to sleep,' says the woman. 'The monsters can't hurt you any more. You've finally arrived.'

Anna's head lolls on the back of the seat. 'What a lovely brooch,' she says. Her eyes follow the curlicues and branches of its elaborate silver setting, until she is hopelessly lost among the numerous bright threads of its filigree.

Also from Awen Publications:

The Tragicall History of Campbell McCluskie

Alistair McNaught

'Alistair McNaught's ingenious fictional biography brings to life not only slain playwright McCluskie but also the mid-twentieth-century Glasgow he inhabited. McCluskie's literary career, social life and erotic escapades are vividly evoked against a backdrop of smoke-filled bars, sombre tenements, and back streets haunted by prostitutes and razor gangs.'
Andrew Crumey

'Replete with a delicious humour and an unerring eye for the extraordinary in the detail … this is a magical jewel of a book wrought with intricacy, many smiles and at heart an awareness of the human condition and all of life's peculiar little twists and turns.' *Andy Swapp*

Fiction ISBN 987-1-906900-55-7

By the Edge of the Sea

Nicolas Kurtovitch

'Nicolas Kurtovitch has been at the forefront of French-language Pacific literature for four decades … This fine collection of short stories, the author's first, takes us from the lagoon of his native New Caledonia to the ocean, from the mainland to the islands, from Kanak fields to Australian desert, from suburbia to the bush … and can now be appreciated for the first time by an English-speaking public thanks to Anthony Nanson's careful and sensitive translation.' *Peter Brown*

'Charm of expression, restraint in tone, precision of line, nuance, and rhythm – these are the prime qualities of the writing of Nicolas Kurtovitch … But beware – the innocuous advance from one line to the next leads us inexorably into profound existential questions, and though his texts may be set in the Pacific this geographical precision can swiftly vanish to evoke the Universal.' *Claudine Jacques*

Fiction ISBN 978-1-906900-53-3

www.ingramcontent.com/pod-product-compliance
Lightning Source LLC
Chambersburg PA
CBHW072349020726
47506CB00004B/1069